VIRTUE

JANE FEATHER

 # VIRTUE

LOVESWEPT®

DOUBLEDAY

NEW YORK LONDON TORONTO SYDNEY AUCKLAND

LOVESWEPT®
PUBLISHED BY DOUBLEDAY
a division of Bantam Doubleday Dell Publishing Group, Inc.
666 Fifth Avenue, New York, New York 10103

DOUBLEDAY and the portrayal of an anchor with a dolphin,
and the word LOVESWEPT and the portrayal of the wave device
are trademarks of Doubleday, a division of
Bantam Doubleday Dell Publishing Group, Inc.

Book design by Patrice Fodero

Library of Congress Cataloging-in-Publication Data
Feather, Jane.
Virtue / Jane Feather. — 1st ed.
p.   cm.
"Loveswept."
I. Title.
PS3556.E22V57   1993
813'.54—dc20   92-30919
CIP

ISBN 0-385-46831-8
Copyright © 1993 by Jane Feather
All Rights Reserved
Printed in the United States of America
April 1993

1   3   5   7   9   10   8   6   4   2

FIRST EDITION

Prologue

THE QUILL SCRATCHED ON THE PARCHMENT. A LOG SPAT IN THE GRATE. THE guttering tallow candle flared as a needle of night wind pierced the ill-fitting shutters.

The man at the table paused in his writing. He dipped his nib in the inkstand and looked around the dim, shabby apartment. The paneled walls were cracked and inlaid with years of grime, the floor sticky beneath his booted feet. He huddled into his cloak and glanced toward the fire. It was low in the grate, and he bent to pick up a log from the basket. Then he let it fall back again. It was an extravagance he didn't need. Not now . . . not in a very few minutes.

He turned back to his writing, and the scratching of the quill was the only sound. Then he reached for the sander and dusted the epistle. Without reading what he had written, he folded the paper with scrupulous care and neatness, dropped a thick blob of candlewax on the folds, and pressed his signet ring into the seal. He sat for a minute, gazing fixedly at the initials imprinted in the wax: G D. Then he wrote again on the front of the sealed paper.

He rose from the table and propped the paper on the mantel-piece against a tarnished candlestick. There was an inch of brandy in the bottle on the table. He poured it into a glass and tossed it back, savoring the rough burn on his tongue, the warmth as it slid down his throat. It was a rough and ready brew for a man who had once known only the finest cognac, and yet it comforted.

He went to the door and opened it softly. The passage outside was dark and quiet. Soft-footed, he crept along the corridor and paused outside the two facing doors at the end. They were securely shut. Gently he turned the knob of the right-hand door. The door swung open and he stood in the opening, looking across the darkness to the shape of the bed and the mound beneath the covers. His lips moved soundlessly as if in benediction, then he closed the door with the same gentleness and repeated the exercise in the other doorway.

He returned to the candlelit apartment, closed the door, and went back to the table. He opened a drawer and drew out the silver-mounted pistol. He spun the chamber. There was one bullet. But he needed no more.

The single shot shattered the silence of the night. The letter on the mantelpiece bore the legend: Sebastian and Judith: My dearest children. When you read this, you will at last understand.

1

WHAT THE DEVIL WAS SHE DOING? MARCUS DEVLIN, THE MOST HONORABLE Marquis of Carrington, absently exchanged his empty champagne glass for a full one as a flunkey passed him. He pushed his shoulders off the wall, straightening to his full height, the better to see across the crowded room to the macao table. She was up to something. Every prickling hair on the nape of his neck told him so.

She was standing behind Charlie's chair, her fan moving in slow sweeps across the lower part of her face. She leaned forward to whisper something in Charlie's ear, and the rich swell of her breasts, the deep shadow of the cleft between them, was uninhibitedly revealed in the décolletage of her evening gown. Charlie looked up at her and smiled, the soft, infatuated smile of puppy love. It wasn't surprising his young cousin had fallen head over heels for Miss Judith Davenport, the marquis reflected. There was hardly a man in Brussels who wasn't stirred by her: a creature of opposites, vibrant, ebullient, sharply intelligent—a woman who in some indefinable fashion challenged a man, put him on his mettle one minute, and yet the next was as appealing as a kitten; a man wanted to pick her up and cuddle her, protect her from the storm . . .

Romantic nonsense! The marquis castigated himself severely for sounding like his cousin and half the young soldiers proudly sporting their regimentals in the salons of Brussels as the world waited for Napoleon to make his move. He'd been watching Judith Davenport weaving her spells for several weeks now, convinced she was an artful minx with a very clear agenda of her own. But for the life of him, he couldn't discover what it was.

His eyes rested on the young man sitting opposite Charlie. Sebastian Davenport held the bank. As beautiful as his sister in his own way, he sprawled in his chair, both clothing and posture radiating a studied carelessness. He was laughing across the table, lightly ruffling the cards in his hands. The mood at the table was lighthearted. It was a mood that always accompanied the Davenports. Presumably one reason why they were so popular . . . and then the marquis saw it.

It was the movement of her fan. There was a pattern to the slow sweeping motion. Sometimes the movement speeded, sometimes it paused, once or twice she snapped the fan closed, then almost immediately began a more vigorous wafting of the delicately painted half moon. There was renewed laughter at the table, and with a lazy sweep of his rake, Sebastian Davenport scooped toward him the pile of vowels and rouleaux in the center of the table.

The marquis walked across the room. As he reached the table, Charlie looked up with a rueful grin. "It's not my night, Marcus."

"It rarely is," Carrington said, taking snuff. "Be careful you don't find yourself in debt." Charlie heard the warning in the advice, for all that his cousin's voice was affably casual. A slight flush tinged the young man's cheekbones and he dropped his eyes to his cards again. Marcus was his guardian and tended to be unsympathetic when Charlie's gaming debts outran his quarterly allowance.

"Do you care to play, Lord Carrington?" Judith Davenport's soft voice spoke at the marquis's shoulder and he turned to look at her. She was smiling, her golden brown eyes luminous, framed in the thickest, curliest eyelashes he had ever seen. However, ten years spent avoiding the frequently blatant blandishments of maidens on the lookout for a rich husband had inured him to the cajolery of a pair of fine eyes.

"No. I suspect it wouldn't be my night either, Miss Davenport. May I escort you to the supper room? It must grow tedious, watching my cousin losing hand over fist." He offered a small bow and took her elbow without waiting for a response.

Judith stiffened, feeling the pressure of his hand cupping her bare arm. There was a hardness in his eyes that matched the firmness of his grip, and her scalp contracted as unease shivered across her skin. "On the contrary, my lord, I find the play most entertaining." She gave her arm a covert, experimental tug. His fingers gripped warmly and yet more firmly.

"But I insist, Miss Davenport. You will enjoy a glass of negus."

He had very black eyes and they carried a most unpleasant glitter, as insistent as his tone and words, both of which were drawing a degree of puzzled attention. Judith could see no discreet, graceful escape route. She laughed lightly. "You have convinced me, sir. But I prefer burnt champagne to negus."

"Easily arranged." He drew her arm through his and laid his free hand over hers, resting on his black silk sleeve. Judith felt manacled.

They walked through the card room in a silence that was as uncomfortable as it was pregnant. Had he guessed what was going on? Had he seen anything? How could she have given herself away? Or was it something Sebastian had done, said, looked . . . ? The questions and speculations raced through Judith's brain. She was barely acquainted with Marcus Devlin. He was too sophisticated, too hardheaded to be of use to herself and Sebastian, but she had the distinct sense that he would be an opponent to be reckoned with.

The supper room lay beyond the ballroom, but instead of guiding his companion around the waltzing couples and the ranks of seated chaperones against the wall, Marcus turned aside toward the long French windows opening onto a flagged terrace. A breeze stirred the heavy velvet curtains over an open door.

"I was under the impression we were going to have supper." Judith stopped abruptly.

"No, we're going to take a stroll in the night air," her escort informed her with a bland smile. "Do put one foot in front of the other, my dear ma'am, otherwise our progress might become a little uneven." An unmistakable jerk on her arm drew her forward with a stumble, and Judith rapidly adjusted her gait to match the leisured, purposeful stroll of her companion.

"I don't care for the night air," she hissed through her teeth, keeping a smile on her face. "It's very bad for the constitution and frequently results in the ague or rheumatism."

"Only for those in their dotage," he said, lifting thick black eyebrows. "I would have said you were not a day above twenty-two. Unless you're very skilled with powder and paint?"

He'd pinpointed her age exactly and the sense of being dismayingly out of her depth was intensified. "I'm not quite such an accomplished actress, my lord," she said coldly.

"Are you not?" He held the curtain aside for her and she found herself out on the terrace, lit by flambeaux set in sconces at intervals along the low parapet fronting the sweep of green lawn. "I would have sworn you were as accomplished as any on Drury Lane." The statement was accompanied by a penetrating stare.

Judith rallied her forces and responded to the comment as if it were a humorous compliment. "You're too kind, sir. I confess I've long envied the talent of Mrs. Siddons."

"Oh, you underestimate yourself," he said softly. They had reached the parapet and he stopped under the light of a torch. "You are playing some very pretty theatricals, Miss Davenport, you and your brother."

Judith drew herself up to her full height. It wasn't a particularly impressive move when compared with her escort's breadth and stature, but it gave her an illusion of hauteur. "I don't know what you're talking about, my lord. It seems you've obliged me to accompany you in order to insult me with vague innuendos."

"No, there's nothing vague about my accusations," he said.

"However insulting they may be, I am assuming my cousin's card play will improve in your absence."

"What are you implying?" The color ebbed in her cheeks, then flooded back in a hot and revealing wave. Hastily she employed her fan in an effort to conceal her agitation.

The marquis caught her wrist and deftly twisted the fan from her hand. "You're most expert with a fan, madam."

"I beg your pardon?" She tried again for a lofty incomprehension, but with increasing lack of conviction.

"Don't continue this charade, Miss Davenport. It benefits neither of us. You and your brother may fleece as many fools as you can find as far as I'm concerned, but you'll leave my cousin alone."

"You talk in riddles," she said. There was no way he could prove anything; no public accusations he could bring, she told herself. But when they went to London . . . supposing he put the word around . . . ?

She needed time to think. With a dismissive shrug, she turned from him, as if intending to return to the ballroom.

"Then allow me to solve the riddle for you." He caught her arm. "We'll walk a little away from the light. You will not wish others to hear what I have to say."

"There is nothing you could say that could be of the remotest interest to me, Lord Carrington. Now, if you'll excuse me . . ."

His derisory laugh crackled in the soft June air. "Don't cross swords with me, Judith Davenport. I'm more than a match for a card-sharping hussy. You may live upon your wits, ma'am, but I can assure you I've been using mine rather longer than you've been using yours."

Judith abruptly dropped a clearly useless pretense. It would only increase his antagonism and thus the danger. She said evenly, "You can prove nothing."

"I'm not interested in proving anything," he replied. "I've said, you may make gulls of as many of these empty-headed idiots as you wish. But you'll leave my family alone." He took her elbow and began to walk down the shallow flight of steps onto the lawn. Twin oak trees threw giant moonshadow at the edge of the grass. In the dim obscurity, the marquis stopped. "So, Miss Davenport, I want your word that you will put an end to Charlie's infatuation."

Judith shrugged. "It's hardly my fault if he fancies himself in love with me."

"Oh, but it most certainly is your fault. Do you think I haven't watched you?" He leaned against the trunk of the oak, folding his arms, his eyes on the pale glimmer of her face, the golden glow of her eyes. "You are a masterly coquette, madam. And I would have you turn your liquid eyes and undeniable arts upon some other young fool."

"Whom your cousin chooses to love is surely his business," she said. "I fail to see how it could have anything to do with you, my lord."

"It has everything to do with me when my ward's embroiled with a fortune-hunting, unprincipled baggage with no—"

Her palm cracked against his cheek, bringing a sudden dreadful silence in which the strains of music drifted incongruously from the house.

Judith spun away from him with a little sob, pressing her hands to her lips, as if struggling with her tears in an excess of wounded pride and sensibility. Marcus Devlin had to be disarmed, somehow, and if honesty wouldn't do it, then she'd have to take another tack. She couldn't run the risk that he would spread his accusations around the London clubs when the Davenports made their entry into London Society. On the spur of the moment, she could think only to offer him the picture of deeply affronted innocence and hope to create if not compassion then some willingness to make amends with his future silence.

"You know nothing of me," she said in stifled tones. "You can know nothing of what we endure . . . of how we are in this situation. . . . I have never knowingly injured anyone, let alone your cousin . . ." Her voice died on a gulping sob.

She was certainly a consummate actress, Marcus reflected, for some reason not deceived for one minute by this masterly display. He stroked his stinging cheek, feeling the raised imprint of her fingers. There had been more conviction there, but such a violent exhibition of outraged virtue seemed hardly consonant with the disreputable woman he believed her to be. Ignoring the bravely stifled sobs, he observed dispassionately, "You've a deal of power in your arm for one so slight."

That was not the response she'd hoped for. Raising her head, she spoke with a brave, aloof dignity. "You owe me an apology, Lord Carrington."

"I rather think the boot is on the other foot." He continued to rub his cheek, regarding her with a penetrating scrutiny that did nothing to reassure her.

It seemed most sensible to escape the close confines of the shadows and an increasingly unstable confrontation that was not following her direction. Judith shrugged faintly. "You are no gentleman, my lord." She turned to go back to the house.

"Oh, no, you're not running off like that," the marquis said. "Not just yet. We haven't concluded our discussion, Miss Davenport." He caught her arm and for a second they stood immobile, Judith still turned toward the house, her captor still leaning against the tree. "That was a singularly violent assault, madam, in response to—"

"To an unmitigated insult, sir!" she interrupted, hoping she didn't sound as back-to-the-wall as she was beginning to feel.

"But one not without justification," he pointed out. "You have admitted by default that you and your brother are . . . how shall we say . . . are expert gamesters, with somewhat unorthodox methods of play."

"I would like to return to the house." Even to Judith's ear, it was a pathetic plea rather than a determined statement of intent.

"In a minute. For such an accomplished flirt, you're playing the maiden of outraged virtue most convincingly, but I've a mind to taste a little more of you than the sting of your palm." He pulled her toward him like a fisherman drawing in his line and she came as reluctantly as any hooked fish. "It seems only right that you should soothe the hurt you caused." Cupping her chin with his free hand, he

9

tilted her face. The black eyes were no longer hard and Judith could read a spark of laughter in their depths . . . laughter, and a most dangerous glimmer that set her nerve endings tingling. Desperately she sought for something that would douse both his laughter and that hazardous glimmer.

"You would have me kiss it better, sir, like a child's scraped knee?" She offered an indulgent smile and saw with satisfaction that she had surprised him, and surprise afforded advantage. Swiftly she stood on tiptoe and kissed his cheek. "There, that'll make it better." After twisting out of his abruptly slackened hold, she danced backward out of the shadows into the relative light of the garden. "I bid you good night, Lord Carrington." And she was gone, flitting under the moonlight, her body lissome as a hazel wand under the fluid silk of her topaz gown.

Marcus stared after her through the gloom. How the hell had such a disreputable baggage managed to win that encounter? He ought to be more than a match for a slip of a girl. He was annoyed; he was amused; but more than anything he was challenged by her. If she wouldn't be warned away from Charlie, then he'd have to find some more potent inducement.

Judith returned to the card room, but only to make her farewells, pleading a headache. Charlie was all solicitude, begging to escort her home, but Sebastian was on his feet immediately.

"No need for that, Fenwick. I'll take m'sister home." He yawned himself. "In truth, I'll not be sorry to keep early hours myself tonight. It's been a hard week." He grinned engagingly around the table.

"A demmed lucky one for you, Davenport," one of the players said with a sigh, pushing across an IOU.

"Oh, I've the luck of the devil," Sebastian said cheerfully, pocketing the vowel. "It runs in the family, doesn't it, Judith?"

Her smile was somewhat abstracted. "So they say."

Sebastian's eyes sharpened and his gaze flickered to the door of the card room, to where the Marquis of Carrington stood, taking snuff. "You look a little wan, m'dear," Sebastian said, taking his sister's arm.

"I don't feel quite the thing," she agreed. "Oh, thank you, Charlie." She smiled warmly as the young man arranged her shawl around her shoulders.

"Perhaps you won't feel like riding tomorrow," Charlie said, unable to hide the disappointment in his voice. "Shall I call upon you—"

"No, indeed not. My aunt detests callers," she broke in, touching his hand fleetingly as if in consolation. "But I shall be perfectly well tomorrow. I'll meet you in the park, as we arranged."

Brother and sister made their way out of the card room. Marcus bowed as they reached the door. "I bid you good night, Miss Davenport . . . Davenport."

"Good night, my lord." She swept past him, then, on an impulse she didn't quite understand, murmured over her shoulder, "I am riding with your cousin in the morning."

"Oh, I fully understand that you've thrown down the glove," he said, as softly as she. "But you have not yet tasted my mettle, ma'am. Take heed." He bowed again in formal farewell and turned away before she could reply.

Judith bit her lip, aware of a strange mingling of apprehension and excitement unlike anything she'd felt before, and she knew it was as dangerous as it was uncomfortable.

"What's amiss, Ju?" Sebastian spoke as soon as they were out of the mansion and on the cobbled street.

"I'll tell you when we get home." She climbed into the shabby carriage that awaited them on the corner, sitting back against the cracked leather squabs, a frown drawing her arched brows together, her teeth closing over her lower lip.

Sebastian knew that expression. It usually meant that his sister's eccentric principles were aroused. She wouldn't say anything until she was ready, so he was content to sit back and wait for her to tell him what was absorbing her.

The carriage drew up outside a narrow house on a darkened lane in a part of town that had definitely seen better days. Brother and sister alighted and Sebastian paid the driver for the evening's work. Judith was already unlocking the front door, and they stepped into a narrow passage, lit by a single tallow candle in a sconce on the stairway wall.

"One of these days someone's going to notice how we never give anyone our direction," Sebastian observed, following his sister up the stairs. "The tale of the irritable aunt won't hold good forever."

"We won't be in Brussels for much longer," Judith said. "Napoleon's bound to make his move soon and then the army will be gone. There'll be no point in our remaining in an empty city." She pushed open a door at the head of the stairs onto a square parlor.

The room was dark and dingy, the furniture shabby, the carpet threadbare, and the gloomy light of tallow candles did nothing to improve matters. She tossed her India shawl on a broken-backed couch and sank into a chair, a deep frown corrugating her brow.

"How much did we make tonight?"

"Two thousand," he said. "It would have been more, but after you'd gone off with Carrington, I lost the next hand by miscounting an ace." He shook his head in self-disgust. "It's always the way; I grow careless if I rely on you for too many hands."

"Mmm." Judith kicked off her shoes and began to massage one foot. "But we need to practice now and again to keep our hands in. In fact, I think we must spend some serious time perfecting the moves because I must have made a mistake, although I can't think how. But the Most Honorable Marquis of Carrington is wise to us."

Sebastian whistled. "Hell and the devil. So now what?"

"I don't know exactly." Judith was still frowning as she switched feet, pulling on her toes with an absent vigor. "He said he'd not call foul on us, but he issued a most direct command that I cure Charlie of his infatuation."

"Well, that's easily done. You've never had any difficulty disentangling yourself from an overzealous suitor."

"No, but why should I? I have no intention of hurting Charlie. In fact, a little sophisticated dalliance will do wonders for him, and if he loses a few thousand at cards, it's not as if he can't afford it. Apart from those few minutes tonight, the only unfair odds he's faced are in your native talent. He plays because he chooses to, and I fail to see why Carrington should be allowed to meddle."

Sebastian regarded his sister warily. It was definitely a case of offended principles. "He is his guardian," he pointed out. "And we're a disreputable pair, Ju. You shouldn't take it too much to heart if someone realizes that and behaves accordingly."

"Oh, nonsense!" she said. "We're no more disreputable than anyone else. It's just that we're not hypocrites. We have to put a roof over our heads and bread on the table, and we do it in the only way we know."

Sebastian went to the sideboard and poured cognac into two goblets. "You could always go for a governess." He handed her one of the goblets, chuckling at her horrified expression. "I can just see you imparting the finer points of watercolors and the rudiments of Italian to frilly little girls in a schoolroom."

Judith began to laugh. "Not at all. I would teach them to play piquet and backgammon for large stakes; to flutter their eyelashes and offer amusing little sallies to gentlemen who might be induced to play; to know when it's time to move on; to find the cheapest lodgings and servants; to slip away in the night to avoid the bailiff; to create a wardrobe out of thin air. In short, I would teach them all the elements for a successful masquerade. Just as I was taught."

The laughter had left her voice half way through the speech and Sebastian took her hand. "We'll be avenged, Ju."

"For Father," she said, lifting her head and taking a sip of her cognac. "Yes, we'll be avenged for him."

Silently Sebastian joined her in the toast, and for a moment they both stared into the empty grate, remembering. Remembering and reaffirming their vow. Then Judith put the glass on a side table and stood. "I'm going to bed." She kissed his cheek and the gesture reminded her of something that brought a glitter of determination to her eyes. "I'm in the mood to play with fire, Sebastian."

13

"Carrington?"

She nodded. "The gentleman needs to be disarmed. He said he wouldn't cry foul on us, but supposing he decided to alert people in London to beware of playing with you? If I can intrigue him . . . engage him in a flirtation . . . he'll be less likely to concern himself with what you do at the tables."

Sebastian regarded his sister dubiously. "Are you a match for him?"

Was she? For a minute she felt again the press of his fingers on her skin, saw again the sharp shrewdness in the black eyes, the unconciliatory slash of his mouth, the prominent jaw. But of course she was a match for any town beau. She knew things, had seen and done things, that had honed her wits to a keenness he would not be expecting.

"Of course," she declared confidently. "And there'll be great satisfaction, I can tell you, in seeing him succumb as easily as his cousin did. It'll teach him to be so high-handed."

Sebastian looked even more dubious. "I don't like it when you mix motives like that. We're so close to catching up with Gracemere, Judith. Don't risk anything."

"I won't, I promise. I'm just going to show the most honorable marquis that I don't take kindly to insults."

"But if you arouse his curiosity, he's going to want to know who we are and where we come from."

She shrugged. "So what? The usual fiction will satisfy him. We're the children of an eccentric English gentleman of respectable though obscure lineage, recently deceased, who, after the death of his wife at a tragically early age, chose to travel the Continent for the rest of his life with us in tow."

"Instead of the truth," Sebastian said. "That we're the children of a disgraced Yorkshire squire, disinherited by his family, driven out of England by scandal and his wife's subsequent suicide, forced to change his name and earn his bread at the gaming tables of the Continent." The story rolled glibly off his tongue, but Judith knew her brother and could hear his pain; it was her own, too.

"And he taught his children all he knew, so that from a horribly precocious age they were his enablers and assistants," she finished for him.

Sebastian shook his head. "Too harsh a truth for the delicate sensibilities of the Quality to handle, my dear."

"Just so." Judith nodded with a return to briskness. "Don't worry, Sebastian. Carrington won't get so much as a sniff at the real story. I'll invent some playful reason for that piece of dubious card play this evening. Mischief rather than need, I think. And if he doesn't catch us at it again and I manage to charm him a bit, I'm sure he won't mention it again."

"I've not yet met the man you can't entangle when you put your mind to it," Sebastian agreed, chuckling. "Just watching you at work is an everlasting delight."

"Wait until I turn my charms on Gracemere," his sister said, blowing him a kiss. "That'll be a treat, I promise you."

She went into her bedroom next door—a room as dingy as the parlor and none too clean. The landlord's serving maid was less than thorough at her tasks, but the Davenports had been living in such lodgings for as long as they could remember and were accustomed to seeing only what they chose to see.

Undressed, she climbed into bed and lay looking up at the faded canopy. Gracemere was in London. They would need maybe twenty thousand pounds in ready money to set themselves up in London in a reasonably fashionable part of town. There would be servants to pay, some form of carriage and horses, even if they were only hired. They would both need large and elaborate wardrobes and at least an illusion of a generous income. The gaming would take care of their everyday expenses once they were established, but they would have to tread a fine line. High-stakes gaming was an accepted activity in Society, for women as well as men, but one must never give the impression that it mattered whether one won or lost.

They would operate their double act only in the final stages of the plan, when it was time to administer the coup de grace. It was too dangerous and powerful a tool to be used except in extremity.

George Davenport had never known of the double act. He had taught his children to rely on wits and skill at the tables, but there had been times of dire necessity . . . those days, sometimes weeks, when he had retreated into the dark world of his soul and there had been no money for food or fuel or even lodging. Then Judith and her brother had learned to fend for themselves.

Tonight they had been practicing, as they did now and again, but somehow she had slipped up and been discovered.

Marcus Devlin, Marquis of Carrington.

Bernard Melville, third Earl of Gracemere.

Her strategem with the one must advance her plans for the other. Sebastian was right about the dangers of mixed motives. She must concentrate only on the need to disarm the marquis in order to guarantee his silence. And any personal satisfaction she might garner from his submission would be a purely private and secondary pleasure. Nothing must be permitted to jeopardize the grand design . . . the driving force behind the life she and Sebastian presently led.

2

"MY DEAR BERNARD, HOW WILL I ENDURE TWO WHOLE MONTHS WITHOUT you?" Agnes Barret sighed and stretched out a bare leg, examining the supple curve of calf, the delicate turn of ankle with a complacent smile. She pinched her thigh several times between finger and thumb; the flesh was as firm as a girl's.

"Your husband's entitled to a honeymoon, my dear." The Earl of Gracemere watched his lady with a knowing smile laced with desire. Agnes's vanity was one of her few weaknesses—her only weakness, in fact, and she was undoubtedly entitled to it. At forty-three she was more beautiful than she'd been at twenty, he thought. Her hair was still as lustrously auburn as ever, her tawny eyes as luminous, her skin as soft and translucent, her figure as lithe and elegant. In truth, there wasn't a woman to touch her, and Bernard Melville had known many women. But always there had been Agnes. She was woven into the fabric of his life as he was woven into hers.

"Oh, Thomas!" Agnes dismissed the inconvenient bridegroom with a languid wave of one white hand. "He's suffering from another attack of gout, would you believe? He can't bear anyone to come within six feet of his left foot, which should rather cut down on the customary activities of a honeymoon." She picked up a glass of wine from the bedside table and sipped, glancing at the earl over the rim.

"Is that a cause for complaint?" Bernard inquired. "I was under the impression that you were dreading the duties of the conjugal bedchamber with an elderly husband."

"Well, so I am, but one must have something to do to while away two months of rustication," Agnes returned, a shade tartly. "I assume *you* will find solace for your empty bed somewhere in Yorkshire . . . a village girl, or a milkmaid, or some such."

"Jealous, Agnes?" He smiled and took up his own glass. He walked to the window, looking down at the sluggishly flowing River Thames below. A horse-drawn barge inched along the south bank of the river. One of London's many church bells pealed on the hot June air.

"Hardly. I don't consider country wenches as rivals."

"My dear one, you have no equal anywhere, so you cannot possibly fear a rival." He took a sip of wine and bent over her, holding the wine in his mouth as he brought his lips to hers. Her mouth opened beneath his and the wine slid over his tongue to fill her mouth with a warm sweetness. His hands went to her breasts in a leisurely caress and she fell back on the bed beneath him.

The evening sun had set, turning the river below their window to a dull, gunmetal gray, before they spoke again.

"I don't know how soon I'll be able to ask Thomas for a sum sufficient to quieten your creditors." Agnes shifted and the bedropes creaked. "It's a little awkward to demand a substantial sum from one's bridegroom as one leaves the altar."

"That's why I'm going into Yorkshire," Bernard said, letting his hand rest on her turned flank. "I can escape my creditors for the summer, while you, my love, work upon the gouty but so wealthy Sir Thomas."

Agnes chuckled. "I have my appealing story well prepared . . . an indigent second cousin, I believe, suffering from rheumatism and living in a drafty garret."

"I trust you won't be required to produce this relative," Bernard remarked with a responding chuckle. "I don't know how good a master of disguise I would prove."

"You are as much a master of deception as I, my dear," Agnes said.

"Which is why we suit each other so remarkably well," Bernard agreed.

"And always have done." Agnes's mouth curved in a smile of reminiscence. "Even as children . . . how old were we, the first time?"

Bernard turned his head to look at the face beside him on the pillow. "Old enough . . . although some might say we were a trifle precocious." He moved his hand lazily to palm the delicate curve of her cheek. "We were born to please each other, my love." Hitching himself on one elbow, he brought his mouth to hers, exerting a bruising almost suffocating pressure as his palm tightened around her face and he held her flat and still with his weight. When finally he released her mouth, there was an almost feral glitter of excitement in her tawny eyes. She touched her bruised and swollen lips with a caressing finger.

Bernard laughed and lay down beside her again. "However," he said as if that moment of edging violence had not occurred, "I shall look around me for a fat pigeon to pluck at the beginning of the Season. I don't wish to be totally dependent upon your husband's unwitting charity."

"No, it would be as well not. It's a pity Thomas is no gamester." Agnes sighed. "That was such a perfect game we once played."

"But, as you say, Thomas Barret is no George Devereux," Gracemere agreed, reaching indolently for his wineglass. "I wonder what happened to that husband of yours."

"It's to be hoped he's dead," Agnes said, taking the glass from him. "Otherwise I am a bigamist, my dear." She sipped, her eyes gleaming with amusement.

"Who's to know but you and I?" Her companion laughed with the same amusement. "Alice Devereux, the wife of George Devereux, has been dead and buried these last twenty years as far as the world's concerned . . . dead of grief at her husband's dishonor." He chuckled richly.

"Not that the world saw anything of her, either before or during her marriage," Agnes put in with remembered bitterness. "Having married his country innocent, George was interested only in keeping her pregnant and secluded in the Yorkshire wilds."

"But with the death of reclusive Alice in a remote convent in the French Alps, the sociable Agnes was born," Gracemere pointed out.

"Yes, a far preferable identity," Agnes agreed with some satisfaction. "I enjoyed making my society debut as the wealthy young widow of an elderly Italian count. Society is so much more indulgent toward women of independent means, particularly if they have a slightly mysterious past." She smiled lazily. "I wouldn't be an ingenue again for all the youthful beauty in the world. Do you ever miss Alice, Bernard?"

He shook his head. "No, Agnes is so much more exciting, my love. Alice was a young girl, while Agnes was born into womanhood . . . and women have much more to offer a man of my tastes."

"Sophisticated, and perhaps a little *outré*," Agnes murmured, again touching her bruised mouth. "But to return to the question of money . . ."

"I still have George's Yorkshire estate," Bernard said.

"But it yields little now."

"No, it's a sad fact that property needs to be maintained if it's to continue to support one," he agreed, sighing. "And maintenance requires funds . . . and, sadly, funds I do not have."

"Not for such mundane concerns as estate maintenance," Agnes stated without criticism.

"True enough, there are always more important . . . or, rather, more enticing ways of spending money." He swung himself off the bed. "On which subject . . ." He crossed to the dressing table. Agnes sat up, watching him, greedily drinking in his nakedness even though his body was as familiar to her as her own.

"On which subject," he repeated, opening a drawer. "I have a wedding present for you, my love." He came back to the bed and tossed a silk pouch into her lap, laughing as she seized it with eager fingers. "You were always rapacious, my adorable Agnes."

"We're well suited," she returned swiftly, casting him a glinting smile as she drew from the pouch a diamond collar. "Oh, Bernard, it's beautiful."

"Isn't it?" he agreed. "I trust you'll be able to persuade your husband to reimburse me at some point."

Agnes went into a peal of laughter. "You are a complete hand, Bernard. My lover buys me a wedding present that my husband will be required to pay for. I do love you."

"I thought you'd appreciate the finer points of the jest," he said, kneeling on the bed. "Let me fasten it for you. Diamonds and naked-ness are a combination I've never been able to resist."

"I don't see your cousin this evening, Charlie." Judith slipped her arm through her escort's as they strolled through the crowded salon. She glanced around, as she had been doing all evening, wondering despite herself why the Marquis of Carrington had chosen not to honor the Bridges' soiree.

"Marcus isn't much of a one for balls and such frippery things," Charlie said. "He's very bookish." His tone made this sound like some fatal ailment. "Military history," he elucidated. "He reads histories in Greek and Latin and writes about old battles. I can't understand why anyone should still be interested in who won some battle way back in classical times, can you?"

Judith smiled. "Perhaps I can. It would be interesting to work out how and why a battle turned out as it did, and to make comparisons with present-day warfare."

"That's exactly what Marcus says!" Charlie exclaimed. "He's for-ever closeted with Wellington and Blücher and the like, discussing Napoleon and what he might decide to do on the basis of what he's done in the past. I can't see why that should be as useful as going out and getting on with the fighting, but everyone seems to think it is."

"Battles aren't won without strategy and tactics," Judith pointed out. "And only careful strategy can minimize casualties." She reflected that perhaps nineteen-year-olds on the eve of battle, drunk on dreams of heroism and glory, probably wouldn't take this particular point.

"Well, I can't wait to have a crack at Boney," Charlie declared, looking a trifle disappointed at his goddess's lack of enthusiasm for the blood and guts of warfare.

"I'm certain you'll have your chance soon enough," Judith said. "As I understand it, Wellington's only waiting for Napoleon to make his approach and then he'll attack before he's properly in position."

"But I don't understand why we can't just go out and meet him. He's already left Paris," Charlie complained in an undertone, glancing around to make sure none of his fellow officers in their brilliant regimentals could overhear a possibly disloyal comment. "Why do we have to wait for him to come close?"

"I imagine it would be rather cumbersome to move 214,000 men at this stage in order to intercept him," Judith said. "They're strung out from Mons to Brussels, and Charleroi to Liege, as I understand it."

"You sound just like Marcus," Charlie observed again. "It seems very poor-spirited to me."

Judith laughed and took the opportunity to return the conversation to its original topic, one that interested her rather more. "So your cousin doesn't care for balls and assemblies. It's perhaps fortunate he doesn't have a wife in that case." She said it casually, with another light laugh.

"Oh, Marcus is not overfond of ladies' company in the general run of things."

"Why not?"

Charlie frowned. "I think it may have something to do with an old engagement. But I don't fully understand the reasons. He has women . . . other sorts of women . . . I mean . . ." He stammered to a halt, his face fiery in the candlelight.

"I know exactly what you mean," she said, patting his arm. "There's no reason to be embarrassed with me, Charlie."

"But I shouldn't have mentioned such a thing in front of a lady," he said, still blushing. "Only I feel so comfortable with you . . ."

"Like an older sister," Judith said, smiling.

"Oh, no . . . no, of course not . . . how could I . . ." Again he fell silent and Judith could almost hear the recognition of what she'd said falling into place like the tumblers of a lock. She chuckled to herself. Charlie was well on the way to curing himself of his infatuation without the heavy-handed intervention of an overanxious guardian. Not that she was about to inform the most honorable marquis of that fact. . . . Not that he was around to be informed, anyway.

Marcus put in an appearance as the clock struck midnight. He could see no sign of his ward or Miss Davenport, although the world seemed gathered in the Bridges' salons. After greeting his hostess he strolled into the card room. The faro table was crowded, the atmosphere lively and good humored. Sebastian Davenport was a steady winner. The marquis stood watching the table intently. There was nothing amiss with the way the man was playing. He certainly had luck on his side, but there was something else. Some innate ability to make judgments on the odds. He examined Sebastian's face. It was quite impassive while he was making his bet, then the minute he'd declared, tossing his rouleaux onto the table, he was as relaxed and lighthearted as ever. A true gamester, Marcus thought. It took a combination of brains and nerve, and Sebastian Davenport had both. Marcus didn't think his sister lacked those qualities either, although he hadn't yet observed her play.

Unprincipled adventurers, the pair of them, he decided. But he could see no reason at this point to expose them. Only the greedy and the foolish fell victim to hardened gamesters, and they got what they deserved. He would take steps to protect Charlie himself.

"Davenport . . . a game of piquet?"

The suggestion surprised Sebastian. He looked up at the marquis, remembering Judith's encounter the previous evening. But the suggestion was seemingly innocuous and piquet was Sebastian's game. "Why, certainly," he said cheerfully. "A hundred guineas a point?"

Marcus swallowed this without a blink. "Whatever you say."

Sebastian settled with the faro table and rose. The marquis was waiting for him at a small card table in a relatively quiet corner of the room. He indicated a fresh deck of cards on the table as he took his place. "Do you care to break them, Davenport?"

Sebastian shrugged and pushed them across to the marquis. "You do the honors, my lord."

"As you wish." The cards were shuffled and dealt and a silence fell between the two men. Sebastian had a full glass of claret at his elbow but Marcus noticed that although he seemed to raise it to his lips frequently, the level barely went down. A most serious gamester. And an expert card player. Marcus, who was no mean player himself, recognized that he was outclassed after the third hand. He relaxed, resigned to his losses, and began to enjoy playing with a master.

"Well, my lord, this is a pleasant surprise." Judith's dulcet tones came from behind him and she offered him her most ravishing smile. "I have been sadly disappointed at your absence."

"Stand behind your brother," he snapped, quite impervious to this coquettry.

"I beg your pardon?" She frowned in puzzlement.

"Stand behind your brother, where I can see you."

Comprehension dawned. She stared at him in dismay, all pretense at flirtation vanishing under the sting of such an unwarranted assumption. "But I wouldn't—"

"Wouldn't you?" he interrupted, without looking up from his cards; it was a damnably difficult discard he had to make. "Nevertheless, I prefer not to take the risk. Now move."

She stepped sideways, struggling for composure, seeking support from her brother. "Sebastian . . . ?"

Sebastian gave a rueful chuckle. "He caught you at it, Ju. I can't call him out for you. Not in the circumstances."

"No, I don't think you can," Marcus agreed, discarding a ten of spades. "Not that you need any help from your sister." He watched with resignation as his opponent picked up the discard. "You'll not even spare me the Rubicon, I fear."

Sebastian totted up the points. "I'm afraid not, Carrington. I make it ninety-seven."

"What were the stakes?" Judith demanded, this issue taking immediate precedence over hurt feelings.

Marcus began to laugh. "What an incorrigibly unprincipled pair you are."

"Not really," Sebastian said. "Ju, at least, has some very strong principles . . . it's just that they tend to be eccentric. Her view of ethics doesn't always coincide with the common view."

"I don't find that in the least difficult to believe," Marcus said.

"That's true of you, too, Sebastian," Judith pointed out. "You should understand, my lord, that we obey our own rules." Maybe a different form of flirtation would work with this intransigent marquis. If he preferred challenge to coquettry, she could offer him that.

Disappointingly, Marcus shook his head. "That's provocation for another day, ma'am. . . . I'll settle up with you in the morning, Davenport." He scrawled an IOU on the pad at his elbow and pushed it over. "Fill in the sum. What have you done with my cousin, Miss Davenport?"

"He's gone off with Viscount Chancet and his friends. They had an engagement. And he is feeling very much in charity with me, my lord."

Marcus stood up. "Mmmm. Somehow that doesn't surprise me. However, don't rest on your laurels, my dear." He pinched her cheek. "As I told you yesterday, you haven't yet tasted my mettle."

"He's damned familiar with you," Sebastian observed as the marquis walked off.

"Yes, and I could cut his throat," Judith declared. "I'm trying to flirt with him and he treats me like a tiresome child in the schoolroom. I think he believes that now he knows what we are, he can be as familiar as he pleases."

Sebastian frowned. "That's perhaps understandable. Just so long as he keeps his knowledge to himself."

Judith sighed. "I don't seem to be doing too well with my present strategy to ensure that he does."

"You were confident enough yesterday," her brother reminded her, gathering up the cards. "And you've never failed yet."

"True." Judith nodded resolutely to herself. "There has to be some way to persuade him to take me seriously. I suspect quarreling with him is the answer."

Sebastian laughed. "Well, you're the fire-eater of the family, Ju."

"Yes, and I intend to put it to good use." A tiny smile flickered over her mouth. She was unable to deny the prickle of excitement at the prospect of joining in a battle of wits and wills with the most honorable marquis.

3

"GOOD MORNING, CHARLIE." MARCUS GREETED HIS COUSIN THE NEXT MORN-ing. Charlie was already at the breakfast table facing a platter of sirloin and mumbled an answering greeting through a mouthful of beef.

"How much did you lose at the tables the other night?" Marcus inquired casually, pouring himself coffee. "When you were playing macao at Davenport's table." He regarded the chafing dishes on the sideboard with an appraising eye.

Charlie swallowed his mouthful and took a gulp of ale. "Not much."

"And how much is not much?" Marcus helped himself to a dish of deviled kidneys.

"Seven hundred guineas," his cousin said with an air of defiance. "I don't consider that beyond my means."

"No," Marcus agreed affably enough. "So long as one doesn't do it every night. Do you play often at his table?"

"That was the first time, I believe." Charlie frowned. "Why do you ask?"

Marcus didn't reply, but continued with his own questions. "Did his sister suggest you play at her brother's table?"

"I don't remember. It's not the kind of thing a fellow does remember." Charlie stared at his cousin in puzzlement and some apprehension. In his experience, Marcus rarely asked pointless questions, and it seemed this series might well be leading up to a stricture on gaming . . . familiar but nevertheless mortifying.

But Marcus merely shrugged and opened the newspaper. "No, I suppose it's not. . . . By the by . . ." He folded back the paper and spoke with his eyes on the page. "Don't you think Judith Davenport's a little too rich for your blood?"

Charlie flushed. "What are you trying to say?"

"Nothing much," Marcus replied, glancing briefly over the newspaper. "She's an attractive woman and a practiced flirt."

"She's . . . she's a wonderful woman," Charlie exclaimed, pushing back his chair, his flush deepening. "You cannot insult her!"

"Now don't fly into the boughs, Charlie. I doubt she'd deny the description herself." Marcus reached for the mustard.

"Of course she's not a flirt." Charlie glared at his cousin over the stiffly starched folds of his linen cravat.

Marcus sighed. "Well, we won't argue terms, but she's too much for a nineteen-year-old to handle, Charlie. She's no schoolroom chit."

"I don't find schoolroom chits in the least appealing," his cousin announced.

"Well, at your age, you should." He looked across the table and said, not unkindly, "Judith Davenport is a sophisticated woman of the world. She plays a deep game and you're way out of your depth. She eats greenhorns for supper, my dear boy. People are already beginning to talk. You don't want to be the laughingstock of Brussels."

"I think it's most unchivalrous, if not downright dishonorable, of you to insult her when she's not here to defend herself," Charlie declared with passion. "And I take leave to tell you—"

"Please don't," Marcus interrupted, waving a dismissive hand. "It's too early in the morning to hear the impassioned rambles of a besotted youth." He forked kidneys into his mouth. "If you want to make a cake of yourself, then you may do so, but do it when I'm not around."

Charlie huffed in speechless indignation, his face burning, then he stormed out of the breakfast parlor.

Marcus winced as the door slammed shut. He wondered if he'd chosen the wrong tactic in this instance. In the past, a cutting comment, a decisively adverse opinion, had been sufficient to bring Charlie back on the right track when he'd been about to stray into some youthful indiscretion. But then Charlie was no longer a schoolboy, and maybe the tactics appropriate for schoolboys wouldn't work with the tender pride of a young man in the throes of first love.

He'd have to try some other approach. His fork paused halfway to his mouth as the approach presented itself, neat and most enticing. What better way to remove Charlie from dangerous proximity to Miss Davenport than to take his place? At present, Marcus had no mistress living under his protection. He had brought his last *affaire* to an expensive close without regret, before coming to Brussels. Supposing he made Judith Davenport an offer she couldn't refuse? It would most effectively remove her from Charlie's orbit. And just as effectively, it would cure Charlie of his infatuation, when he saw her for what she was. And for himself . . .

Dear God in heaven. Images of rioting sensuality suddenly filled his head as he found himself mentally stripping her of the elegant gowns, the delicate undergarments, the silken stockings, revealing the lissome slenderness, the supple limbs, the white fineness of her skin. Would she be a passionate lover or passive . . . no, definitely not passive . . . wild and tumbling, with the eager words of hungry need, the tumultuous cries of fulfillment unchecked upon her lips. Impossible to believe she could be otherwise.

Marcus shook his head clear of the images. If they alone could arouse him, what would the reality do? The proposition took concrete shape. Yes, he would make Miss Judith Davenport an offer she couldn't possibly refuse: one beyond the wildest dreams of a woman who earned her bread at the gaming tables.

An hour later, in buckskin britches and a morning coat of olive-green superfine, his top boots catching the sunlight like a polished diamond, his lordship set out in search of Miss Davenport. There was a powerful tension in the Brussels' air, knots of people gathered on street corners, talking and gesticulating excitedly. He discovered the reason in the regimental mess.

"It looks like Boney's going to attack," Peter Wellby told him as he joined the circle of Wellington's staff and advisors deep in an almost frenzied discussion. "He issued a *Proclamation à l'armee* yesterday, and it's just come into our hands." He handed Marcus a document. "He's reminding his men that it's the anniversary of the battles of Marengo and Friedland. If they've succeeded in deciding the fate of the world twice before on this day, then they'll do it a third time."

Marcus read it. "Mmm. Napoleon's usual style," he commented. "An appeal to past glories to drum up spirit and patriotism."

"But it usually works," Colonel, Lord Francis Tallent observed a touch glumly. "We've been sitting on our backsides waiting to catch him off guard, and the bastard takes the initiative right out from under our noses. We're prepared to attack, not defend."

Marcus nodded. "It would have been worth remembering that Napoleon has never waited to be attacked. His strategy has always been based on a vast and overwhelming offensive."

There was a moment of uncomfortable silence. Marcus Devlin had been vociferous in this view for the last week, but his had been a lone voice crying in the wilderness. "We did receive a report from our agents that he was taking up the defensive on the Charleroi road," Peter said eventually.

"Agents can be fed mistaken information." Marcus's wry observation generated another silence.

"Marcus, I'm glad to see you, man." Arthur Wellesley, Duke of Wellington, came out of a next-door office, a chart in his hand. "You seem to have had the right idea. Now, look at this. He can attack at Ligny, Quatre Bras, or Nivelles. Do you have an opinion?" He laid the chart on a table, jabbing at the three crossroads with a stubby forefinger.

Marcus examined the chart. "Ligny," he said definitely. "It's the weakest point in our line. There's a hole where Blücher's forces and ours don't meet."

"Blücher's ordered men up from Namur to reinforce his troops at Ligny," the duke said. "We'll concentrate our army on the front from Brussels to Nivelles."

"Supposing the French swing round to the north toward Quatre Bras," Marcus pointed out, tracing the line with a fingertip. "He'll separate the two forces and force us to fight on two fronts."

Wellington frowned, stroking his chin. "Can you join me in conference this afternoon?" He rolled up the chart.

"At your service, Duke." Marcus bowed.

His own plans ought to seem less urgent in the face of the present emergency, but for some reason they weren't. He would see Judith tonight, of course, at the Duchess of Richmond's ball, but he was in a fever of impatience, almost as if he were still a green youth pursuing the object of hot and flagrant fantasy. Reasoning that he could be of little use until the afternoon's conference, he decided to continue his search.

He ran her to earth at the lodgings of one of Wellington's aides-de-camp. It seemed as if half Brussels were gathered there, chattering and exclaiming over the news that, incredibly, Napoleon had taken Wellington by surprise and was even now preparing for an attack on the city.

"But the duke has all well in hand," a bewhiskered colonel reassured a twittering, panicked lady in an Angoulême bonnet. "He'll concentrate his troops on the Nivelles road to meet any attack on the city."

"I'm sure there's nothing to concern us, dear ma'am," came the dulcet tones of Miss Davenport. She was standing by the window and a shaft of sunlight ignited the rich copper hair braided in a demure coronet around her head. She was in flowing muslins, a wisp of lace doing duty as a hat, and Carrington regarded her for a minute in appreciative silence. There was something wonderfully tantalizing about the contrast between her demurely elegant dress and the wicked gleam in the gold-brown eyes as she surveyed the room and its alarmed inhabitants with the faintest tinge of derision. A jolt of anticipatory excitement surprised him. He didn't think he'd felt such powerful lust since his youth.

He crossed the room toward her. "Your sangfroid is estimable, ma'am. Don't you feel the slightest tremor at the thought of the ogre?"

"Not in the least, sir." Idly she twirled her closed parasol on the floor. "I trust you've recovered from your losses last night. They were rather heavy, I believe."

"Are you referring to my losses to your brother, or to his sister, ma'am?" His eyes narrowed as he flipped open his snuff box and took a delicate pinch.

"I was not aware of any winnings, sir." She looked up at him through her eyelashes. "Only of the need to keep up my point."

"I'm hoping to persuade you to lower that point." He replaced the enameled snuff box in the deep pocket of his coat. "I have a proposal to make, Miss Davenport. May I call upon you this afternoon?"

"Unfortunately, my aunt, who lives with us, is indisposed and visitors quite put her out of curl. The sound of the door knocker is enough to throw her into strong hysterics," she said with a bland smile.

"What a masterly fibber you are, Miss Davenport," he observed amiably. "I won't ask why you see a need to keep your direction a close secret."

"How gentlemanly of you, Lord Carrington."

"Yes, isn't it? But perhaps I could induce you to call upon me."

"Now, that, my lord, is not a gentlemanly suggestion."

"I was, of course, assuming your aunt would escort you as chaperone," he murmured.

An appreciative twinkle appeared in her eyes. This was much more amusing than an ordinary flirtation. Marcus Devlin was certainly an entertaining opponent when it came to challenges. "I'm afraid she doesn't go out of doors, either."

"How very inconvenient . . . or do I mean convenient?"

"I don't know what you could mean, Lord Carrington."

"Well, what's to be done? I wish to have private speech with you; how is it to be contrived?"

"You seemed remarkably expert at abduction the other evening," Judith heard herself say, astonished at the recklessness of her response.

He bowed, and his black eyes glittered. "If that's how you'd like to proceed, I am always happy to oblige. Make your farewells, we're going in search of privacy."

"You would find it difficult to abduct me from this room, I think, sir." She gestured to the crowd.

"Do you care to make a wager, ma'am?"

She caught her lower lip between her teeth, putting her head on one side as she considered the question. This was infinitely more entertaining than simple flirtation. "Twenty guineas?"

"We have a wager, Miss Davenport." The next instant, he had swept her off her feet and bundled her into his arms. It was so startling, she was momentarily speechless. And then he was pushing through the crowd with his burden. "Miss Davenport is feeling faint. I fear the news of Napoleon's advent has quite overset her."

"Oh, goodness me, and it's no wonder," the bewhiskered colonel said. "We must protect the delicate sensibilities of ladies from such news."

"Just so, Naseby," Marcus agreed. "I'm going to take her into the air. It's very close in here." People fell back, clucking solicitously, clearing his path to the door. Judith, recovered from her surprise, still found it impossible to say anything that wouldn't make the situation even more farcical, and was obliged to close her eyes tight and remain still as he carried her out of the house and into the street.

There he set his seething burden on her feet, dusted off his hands with great satisfaction, and said, "You owe me twenty guineas, Miss Davenport."

"That was shameless!" she exclaimed. "And to say I was swooning with fear of Napoleon was . . . was . . . was . . . Oh, I can't think of the right words."

"Dastardly," he supplied helpfully. "Despicable, shabby . . ."

"Unsporting," she snapped. "Adding insult to injury."

"But irresistible, you must admit."

"I admit nothing." She smoothed down her skirts and adjusted a pin in the diminutive lacy cap, before putting up her parasol. "I don't have twenty guineas with me, my lord. But I will send it around to your house this afternoon."

"That will be quite convenient." He bowed. "However, I'm more interested at the moment in finding somewhere private. We'll walk in the park, I think." He drew her arm through his.

"I don't care to walk in the park." Petulance seemed to have replaced mature challenge.

"Would you prefer me to escort you home?" he offered with prompt courtesy.

"You know I would not."

"Then it must be the park."

And that seemed to be that. Short of turning and running, which would be ridiculously undignified, there seemed no alternative but to do as he said. She'd husband her resources for the time being.

They passed through the iron gates at the entrance to the park and Lord Carrington directed their steps unerringly to a small copse.

Judith hesitated as they moved into the cool, green seclusion. Something didn't feel right. "Can't we have this discussion in the open, my lord?"

"No, because I can't be walking around when I say what I wish to say, and if we were to stand still in the middle of the path it would look very odd." Releasing her arm, he sat down on a stone bench encircling the trunk of a pine tree and patted the space beside him.

Judith was unsure whether it was invitation or command, but it didn't seem to matter. She sat down, curiosity now getting the better of unease.

"I'll come straight to the point," he said.

"Do."

He ignored the sardonic interjection. "A house and servants in Half Moon Street; a barouche and pair, or laundelet, if you prefer; a riding horse; and a quarterly allowance of two thousand pounds."

"Good God," Judith said. "Whatever are you saying?" She turned to look up at him, her eyes wide. "I think you are run mad."

"It seems reasonable," he said. "Such an allowance should be more than enough to keep you in style . . . of course, there'll be presents. You'll not find me ungenerous, my dear."

"Sweet heaven." The color had drained from her cheeks. "Could you be utterly precise about what you're offering me, my lord?"

It struck him she was being unusually obtuse. "A carte blanche," he elucidated. "And I will make provision for your future should we . . . should we tire of one another." He smiled. "There now, what could be fairer than that?"

Judith rose from the bench. Turning her back on him, she walked a few paces away. Her game of intrigue had suddenly got out of hand. It was one thing to engage a man in a pointful flirtation, quite another to be his paid whore. *How dared he make such a proposition . . . make such assumptions about her?*

Marcus watched her fumble in her reticule and thought perhaps she was looking for her handkerchief. Such an offer would be sufficient to bring tears to the eyes of the most grasping female.

"I don't have anyone to defend my honor, Lord Carrington, so I must do it for myself." She turned. In her hand was a small, silver-mounted pistol, and it was pointed in the most workmanlike fashion at his heart. "You have insulted me beyond bearing. Davenports are not whores. Even highly paid whores."

Carrington was vaguely aware that his jaw had dropped and his mouth was hanging open as he stared in shocked amazement, his eyes riveted to the small, deadly muzzle pointing at his chest. "Don't be ridiculous," he said, swallowing hard. "Put the gun away, Judith, before you do something stupid."

"I am an excellent shot, I should tell you," she said. "I'm not about to do anything stupid. Indeed, I consider putting a bullet in you, my lord, to be one of my more sensible notions."

"God in heaven," he whispered, trying to order the turmoil raging in his brain. For some reason, he had the unshakable conviction that Judith Davenport was more than capable of pulling the trigger. "I intended no insult," he tried. "Not to you or to your family. The manner in which you and your brother live led me to assume you wouldn't be averse to an unconventional but nevertheless convenient source of income. You don't live like a woman of virtue, ma'am, however skillful you are at the masquerade. You and your brother lead a raffish, hand-to-mouth existence in the shadows of the gaming tables. Can you deny that?"

Judith didn't attempt to do so. "That doesn't justify offering me such a dishonorable proposal. My circumstances are not of my own making. You can know nothing of them."

Marcus swallowed again. His mouth was very dry. He wondered if he could cross the space between them before she pulled the trigger. He couldn't. He watched, mesmerized, as she squinted down the barrel, extending her hand with the pistol straight in front of her. The sharp report and the flash of fire from the barrel were simultaneous. The smell of cordite hung in the muggy air. He waited for the pain, but there was nothing. He followed the direction of her eyes, between his feet. The bullet had dug a neat hole in the ground, directly in the middle of the space between his boots. It was no accident.

"I decided you weren't worth hanging for," Judith said coldly. She dropped the pistol in her reticule. "I'll send the twenty guineas to your house as soon as I return to my lodgings."

Marcus cleared his throat. "In the circumstances, I am prepared to forgo the wager."

"I always pay my debts of honor," she said. "Or did you think that I was without honor in that respect also?"

He waved his hands in hasty retraction. "It was only a suggestion. One quite without merit, I realize."

Judith glared at him for a minute, then she turned and marched away through the trees.

Marcus let out his breath on a slow exhalation, running his hands through his hair. He had assumed she received such proposals often enough. She lived by her wits, it was only to be expected that she might use her body, too. But what had her brother said? Something about his sister's eccentric principles. Presumably, he'd just been given a lesson in them.

Sweet heaven, what an exciting partner in passion such a woman would make. Perversely, he found he had not the slightest intention of giving up his pursuit.

"Good God, what's happened to send you into such a temper, Ju?" Sebastian looked up from the chess board as his sister banged fuming through the door of their living room.

"I don't think I have ever been angrier," she said, drawing her gloves off her trembling hands. "Lord Carrington has just had the . . . the unmitigated gall to offer me a carte blanche." She tossed her gloves onto the sofa and pulled the pins loose from her hat.

Sebastian whistled. "What did you say?"

"I shot him." She pulled the pistol from her reticule and hurled it onto the sofa.

Her brother reached over and picked up the weapon. The smell of cordite was acrid on the muzzle. He spun the chamber. It was empty. "Well, you certainly shot something," he observed. "But somehow I doubt it was the marquis. You've the devil of a temper, but I don't see you as a murderess."

Judith bit her lip. Sebastian could always bring her down to earth. "I shot between his feet," she said. "But I frightened him, Sebastian. He really thought for a minute he was about to meet his maker." She chuckled suddenly, relishing the memory. "Pour me a glass of sherry, love. It's been a most trying morning, one way or another."

Sebastian filled two sherry glasses from the decanter on the sideboard. "What were the terms of the carte blanche?" he asked with a bland look. "Just as a matter of interest, of course."

When she told him, he whistled once more. "If it weren't for Gracemere, it might have done very well for both of us."

"You would sell your own sister?" she exclaimed.

"Oh, only to the highest bidder," he assured her solemnly.

Judith threw a cushion at him, then bent to examine the chess problem positioned on the board. Chess was a way of sharpening their wits, particularly before an evening's gaming.

"Of course, if anyone suspects for one second that we're not what we seem when we get to London, we'll never be able to move in Gracemere's circles," Sebastian said, serious now. He sipped his sherry. "You've inadvertently given Carrington the wrong impression. I think, m'dear, that it may be time to cultivate higher necklines and a pious air."

"And what will you cultivate, brother?" She regarded him over the lip of her glass.

"Oh, I shall be a most serious student of foreign parts," he declared. "I shall have traveled extensively and be most amazingly knowledgeable, and most amazingly boring, as I prose on and on about the flora and fauna of exotic places."

Judith chuckled, imagining her good-humored, insouciant sibling in such a guise. "You'd have to forsake striped waistcoats and starched cravats, and play whist for penny points."

"Well, that I don't think I could manage," he said. "Not if we're to have enough to pay our expenses." He came to look at the chess board with her. "Can you see it? White to move and mate in three. I've been looking at it for half an hour and can't get beyond queening the pawn. But then it's stalemate."

Judith frowned, considering. What if the pawn knighted, instead? She ran through the consequences in her head. "Let's try pawn to queen seven."

Sebastian moved the pieces, following the logic now on his own, bringing the problem to solution. "Clever girl," he said, toppling the black king with a fingertip. "You've always been able to see farther than I can."

"At chess, but you're better at piquet."

Sebastian shrugged, but offered no disclaimer. "Shall we have nuncheon?" He gestured to the table.

Judith wrinkled her nose at the dull and insubstantial repast laid out by their landlady. "Bread and cheese again."

"But we're dining with the Gardeners," he reminded her, cutting into the loaf. "And supper at the Duchess of Richmond's ball should be more than palatable."

"And I daresay the Most Honorable Marquis of Carrington will be present." Judith sat down and dug a knife into the wedge of cheese. "I don't seem to have done too well at disarming him, do I?" She frowned. "Threatening to shoot a man isn't very flirtatious." She took the cheese off the knife with her fingers and absently popped it into her mouth. "Oh." She was suddenly reminded. "I have to settle a debt of honor. I owe Carrington twenty guineas."

4

IT HARDLY SEEMED POSSIBLE THAT NAPOLEON AND HIS ARMY WERE GATHERED a stone's throw from the city, Judith thought, as she and Sebastian joined the receiving line that night, slowly progressing up the wide shallow staircase, to be announced to the Duchess of Richmond standing at the head.

There were more men in uniform than in civilian evening dress. The women glittered under the brilliant chandeliers—a swarm of jeweled butterflies in gowns every shade of the rainbow. But something lurked beneath the gaiety—a feverishness to the conversations, a slightly shrill pitch to the laughter, the distracted darting of eyes around the room, on the watch for a sign, a hint of new information. The world contained in the Duchess of Richmond's salons this hot June night was in waiting.

The Marquis of Carrington was speaking with the Duke of Wellington and General Karl von Clausewitz across the salon from the double entrance doors as Judith and Sebastian entered the room. Judith glanced sideways into the massive gilt-framed mirror on the wall, checking her reflection. She was abruptly annoyed with herself. After this morning's debacle, Carrington was unlikely to approach her, and why did she want him to? The man had offered her the most offensive insult imaginable. She turned to her brother. "Dance with me, Sebastian."

"If you wish." He looked at her quizzically. "But since when have you been dependent on your brother for a partner?"

"My card is filled from the third cotillion," she said, taking his arm. "I refused partners until then because I didn't think I'd want to dance immediately. But I find that I do."

Sebastian said nothing, merely clasped her waist lightly and whirled her into the dance.

They were a strikingly handsome couple, Carrington reflected, watching them, his mind wandering from the discussion of the need for latitudinal support for the Prussians behind the Sambre. Copper-haired and with those fine golden-brown eyes, flecked with green, they could almost be twins. There must be barely a year between them. Judith's chin was slightly more rounded than her brother's, but they both had straight, well-proportioned noses and generous mouths, slanting cheekbones and firm jawlines. An elegant pair of disreputable adventurers. Who were they? And where the devil had they sprung from?

Would she refuse to dance with him after the morning's fiasco? A man's pride could take only so many defeats at the hands of an impudent, though admittedly clever, baggage.

After excusing himself from his companions, he moved around the dance floor until the Davenports were abreast of him. Then he weaved his way deftly between dancing couples and lightly tapped Sebastian's shoulder. It was a most unorthodox procedure, but sometimes a man must be creative.

"Will you yield your sister, Davenport? It seems a crying shame that you should keep her to yourself when you have the advantage of her company at all other times."

Sebastian grinned. "Well, as to that, Carrington, it's for Judith to say."

"Ma'am?" Carrington bowed with a self-mocking gallantry. His eyes smiled, both colluding and conciliatory.

Judith glanced around, well aware of the notice the byplay was attracting. Marcus Devlin had rather cleverly cornered her.

"I suppose a woman must grow accustomed to being passed from hand to hand like a parcel," she said, gracefully moving out of Sebastian's encircling arm and turning into her new partner's hold.

"Baggages are usually handled in such fashion," Marcus murmured, savoring the feel of her. She was light and compact . . . and as sleek and dangerous as a lynx.

Judith drew a sharp breath. "I suppose, after this morning, I must expect such an insult from you, sir."

"Is that the best you can do?" His eyebrows lifted quizzically. "You disappoint me, Judith."

"Unfortunately, I don't have my pistol with me," she returned. "I trust you've recovered your equilibrium, sir."

"It took awhile," he admitted. "I've never had dealings with a lynx before, you see."

"A lynx?" She was betrayed into looking up at him. His black eyes laughed down at her, rich with enjoyment.

"Yes, my lynx, exactly so."

A tinge of pink appeared on her high cheekbones. It seemed sensible to ignore such a statement. "You received the payment of my debt of honor, I trust, sir."

"I did indeed. I am grateful for the improvement in my financial state."

She caught her lip between her teeth and resolutely fixed her gaze in the middle distance over his shoulder. But it was impossible, and finally she chuckled and he felt the tension leave her body.

"Am I forgiven?" he asked, suddenly serious.

"For what, my lord?"

"I'm not playing games now, Judith. I have begged your pardon for this morning. I should like to know if my apology is accepted."

"It would be ungenerous of me to refuse to do so, my lord."

"And you are not, of course, ungenerous."

She met his eye then. "No, I am not. It's not the Davenport way. Any more than it's our way to be dishonorable."

"Card sharping is honorable then?" It was not a playful question and she bit her lip again, but not this time to hide her laughter.

"I can't explain about that."

"No, I should imagine it's very difficult to explain."

"We don't make a habit of it," she said stiffly.

"I'm relieved to hear it."

"When we win at the tables, we win on skill and experience," she said. "What you saw . . . or thought you saw—"

"I saw it."

"We were merely practicing for a couple of hands. The money involved was insignificant."

"You'll forgive me if I remain unconvinced of the scrupulous purity of your play."

Judith was silent. There seemed nothing more to say.

When he spoke again, the hard edge had left his voice. "I might, however, be induced to understand why you were obliged to learn such dubious arts."

Her chin went up and for the first time he saw the shadows in the lynx eyes. "Would you, my lord?" she said coldly. "That's really too kind of you. But I hope you won't consider me discourteous if I tell you my business is my own. Your understanding is a matter of complete indifference to me."

Marcus drew breath in sharp anger. His hand tightened around hers, crushing the slender fingers. Then the dance ended and she had pulled free of him. Fighting his anger, he watched her walk off the floor, her gown of ivory spider gauze over deep cream satin setting off the rich burnished copper hair falling in delicate ringlets to her shoulders. He wondered whether the topaz necklace and earrings were paste. If they were, they were remarkably good copies. But then he couldn't fault the skill with which the Davenports conducted their masquerade.

Who the devil were they? And why did she arouse in him this savage hunger?

He shook his head impatiently and stalked off the dance floor. An image of Martha drifted into his head: soft, brown-haired, doe-eyed

Martha, who wouldn't say boo to a goose. Gentle, simple Martha . . . the perfect prey. A lamb on the one hand and an untamed lynx on the other. There must be a middle course.

Judith retreated to the retiring room. She was more shaken than she cared to admit by the intimacy of Carrington's questions. They trespassed on the darkness, the darkness that only Sebastian could ever truly know and understand, because he shared it. She confided only in her brother. It was the way it had to be. Their secrets and their griefs and their plans were their own. They knew no other way of living.

She bent to the mirror, adjusting a pin in her hair. The room was filled with chattering women, making repairs to dress or countenance. The talk was all of what they would do when the battle was joined.

"I'm not staying here to be raped by a horde of Frenchmen," one lady declaimed, fanning herself vigorously as she sat on a velvet stool in front of a mirror.

"Oh, dear countess, how could you imagine such a thing happening?" squeaked a dim, brown mouse of a woman, dropping a comb to the floor. "The duke would never leave us to the mercies of the ogre."

"Once our own men have left the city, those Frenchies will be here, you mark my words," the countess said with an almost salacious dread as she brushed a haresfoot across her rouged cheeks.

"Well, they do have to defeat our own armies first," Judith pointed out demurely. "One mustn't presume disaster too quickly."

"Indeed not," the stout wife of a colonel put in. "You're quite right, Miss Davenport. Our men need our support, not whining snivels. Of course they'll defeat Boney."

"Of course," Judith agreed. "No purpose is served by panic."

Thus chastised, the countess and the brown mouse fell into an injured silence.

"There'll be a run on horses once the battle's joined," another woman remarked calmly. "Alfred's hidden away our carriage horses in a stable outside the city. Once he's left for the front, he's instructed me to leave the city. Just in case," she added, with a smile at Judith and the colonel's wife. "Sensible people make provision for every eventuality."

"You wouldn't find me leaving Colonel Douglas in the heat of battle," Colonel Douglas's wife declared, disappearing behind the commode screen, her voice rising above the stiff rustlings of her taffeta skirts. "It's the duty of a soldier's wife to wait behind the lines and the heartbreak of a soldier's wife to wait in fear. I've been at the colonel's side through every battle on the Peninsula and I'm not running shy now . . . damned Frenchies or not. I'd like to see them try their tricks with me."

Judith chuckled, her composure restored, and left the retiring room. As she was making her way back to the ballroom she ran into Charlie.

"I saw you dancing with Marcus," he said accusingly. "You said you wouldn't agree to dance until the third cotillion."

"I wasn't intending to," she replied with a reassuring smile. "But my brother persuaded me to waltz and your cousin cut in on us."

"Marcus can be rather high-handed," Charlie said, slightly molli-fied. "Though I've noticed that women seem to like that sort of thing."

"My dear Charlie," she said with asperity. "We're not all ac-cepting of the yoke."

Charlie looked startled at such a novel thought. His tentative laugh was unconvincing. "You're always funning."

"Oh, make no mistake, Charlie, I was not funning." She tapped his arm lightly with her fan. "You haven't known many women yet, but that'll change."

"You think me a mere greenhorn." Disconsolately he remem-bered his cousin's words over the breakfast table.

Judith smiled to herself and made haste to bolster his wounded self-esteem. "No, of course I don't. But a soldier has little time for dalliance."

"Yes, that's certainly so." Charlie brightened. "We have other things on our minds. The duke is wonderfully calm, don't you think?

He says he's made his dispositions and is perfectly certain of how things will develop."

Judith glanced thoughtfully across the room to where Wellington was laughing with a group of his officers in the midst of an admiring circle of ladies. He had a glass of champagne in his hand and certainly didn't appear a man whose mortal enemy was drawing up battle lines a few miles away. Was he a fool or a genius? The latter, it was to be hoped. Otherwise Brussels could become rather uncomfortable.

"Miss Davenport, have you been introduced to the Duke of Wellington?"

The Marquis of Carrington's voice at her shoulder startled Judith into a betraying flush. "No," she said, fanning herself vigorously. "Must you creep up on me like that?"

Marcus glanced around the crowded salon and raised his eyebrows. "Creep up on you in this crowd? Come now, Miss Davenport, I didn't intend anything so theatrical." He drew her arm through his. "Allow me to introduce you to the duke. He flirts outrageously with all pretty women, but he appreciates a nimble wit as well as a pretty face."

Judith allowed herself to be swept off. The introduction was a great honor, and perhaps Carrington intended it as a peace offering of some sort. It would be churlish to reject it. Her escort cleared a path for them through the crowd with a touch on a shoulder, a soft excuse, an occasional bow, until they reached the corner where the duke was holding court.

"May I introduce Miss Davenport, Duke." Marcus drew Judith forward.

"Delighted, ma'am." The duke bowed over her hand, his eyes twinkling appreciatively over his prominent nose. "Quite charming . . . I have been watching you all evening and wondering how to effect an introduction. Fortunately, my friend Carrington tells me he has the great good fortune to be a friend of yours."

So it wasn't a peace offering at all. She'd been commandeered—if not procured—for the great man's entertainment.

"It's the barest acquaintanceship, sir," Judith said, smiling brilliantly at the duke over her fan. "But I'm honored his lordship considered it sufficient to bring me to you. I stand in his debt."

"No, no, ma'am, it's I who stand in his debt," the duke said expansively. "A glass of champagne now. And we shall have a good talk." Linking his arm in hers, he drew her out of the circle, gesturing with his free hand to a servant bearing a tray of glasses.

Barest acquaintanceship indeed! The insolent baggage had made him out to be a coxcomb who fancied an intimacy that didn't exist. Torn between amusement and annoyance, Marcus watched her walk off on the duke's arm.

It was almost three o'clock in the morning when the Duchess of Richmond's grand ball disintegrated into a confusion of panicked civilians and galvanized officers. An equerry had entered the ballroom and stood for a minute with his gaze raking the glittering throng in search of the commander-in-chief. Then he hurried through the crowd to where the duke was sitting on a window seat beside Judith.

Wellington was delighted with his companion, who was not in the least prudish and quite prepared to flirt as openly and outrageously as he was.

"I do enjoy women of the world, my dear," he said, patting her hand. "None of these die-away airs and touch-me-nots about you, Miss Davenport."

"Shame on you, Duke." Judith laughingly chided without moving her hand from his. "You'll ruin my reputation."

"Not so, ma'am. Your reputation's safe enough with me."

Judith put her head on one side and gave him an arch smile. "More's the pity."

Wellington roared with laughter. He was still laughing when the equerry reached him.

"Duke?"

"What is it, man?" he demanded testily.

"Dispatches, sir." The equerry looked around the room. "In private, my lord."

Wellington stood up immediately. "Excuse me, Miss Davenport." He was suddenly a different man, his face as somber as if it had never known laughter.

Judith rose with quick understanding, holding out her hand. "I'll leave you to your business, Duke."

He took her hand and kissed it, then strode off, beckoning to members of his staff as he made his way to a small room off the ballroom. "Ask Lord Carrington to join us," he said to an aide.

Marcus entered the salon a few minutes later, closing the double doors behind him. "Quatre Bras?" he said immediately.

"You were damned right, Marcus. Boney's left has swung round to the north. The Prince of Orange has him checked at Quatre Bras, but Napoleon's preparing to open the attack."

"And with his right, simultaneously attack the Prussians at Ligny," Marcus said.

"Ligny to the east and Quatre Bras to the west," Wellington agreed, bending over a chart. "Sound general quarters. We'll make our stand at Quatre Bras."

Outside the small salon, the ballroom buzzed. The musicians continued to play, but dancers were few as knots of people gathered in corners and the officers discreetly melted away. Judith was searching for Sebastian when Charlie approached her, his expression radiating excitement.

"Judith, I must go and join my regiment."

"What's happened?"

"General quarters has been sounded and we're to march to Quatre Bras."

He couldn't conceal his eagerness and Judith felt a great surge of affection for him, followed by apprehension. So many young men all so ready to find a bloody death on the battlefield.

"My first battle," he said.

"Yes, and you will be brave as a lion," she said, smiling with a great effort. "Come, I'll see you off."

She walked with him downstairs. Men in uniform milled around the hall. Orders were hastily and quietly given. Groups of soldiers took their leave, trying to appear as if nothing out of the ordinary had happened as they went through the great doors standing open to the stone steps outside. Once outside, however, discretion went to the four winds and they were off and running, calling for carriages, yelling orders and information.

Judith reached up and kissed Charlie lightly on the corner of his mouth. "Be safe."

"Oh, yes, of course I shall." He was impatient to be off, his eyes chasing around the hall. "Oh, there's Larson. He's in my company."

"Off you go, then." She gave him a friendly little push. He gave her a rueful, slightly guilty smile, then ducked his head and kissed her with a jerky bob.

"I do think you're wonderful, Judith."

"Of course you do," she said. "Be off with you. You have more important things on your mind now than dalliance."

"Yes, yes I have. That's quite true."

She waggled her fingers at him as he backed away into the crowd. He grinned suddenly, blew her a kiss, and then turned and plunged into the melee, calling for his friend.

Feeling stricken, Judith turned and went back up the stairs. Sebastian was looking for her. He held her cloak, his own already around his shoulders. "Judith, I must take you home."

She glanced around at the emptying salons. "Yes, there seems little point remaining. Although maybe we might hear some more news."

"There'll be no more news to be had here." Her brother draped the gold taffeta cloak around her shoulders. "Wellington and Clausewitz have left with their entourages. They're to set out for Quatre Bras within the half hour." He urged her down the stairs with an impatient hand under her elbow.

"What's your hurry, Sebastian?"

"Oh, come on, Ju." He looked anxiously around. "I don't want to miss anything."

"Miss what?"

"The battle," he said, again propelling her down the stairs.

"You're going?" But she knew the answer. It would be impossible for Sebastian to kick his heels in Brussels while the fate of Europe was being decided such a short distance away.

He gave her the same rueful, slightly guilty smile she had received from Charlie. "I'd give my eye teeth to have a crack at Boney myself, Ju. Since I can't do that, I must at least *be* there."

She made no attempt to dissuade him. If their lives had been different—had been as they should have been—her brother's birthright would have included a pair of colors in the Scots Greys, the regiment that had seen the service of generations of Devereux. It must be torment for him to be forced to stand on the sidelines while his peers in their brilliant regimentals plunged into the fray.

But soon it would be put right. Soon Sebastian would reclaim his birthright. She linked her arm through his and squeezed it tightly. He returned the squeeze absentmindedly and she knew that for once his thoughts were a great distance away from her own.

5

AT THEIR LODGINGS, JUDITH WAITED IN THE SITTING ROOM WHILE SEBASTIAN
changed out of his evening dress and into buckskins and riding
boots.

"Where are you going to find a horse?"

"Steven Wainwright has offered to mount me on his spare nag."
He checked through his pockets, counting the bills in his billfold.
"You'll be all right, Ju?"

She wasn't sure whether it was statement or question. "Of course.
We'll meet here when it's all over."

He bent to kiss her. "I hate to leave you . . . but . . ."

"Oh, go!" she said. "Don't give me a second thought. But just be
careful. We have things to do and we can't risk a stray bullet."

"I know. Do you doubt me?" The excitement faded in his eyes to
be replaced by the shadowed intensity so often to be found in his
sister's.

She shook her head. "Never."

Judith listened to his booted feet on the stairs and the slam of the front door. She went to the window overlooking the narrow lane and watched as he strode, almost at a run, toward the center of town.

It was four o'clock in the morning and the city was as alive as if it were midday. Bells were ringing; people leaned out of windows in their nightcaps, shouting across the narrow lanes. She could hear the roar of the crowds in the streets a short distance away, a roar edged with hysteria. The citizens of Brussels were terrified.

Judith had no intention of missing the drama herself, although she couldn't have told Sebastian that. It would have ruined his own adventure. Swiftly she changed out of her ball dress into a dark-blue riding habit of serviceable broadcloth and drew on her York tan gloves. She unlocked the wooden chest under her bed, put away the paste jewelry she had been wearing, and took a wad of bank notes from the supply, tucking them away in the deep pocket of her coat. Into the other pocket went her pistol, cleaned and primed.

She let herself out of the house, locking the door behind her, then hesitated, wondering which direction to take. She needed transport, but she suspected that tonight horses couldn't be acquired for love or money. The inhabitants of Brussels would be holding onto their horseflesh in preparation for flight.

Following a hunch, she turned into an alley that would lead her even farther away from the fashionable part of town, into the poorer commercial areas. The people here would see less need to run from the ogre.

Raucous shouts, singing, and laughter came from a tavern at the end of the lane, yellow light spilling from the open door onto the mired cobbles. Some people were not intimidated by the prospect of battle on their doorstep. A farmer's cart stood in the shadows and her heart leaped exultantly. Between the shafts, a thin horse hung a weary head.

Judith crept up to the cart, patting the nag's hollowed neck. The cart was empty so presumably its owner had sold his produce that evening and, judging from the noise within the tavern, was probably drinking up his profits. With luck he wouldn't surface for hours and she could return the horse before he'd missed it. She unhitched the bridle from the post. Cautiously she backed the horse and cart away from the tavern. Then she sprang onto the driver's seat, shook the reins gently, and clicked her tongue. With a heavy sigh, the horse pulled away down the lane.

As soon as she emerged from the poorer sections, Judith realized the panic in the city was full blown. Houses stood open as their residents ran back and forth with possessions, filling carriages and dog carts. Men and women hurried through the streets, and every-where was heard the cry for horses.

As she drove down a narrow cobbled lane, two men came out of the shadows, seizing her nag by the bridle, close to the bit. The horse came to an immediate stop with a snort indicative of relief. "All right, miss, we're requisitioning your horse," one of the men said. He wore the baize apron of a servant, but the man accompanying him was a stout, florid gentleman in satin waistcoat and knee britches. He stood breathing heavily, hanging onto the bridle for dear life.

"On whose authority?" Judith demanded, her hand moving to her pocket, closing over the pistol.

"Never you mind on whose authority," the stout gentleman wheezed. "I need that horse."

"Well, so do I," Judith pointed out. "Let go of the bridle, if you please, sir."

The man in the baize apron came round to the side of the cart, his expression menacing. In his hand, he held a club. "Now, don't make trouble for yourself, miss. You step down from there nice and quick, and no one's going to get hurt."

"I hate to disillusion you, but someone is most definitely going to get hurt." Judith drew the pistol from her pocket, leveling it at the man with the club. "Step away from the cart, and you, sir, release the horse."

The stout man dropped the bridle on a wheezing gasp, but his servant was made of sterner stuff. "She won't use it, sir. Never met a woman yet who could stand to hear the sound of a gun, let alone fire one."

"Well, let me introduce you to a new experience, my good man."

For the second time that day, Judith fired her pistol. The bullet whistled so close to the servant's ear, he could feel the breeze. With a foul oath, he jumped back. The startled horse leaped forward at the same moment and Judith snapped the reins in further encouragement. The ancient nag fairly galloped down the cobbles, the cart swinging and bouncing on its iron wheels behind him.

Judith laughed with pure exhilaration, then she noticed that her hands were gripping the reins so tightly they were numb. She hadn't been conscious of fear during the confrontation, but now her heart began to pound. She drew back on the reins as they left the cobbled alley behind them and took several deep breaths until she felt calmer.

She turned down the broad, tree-lined thoroughfare that would take her to the Quatre Bras road.

Lord Carrington was standing outside a tall town house, observing the antics of his fellow man with both astonishment and amusement. He was in riding dress, tapping his whip against his boots, as he waited for his horse to be brought round from the mews. He had no difficulty recognizing the driver of the cart turning onto the street. She was hatless and the tumbling copper ringlets were unmistakable in the moonlight.

Where the devil was she going? Without conscious purpose, as she came abreast of him, he moved to intercept her. He swung himself upward with an agile twist, and landed on the seat beside her. "Whither away, Miss Davenport? I find it hard to believe you're running."

Judith blinked at him, bemused by this abrupt, unexpected manifestation. "No, of course I'm not, but Sebastian has gone to view the battle and I'm not to be left behind to cool my heels while the men have all the excitement. What are you doing in my cart?"

"Hitching a ride," he said shortly. "What the hell do you think you're doing, going to Quatre Bras?"

"What's it to you, Lord Carrington, where I go?"

He didn't trouble to answer that question. "You're an irresponsible madcap, Miss Davenport," he roundly informed her. "What was your brother about to leave you to brew such mischief alone?"

"I am perfectly able to have a care for myself, my lord, as I rather think you're aware." She glared at him in the gray light of the false dawn.

"Against one unarmed man, maybe. But facing a rabble of looting, rapine soldiery in the aftermath of battle? Permit me to doubt it, ma'am."

"I've just protected myself and my horse most satisfactorily against two armed men," she retorted.

"Pray accept my congratulations," he said caustically. "However, I am not in the least impressed by your powers of self-defense, or your foolhardy courage."

"This is no business of yours!"

"On the contrary, you seem to be becoming my business with dismaying speed." He stretched his long legs in front of him, settling down with every appearance of permanence. "I've a mind to further our *bare* acquaintance." He cast her a sharp look and she had the grace to blush. "I should have expected a hornet's response from you to something kindly meant," he said, rubbing in salt.

Judith took a deep breath. "Maybe I seemed ungracious, but I don't much like being procured."

"Being what!" he exclaimed. "Well, of all the . . ." His shoulders began to shake. "What an eccentric vocabulary you have, lynx. Or perhaps it's just the product of an overactive imagination."

"I don't like being laughed at, either," Judith said crossly.

"Well, you shouldn't be so absurdly insulting."

Judith gave up a battle in which she seemed to be severely handicapped. The road for the moment was deserted, a pale glimmering ribbon ahead of them, the trees and hedgerows slowly taking shape as the night faded. The sky was a deep blue, the North Star a brilliant pinprick, and she had the sensation that they were alone together at the edge of the universe . . . alone and waiting for something to which she could attach no name. She had a slight sinking feeling in her belly and her skin seemed to have a life of its own. The tautly muscled thigh beside her suddenly touched hers on the narrow seat and her whole body jolted with a current of unidentifiable energy.

Marcus felt the jolt deep in his own body, the energy emanating from her, joining with his own. He increased the pressure of his thigh against hers. A recklessness had entered his soul. He wanted this woman as he didn't remember wanting any other, and he didn't care what he had to do to possess her. If he could take advantage of the strange magic of this dawn journey, the apprehension and excitement and drama of events shaping the present moment, then he would. He felt the tension building in the body so close to his and kept silent for a long while, letting her grow accustomed to arousal. When he spoke, it was with a cheerful nonchalance, quite at odds with the brooding tension of the previous silence.

"How did you manage to come by this dog-eared conveyance?" he inquired, watching her hands on the reins.

Judith stared out between the horse's ears, the ordinary question offering a breathing space. After a minute she replied calmly, "Oh, I found it outside a tavern. The owner is probably so far under the hatches by now, he won't notice its absence for hours."

Marcus sat up straight. "Are you telling me you *stole* it?"

"No, I just borrowed it," she said with an airy wave of a hand. "I'll put it back when I've finished with it."

"You are an incorrigible, unscrupulous, card-sharping, horse-thieving hussy!" Marcus declared, truly shocked. "By God, someone had better take you in hand, before you do some serious damage and find yourself at the end of the hangman's rope."

He jerked the reins from her grasp and guided the horse over to the side of the road, in the shadow of a bramble hedge. The horse dropped his head and began to crop at the grassy verge.

"What are you doing?" Judith demanded.

"I don't know yet." He turned on the bench, catching her shoulders, and the minute he touched her that jolting current surged between them. Judith looked into his eyes, glittering with purpose, and she shivered, feeling the heat in her belly slowly turning bone and sinew to molten lava.

"You weave the strangest magic, Judith," he said, his voice a husky murmur, his eyes holding hers. "You confuse me so much I don't know whether I want to beat you or make love to you . . . but I have to possess you one way or the other."

Judith shook her head dumbly. She seemed to have forgotten how to speak. She knew only that she wanted his hands on her; rough or gentle, it was immaterial.

Marcus groaned in defeat and pulled her against him, his mouth coming down on hers with a crushing violence akin to punishment. Judith responded unhesitatingly to the bruising pressure, her lips parting for the determined thrust of his tongue. Her hands found their way around his neck, her fingers raking through the thick, dark hair. Deep within her was a warm, throbbing core of excitement and wanting that seemed to spread in waves through her body. She had never felt anything like it before and she yielded to the hot, red sensation, reaching against him as if she would be a part of him as his hands moved over her, outlining her body, learning its contours.

Slowly Marcus released her mouth for as long as it took him to readjust his hold so that he could pull her sideways onto his thighs. "I need a little more of you," he said softly, finding her mouth again. Her head rested against his shoulder, her mouth below his now more vulnerable and accessible to the deepening exploration of his tongue. His hands found her breasts, molding the soft swell beneath her jacket, and she felt in some way opened to him. She stirred on his lap, her thighs parting without volition as the deep red heat within her threatened to consume reason and reality.

"Dear God, but there's a passion in you, my lynx." He raised his head, gazing down into the bemused but desirous golden eyes.

"It must be the champagne," Judith murmured, reaching for his head again, bringing it back to her.

Marcus pulled back, laughter sparking in his gaze, rippling in his voice, lust's flame abruptly reduced to a smolder. "Did I hear you aright? You attribute such a passionate response simply to an excess of champagne?"

"I think it must contribute," she said, grinning up at him. But the mischief couldn't hide the banked fires in her eyes, the deeply sensual curve of her mouth.

"Wretch," he said softly. "I don't know what you deserve for interrupting me like that." His hand moved again to her breast, fingers deftly unhooking the frogged buttons of her jacket. Judith quivered, the moment of levity past. The tiny buttons on her lawn shirt flew apart and his fingers were on her skin, warm, firm, knowing. She raised one hand to caress his head, her body arching upward into his hand with the swelling urgency of her wanting.

"I have never felt like this," she whispered on a tiny gasp of excitement.

"That's much better," he murmured. "We'll have no more nonsense about the uninhibiting effects of champagne." He smiled at her, a glinting smile of male satisfaction. Holding her gaze, he dropped one hand to her knee, hitching up her skirt inch by inch. The warm breath of a summer's night brushed her bared legs as the skirt reached her thighs. His palm cupped her knees and slid upward beyond her stocking tops, over the satin softness of her inner thighs.

"If you knew how often I've dreamed of this," Marcus said, still smiling, still watching her face, as his fingers crept upward on an intimate, tantalizing invasion. "While you've been treating me to the sharpest edge of your razor tongue, I've been tormented with visions of your body, with fantasies of how your body would respond to mine."

Judith made no response, but her tongue touched her lips, her eyes narrowing as she drifted in sensation, the rapid rise and fall of her bosom the only indication of her mounting excitement.

Abruptly the self-enclosed world of arousal was shattered by the sound of voices, the tramp of feet, a harsh clarion call of a bugle. The horse between the shafts started and plunged forward into the hedge. Judith fell off Marcus's knee with a thump and a yowl of indignant surprise. Marcus, swearing, grabbed up the reins he had negligently let fall and hauled back on them, dragging the terrified horse out of the hedge.

"Hell and the devil!" Judith expostulated, clambering back onto the bench.

"Nicely put," Marcus approved, looking over his shoulder. "We appear to find ourselves in the midst of a regiment on the way to battle."

"Well, it's most inconvenient of them," grumbled Judith, smoothing down her skirt.

Marcus shot her a sideways glance, radiating amusement. It seemed they must take a brief respite from passion.

"Tell me," he said with deceptive innocence. "Why would you consider my proposal this morning to be without honor, whereas a scrambling tangle in a hedgerow like a milkmaid and her swain on May Day is perfectly acceptable?"

Judith combed her fingers through her disordered curls. "Is that a serious question, my lord?"

"Most certainly."

"You haven't offered to pay for my services on this occasion. Surely you can see the difference between a whore and a lover."

Marcus inhaled sharply and then slowly exhaled, steadying himself. Eccentric principles were at work again. But he didn't care on what terms they conducted their liaison, only in its fact.

"And you are willing to be my lover?" he asked quietly. "I want you, Judith, with the most powerful hunger. If you say so, I'll get down here and leave you to continue your journey, and I will never interfere in your life again. Otherwise . . ." There was no need to complete the sentence.

"I don't want you to leave," she said, meeting his eye with clear candor.

"And you know what that means?"

"I know what that means."

Relief swamped him. It was a pleasure to deal with a woman who was plain speaking and unvirtuous. He'd never had a taste for ingenuous, virginal misses, and found sophistication and honesty infinitely more arousing.

He glared impatiently at the ranks of men marching along the road. How the hell long was the column?

Judith shifted on the bench. "Where are we going?" The die was cast, and yet she was suddenly apprehensive.

"There's an inn up ahead," he said. "If I remember the road aright. . . . Thank God, I think the column's passed."

He drove the cart back onto the road and resumed the journey toward Quatre Bras. Full dawn was breaking. Red streaks slashed the sky, finally permeating the gray with a deep rosy glow.

"How beautiful," Judith said. "I've always loved traveling in the dawn."

He glanced sideways at her. "It's an unusual time of day for travel."

She shrugged. "Perhaps. For other people."

Marcus said nothing. He didn't want her to expand on that . . . not now . . . not at a moment when he wanted her to forget the constraints of the past, to be driven only by the urgent desire that he knew matched his own. She was an adventuress, wicked and unfettered, and right now he wanted her just as she was.

A thatched-roof building loomed ahead in the gray light, a creaking sign swinging in the dawn breeze.

"Journey's end," he said quietly.

Or journey's beginning, Judith thought. Her head swirled with an intoxicating brew: equal parts excitement, apprehension, anticipation. She didn't question her actions or her motives. She was accustomed to following instinct, but even if she hadn't been, she knew she was in the grip of a compulsion that must be satisfied. She wanted the man beside her, his body on hers, within hers. She wanted to feel his skin, to touch every part of his body, to know his body as she knew her own. It was a primitive bodily hunger, and at this moment she was as red in tooth and claw as any lynx in the jungle.

6

THE WHITEWASHED BEDROOM BENEATH THE EAVES WAS SPARSELY FURNISHED but clean. A rush mat covered the uneven planking, faded muslin curtains blew at the open dormer window, matching the tester of the poster bed. Judith walked across to the window, noticing distantly that her hands were shaking as she drew off her gloves. She looked out unseeing over the kitchen garden and the panorama of fields beyond. Behind her Marcus patiently dismissed Madame Berthold, the innkeeper's wife, whose anxious descriptions of the room's amenities were interspersed with dread predictions on the possible outcome of the coming battle.

Finally Madame was induced to leave and Marcus leaned against the closed door, regarding Judith's turned back, allowing the silence to fill the room, the anticipation to build again. He tossed his whip onto a chair and slowly drew off his own gloves. Judith didn't move.

Marcus came up behind her. He lifted the massed copper curls from her neck and laid his lips softly on her warm nape. A shudder went through her and he felt again that jolting surge of energy that met and matched his own. His lips moved to the soft vulnerable spot behind her ear, his breath whispering over her skin.

"My beautiful lynx, I want to see you naked." He drew her backward into the room, turning her to face him, taking her chin between thumb and forefinger. Judith read the brilliant sensual sheen in his eyes, as vibrant with longing as his words, and she felt herself slipping into some half world where the only reality was contained within the powerful surges of her responses. Her need and her hunger was his. She whispered that she wanted his nakedness as he wanted hers, and she ran her flat palm over his cheek, lightly tracing his mouth with her little finger. His hand came up to grasp her wrist, holding her hand steady, and he sucked her probing finger into his mouth, delicately nibbling the tip.

It was an exquisite sensation. The nerve endings in the tip of her finger seemed to be connected to other parts of her body. Her tongue ran over her own lips and her eyes glowed up at him, the sensual currents as frank and clear as his own.

"Sweet heaven, but I want you, Judith." His loins were on fire with wanting. "I have to look at you." He lifted her, feeling again her light, tensile muscularity. A true golden-eyed lynx.

He carried her to the bed and sat her on the edge, dropping to his knees to pull off her boots. He rose and drew her to her feet again. "I'll find it easier to undress you standing up," he said with a smile, kissing the corner of her mouth.

"I could do it more quickly," Judith offered.

Marcus shook his head, taking a handful of her hair in each fist, holding her face steady as he kissed her mouth. Her breasts pressed against his chest and she moaned softly beneath his lips. With a sharply in-drawn breath, he released her head. His fingers, swift and deft, moved to her jacket. The buttons flew undone and he pushed the garment off her shoulders with rough haste, before turning his attention to the buttons of her lawn shirt.

The soft mounds of her breasts, the nipples hard and erect with desire, disappeared into his warm palms. Judith closed her eyes on a deep shudder of pleasure as his fingertips teased the taut crowns. He ran his hands down the narrow rib cage, feeling the shape of her, the smoothness of her skin, the delineation of her ribs, until he spanned her waist. He took a step backward and looked at her, bared to the waist for his hungry gaze, her hair lustrous against the whiteness of her skin, her breasts moving gently with her swift breath.

She smiled, a deep, self-absorbed smile, her eyes hooded as she ran her own hands over her bared breasts in offering. "Take your skirt off," he rasped.

She unfastened the hooks at the back of her skirt, sliding her hands into the loosened waistband, easing the garment over her hips, until it slithered to her ankles. She stood in front of him, clad only in her thin cambric petticoat. Putting his hands on her hips, he turned her. Judith shivered at his touch, at the warm imprint of his hands through the thin material. He ran a flat finger down her spine, feeling her skin ripple. Holding her shoulders, he bent his head and his tongue followed the path of his finger, a hot, moist stroke that brought a low moan to Judith's lips. She tried to keep still, but her feet shifted restlessly on the wooden floor.

The button at the waist of her petticoat came undone and the garment slipped to her ankles. Marcus ran his hands in a lingering caress over the curve of her hips, the firm rise of her buttocks, the supple slenderness of her thighs. Then, with his hands on her hips, he turned her around to face him.

Again stepping backward, he took in her body, from the tip of the burnished head to the toes of her still-stockinged feet. Lacy garters banded her thighs, just above the knee, and he decided he would leave them there. There was something rather wonderfully wicked about them, something that went with the essential Judith he thought he was beginning to know.

"So beautiful," he said. "As beautiful as in my wildest imaginings."

Judith stepped toward him, reaching her arms around his neck, pressing her nakedness against the slight roughness of his coat, feeling the smooth leather of his britches against her thighs. Her head fell back, offering him the porcelain column of her throat, her hair cascading in a burnished river over her shoulders, her loins pressed hard against him in a gesture as eloquent as any words of arousal.

"Dear God, Judith," he whispered, cupping her buttocks and lifting her against him. "Dear God, lynx. What are you doing to me?" He took a step to the bed and let her fall onto the coverlet. He stood looking down at her for a second, then began to throw off his own clothes.

Judith watched. She gazed with a predator's lustful greed as the powerful, athletic body was revealed. When he shrugged out of his shirt, she dwelled on the broad chest, lightly dusted with dark curls, the narrow waist, and then stared with uninhibited curiosity as he unfastened his belt and pushed off his britches; a concave belly, slim hips, long muscular legs, the hard, erect evidence of his arousal . . . He turned to throw his britches on the chair, revealing taut-muscled buttocks, and she drew in a sharp breath, her body stirring on the coverlet.

He came down to the bed, stretching himself beside her, kissing the soft pulse at the base of her throat as he caressed her belly, tickled a fingertip in her navel, inhaling the scents of her body. He touched the line of her body, from below her ear to her hip, feeling the tender curves, the deep indentations, and she moaned beneath his hand, whispering his name. His mouth moved to her breasts, his teeth lightly grazing her nipples, and Judith was awash in sensation, the liquid fullness in her loins a near unendurable urgency. Shifting her body, she felt his hardness against her thigh and reached down to take the turgid, ridged flesh in her hand, feeling the blood pulsing strongly against her palm. It was a curious and wonderful sensation as she curled her fingers around him, enclosing him in a warm grip.

Marcus groaned softly under the knowing caress, and his tongue trailed a moist and fiery path over her belly. She opened her thighs in sudden demand, still caressing his flesh, her fingers now conveying an acute urgency in their tips.

"Such impatience," he whispered, slipping a hand beneath her, his fingers closing like pincers over the firm, sweet flesh of her buttocks. "Slow down, sweetheart." He pinched just hard enough to pierce the self-enclosed trance of her need and her eyes opened, focusing fully on the face hanging over her. "You'll have me over the edge in a minute," he said, smiling. "And that would be a great pity for both of us."

She nodded in fierce understanding, clenching the cheek of her captured backside against his fingers.

Marcus moved his hand, flipping her onto her stomach. And now his lips were cool, his breath warm, erasing the marks of his fingers on the imprisoned flesh. His hand slid between her thighs, delicately probing, opening the soft swollen petals, feeling her warm readiness. She opened to his touch, moving her body backward against his hand, her little whimpers of pleasure filling the room.

"Turn over now," he said softly, moving his hand, kissing the nape of her neck. "I want to look into your eyes when I'm a part of you."

She rolled onto her back and gazed up at him through half-closed eyes. "I cannot describe how I feel." It seemed to both of them the first time she'd spoken in an eternity, and her voice sounded to Judith rusty and thick from disuse.

Marcus kissed her again, his pleasure in her pleasure glowing in his eyes as he eased himself between her legs with a low sibilant murmur of fulfillment. She felt the press of his manhood against the cleft of her body and instinctively tightened against him. Surprise skimmed his eyes, and then he touched her again with his hand, and her body surged against him, her legs lifting to receive him as he pressed within her, her heels gripping his buttocks with a wild urgency. Too late he became aware of her tightness, of the thin membrane momentarily barring his entrance. And then he was deep within her, his body a part of hers, and the tears glittered in her eyes, but her lips were parted on an exultant little cry and she was moving with his rhythm and the full force of Napoleon's Imperial Guard couldn't have stopped either of them then.

A look of astonishment appeared in her eyes, her head fell back, her throat arching, and her legs curled around his waist, pulling him into the cleft of her body. With a supreme effort of will, he held himself still, glorying in her velvet warmth as her climax surged around him. He wanted to stay forever on the precipice, reveling in the feel of her, the grip of her body around him, but the deep spiraling urgency could not be controlled. With a sharp stab of loss, he forced himself to withdraw from the tight sheath in which she held him, gathering her against him as his own climax throbbed.

"Sweet heaven." Judith gasped. "What a wondrous thing."

Marcus fell back on the bed beside her, his eyes tightly closed, and for a long minute he didn't say anything. Then finally he asked in a curiously flat voice, "Why didn't you tell me?"

"Tell you what?"

He rolled over, propping himself on an elbow. "That you were a virgin." His gaze fell on the bright blood smearing her thighs as she lay sprawled in wanton abandonment beside him. "Why the hell didn't you tell me?" he demanded, his eyes hard as the shared glory of that union was abruptly tarnished by a wash of guilt and confusion.

"Did you think I wasn't?" she asked.

"How could I think you were? You behaved like an experienced woman. How could I possibly have imagined you to be still virtuous?"

"Does it matter?" Judith sat up, unease puncturing her euphoria.

"Of course it matters." He fell back on the pillows again. "I don't make a habit of deflowering virgins."

"But we only did what we both wanted." She was genuinely puzzled. "Nothing happened that wasn't supposed to happen."

He looked at her closely. "No," he said slowly. "Perhaps that's true. Nothing happened that wasn't supposed to happen."

There was an edge to the flat statement that was as confusing to Judith as it was dismaying. She slid off the bed and went to the dresser, pouring water from the ewer into the basin. "You sound angry. I don't seem to understand why." She squeezed a cloth in water and sponged her thighs. "How have I upset you?"

Marcus stared up at the flowered canopy, trying to sort out the raging confusion in his brain. Perhaps he was wronging her. Why would she have contrived such a happening? And surely not even the most consummate actress could have faked her passion, her need, her fulfillment?

"Come to bed," he said. "It's well past dawn and we need to sleep."

"But won't you explain?" She came across to the bed, her eyes huge with tiredness and a distress that he would swear was genuine. With a wash of remorse, he reached up and drew her down beside him.

"Tristesse de l'amour," he said gently. "Forgive me. It happens sometimes, and you did take me by surprise. I feel a little guilty, but it'll fade after a few hours' sleep. Close your eyes now." He closed her eyelids with his fingertips, stroking her cheek until he felt her relax against him, yielding anxiety to the soft billows of exhaustion.

Judith breathed deeply of the sweat tang of his skin and the lingering perfume of their loving as she slipped into unconsciousness. The whole business was so new to her it was no wonder it had some puzzling aspects.

She awoke to a rumbling, booming roar. For a moment she lay, disoriented, aware of the contours of an unfamiliar bed, staring up at the muslin canopy. Then memory rushed back and she sat bolt upright. "Whatever is that noise?"

"Guns." Marcus was standing at the window. He had on his britches and was in the act of putting on his shirt. "The battle has been joined."

"What time is it?"

"Four o'clock." He turned to the bed. Judith was an artless yet bewitchingly wanton sight, sitting up, her hair tumbling around her shoulders, the sheet tangled around her thighs. He remembered the abandonment of her responses, the wild and glorious honesty of her desire. Honest . . . except that she hadn't told him of her innocence, had left him to discover it when it was too late for control or caution. But perhaps that was part of the openness of her response; she genuinely hadn't given it a second thought in the blind world of arousal. She was an adventuress, after all. He allowed doubt and confusion to fade and enjoyed the sight of her as she blinked and shook her head in some bemusement, struggling to come back to the bright world of daytime reality.

"We've slept the day away," she said finally.

"So it would seem." He crossed the room and bent to kiss her. "How do you feel?"

Judith took stock. "A little sore," she said, after due consideration.

He winced and said wryly, "I did ask, I suppose. There's hot water in the ewer. But how do you feel in yourself?" His voice was serious, telling her he wanted an equally serious answer.

"Wonderful," she declared. "Virginity is a much overprized condition." She smiled up at him. "Why were you worried about it last night? There's no need to feel guilty; you weren't responsible."

Marcus frowned. "Of course I was responsible." He caught a tangled ringlet and twisted it around his finger. "Things happened very fast . . . perhaps too fast."

"Oh, I don't know," she said, putting her head on one side. "I rather thought it was a very leisurely business."

Marcus gave up trying to persuade her to feel badly about something she clearly didn't regret in the least. Any regrets he might have would fade soon enough. It was done now, and there was nothing to hinder the progress of this liaison. Indeed, if it wasn't for the sound of cannon and the knowledge of what that meant, not to mention his own very empty belly, he'd be back in bed with her in a trice.

He laughed and pulled the sheet away from her legs. "Get up! Shameless wanton! I'm going belowstairs in search of an extremely delayed nuncheon."

"Good, because I am starving. Are we going on to Quatre Bras, then?"

He was, but he had no intention of taking Judith into the theater of war. However, that tussle could wait on a full stomach. "As soon as possible. I'll be needed at Wellington's headquarters. I should have arrived there last night, but I daresay I'll think of some excuse other than the truth: that I was delayed by delight." He chuckled and drew the heavy, gold signet ring from his finger. "You had better wear this while you're here, for appearance's sake. Madame Berthold is sure to notice such an absence."

"Yes, of course. I hadn't thought," she said, slipping the ring on her finger. "It's a bit big, but I can hold it on." She poured water from the ewer into the basin.

Marcus stood transfixed by the door, watching the matter-of-fact manner in which she sponged her body. His loins stirred anew and, with a muttered oath, he fled the webs of enchantment and went down to the taproom that served as parlor and dining room.

"Oh, there you are, my lord. I was just explaining to these officers that we had a benighted gentleman and his wife as guests." Madame Berthold, the innkeeper's wife, looked up from the keg of ale from which she was drawing foaming tankards. She looked frightened. "The battle has begun, my lord. All day we've been waiting for the sound of the guns, only it didn't start till but an hour or two past. Boney's been delaying his attack, these gentlemen say."

"Carrington, good God, man, what brings you here?"

Marcus silently swore every oath he knew as he recognized the Dragoon officer and his two companions, lounging against the bar counter. "I'm on my way to Wellington's headquarters, Francis." He stepped into the room, nodding at the other men. "Whitby, George. Good day."

Colonel, Lord Francis Tallent, looked at his old friend with a suddenly arrested expression. "Wife?"

"We all have our secrets, Francis," Marcus said casually. His friends would draw the correct conclusion and discreetly drop the subject. A man's amorous adventures were his own concern. He turned to the innkeeper's wife. "Could you have a nuncheon taken abovestairs, madame?"

"And would your good lady like a dish of tea with that, sir, or perhaps a glass of sherry?" The woman bobbed a curtsy, looking helpful.

"Oh, there's no need to wait upon me. I can perfectly well be served in the taproom. I'm so hungry, I could eat a horse."

Judith Davenport swept smiling into the room. She was still putting up her hair as she walked, blind fingers twisting the ringlets into a knot, pushing in securing pins. She wore no jacket and her lawn blouse was carelessly opened at the neck, her breasts lifted by her upraised arms. "Marcus, I was thinking . . ." Her voice died as she took in the room's other inhabitants, all of whom had turned the color of beetroot. Her hands dropped to her sides.

Had she heard the voices? How could she not have heard them as she came down the stairs? The world spun on its axis as Marcus faced what had happened and its immutable consequence. He'd once found a poacher caught in the steel jaws of a man trap. His sick horror at the man's plight was what he now felt for himself as the vicious jaws of his own trap clamped. He had no choice . . . no choice whatsoever. Adventuress she may be, but he'd taken her virginity and knew she was no whore . . . not unless he made her one.

"You know my wife, of course, Francis," he said. He crossed to the door and took her hand, drawing her into the room. "My dear, are you also acquainted with Viscount Whitby and George Bannister?"

"We have met, I believe," Judith replied distractedly, her head spinning as she took in the disaster. These men were all prominent members of London Society. The story of this encounter would be on everyone's lips and she'd never be able to enter the hallowed portals of the ton . . . and neither would her brother. And her father would go unavenged. Marcus's fabrication was her only protection at the moment, and she had to go along with it until she could think things through clearly.

"Devil take it, Marcus, but you're a dark horse!" Francis exclaimed. "Secrets, eh? Pray accept my congratulations, Lady Carrington."

"Yes, indeed. This calls for a bottle," Bannister announced. "My good woman, champagne."

"Well, I don't know as we've got any, sir," the flustered woman said. "I'll go and ask Berthold." She hastened out of the room and a short silence fell. The puzzlement of the other men was evident, although they were trying politely to disguise it.

"So, you're taking Lady Carrington to Quatre Bras?" Whitby said, raising his tankard of ale to his lips.

"In the manner of a honeymoon," Marcus agreed without blinking. "A little unusual, but then the times are not exactly accommodating." His smile was a trifle twisted.

"Quite so," Lord Francis said.

"What news of the battle?" Marcus changed the subject abruptly.

"As expected, he's attacking Blücher at Ligny and Wellington at Quatre Bras."

"Why did he wait so long to attack? He's left himself but five hours until sunset."

"According to our agents, he didn't make his usual early-morning reconnaissance and thought he was only facing Blücher's one corp at Ligny. He didn't realize Ziethen's forces had come up in support, so he didn't see any need to hurry," Francis replied.

"But despite the delay, we're being mangled on both fronts," Whitby said somberly. "Wellington's taking very heavy losses at Quatre Bras and we've orders to call up reinforcements at Nivelles."

"Here's a nuncheon, my lord, and a bottle of Berthold's best claret." The innkeeper's wife came in with a heavily laden tray. "I hope it'll do. We've no champagne, sir."

"It will do very well," Carrington reassured. He drew out a chair at the table. "Judith, come and sit down. Gentlemen, will you join us?"

"Thank you, no, Carrington. Beg you'll excuse us, ma'am." Whitby bowed formally. "Fact is, had nuncheon some time ago."

"It is rather late in the day," Judith managed to say. She took the chair Marcus held for her, casting him a quick glance as she did so. His expression was impassive, his eyes unreadable.

"May I carve you some ham?" he asked with a distant courtesy.

"Thank you, sir." A pink tinge touched her cheekbones.

"A morsel of chicken also?"

"Please." She dropped her eyes to the tablecloth, feeling as if she had committed some dreadful crime for which retribution waited in the wings.

Wretched, she concentrated on her food and left the conversation to the men. The steady booming of the guns continued until the sound was abruptly overtaken by a swelling roar from outside. The roar gradually separated itself into shouts, screams, and pounding feet.

Lord Francis ran to the inn doorway, followed by the others. A torrent of humanity, some on horseback, some in gigs and dog carts, but most on foot, poured down the lane toward Brussels. Women carried babies, small children clinging to their skirts, stumbling on the hard mud-ridged road; the men were armed with whatever they had been able to grab in their haste: staves, knives, a blunderbuss.

"What the devil?" Marcus exclaimed.

"Looks like a rout," Whitby said. "Wellington must be retreating."

"Napoleon's not beaten him so far," Marcus said. "I can't believe he'll do it this time."

"Oh, sirs, they say the army is retreating!" Berthold, the innkeeper, came running in from the road, where he had been chasing after information among the fleeing crowd. "Wellington's falling back on Brussels. The Prussians are retreating to Wavre."

"Hell and damnation!" George Bannister grabbed up his hat. "We'd best be about our business."

"Berthold!" Marcus bellowed as the innkeeper ran for the door again. "Have my nag put to the cart." He strode to the stairs leading to the bedchamber and took them two at a time. Judith stood in the now-empty taproom, listening to the roar of humanity outside. Then she ran up the stairs after Marcus.

He was shrugging into his coat, checking the contents of his pockets. He glanced up as she came in and said curtly, "I'm going to Quatre Bras. You'll stay here. I'll pay our shot when I come back for you."

"You seem to be forgetting that *I* was going to Quatre Bras, too," she said, swallowing the lump that seemed to be blocking her throat. With what was happening at the moment, it was hardly feasible for them to discuss the personal mess they were in, but the coldness of his voice was surely unwarranted. And she couldn't believe he intended simply to take off and leave her stranded, cooling her heels in a lonely inn, not knowing anything of what was happening.

"Well, you're not going now," he said in clipped accents. "It's too dangerous with that horde out there, and you'll only be in the way."

Judith lost her temper. It was a relief to do so since it banished her feeling of helplessness and concealed for the time being the apprehension that something very hurtful lurked around the next corner of her relationship with Marcus Devlin.

"That's *my* horse and *my* cart," she said with furious emphasis. "And I'll have you know, Lord Carrington, that I go where I please. You have no right to dictate to me." She snatched up her jacket and gloves. "If you wish to hitch another ride in my cart, then you're welcome to do so. Otherwise, I suggest you find your own transport."

Before he could respond, she had turned and run from the room. With a muttered oath, Marcus grabbed up his whip and sprang after her. He reached the stableyard on her heels. Judith leaped onto the driver's seat of the cart, standing ready as ordered, and snapped the reins. Marcus grabbed the bridle at the bit and held the horse still.

"You're behaving like a spoiled child," he said. "A battlefield is no place for a woman. Now get down at once."

"No," Judith snapped. "You really are the most arrogant, high-handed despot! I told you, I go where I please and you don't have any right of command."

"At this moment, I'm exercising a husband's authority," he declared. "A battlefield is no place for a woman and most definitely not for my wife. Now, do as you're told."

For a moment Judith was speechless. "I am not your wife," she managed to get out finally.

"To all intents and purposes you are now. And as soon as I can find a damned priest, you will be in the eyes of the church."

It was too much for a saint to bear. "I wouldn't marry you if you were the last man on earth!" she cried.

"As far as you're concerned, my dear Judith, that's exactly what I am," he announced aridly. "The first and last man you will know, in the fullest sense of that word."

White-faced, Judith stood up in the cart and whipped at the horse with the reins. The animal plunged forward with a snort, catching Marcus off guard. He stumbled, still holding the bit as the horse lunged. He regained his balance just in time and released the bit before he was dragged forward by the now caracoling animal. He grabbed the side of the cart and sprang upward, seizing the reins from her. The horse shot off as if a bee were lodged beneath his tail.

"Monsieur . . . monsieur . . ." came the outraged screams of the innkeeper's wife behind them.

Judith looked over her shoulder. Madame Berthold was pounding up the road in their wake, waving a skillet at them, her apron flapping into her face. Her cap flew off into the ditch but her charge continued regardless.

"I think you forgot to pay your shot," Judith said on a strangled gasp, an almost hysterical laughter suddenly taking the place of her rage.

"Damnation!" Marcus hauled back on the reins, and the near-demented horse reared to a snorting halt. He turned to look at Judith, who was now doubled over, weeping with laughter. His lip quivered and his shoulders began to shake at the absurdity of the scene. He glanced over his shoulder to where Madame Berthold still pounded, panting, toward them.

"One of these days, I really will wallop you," he commented to the gasping Judith, as he reached into his pocket for his billfold. "You nearly had me taken up for a thief." Leaning down to the red-faced, indignant Madame Berthold, he gave her his most charming smile and poured forth a flood of apologies, blaming the urgency of the moment for his forgetfulness.

Madame was appeased with a handful of sovereigns that more than compensated for her hospitality, and stood breathless and perspiring in the road as Marcus started the cart again.

"Now, where were we?" he said.

Judith had finally stopped laughing and leaned back against the rough wooden seat back. "On the road to Quatre Bras. Where we're *both* going against the traffic."

"So it would seem. We'll find a priest there."

"There must be some other way," she said, biting her lip. But she couldn't think of one that wouldn't ruin everything. How could Sebastian ever forgive her for destroying months and months of planning in the willful pursuit of passion?

"I took your maidenhead and we were discovered in a situation that would ruin you. In such a circumstance, there is no honorable alternative." He stated the facts bluntly, without inflection.

"But have you forgotten, my lord, that I am a card-sharping, horse-thieving, disreputable hussy, living on the fringes of Society, in the shadow of the gaming tables?" Her voice thickened and she swallowed crossly.

"No, I haven't forgotten. I'll just have to wean you away from your undesirable pursuits."

"And if I am not to be weaned, my lord?"

He shrugged. "It's not a matter for jest, Judith. As my wife, you will have responsibilities to my name and my honor. You'll accept those responsibilities as your part of the bargain."

Bargain? Judith turned away from him, trying to sort out the maelstrom raging in her head. Marriage to the Marquis of Carrington would work beautifully for both herself and Sebastian. Installed as the Marchioness of Carrington, she would have immediate and natural access to the circles frequented by Gracemere, as would Sebastian as the marquis's brother-in-law. Their position in Society would be assured and their present funds would be more than ample to set Sebastian up as a bachelor in London. He would need fashionable rooms instead of a house; one servant instead of a houseful. Their accumulated money would go much farther. It would mean they could begin to enact their revenge so much sooner than they'd antici-pated. And when it was over, Sebastian would be established in his own right. This card had been dealt to her hand; only a fool would refuse out of scruple to play it.

But Marcus mustn't know anything of that. There was a lifetime of secrets he couldn't know. So how could she fulfill her side of this bargain?

"I know nothing of you," she said aloud. "Why have you never married?"

There was silence. Marcus stared across the past and contem-plated the truth . . . and the half-truth that had become the truth. Honor still bound him to the half-truth, for all that the one who could be most damaged by the whole story had been in her grave these many years past. The full truth was known now only to himself and one other. But it was a fair question.

"It's a plain and unremarkable tale, but pride is a devilish thing, and I have more than my fair share. Ten years ago I was to be married. A woman your antithesis in every way. I had known her since childhood and it didn't occur to me to woo her. She was a sweet, meek soul who I assumed would make me a compliant and exemplary wife. Instead, she fell wildly in love with a fortune-hunting gamester, who most skillfully swept her off her feet. She cried off."

His voice was perfectly level, almost bland as he continued. "The role of jilted fiancé was a hard and humiliating one for me. I was rather young to face such public mortification with equanimity. I decided then that a man could live in perfect contentment without a wife."

"Did she marry the fortune hunter?"

What choice had she had . . . ? Poor little dupe. Marcus closed his eyes on the memory of Martha's battered face, closed his ears to the sound of her broken whimpers. An untamed lynx would never get herself into such a predicament. An unprincipled adventuress would arrange matters to suit herself. *Had she heard those voices on the stairs? Had she known who was in the taproom before she'd walked in, her clothes almost disheveled, the aura of a satisfied woman clinging to every curve and line of her body? Had she contrived this?* But even if she had, a man of honor had no choice.

"Yes, she married him," he said, "and died in childbed nine months later, leaving him to game away her fortune." He shook his head in a dismissive gesture. "I don't wish to talk of Martha ever again. You and she are so different, one could almost believe you to be different species."

She wanted to ask him if he believed he could be happy married to her, but deep in her soul she knew the answer. His hand had been forced; he was making that clear with every word and intonation.

If it wasn't for Gracemere, it would be easy to let him off the hook. She'd be able to say that in her circles, reputation didn't matter, that she'd be perfectly happy to be his lover for as long as it suited them both. But she wasn't going to say any of those things. She was a gamester and she'd been dealt a perfect hand.

She turned her head and met his cool gaze. "We have a bargain, then, my lord Carrington," she said simply. Marcus nodded in brief affirmation and returned his attention to the road.

Judith closed her eyes, listening to the roar of cannon growing ever closer. The road was thronged with columns of soldiers, horses and limbers, fleeing civilians mingling with the detritus of a retreating army. Suddenly all thought of passion and revenge seemed trivial in the midst of an event that would obliterate thousands of lives and shape the future of their world.

7

THE VILLAGE OF QUATRE BRAS STOOD AT A CROSSROADS. TO JUDITH'S EYES IT was a village out of Dante. The battle still raged and a heavy pall of gunsmoke hung over the shattered cottages and farmhouses along the road. The dead and the wounded lay anywhere a spare place could be found for them, and from the surgeons' field hospital, the sounds of agony rose, pitiable, on the evening air.

The main street of the village was clogged with men and horses; a wounded horse struggled in the traces of an overturned limber, screaming like a banshee as a group of soldiers fought to cut the traces and right the cannon.

"Dear God, you shouldn't be here," Marcus muttered to Judith. "What the devil am I going to do with you?"

"You don't have to do anything with me," Judith declared. "I'm getting down here. There's work to be done."

Marcus glanced sideways at her, took in the resolute set of her white face, and drew rein. They were behind the front line but still close enough for danger. He laid a restraining hand on her arm as she prepared to jump from the cart. "Just a minute."

"We're wasting time," she said impatiently.

"It's not safe," he said.

"Nowhere's safe," she pointed out, gesturing to the chaos around them. "I'll be careful."

Marcus frowned, then shrugged in resignation. "Very well, then. Keep your head down and stay out of the open as much as possible. I'm going to Wellington's headquarters. Stay in the village and I'll find you when I know what's happening."

She nodded and jumped down. Gathering up her skirt, she ran across the narrow street to where a group of unattended wounded lay in the shade of a hedge.

For many hours, long after sunset brought an end to the day's fighting and the incessant bombardment of the cannon finally ceased, Judith fetched water for the parched, bandages from the field hospital to staunch the more accessible of wounds, and sat beside men as they died or drifted into a pain-filled world of merciful semiconsciousness. She heard dreams and terrors, confessions and deepest desires, and her heart filled with pity and horror for so much suffering, for such a waste of so many young lives.

Throughout the endless evening she was constantly on the watch for Sebastian, her ears pricked for the sound of his voice. He must surely be somewhere in this carnage. Unless he'd found his way to the battlefield, and some stray shot had . . . but she couldn't allow herself to think such a thought.

Marcus found her in the field hospital, holding the hand of a young ensign while a surgeon amputated his leg. The lad bit down on a leather strap and his fingers were bloodless as they clutched Judith's hand. Marcus watched from the shadows until the moment came when the patient entered the dark world beyond endurance and his hand fell inert to the table. Judith massaged her crushed fingers and looked around for where she might be most useful next.

She saw Marcus and gazed at him wearily as he came over to her. Her face was streaked with dust and soot from the gunfire, her skirt caked with blood, her eyes filmed with exhaustion. She brushed her hair away from her forehead, where it clung, lank with sweat, in the fetid heat of the hospital tent.

"What's happening?"

"The army's retreating to a new line at Mont St. Jean," Marcus said. "Wellington and his staff are still here, taking stock." He pulled out his handkerchief and mopped her forehead, then took her chin between finger and thumb and wiped a black streak off her cheek. His eyes were somber. "I'm trying to find some news of Charlie. The losses have been horrendous."

"I've been hoping to come across Sebastian." Judith glanced around the hospital. Lanterns now cast a bloodred glow over the scene, throwing huge shadows against the tent walls as the surgeons and their assistants moved between the tables laden with wounded. "What do we do now?"

"You're exhausted," Marcus said. "You need food and rest."

Judith's head drooped, as if her neck were no longer strong enough to support it. "There's still so much to do here."

"No more tonight. There'll be as much and more to do tomorrow." He took her arm, easing her toward the tent opening. Her foot slipped in a pool of blood and she clutched at him desperately. His arms came strongly around her, holding her up, and for a moment she yielded to his strength, her lithe, tensile frame suddenly without sinew.

Marcus held her against him, feeling the formlessness of her body, like a small animal's. She smelled of blood and earth and sweat, and he was surprised by a wash of tenderness. It was not an emotion he was accustomed to, and certainly not with Judith, who aroused him, annoyed him, challenged him, amused him—often all at once—but hadn't sparked a protective instinct before. He dropped a kiss on her damp forehead and led her outside into the relatively cool night air.

"Before we do anything else," he said, "there's some business we have to attend to. I've arranged matters so that it'll be very discreet."

"What business?"

He took her left hand, which still bore his signet ring, and frowned down at her. "Your presence here with me has to be explained, and there is only one explanation. I intend to make it good without delay. There's a Belgian priest in the village who's prepared to perform the ceremony. It won't take long."

Judith realized that for some reason she'd expected the traditions to be observed when they formalized their relationship. Marcus was obviously interested only in expediency. It hurt, even though she told herself that her own motives were purely pragmatic. This was no love match. It was a simple bargain. But she couldn't help asking "Must it be now? In the midst of all this carnage?"

"It's a matter of honor," he replied curtly. "Mine . . . if not yours."

Judith detected his sardonic inflection and flushed with annoyance. "The last time we discussed my honor, I had a pistol in my hand," she reminded him, squaring her shoulders despite her weariness.

Marcus's reply was cut off at birth by a loud hail.

"Judith . . . Ju—!" They both turned to see Sebastian in the shadow of a doorway.

"Sebastian!" Judith ran toward her brother, forgetting about Marcus and disputed honor. "I've been looking everywhere for you."

"What the devil are you doing here?" he demanded, hugging her. "I left you in Brussels."

"You didn't expect me to stay there, did you?" she retorted with a tired grin.

He shook his head ruefully. "Knowing you, I suppose I shouldn't have." He noticed Marcus for the first time, and his eyebrows lifted. "How d'ye do, Carrington."

"You haven't seen Charlie, have you?" Judith asked her brother abruptly before Marcus could respond to Sebastian's greeting. "Marcus has been trying to get news of him."

"Oh, I saw him a few hours ago," Sebastian replied. "He was with Neil Larson. Larson was wounded and Charlie carried him off the field. They were putting Larson into one of the wagons heading back to Brussels."

Judith felt the tension leave Marcus as if a black goblin had leaped from his shoulders. "Thank God for that," he murmured, the hardness gone from his eyes, the tautness from his mouth. His gaze suddenly focused on Sebastian. "Davenport, you're just in time to perform a very useful service."

"Oh?"

"Yes, you may give your sister away."

"I may *what?*"

"Marcus, would you mind if I talk with my brother privately for a few minutes?" Judith said quickly.

Marcus made a rather formal bow. "Of course not. The curé's house is beside the church, as you might expect. I'll meet you both there when you've done your explaining."

Judith watched him stroll off in the direction of the small road-side church, its steeple tumbled by a cannon ball earlier in the day.

"Tell," her brother demanded.

Judith explained as best she could. But it was awkward, for all her intimacy with her brother, to admit to the compulsion of that wild passion that had thrown her so far from their chosen track.

Sebastian was very still as he listened, his expression giving no indication of the turmoil of his emotions. He was astounded that his usually clear-headed sister could have lost her grip on reality so completely, yielding to a moment of madness that now bade fair to ruin everything they'd worked for. He tried to see Marcus Devlin as his sister's lover, to understand what it was about the man that could arouse such passion in Judith, but the image filled him with such a confusion of dismay and discomfort that he pushed it from him.

When he remained silent at the end of her story, Judith said tentatively, "Are you angry?"

"I don't know if that's the right word," he said slowly. "But, yes, I suppose I am." Angry and something else, he recognized. He was jealous of Marcus Devlin, who had broken into the tight exclusivity of their relationship. He didn't want to share his sister, Sebastian realized with a shock. He was ten months older than Judith and couldn't remember a time in his life when she had not been there, so close to him that sometimes it seemed as if they inhabited one skin. They shared everything: thoughts, dreams, desires, nightmares. They laughed at the same things and cried at the same things. And now Judith would have someone else to turn to . . . to share these things with.

"Do you *want* to marry him?" he asked abruptly. "Or are you doing this because you must?"

Judith bit her lip. "It doesn't really matter how I feel. I created this mess and I have to put it right. This is the only way we have open to us now to do what we must. And it'll be perfect, Sebastian. As Marchioness of Carrington, I'll be perfectly placed to befriend Gracemere, and as my brother, your position in Society will be assured. Nothing could be better, could it?"

"No, I suppose not." He stared, frowning into the darkness. Maybe if he could put it into the context of furthering their plan, it would hurt less. "What if Carrington ever discovers that you've used him?"

Judith shrugged. "Why should he?"

Sebastian ran his hands through his hair, clasping his temples with a distracted frown. "We'll have to make damn sure he doesn't, Ju. I don't know the man, but I'll lay odds he'd be a devilishly uncomfortable adversary."

Judith had formed a similar opinion, but she tried to make light of it. "Oh, the worst I know of him is that he's an autocrat. But I ought to be able to handle that. I'm sure he doesn't have any hideous vices or perversions." She laughed a little nervously. "I'm sure I'd sense something like that after . . . I mean, when . . ."

"Yes, I know what you mean," Sebastian interrupted dryly. "And if it's all the same to you, I prefer not to dwell on it."

"Sorry," she said. "I didn't mean to embarrass you."

"Oh, well, I'll get used to it," he said, suddenly all business. "And if you're sure about going through with it, we can certainly turn your position to good use. Besides, you have to get married sometime. I ought to be relieved to see you well established."

Judith was not wholly convinced by her brother's sudden briskness, but chose not to question it. "Let's go and do it, then," she said with matching determination.

Marcus was waiting for them in the little garden of the priest's house. He watched them come down the road, arm in arm, heads together, deep in conversation. What were they discussing—him? How easily he'd been manipulated?

He abruptly dismissed his suspicions. Judith and Sebastian understandably had a great deal to discuss. It was perfectly natural and didn't mean anything sinister. Judith was unconventional and unscrupulous, but that didn't mean she was a designing Delilah.

And despite everything, as he looked at her, at her luminous beauty barely dimmed by the blood and sweat of her day among the wounded, at the lithe frame, still graceful despite her bone-deep weariness, he wanted her now as powerfully as he had wanted her the night before. She would make him no ordinary wife, of that he was certain. She was too mercurial, had as many facets as a polished diamond, and he couldn't imagine tiring of her.

He stepped toward them as they turned into the garden, and held out his hand. "Well, Sebastian, I hope your sister has your permission. I suppose I should have asked for it formally myself."

Sebastian took the offered hand in a firm clasp. "Ju's never needed anyone's permission to do anything. And anyway," he said with a slight smile, "in the circumstances . . ."

Marcus found himself responding to the infectious, colluding smile, so like Judith's. "Quite so," he agreed. "Shall we go in? Oh, Judith, you'd better give me back the ring."

The curé seemed to consider this duty no more out of the way in the middle of a battle than ministering to the dying, as he'd been doing all day. He was as weary as the rest of them, took in Judith's blood-smeared, bedraggled state with a comprehending nod, summoned an ancient crone from the kitchen to act as the second witness, and escorted them into the ruined church. He mumbled through the service at high speed, his accent so local that even Judith, who had been speaking French from earliest childhood, had difficulty following.

But there amid fallen masonry, before an altar standing open to the sky, in the middle of a battlefield, surrounded by the hideousness of war, Judith Davenport married Marcus Devlin, Marquis of Carrington, in the eyes of the church. He placed his signet ring upon her finger, saying quietly, "We'll find something more suitable when we get to London." Following convention, he laid his lips lightly on hers.

"*M'sieur . . . madame . . . s'il vous plaît . . .*" The priest appeared from the vestry, carrying a leather-bound tome. "*Le registre.*"

Judith and Marcus signed the book under the scrawled and mostly illegible marks of their predecessors.

"*Eh, vous aussi, m'sieur.*" The priest nodded at Sebastian, who wrote his name beneath his sister's. The crone put a large X.

An awkward silence fell suddenly in the dark, ruined church. Judith cleared her throat just as Sebastian said with an unconvincing heartiness, "Well, that seems to be that. Congratulations." He kissed his sister and shook his brother-in-law's hand. "I've a bottle of cognac in my saddlebag. We should drink a toast."

Marcus nodded. "Why don't you two go outside while I settle up with the curé?"

Judith was staring down at the page on the register, at the three signatures. A curious cold crept up the back of her neck, and her scalp crawled.

"Let's go outside," Sebastian said, taking her arm. Numbly she let him lead her out into the garden.

"It's not legal," she said in a shaky whisper.

He stared down at her. A fine crescent moon was just visible through the cloud and smoke pall. It gave her pallor a waxen hue. "Whatever do you mean?"

"The names," she whispered. "They're not our legal names."

"Sweet Jesus!" Sebastian whistled softly. "We haven't been known by our baptismal names since we were babies. I never even think about it."

"What should we do?"

"Nothing," he said. "No one will ever know. If we go back in there and try to put it right, Marcus will have to know everything."

Judith shivered. "This is absurd. I'm married but I'm not."

"Judith Davenport is married," Sebastian said firmly. "Charlotte Devereux hasn't existed since she was two years old."

"But what about children?" she said almost wildly. "They'll be illegitimate."

"No one knows except the two of us," her brother stated, gripping her hands in a hard clasp. "No one will ever know. We create our own facts . . . our own truths. . . . We always have."

"Yes," she said, taking herself in hand. "Yes, you're right. What's in a piece of paper?"

The door of the church banged shut, and in startled reflex they jumped guiltily apart. Frowning, Marcus came toward them, his suspicions flaring anew. "Am I intruding on family secrets?" His voice was stiff.

Desperately, Judith sought an answer that was not wholly an untruth. Her smile was strained, but she made an effort to speak naturally. "We were talking about our father. He died last year in Vienna."

"He would have been happy to see Judith married." Sebastian stepped in smoothly. "He didn't have much happiness in his life."

"No," Judith agreed. "Our mother died when we were babies and he never recovered." She passed the back of her hand over her forehead. "If I don't sit down soon, I think I'm going to fall over."

"You need to eat," Marcus said immediately, the gnawing rat of mistrust for the moment appeased. "We'll go to the duke's headquarters."

Sebastian chose to return to his friends in the village tavern while Marcus hustled Judith into a stone farmhouse, one of the few buildings with its roof still intact, where they found Wellington's staff sitting around a table. The duke himself was chewing a hunk of barley bread as he fired off dispatches to a steady stream of runners.

Francis Tallent offered Judith a pewter cup of rough red wine, greeting her pleasantly and without surprise. Fleetingly, Judith wondered what he must have thought that morning when she'd drifted into the taproom with her shirt unbuttoned and her hair tumbling about her ears. It was best not to speculate, she decided, taking a seat at the table.

It didn't take long before she was completely at ease. The condition of her clothes, her exhaustion that matched their own, the part she'd played in the last hours, provided her pass into this group of battle-weary veterans. Even Wellington greeted her with an absent yet friendly acceptance, accused Marcus of being a secretive dog to keep his marriage plans under wraps, and suggested she try to wash the blood from her skirt with a mixture of salt and water.

Judith spent what was left of her wedding night wrapped up in a military greatcoat, asleep on a table at the end of the room, while the military conference went on around her. Marcus looked across at her and tried not to dwell on how they would have been spending this night in more traditional circumstances. He took off his coat, rolled it up into a pillow, and gently lifted her head, slipping it beneath her. Her eyelids fluttered, and she mumbled something inarticulate. He smiled, stroked her hair, its usual burnish faded, and returned to the table.

Judith was awakened just before dawn by an orderly, who touched her shoulder tentatively. "Ma'am . . . there's coffee, ma'am. We're on the move."

She opened her eyes and blinked up at him in bemusement. Slowly memory returned and she struggled into a sitting position, swinging her legs over the edge of the table. She took the steaming mug from the orderly with a grateful smile. Apart from the two of them, the room was empty.

"Where is everybody?"

"Outside, ready to move, ma'am," he said. "His lordship's waiting for you."

"Thank you." She slid off the table and made her way outside into the damp, gray light, her hands cupped around the comforting warmth of the mug.

Men and horses milled around the front door. Wellington was mounted on Copenhagen, his favorite charger, and the beast pranced impatiently, tossing his head, sniffing the wind. The village seemed quiet, after the frenzy of the previous evening, and a line of wagons moved away from the field hospital toward Brussels, transporting those the surgeons had managed to patch up. Burial parties were at work in a neighboring field, turning the sod with their shovels, wraithlike figures in the dawn mist.

Marcus, holding the bridle of a black stallion, stood talking with Francis Tallent. Judith hurried over to him. Colonel Tallent greeted her cheerfully, then made his excuses and went to join the duke.

Judith examined her husband. He looked tired but calm. "Are we to leave straightaway?"

Marcus gave her his own searching look. "As soon as you're ready. Are you rested at all? The table made a hard bed."

She laughed. "I've slept in many a hard place in my time, sir. Indeed, I'm very rested. I must have slept for three hours." She took an appreciative gulp of the coffee. "This is the elixir of the gods."

Marcus smiled. "A lifesaver I agree. You'll have to manage the cart today on your own, I'm afraid. Just keep up as best you can."

Judith looked at the stallion. "You're riding?"

"Yes, one of Francis's spares."

"I suppose he doesn't have one for me," she said disconsolately.

Marcus regarded her calmly. "It wouldn't matter if he did. After 'borrowing'—as you so charmingly put it—the cart and horse, it's your responsibility to look after it and make sure it's returned to its owner no worse for wear."

Judith pulled a face but couldn't dispute the justice of this. "I hadn't expected to keep it for so long."

A glimmer of amusement appeared in the ebony eyes. "No, I'm sure you hadn't. But then, rather a lot of unexpected things have happened in the last day or so."

"They have," agreed Judith with a tiny answering smile. "But I daresay the owner will be happy with a handsome compensation. I'm sure the tavern keeper will find him for me when we get back to Brussels."

"Conscience conveniently quietened?" he mocked.

Judith laughed. "My conscience was never uneasy. However, if I can't ride with you, then I'll stay here today. There's still work to be done at the hospital."

Marcus frowned, considering. She'd proved herself competent enough yesterday. "I suppose I could allow you to do that. I'll send someone for you later. When he comes, though, you're to go with him without delay. He'll have orders to bring you to me at once, because there's no knowing how long we'll be in any one place. If you delay, I may lose you. Is that clear?"

It had been a short moment of accord. "Yes, it's perfectly clear, and would have been equally so without your sounding so autocratic," she pointed out, reflecting that it was never too early to start her program of reform. "I'm not in the schoolroom."

"For heaven's sake, Judith, I don't have time to squabble with you in the middle of a war!"

"Oh, listen to you!" she exclaimed in a fierce undertone. "That's exactly what I mean."

Taking her shoulders, he pulled her toward him. "Maybe I am a trifle autocratic, but you're as bristly as a porcupine this morning." Despite the irritation in his voice, he couldn't control the flicker of desire in his eyes. Although her cheeks were flushed with indignation, dark currents of promise lurked below the surface of her eyes, and he could feel in memory the print of her soft mouth on his. "Porcupine or not, I want you," he murmured. "Somehow, I'll contrive something for later." He ran his finger over her mouth. "And we'll be a world away from any schoolroom, I can safely promise you that." His eyebrows rose and his eyes gleamed. "Will that guarantee your obedience, lynx?"

Judith grinned, her irritation vanished. "I'll come when I'm called, sir."

He caught her face and kissed her, a hard, assertive salute that left her lips tingling and heated her blood. "A further promise," he said, then turned, swung onto his horse, and rode off with a backward wave.

8

As the day wore on, passion became the last thing on Judith's mind. She was soon moving in a trance of fatigue, blindly putting one foot in front of the other, driven by the overpowering need and suffering around her. Wellington had lost five thousand men the previous day and they were still bringing in casualties from the battlefield, men who had lain outside all night. It began to seem as if the stream of wounded bodies would never cease.

The sky darkened toward the middle of the morning and within minutes was shot with jagged forks of lightning. The thunder was almost as violent as the gunfire of the preceding day, Judith thought, standing for a moment in the entrance of the hospital tent looking out at the sheeting rain.

All day the downpour was relentless. Judith was soon soaked to the skin, but was barely aware of it. Wagonloads of patched wounded continued throughout the day to bump along the road to the safety of Brussels, and toward evening Judith was trying to make some of the casualties more comfortable under a tarpaulin in one of the wagons when a hesitant voice called her.

"Charlie!" She looked up in glad surprise, water dripping from her hair. "Thank God, you're safe."

"Yes," he said, blushing crimson over his tunic as he stammered, "Um . . . Miss Daven . . . um . . . Jud . . . um . . . my cousin . . . my cousin sent me to fetch you. He's with the army at Waterloo. We're to go at once."

Judith climbed wearily down from the wagon. What had Marcus told Charlie? "Is it far?"

"No, a couple of miles. The army's in position across the Brussels road," Charlie said. "There's been no fighting today, because of the storm."

"I have to find my horse and cart."

"I have it," Charlie said. "Over by that farmhouse. Marcus told me where it would be." He stared into the middle distance, unable to meet her eye. "He said you . . . well, I gather congratulations are in order."

"Oh, Charlie, it's too difficult to explain at the moment," she said, taking his arm. "In fact, I don't know whether I *can* explain it. It happened very quickly."

"In Brussels, you weren't thinking of—"

"No," she interrupted, recognizing his mortifying suspicion that he'd been played for a fool by his elders, who'd had their own secret liaison all along. "No. It just happened very suddenly. I don't know how to ask you to understand it when I don't myself."

"Oh." Charlie still seemed unconvinced as he handed her up into the cart. "I'll tether my horse to the back and sit beside you. There's a tarpaulin we can put over us."

Judith took the reins. They both huddled beneath the tarpaulin, although they were already so wet it seemed rather pointless. After a minute Charlie said hotly, "My cousin never does surprising things. Why would he suddenly get married in the middle of a battle? I thought people only fell in love like that in Mrs. Radcliffe's romances."

Judith smiled and patted his hand. "You know what they say about truth being stranger than fiction." If that was the explanation he'd hit upon, then she'd leave him with it. He obviously wouldn't be able to handle the truth: violent passion, mutual seduction, inconvenient encounters, and a most scrupulous sense of honor . . . along with a quite unscrupulous seizing of an opportunity.

Wellington's army was drawn up outside the village of Waterloo, straddling the Brussels road behind the shelter of a small hill that would protect them from enemy observation and gunfire. It was a relatively strong position, and the duke was in cheerful mood when Judith, escorted by Charlie, walked into one of the string of farm buildings that protected both the army's flanks. A fire burned in the grate and the smell of gently steaming wet wool filled the air as the soaked inhabitants of the farmhouse jostled for position near the heat.

"We'll stand where we are, if Blücher promises us one corp in support," the duke was declaring, over a table laden with supper dishes. "Ah, Lady Carrington, you've been in the field hospital at Quatre Bras, your husband says." He waved a chop bone at her in greeting. "Come to the fire and dry off. Carrington's taking a look at the field. Boney's ensconced on the other hilltop."

Judith dropped onto a bench at the table, exhaustion flooding her so she couldn't even summon up the energy to reach the fire. Charlie murmured his excuses and went off into the rain again to rejoin his regiment. Someone pushed a pewter mug of wine toward her, and she buried her nose in it with a grateful groan. As with last night, her presence was completely accepted. This didn't seem as surprising to her now that she'd met several women that day, laboring beside her in the hospital, all wives of soldiers, all accustomed to following the drum and enduring the same privations as the army while they waited behind the lines for their men. That Lord Carrington's wife chose to do the same was a little more remarkable, but then so was the marquis's position with Wellington's army as a civilian tactician.

Marcus came in a few minutes later, shaking water off his coat, tossing his soaked beaver hat onto a settle. "It's raining cats and dogs," he said. "The roads are enmired and the field's a mudbath." He saw his wife and came quickly to the table. "How are you?"

"Dripping," she said, smiling wearily. "But well enough. I'll be even better for another cup of wine."

"Take it easy," he cautioned, reaching for the bottle and refilling her cup. "Exhaustion and wine make the devil's own combination. Have you eaten?"

"Not yet," she said. "I think I'm too tired."

"You must eat. Then I'll show you to the chamber I've managed to lay claim to, and you can get out of those clothes."

Judith toyed with a cold mutton chop and listened to the conversation. Marcus sat beside her on the bench and, when her head drifted onto his shoulder, put an arm around her in support. Her clothes dried a little in the steamy warmth of the crowded room and she sipped wine sleepily, trying to make some sense of the discussion. Everything seemed to hang on the Prussians. Could they send a corps in support? If not, Wellington's army was alarmingly outnumbered by the French across the hill.

The tension in the room was too powerful for her to wish to go to bed, and she shook her head when Marcus suggested he show her to the bedchamber he'd found in a cottage across the yard. At three in the morning, a drenched runner tumbled through the door bearing the message they'd all been waiting for. At dawn, two corps of the Prussian army would move from Wavre against Napoleon's right flank.

"Twice as good as we'd hoped for!" Peter Welby exclaimed.

Marcus examined a map with a pair of compasses. "It's ten miles from Wavre to Waterloo and it'll be slow going during this terrible storm on muddy roads. I expect they'll be here midday."

"If the French attack before then, we'll have to hold the field until they get here," the duke said.

But there was renewed confidence in the low-ceilinged room and men rose from the table, intending to snatch what hours of rest they could before the attack opened.

"Come, Judith." Marcus shifted her head from his shoulder and stood up, pulling her with him. She obeyed readily, stumbling slightly as he led her out into the storm, across the swamped stableyard, and under the low lintel of a small cottage.

Men were asleep on the earth-packed floor and Judith trod delicately over them as Marcus hushed her with a finger on his lips. They climbed a rickety staircase and entered a tiny loft, smelling of apples and hay. A blanket-covered straw mattress lay on a roped bedframe. To Judith at that moment, nothing could have seemed more luxurious.

"Are the French expecting the Prussians?" she asked, sinking onto the mattress. There was another violent crash of thunder from outside.

"We're calculating that they won't be." Marcus bent to pull off her boots. "Napoleon's had Grouchy chasing a phantom Prussian retreat toward Liege, when in fact Blücher's been moving toward us. I think we've caught him unawares." He sat on the edge of the bed to pull off his own boots. "I *hope* we've caught him unawares. . . . You can't sleep in wet clothes."

"Neither can you," she responded, struggling upright again, fumbling with the buttons of her jacket. "My fingers are all thumbs."

"Let me do it." He pushed her hands away and unbuttoned her jacket. His hands brushed her breasts as he pushed the coat off her shoulders and her nipples instantly hardened, pressing darkly against the thin lawn of her shirt. Slowly he laid his hands over the soft mounds. Her tongue touched her lips as she stood immobile, her eyes locked with his. The rain beat against the closed shutters of the tiny window. Downstairs a soldier stirred and groaned in his sleep, the hilt of his sword scraping on the floor.

With abrupt urgency, and in total silence, Marcus stripped the clothes from her body. Her eyes were on fire but her skin was cold as he ran his hands over her nakedness. "Get under the blanket!" he rasped, pushing her to the bed.

Judith obeyed, huddling under the scratchy wool, watching as he threw off his own clothes. She held up the blanket for him as he slid beneath, pulling her against him, fitting her body to his. Soon there was warmth where her skin touched his and cool places where they were apart. His palm cupped the flare of her hip, flattened against her thigh, drew her leg across his own thighs, opening her body.

Judith shuddered, unfolding to the fervid, searching caress, the deep exploration of the heated furrow of her body. Her thighs slithered against the muscular hardness of his and her tongue dipped into the hollow of his shoulder, tasting the salt on his skin before her mouth locked with his. Their tongues warred, danced, plunged in a wild spiral of passion that excluded all but their partnered bodies and their frantic need.

"Love me," Judith whispered against his mouth. "Now, it must be now."

Marcus drew her beneath him. He parted her thighs, then paused for an instant on the threshold of her body. Her eyes were closed, her face lost in joy, but as he gazed down at her, the luxuriant fringe of her eyelashes swept up, showing him those great golden-brown lynx eyes awash with passion. "Love me," she whispered again.

With a little sigh he entered the moist tenderness of her core, and she closed around him. He eased deeper, feeling the suppleness of her body, and bent to brush her damp temples with his lips, to touch the corners of her eyes, trailing his tongue over the sensitive corner of her mouth. She smiled at the caress and reached down to touch him where his body was joined with hers. He drew breath as his pleasure surged. His hands closed over her buttocks, lifting her to meet him as he plunged to the very center of her being. The blossom of delight within her burst into full bloom, and she cried out against his mouth.

Marcus thrust once more, deep within her, feeling in his own flesh the pulsating throb of her climax. As he moved to withdraw from her, her arms tightened around him as if to hold him within, but he resisted the pressure, leaving her body the instant before his own core burst asunder.

They lay entwined as the fever abated, and Marcus felt Judith's heart slow as she slipped into sleep. He held her, wondering why he had withdrawn at the last. She was his wife now. She could carry his child. But the truth was that he hardly knew her, and had little reason to trust her.

He awoke slowly, wonderfully, to the awareness of his body coming alive beneath whispering caresses. He heard Judith's soft murmur of satisfaction as he rose beneath her ministering hands, and he reached down dreamily to twine his fingers into the curls resting on his belly as she concentrated on her task. In the aftermath of passion's extremity, she made love to him now with a languid pleasure, learning his body as she tasted every inch of him, exploring his planes and hollows, and he yielded to her orchestration before conducting his own symphony on her delicate, thrumming femininity.

Beyond the shuttered windows the rain-soaked sky lightened on the morning of Sunday, June 18, 1815. The storm had passed and a bird in the ivy began an insistent, stubborn song.

Judith stretched luxuriantly beneath the rough blanket, glorying in her body's satiation, its complete relaxation. She was warm and dry and thought life could hold no greater joy than to spend the day in this loft with Marcus, sharing and exploring their bodies. But her husband was already pushing aside the blanket.

"Must you?" she asked with a tenderly inviting smile.

"Yes, I must." He bent to kiss her. "But you stay here and sleep. I'll see what I can find in the way of breakfast." He stood up, shivering in the damp chill of early morning. He picked up his clothes and grimaced. "Everything's still wet. Stay under the blanket, and I'll take your clothes to dry by the fire."

"You can't hang up my clothes in front of all those men," Judith squeaked.

"This is neither the time nor the place for such niceties," he said, shuddering as he fastened his britches. "Now stay put and I'll be back soon."

"Yes, sir," Judith murmured, pulling the blanket over her head. "Without any clothes, I don't have much choice." His laugh hung in the air for a minute, then the door closed and she heard his booted feet on the staircase.

She fell asleep again for an hour and woke to the sound of a bugle and the tramp of feet. After struggling up on the bedframe, she pushed open the shutters and gazed down at the courtyard where men and horses were splashing purposefully through the puddles. The bugle sounded again, an urgent clarion call that stirred her blood with both fear and excitement.

The door banged closed below and Marcus's step sounded on the stairs. He came in with her clothes and a basket. "Good, you're awake," he said briskly. He looked distracted as he put the basket on the floor and dropped the bundle of clothes on the bed. "Your clothes are dry, at least. Other than that, there's not much I can say for them. There's coffee, bread, and jam in the basket. I'm going to have to leave you now."

"What's happening?" She sat on the bed, wrapping the blanket tightly around her.

"The French are advancing. We're—" A roll of cannon fire shattered the air, and for a second there was an eerie silence. Then it came again. "We've opened the attack," Marcus said, his mouth grim. "I don't know when I'll be back. You're to wait for me here."

"Where will you be?"

"With Wellington."

"On the field?" Her heart lurched. Somehow she hadn't thought of him under fire.

"Where else?" he said shortly. "Tactics change constantly as the position changes." Bending, he caught her shoulders and held her eyes with his. "I'll come back for you. *Be here.*"

"Don't go just yet." She put a hand on his arm.

His expression softened. "Don't be frightened."

"It's not that . . . not for me . . . but for you," she said hesitantly. "I want to be where you are."

"It's not possible, lynx. You know that." He brushed the line of her jaw with a gentle finger.

"Answer me a question." She didn't know why she was going to ask this question now; it was hardly an appropriate time or place for discussion of something so serious. But for some reason, after the passion of the night and in their present warm accord, she desperately needed to know his answer.

He waited.

"Why did you withdraw from me last night?" She regarded him steadily, waiting for his reply. When, last night, instinctively, she had tried to hold him within her and he had resisted, she had been drowning in the sensate glory of loving and had felt only the barest flicker of loss. In the cool clear light of day, she knew she was not ready for pregnancy herself; there was Gracemere to deal with before she could be ready for other responsibilities. And a husband to get to know before he could be the father of her child. Did Marcus feel the same way about her? About their situation? Or was it something else?

Marcus didn't immediately reply. He stood looking down at her, his black eyes searching hers, almost as if he would look into her soul. Judith shivered, abruptly convinced that she was hovering on the edge of a chasm where something dark and repellent lurked.

Then Marcus turned and went to the door. He paused, his hand on the latch, and didn't turn to look at her as he said, "I'll answer that question with one of my own. Did you know who was in the taproom yesterday before you made such a dramatic entrance?"

The shocked silence stretched between them, and when she didn't answer him, he quietly opened the door and left.

He believed she had trapped him into marriage. Cold nausea lodged in her throat. Of course he wouldn't want children by a woman capable of such calculating deceit. How he must hate her. But it was a hatred and contempt that didn't extend to her body. As far as Marcus was concerned, she was his wife in name but his whore in body and soul.

Bitter bile rose into her mouth, and her head began to pound. Why hadn't she denied it? Why hadn't she poured out a torrent of violent denial, protestations of innocence, anger that he could think such a thing? But Judith knew why she had sat in silence. Because in essence he was right. He believed she had married him for his fortune and his position, and so she had. What did it matter that she hadn't known who was in the taproom when she'd strolled in. She'd still taken advantage of the situation . . . of Marcus's sense of honor. Why should he ever see her as anything other than a grasping, deceitful gold-digger?

Shivering and queasy, she dressed in her crumpled, stained riding habit. The ring on her finger caught a shaft of sunlight and the gold glowed dully. Once she and Sebastian had done what had to be done —once Sebastian was again in possession of his birthright, their father avenged, and Gracemere defeated—she would tell Marcus that no legal ties bound them. She would set him free. But until then, she must play out the masquerade. And what else was new? she thought with grim cynicism. Her whole life had been a masquerade.

Outside, she stood looking around, trying to decide where to go. The sounds of battle were loud and terrifying, the clash of steel, the boom of the cannon, the sharp volley of muskets. Men were running backward and forward, and wounded were beginning to trickle in.

Judith ran out of the yard and behind the group of farmhouses to a small hill. When she reached the top, she gazed in fascinated horror at the scene spread out before her. It was a field, bounded by hedgerows. Swaying backward and forward over those few acres were two massed armies, banners waving in the breeze, trumpets blaring. Wellington's infantry charged the squares of French soldiers. Cavalry rode over men and guns, lance and sword hacking and thrusting. Lines of infantry dropped to their knees, muskets aimed, there was a crashing boom, and the line of advancing French was decimated.

From the distance of her observation post, the scene looked like some kind of anarchical play, wrested from the twisted imagination of a demented playwright. What must it feel like to be in the middle of that hand-to-hand melee, men facing men with but one intention —to kill? Bodies carpeted the field, men and horses falling on all sides, and it was impossible to believe there was any direction, any coherent strategy to the killing on either side. And yet there had to be. Marcus was somewhere in that murderous scrimmage, presumably making some kind of sense of it.

She went back to the yard to work with the wounded but in the late afternoon climbed the hill again. The Prussian advance on Napoleon's flank was beginning to have its effect now, although Judith didn't know that. But she could tell that the French seemed to be falling back, or at least that there seemed to be fewer of them. Peering into the melee, she distinguished a massive cannonade centered on a small rise, behind which a brigade of British Foot Guards sheltered. It seemed to Judith that the cannonade must split the earth with its violence. And then, abruptly, the firing ceased. There was an unearthly moment of silence. Then the smoke of the guns wafted away and she stared, transfixed, at the column of French Grenadiers, Napoleon's Imperial Guard, advancing toward the rise. A great cry of *"Vive l'Empereur"* seemed to reach the heavens as the column moved forward in deadly formation.

It was six o'clock in the evening.

Suddenly, from behind the little hill, the brigade of Foot Guards who had been sheltering from the cannonade rose seemingly out of the ground and fired round after round into the Imperial Guard. The effect was as if the fire itself was a battering ram, bodily forcing the front line of the French column backward. They began to fall like ninepins at a terrifying rate. The divisions at the rear began to fire over their comrades' head, the formation wavering as they milled in confusion. With an almost primeval scream that lifted the tiny hairs on her skin, the brigade of Foot Guards sprang forward, swords in hand. As Judith watched, the unthinkable happened. Napoleon's Imperial Guard, his last hope, his tool for certain victory, the veterans of ten years of war and innumerable triumphs, broke rank, turned, and ran, pursued by the bellowing brigade.

Slowly Judith turned and went back down the hill, unable to believe what she'd seen. But it seemed it was over. Wellington and Blücher had won the Battle of Waterloo. The atmosphere in the stableyard was one of exhausted jubilation as the sun set and the sound of firing became sporadic. The death toll was horrendous and the wounded were brought in in wagonloads; but Bonaparte had been defeated for the last time. The Prussians were pursuing the fleeing French army, leaving the depleted British to gather themselves together, recover their strength, and take stock of their losses.

Marcus rode into the stableyard toward midnight. He'd accompanied Wellington to his post-victory meeting with Blücher. The two men had kissed each other and Blücher had summed up the day's events in his sparse French. *"Quelle affaire!"*

Adequate words, it seemed to Marcus. Superlatives somehow wouldn't capture the sense of finality they all felt. The world as they knew it could now return to peace again.

He looked for his wife in the torch-lit stableyard. Finally, he saw her bending over a stretcher in the corner of the yard. As if she were aware of his arrival, she straightened, pushing her hair out of her eyes, turning toward him. His heart leaped at the sight of her. The bitterness of their parting, the sourness of suspicion, faded, and he wanted only to hold her.

"You're safe," she said, her voice shaky with relief as he dismounted beside her. There was a shadow of sorrow in her eyes as she met his gaze, a questioning apprehension that harked back to the wretchedness of the morning.

He was filled with an overpowering need to kiss the sadness from her eyes, the tremor from her soft mouth. Suddenly, nothing seemed to matter but that she was there for him. "Yes," he said, pulling her into his arms. He laid his lips against her eyelids, feeling their rapid flutter against his mouth. "Safe and sound, lynx."

Her arms went around him, and she reached her body against his, her head resting on his chest, the steady beat of his heart thudding against her ear. Her eyes closed and for this moment she lost herself in the security of his hold, the warmth of his presence, the promise of passion.

9

"THAT NEW BUTLER OF YOURS SEEMED INCLINED TO DENY ME." BERNARD Melville, third earl of Gracemere, entered Lady Barret's boudoir without ceremony. "I trust it doesn't mean the gouty Sir Thomas is turning suspicious."

"No. He's at Brooks's, I believe. Snoring over his port, probably." Agnes stretched languidly on the striped chaise longue, where she had been taking a recuperative afternoon nap. "Hodgkins is overly scrupulous about his duties. He knew I was resting." She held out her hand. "I wasn't expecting you to return to town for another week."

He took her hand, carrying it to his lips. "I couldn't endure another day's separation, my love."

Agnes smiled. "Such pretty words, Bernard. And am I to believe them?"

"Oh, yes," he said, bending over her, catching her wrists and holding them down on either side of her head. "Oh, yes, my adorable Agnes, you are to believe them." His hard eyes, so pale their blueness was almost translucent, held hers, and she shivered, waiting for him to bring his mouth to hers, to underwrite his statement with the fierce possession of his body.

He laughed, reading her with the ease of long knowledge. "Oh, you are needy, aren't you, my love? It's amazing what an absence can do." Still he held himself above her, taunting her with promise.

"And you are cruel, Bernard," she stated softly. "Why does it please you to taunt me with my love?"

"Is it love? I don't think that's the right word," he murmured, bringing his face closer to hers but still not touching her. "Obsession, need, but not love. That's too tame an emotion for such a woman as you."

"And for you," she whispered.

"Obsession, need," he responded with a smile that did nothing to soften the cruel mouth. "We feed on each other."

"Kiss me," she begged, twitching her imprisoned hands in her need to touch him.

He let his weight fall onto her hands so that her wrists ached and very slowly brought his mouth to hers. She bit his lip, drawing blood, and he pulled back with a violent jerk of his head. "Bitch!"

"It's what you like," she said, with perfect truth.

He slapped her face lightly with his open palm and she gave an exultant crow of laughter, bringing her freed hand to his face, wiping the bead of blood from his lips with her fingertip and carrying it to her own mouth. Her tongue darted, licking the red smear, and her tawny eyes glittered. "Shall I come to you tonight, my lord?"

He caught her chin with hard fingers and kissed her, bruising her lips against her teeth in answer. A knock at the door brought him upright. He swung away from her, picking up a periodical from a drum table, idly flicking through the pages as a footman silently mended the fire.

"What's this I hear about Carrington taking a wife in Brussels?" Gracemere asked casually. "It's the talk of the town. Some nobody, I gather."

"Yes, I haven't met her yet. We came up to town ourselves only yesterday," Agnes said in the same tone. "Letitia Moreton says she's stunning and seems very much up to snuff. She's charmed the Society matrons at all events. Sally Jersey raves about her."

"Not another Martha, then?" He tossed the periodical onto the table again as the footman left, and he sat down, carefully smoothing out a crease in his buff pantaloons.

"Hardly," Agnes said. "No little brown mouse this, as I understand it. But no one knows anything about them . . . there's a brother too. Equally charming, according to Letitia."

"Plump in the pocket?" There was an arrested look in the pale eyes, a sudden predatory hunger.

Agnes shook her head. "That I don't know. But if he's Carrington's brother-in-law . . . why?"

Gracemere's manicured fingernails drummed on the carved arm of his chair. "I'm looking for another pigeon to pluck. Newcomers to town tend to provide the easiest pickings. I wonder if he plays."

"Who doesn't?" Agnes said. "I'll see what I can find out this evening at Cavendish House. But I have another idea for improving your financial situation, my love." She sat up, her tone suddenly brisk.

"Oh?" Gracemere raised his eyebrows. "I'm all ears, my dear."

"Letitia Moreton's daughter, Harriet," Agnes announced, and lay back again on the piled cushions with a complacent smile. "She has a fortune of thirty-thousand pounds. It should last you quite a while, I would have thought."

Gracemere frowned. "She must be barely out of the schoolroom."

"All the better," Agnes said. "She'll fall easily for the flattering attentions of a charming older man. You'll be able to sweep her off her feet before she has the chance to lay eyes on anyone else."

The earl tapped his teeth with a fingernail, considering. "What about Letitia and the girl's father? They'll be unlikely to look kindly on the suit of a fortune hunter."

"They don't know you're a fortune hunter," Agnes pointed out. "And you have the earldom. Letitia will jump at an earl for her daughter so long as you behave with circumspection. I've already become fast friends with the lady." She laughed unkindly. "Such a nincompoop she is, with die-away airs. She professes to be an invalid and can't chaperone her daughter as much as she should. So who do you think has offered to take her place?" Her eyebrows rose delicately, and Gracemere laughed.

"What a consummate plotter you are, my dear. So I can expect to meet the sweet child in your company."

"Frequently," Agnes agreed with another complacent smile.

"In the meantime, bring me your impressions of Carrington's brother-in-law. I might as well pluck a pigeon while I'm waiting for the heiress to ripen and fall," he said, rising. "I'm not invited to Cavendish House, since I'm still supposed to be in the country, so I'll rely on your acute senses, my love." He bent over her again, laying one hand on her breast, feeling the nipple rise in immediate response. "Adieu, until later."

Agnes shifted on the couch, one leg dropping to the floor. The earl moved his hand down, pressing the thin silk of her negligee against the opened cleft of her body, feeling her heat. "Until later," he repeated, and then left her.

Marcus tossed the reins to his tiger and alighted from his curricle in Berkeley Square.

"Take a good look at the leader's left hock when you get them to the mews, Henry. I sensed a slight imbalance as we took that last corner."

"Right you are, governor." The lad tugged a yellow forelock before going to the horses' heads.

Marcus strolled up the steps of the handsome double-fronted mansion. The front door opened just as he reached the head.

"Good afternoon, my lord. And it's a beautiful one, if I might be so bold." The butler's bow was as ponderous as his words.

"Afternoon, Gregson. Yes, you may be so bold." Marcus handed him his driving whip and curly-brimmed beaver hat. "Bring a bottle of the seventy-nine claret to my book room, will you?" He crossed the gleaming marble-tiled expanse of hallway and went down a narrow passage behind the staircase to a small, square room at the back of the house, where a young man was arranging papers on the massive cherrywood table that served as desk.

"Good afternoon, my lord." He greeted his employer's entrance with a bow.

"Afternoon, John. What are you going to entertain me with now?"

"Accounts, my lord," his secretary said. "And Lady Carrington's quarterly bills. You did say you wished to settle them yourself." His tone conveyed a degree of puzzlement, since in general he was responsible for settling on the marquis's account all the bills that came into the house.

"Yes, I did," Marcus said absently, picking up a neat pile of bills. "Are these they?"

"Yes, my lord. And there are some invitations you might want to look at."

"I can't think of anything I'd like to do less," Marcus said, leafing through the bills in his hand. "Give them to Lady Carrington."

"I did, my lord. But she said she didn't feel able to make up your mind for you." John blushed and he pulled awkwardly on his right ear, wishing he hadn't been put in the position of conveying Lady Carrington's forthright opinion to her husband. But his lordship merely shrugged.

"Very well. I'll discuss them with her." He dropped the bills to the table and picked up the pile of embossed cards, wrinkling his nose in distaste. The number of irksome invitations that came into the house of a married man far exceeded those he'd received as a bachelor. Everyone knew he didn't care for social events, and he couldn't understand why all these overzealous Society matrons now soliciting his company imagined that marriage would change the habits and interests of a lifetime.

"If that'll be all, my lord, I'll go and work on your speech to the House of Lords on the Corn Laws."

Marcus grimaced. "Can't you find something more interesting for me to talk on than the Corn Laws, John?"

His secretary looked startled. "But there is nothing more important at the moment, my lord."

"Nothing to do with the army or the navy . . . further reforms in the Admiralty, how about that?"

"I'll do some research, my lord." With a hurt look, John left the book room.

Marcus smiled. John's political interests were unfortunately not his employer's. He turned back to the papers on the desk, picking up the pile of bills again.

Gregson came in with the claret. "Is her ladyship in, Gregson?"

"Yes, my lord. I believe she's in the yellow drawing room." The butler drew the cork, examined it carefully, poured a small quantity of claret into a shallow taster, and sniffed and sipped with a critical frown.

"All right?"

"Yes, my lord. Very fine." He filled a crystal goblet and presented it to his employer. "Will that be all, sir?"

"For the moment. Thank you, Gregson."

Marcus took the scent of his wine before sipping appreciatively. He wandered over to the long narrow windows overlooking a small, walled garden. The leaves of a chestnut tree drifted thickly to the grass under the brisk autumnal wind. A gardener was gathering the richly burnished mass into a bonfire. Marcus was abruptly reminded of Judith's hair, glowing in the candlelight, spread over the white pillows . . . the silky matching triangle at the apex of those long, creamy thighs . . .

Abruptly he turned back to the desk and picked up the pile of bills again, tapping them against his palm. Judith certainly didn't count the cost when it came to her personal expenditures. *She was beautiful and passionate in bed and he paid her well for it.*

Why in God's name did he resent it? He was a generous man and always had been. Money had never concerned him—his fortune was too large for it ever to be an issue. And yet, as he looked through his wife's bills, saw what she'd spent on her wardrobe, he could think only of how different it must be for her now, after all those years of living from hand to mouth, of making over her gowns and wearing paste jewelry, of living in cheap lodgings . . . of pretending publicly that she had access to all the things she now had at her fingertips.

A house in Berkeley Square, a country estate in Berkshire, an unassailable social position . . . She must congratulate herself every moment of every day on how well her strategem had succeeded.

Marcus drained the claret in his glass and refilled it. Since Waterloo, they'd skimmed the surface of their relationship. There had been no further mention of the encounter in the taproom. And no reference in their lovemaking to his continued precautions against conception. Socially, they obeyed convention and went their separate ways. Except during the quiet, private hours of the night. Then the needs of their bodies transcended the bleak recognition of the true nature of their partnership, so that he would wake in the morning, filled with a warmth and contentment, only to have it destroyed immediately with the full return of memory.

She never talked of her past and he never asked. In all essentials they remained strangers, except in passion. Was that enough? Could it ever be enough? But it was all he was going to have, so he'd better learn to be satisfied.

He put his glass down and left the book room, still holding the sheaf of bills. The yellow drawing room was a small salon upstairs, at the back of the house. Judith had laid claim to it immediately, eschewing the heavy formality of the public rooms: the library, main drawing room, and dining room. He opened the door, to be greeted by a light trill of feminine laughter; it was abruptly cut off as the three women in the room saw who had entered, and for an instant he felt like an intruder in his own house.

"Why, Carrington, have you come to take a glass of ratafia with us?" Judith said, quirking her eyebrows with her habitual challenge.

"The day I find you drinking ratafia, ma'am, is the day I'll know I'm on my way to Bedlam," he observed, bowing. "I give you good afternoon, ladies. I don't wish to intrude, Judith, but I'd like to see you in my book room when you're at liberty."

Judith bristled visibly. She hadn't yet succeeded in moderating her husband's autocratic manner. "I have an appointment later this afternoon," she fibbed. "Maybe we could discuss whatever it is at some other time."

"Unfortunately not," he replied. "It's a matter of some urgency. I'll expect you in—" He glanced at the clock on the mantelpiece. "—within the hour, shall we say?"

Without waiting for her response, he bowed again to his wife's guests and left, closing the door gently behind him.

Judith seemed to have a natural talent for making friends, he reflected, and the door knocker was constantly banging, female trills and whispers filling the corners and crevices of his previously masculine-oriented house. Not only women either. There were men aplenty, anxious to play cicisbeo to the Marchioness of Carrington. Not that Judith had so far stepped out of line with her courtiers. Her flirtations were conducted, as far as he could see, with the light hand of an expert. But then that's only what he would expect from an expert.

As he reached the hallway, the door knocker sounded. He paused, waiting as the butler greeted the new arrival. "Good afternoon, Lady Devlin."

"Good afternoon, Gregson. Is her ladyship at home?" The visitor nervously adjusted the ostrich feather in her hat.

"In the yellow drawing room, my lady."

"Then I'll go straight up. There's no need to announce me. . . . Oh, Marcus . . . you startled me."

Marcus regarded his sister-in-law in some puzzlement. Sally's complexion was changing rapidly from pink to deathly white and back again. He knew she tended to be uncomfortable in his company, but this degree of discomposure was out of the ordinary.

"I beg your pardon, Sally." He bowed and stood aside to let her pass him on the stairs. "I trust all's well in Grosvenor Square." He waited with bored resignation to be told that one of his nephews had the toothache or come down with a chill.

To his surprise, Sally looked startled and, instead of launching into one of her minute descriptions of childish ailments, said, "Yes

. . . yes, thank you, Marcus. So good of you to be concerned." Her gloved hand ran back and forth over the banister, for all the world as if she were polishing it. "I was hoping to see Judith."

"You'll find her in her drawing room."

Sally almost ran up the stairs, without a word of farewell. Marcus shook his head dismissively. He didn't object to Jack's wife, but she was a pretty widgeon with no conversation. Judith seemed to like her, though. Which was interesting, since he'd noticed that his wife didn't suffer fools gladly.

"Sally . . . why, whatever's the matter?" Judith jumped up at her sister-in-law's precipitate entrance.

"Oh, I have to talk to you." Sally grasped Judith's hands. "I don't know where to turn." Her eyes took in the other two women in the room. "Isobel, Cornelia . . . I'm at my wit's end."

"Good heavens, Sally." Isobel Henley examined a plate of sweet biscuits and took a macaroon. "Is it one of the children?"

"I wish it were as simple as that." Sally sat down on a sofa, gazing tragically around the room. Her usually merry blue eyes glittered with tears. She opened her reticule and dabbed at her eyes with a lacy scrap of handkerchief.

"Have some tea." Practically, Judith filled a teacup and passed it to her sister-in-law. Sally drank and struggled to pull herself together. She put the cup back on the table and took a deep breath.

"I've been racking my brains for three days until I think my head is about to explode. But I can't think what to do." The scrap of lace tore under her restless fingers.

"So tell us." Cornelia Forsythe leaned forward, patting Sally's hand reassuringly. Her lorgnette swung into her teacup, splashing her already slightly spotted gown. "Oh, dear." She dabbed ineffectually at the spots. "I was perfectly clean when I left the house."

Judith swallowed a smile. Cornelia was a large, untidy woman who never seemed in control of her dress, her possessions, her hair, the time, or her relationships. She was, however, possessed of a quick wit and an agile brain.

"I don't see how, unless you can put me in the way of acquiring four thousand pounds by tomorrow morning."

"Four thousand?" Judith whistled in the manner she'd picked up from Sebastian. "Whatever for?"

"Jeremy," Sally said. Her younger brother was an impoverished scapegrace. "I had to lend him four thousand pounds or he'd have been imprisoned for debt in the Fleet and now I have to get my money back. But what else could I have done?"

"Your husband?" Cornelia suggested.

Sally looked at Judith. "Jack might have helped him, but you know what Marcus thinks of Jeremy."

Judith nodded. Marcus had no tolerance for the dissipated excesses of young men with breeding and no fortune. He was inclined to declare that a career in the army was the answer for all such young fools. Either that, or politics. Judith didn't disagree with him. The reckless and undisciplined pursuit of pleasure was as alien to her as the man in the moon. However, saying so wouldn't help Sally at the moment.

"I suppose Marcus's advice to Jack is to let Jeremy suffer the consequences," Judith said.

Sally nodded. "And in truth, I can't really blame him. Jeremy's always going to be wanting more."

"So, how did you furnish him with four thousand pounds?" Isobel brought the conversation back to the point as she took another macaroon. She had an inveterate sweet tooth, but, much to Judith's amusement, even Isobel's lamentable fondness for ratafia couldn't sugar her tongue.

"I pawned the Devlin rubies," Sally said flatly.

Isobel dropped her macaroon to the carpet. "You did what?"

Judith closed her eyes for a minute, absorbing the full enormity of this.

Sally continued in a voice devoid of expression. "I didn't know what else to do. Jeremy was desperate. But Marcus has asked for them. Jack thinks they're being cleaned."

"Why has Marcus asked for them?" Judith asked.

Sally looked at her sister-in-law as if the answer were self-evident. "Because they're yours, Judith."

"Mine?"

"You're the Marchioness of Carrington. The Devlin jewels are rightfully yours. Marcus only loaned them to me . . . although no one expected him to marry, so I thought . . ." Her voice died.

A silence fell as her three companions contemplated the situation. "What a pickle," Cornelia said finally. "You should have had them copied."

"I did," Sally said. "But the copy won't fool Carrington."

"No," Judith agreed, thinking about her husband's sharpness of eye and intellect. "I suppose I could say I don't like rubies and I'm quite happy for you to keep them. . . . But no, that won't work. Marcus is still going to want to see them."

She stood up and walked around the room, thinking. There was one way to help Sally. It was risky. If Marcus found out, what little accord they had would be destroyed. But she could do it, and surely, if you had the means to help a friend, then you were honor bound to do so. At least, by her code of honor.

"When must you redeem them, Sally?"

"Jack said he wanted to return them to Marcus tomorrow." Sally wrung her hands. "Judith, I feel so terrible . . . as if I stole something that belonged to you."

"Oh, nonsense!" Judith dismissed this with a brisk gesture. "I don't give a tinker's damn for rubies. Your brother needed help and you gave it to him." This she understood as an absolute imperative. "I only wish you'd said something earlier. It'll be noticeable if I win such a sum in one evening. I would much prefer to have won it over several occasions. It looks rather singular to be spending the entire evening in the card room playing only for high stakes."

"What are you saying? I know you're fond of gaming, but—"

"Oh, it's a little more than that," Judith said. "I'm actually very skilled at cards."

"I had noticed." Cornelia surveyed Judith through her lorgnette. "You and your brother."

"Our father taught us," Judith said. Even in this company, she wasn't prepared to expand on her background. "We were both apt pupils and I enjoy it."

"But I don't fully understand . . ." Sally said hesitantly.

"If I went to Mrs. Dolby's card party this evening, I could probably win such a sum," Judith explained succinctly. "And it would draw no attention in such a place."

"But you can't play on Pickering Street, Judith." Isobel was shocked. The widow Dolby's card parties were notorious for their enormously high stakes and loose company.

"Why not? Many women do."

"Yes, but they're generally considered fast."

"Sebastian will escort me. If I go in my brother's company, there should be no gossip."

"What about Carrington?"

"There's no reason why he should discover it," Judith said. "It will serve very well. There's bound to be a table for macao." She smiled at Sally. "Cheer up. You will redeem the rubies in the morning."

"But how can you be so confident?"

"Practice," Judith said a touch wryly. "I have had a great deal of practice."

They left soon after, Sally looking a little more cheerful. Judith's confidence was infectious, although it was difficult to trust in such a promise of salvation.

Judith stood frowning in the empty salon. Since her marriage, she'd played only socially, for moderate stakes. Serious gaming was something quite different. Was she out of practice? She closed her eyes, envisioning a macao table, seeing a hand of cards. The old, familiar prickle of excitement ran down her spine and she smiled to herself. No, she'd never lose the touch.

She'd have to have Sebastian's escort. He would probably have plans of his own for the evening and would need time to alter them. It didn't occur to her that her brother would fail her. She'd go to his lodgings right away . . . but, no. Marcus was waiting for her. Just what lay behind this brusque summons to his book room? For a minute, she toyed with the idea of ignoring the summons, then dismissed the urge. Matters were delicate enough between them as it was, without deliberately stirring things up.

Marcus opened the door himself at her brisk knock. "I was wondering how long your friends would keep you."

"They had the prior claim on my attention, sir," she said. "It would have been unpardonably rude to have asked them to leave prematurely . . . although you don't seem to share that opinion. You made it very clear they shouldn't prolong their visit."

Marcus glanced at the clock, observing wryly "I can't have been very persuasive. I've been waiting for you for well over an hour."

Judith put her head on one side, surveying him through narrowed eyes. "And what else did you expect, Carrington?"

That surprised a reluctant laugh from him. "Nothing else, lynx." A wispy strand of copper hair was escaping from a loosened pin in the knot on top of her head. It was irresistible, and without conscious decision, he pulled the pin out. Then it seemed silly to stop there and his fingers moved through the silken mass, finding and removing pins, demolishing the careful coiffure.

Judith made no protest. Whenever he put his hands on her, it was always the same. She became powerless to do anything but respond. As the hair tumbled around her face, he ran his hands through it, tugging at tangled ringlets with a rapt expression. Then he stood back and surveyed his handiwork.

"What did you do that for?" Judith asked.

"I don't know," he said with a puzzled headshake. "I couldn't seem to help myself." Cupping her face, he kissed her, a long, slow joining of their mouths that as always absorbed them totally.

Slightly breathless, Judith drew back from him when he let his hands fall from her face. "You do kiss remarkably well, husband," she observed with a tiny laugh.

"And you have, of course, vast experience from which to draw your comparisons."

"Now, that, sir, is for me to know and you to find out."

"I'm not sure this is the time or the place for such a discovery. I shall postpone the exercise until later."

"So what lies behind this urgent summons?" Judith asked, changing the subject in the hope that it would allow her heated blood to cool and put the stiffness back in her knees.

"Ah." Leaning against the desk, crossing his long legs in their fawn pantaloons at the ankles, he reached behind him for the pile of bills. "I've been examining your quarterly bills and I think . . . I really think you need to explain some of them."

"Explain them?" She looked at him in genuine confusion, arousal quenched as thoroughly as if she'd been dipped in an icy stream.

"Yes." He held out the bills and she took them, staring down at the sheet on top bearing columns of John's neat figures. The total was extravagant, certainly, but not horrendous . . . at least not by the standards of London Society.

"So what do you want me to explain?" She leafed through the bills. "They all seem quite straightforward."

"Do you usually spend four hundred guineas on a gown?" he asked, taking the sheaf from her, riffling through them until he found the offending document. "Here."

"But that was my court dress," she said. "Magarethe made it."

"And this . . . and this . . ." He held out two more. "Fifty guineas for a pair of shoe buckles, Judith!"

Judith took a step back. "Let me understand what's happening, Marcus. Are you questioning my expenditures?"

He pursed his lips. "That would be an accurate interpretation of this interview."

"And you're accusing me of extravagance?" There was a faint buzzing in her ears as she grappled with the humiliation of this: to be chastised like a child who's overspent her pin money. No one, ever, had questioned her expenditure. Since she had first put up her hair, she had been managing her own finances as well as those of their small household. She had juggled bills, paid rent, ensured food of some kind appeared on the table; and in the time since her father's death, she had managed the growing fund that would underpin the plan for Gracemere's downfall.

"In a word, yes."

"Forgive me, but just how much would it be reasonable for me to spend in a quarter?" Her voice shook. "You neglected to give me a limit."

"My error," he agreed. "I'll settle these bills and then I'll instruct my bankers to make you a quarterly allowance. If you overspend, then I'll have to ask you to submit all bills to me for prior approval."

He stood up, tossing the bills on the desk as if to indicate the interview was over. "But I'm sure you'll remember how to put a rein on your spending, once you understand that marriage has not opened the gates to a limitless fund. I'm sorry if you didn't realize that earlier." He could hear the bite in his voice, could almost see the ugly twist to his mouth, and yet he couldn't help himself.

Afraid of what she would do or say if she stayed another minute in the same room with Marcus, Judith turned and left, closing the door with exaggerated care behind her. Her cheeks burned with humiliation. He was accusing her of taking advantage of her position to satisfy her own greed. What kind of person did he think she was? But she knew the answer: a conniving, unprincipled trickster who would stoop to anything to achieve her ambition.

But it wasn't true. Oh, on the surface, maybe. She wasn't dealing the cards of her marriage with total honesty. But she wasn't the despicable person he believed her to be.

And she wasn't going to submit to a meager allowance and a controlling hand on her purse strings. Her lips tightened with determination. What she could do for Sally, she could do for herself. She would simply return to the old days: Pay her own way at the tables. And Marcus Devlin and his quarterly allowance could go to the devil.

Half an hour later, footman in tow, she walked to her brother's lodgings on Albemarle Street. Sebastian was on his way out for a five o'clock ride in Hyde Park, but with customary good nature postponed the excursion and ushered his sister into his parlor.

"Sherry?"

"Please." She took the glass he handed her.

"So, what can I do for you, Ju?"

"Several things." She explained the matter of Sally and the four thousand pounds.

Sebastian frowned. "That's a devil of a haul in one night, Ju."

"I know, but what else is to be done? If Marcus ever discovered what she'd done, I can't think how he'd react. Jack might be a bit more understanding, but he'll follow Marcus's lead, he always does."

"He wields a lot of power, that husband of yours," Sebastian observed.

"Yes," Judith agreed shortly. "Jack's elder brother, Charlie's guardian . . . my husband," she added in an almost vicious undertone.

"What's happened?" Sebastian asked without preamble.

Judith told him, trying to keep her voice steady, but her anger surged anew as she recounted the mortifying interview. She paced Sebastian's parlor, the embroidered flounce of her walking dress swishing around her ankles. "It's intolerable," she finished with a sweep of her arm. "Marcus is intolerable and the situation is intolerable."

"What are you going to do about it?" Sebastian knew his sister well enough to know she would never submit meekly to her husband's edict.

"Provide for myself," she said. "At the tables. Just like before."

Sebastian whistled softly. "I suppose you couldn't just tell him that you didn't know who was in the taproom at Quatre Bras? Since that's what's causing the mischief."

Judith shook her head. "It wouldn't do any good. He's determined to believe the worst of me, and the truth's dubious enough, anyway." She looked helplessly at her brother. "Supposing I say: I didn't deliberately trap you into marriage, but it was too good an opportunity to pass up, for an adventuress in need of a good establishment in order to pursue her secret goal. And anyway, we're not really married, but I didn't want you to know that." She raised her eyebrows at her brother.

Sebastian pretended to consider this. "No, I'm afraid that wouldn't go over too well. At any rate, you know you can count on me. The deep play doesn't begin at Dolby's until the early hours. If you're going to Cavendish House, I'll escort you from there. Will that serve?"

"Perfectly. Marcus doesn't intend to put in an appearance at Cavendish House, and he'll not be surprised if I don't return home until near dawn. We always go our separate ways."

"You'd better dip into the 'Gracemere fund,' " Sebastian said. "You'll need decent stakes at the start, and clearly your husband isn't going to furnish them." He went into the next-door bedroom and returned with a pouch of rouleaux. "Eight hundred." He dropped it into her hand and grinned. "If you don't turn that into four thousand in one evening, I'll know you've lost your touch."

She smiled, weighing the pouch on the palm of her hand. "Never fear. Now, there's another matter in which I need your help." She put down her sherry glass. "Since I'm declaring war, I might as well do it properly. I wish you to acquire a high-perch phaeton and pair for me. Marcus has expressed himself very vigorously on the subject of loose women who drive themselves in sporting vehicles, so my driving one should nicely confirm his flattering opinion of me."

Sebastian scratched his nose and refilled his glass. Judith had lost her temper, and once she'd taken the high road, as he knew from a lifetime's experience, there was little he could do to turn her from the path. She'd pursue it until the momentum died. "Is it wise to be so blatantly provoking?" he asked, without much hope of success.

"I don't much care," his sister responded. "He thinks I'm a designing, conniving baggage, with no morals and no principles. And so I shall be."

Sebastian sighed. "How much do you want to spend for the pair?"

"Not above four hundred . . . unless it would be a crime to pass them up, of course."

"Grantham's in debt up to his neck . . . I could probably acquire his match bays for around four hundred."

"Wonderful. Pay for them out of the 'fund,' and I'll replace it as soon as I've earned it."

She reached up and kissed him. "Now I'll leave you to Hyde Park."

"Ju?"

"Yes?" She stopped as she reached the door.

"Gracemere's in town."

"Ahhh. Have you seen him?"

"No, but Wellby was talking of him in Whites this morning."

"Ahhh," said Judith again, as a prickle of anticipation crept up her spine. "Then soon we begin, Sebastian."

"Yes," he agreed. "Soon we begin."

Judith stood on the pavement for a minute, gazing sightlessly down the narrow road. The footman waited patiently. A sudden gust of wind picked up a handful of fallen leaves from the gutter and sent them eddying around her. Absently she reached out and caught one. It was dry and crackly and crumbled to dust as her hand closed over it. Once the game with Gracemere was played out, there would be no need to continue the illegal charade of her marriage. Marcus would have his freedom from her. But not before she'd taught him a lesson.

10

MARCUS COULD HEAR JUDITH'S VOICE THROUGH THE DOOR CONNECTING their bedchambers, talking with her maid as Millie dressed her for the evening. The afternoon's unpleasantness had left him with a sour taste in his mouth. He was perfectly entitled to keep a close hand on his wife's pursestrings, but he couldn't rid himself of the feeling that he wasn't behaving like himself. What difference did it make what she spent? It would take more than one lifetime of extravagance to run through his fortune. But disillusion had soured his customary generosity. This wasn't about Judith's spending habits. He wanted to punish her. It was as simple as that. And as disagreeable as that.

He inserted a diamond pin carefully into the snowy folds of his cravat. "You needn't wait up for me, Cheveley."

"No, my lord." The valet turned from the armoire where he was rearranging his lordship's wardrobe with loving care. "If you say so, my lord," he said woodenly.

"I do," Marcus affirmed, a smile tugging at the corners of his mouth. Cheveley's sensitive dignity was always seriously affronted at the slightest hint that his employer could manage without him. "That cough of yours needs a hot toddy and an early bed, man."

Cheveley's thin cheeks pinkened and his stiffness vanished at this solicitude. His lordship was a considerate and just employer, quick to notice signs of discontent or ill health, and quick to act upon both. "That's too good of you, my lord. But I'll be right as a trivet in a day or so."

"Yes, I'm sure you will. But you don't want to take any chances with that weak chest. Leave that now, and take yourself off to bed."

He waited until the valet had left the bedchamber, then opened the door onto his wife's apartment. Judith was sitting at the dressing table, watching critically in the mirror as Millie threaded a gold velvet ribbon through her ringlets.

"Good evening, my lord." For form's sake, Judith offered him the semblance of a smile in the mirror, but didn't turn to greet him.

"Good evening, Judith." Marcus sat down in a velvet chair beside the crackling fire in the hearth. Millie turned her attention to the row of tiny buttons on the tight sleeves of the gown of pale-green crape. It was a color that suited his wife's vibrant coloring to perfection, Marcus reflected, and the thin silk cord circling her waist emphasized her slenderness.

"Did you wish to speak with me?" Judith asked after a few minutes, wondering what could have brought him to her bedchamber in this conjugal fashion. They were hardly in charity with each other at the moment.

"Not about anything in particular," he said, observing without due consideration, "that's a delightful gown."

Judith's expression registered complete disbelief. She blinked and dismissed her maid. "Thank you, Millie, that will do very well. You may go."

The maid curtsied and left. Judith turned on her stool to survey her husband. He was impeccably dressed as always in black satin knee britches and white waistcoat, his only jewelry the diamond pin in his cravat and his heavy gold signet ring, now returned to him. His black hair was brushed *à la Brutus* and there was a distinct frown in the ebony eyes, but it didn't seem to be directed at her.

"Did I hear you aright?" she demanded, raising her eyebrows. "You approve of my gown, sir. Well, that's fortunate, since I daresay you'll be seeing it on many occasions over the next few years. I shall wear it until it falls off my back in shreds. That is what you intend, isn't it?"

"Don't be silly," Marcus said. He'd come in with the vague intention of making peace, but it looked like a forlorn hope. "You know perfectly well that was not what I meant this afternoon. Your allowance won't be ungenerous."

Judith swung back to the mirror. "Your kindness overwhelms me, my lord." She licked her finger and dampened the delicate arch of her eyebrows, struggling to calm herself. Losing her temper again would play havoc with her equilibrium and she needed a cool head tonight, if she was to win for Sally.

Marcus sighed and tried a new tack. "I thought I would accompany you to Cavendish House this evening." Judith knew how he loathed such social engagements; she would surely understand the sacrifice as the peace offering it was meant to be.

He had expected her to be surprised. He had not expected to see a flash of shock in her eyes. It was replaced almost immediately by something that looked unnervingly like calculation.

"Such gallantry, my lord. But quite unnecessary." She laughed lightly, continuing to examine her reflection critically in the mirror. "It would be a sure way to ruin my evening . . . or perhaps that was your intention."

"My apologies, ma'am." He stood up, his lips thinned. "I wasn't intending to ruin your evening. Forgive me."

Judith relented slightly. She half turned on the stool again. "I only meant that I won't be able to enjoy myself because I'll know how bored you are."

She turned back to the dressing table and began tidying a pot of hairpins. "None of your friends will be there and mine won't amuse you."

She didn't want his company; it was as simple as that. Marcus bowed and said coldly, "As you wish. I'm sure you know best." He returned to his own bedchamber without a backward glance.

Oh, Lord, Judith thought miserably. Surely not even a forced marriage should be conducted in this sniping wasteland. She and Marcus were simply the wrong people to have chained themselves in this mutual bondage. The sooner she left him to his own devices the better.

It was after two o'clock when a hired hackney drew up outside Number 6, Pickering Street. Sebastian sprang down and assisted his sister to alight. Judith smoothed down her cloak of gold taffeta and adjusted the puffed muslin collar, looking up at the tall, narrow house. So this was London's equivalent of the more genteel gaming hells. She had frequented such places in most of the capitals of the Continent and was more than a little curious to see what London could produce.

A liveried footman admitted them, took their cloaks, and escorted them up the narrow staircase to a square hall at the head. Three brightly lit salons opened off the hall, all thronged with men and women in evening dress, flunkeys moving among them bearing trays of glasses. Above the relatively subdued level of conversation, the groom-porters could be heard calling the odds at the hazard table.

Judith glanced up at Sebastian and he grinned down at her in instant comprehension. They were home.

"Why, Mr. Davenport, I'm delighted you could honor us. And, Lady Carrington . . ." Amelia Dolby drifted toward them from the quinze table. She must be more than sixty, Judith thought, despite the heavy rouge, absurdly youthful hairstyle, and semitransparent gown. Harsh-featured, sharp-eyed, she offered Judith the piranha's smile of one welcoming a victim. Judith had received many such smiles in her life, and offered her own bland version. For the next few hours, her face would be a mask, revealing nothing.

"What's your game, Lady Carrington?" Amelia Dolby inquired. "Hazard, perhaps?"

Judith shook her head. She and Sebastian only ever played the dice for pleasure; there was no skill to counteract the element of chance. Only a fool would bet seriously on pure luck. "I'm not sure. What are you playing, Sebastian?"

"I've a mind to try the quinze table," he said carelessly, slipping black velvet ribands around his ruffled cuffs to keep them from flopping over his hands.

"Then I'll play macao." They never played at the same table; it would rather defeat the object of the exercise.

Amelia Dolby escorted her to the macao table, introducing her to the other players. Judith was slightly acquainted with several of them. They were all hardened gamesters and accepted Judith in their midst with the unquestioning assumption that she too was a slave to the cards and dice. She wouldn't be there if she wasn't in a position to play high, and that was all that interested any of them.

Three hours later she had won almost five thousand guineas. Enough to redeem the Devlin rubies and purchase her phaeton and pair. It was all very satisfactory and very exhilarating. She felt amazingly revivified and wondered why she'd taken so long to get back to serious play. Some pointless sense of obligation to Marcus, of course. She'd thought it might upset him. Laughable really, in the circumstances. Everything about her upset him anyway. Except in bed . . .

Swallowing that thought, Judith gathered up her winnings and excused herself from the macao table.

Sebastian was still heavily engaged at the quinze table, where silence reigned, and most of his fellow players wore masks to hide any emotional response to the fall of the cards. Recognizing that she couldn't expect him to leave yet, Judith strolled through the salons, relaxed now that her goal was achieved, and prepared to play purely for pleasure if a place opened up at one of the other tables.

"Lady Carrington . . ." A woman's voice hailed her from a faro table. "Do you care to join us?"

"If you've a place." Smiling, Judith went over to the table. She didn't recall meeting the woman before. "You have the advantage of me, ma'am."

"Oh, permit me to perform introductions." Amelia was at her elbow. "Lady Barret . . . Lady Carrington."

"I only arrived in town the other day," Agnes Barret said. "My husband has been indisposed and it delayed our return from the country." She gestured to the chair beside her at the table. "Do, please. . . . I was hoping for an introduction at Cavendish House," she went on as Judith sat down. "But you were so surrounded by admirers, my dear, I couldn't come near you." She held out her hand with a laugh.

"You flatter me, ma'am," Judith demurred, taking the hand. As Lady Barret held her hand, she regarded Judith with an intensity that seemed to exclude the rest of the room. Judith's skin crawled and her scalp contracted. The buzz of voices, the calls of the groom-porters, faded into an indistinguishable hum; the brilliance of the massive chandeliers dimmed, became fuzzy.

It was as if she were held in thrall by some species of witchcraft. And then Lady Barret smiled and dropped her hand. "So you're a gamester, Lady Carrington. Does your brother share the passion?"

Judith forced herself to respond naturally, wondering what on earth was the matter with her. What kind of fanciful nonsense had gripped her? "He's at the quinze table," she said, laying her rouleaux around her selected cards.

Faro was essentially a game of chance and, in general, if her luck was out, she would move on to something else. But it was impossible to concentrate and she lost far more than she'd meant to risk before she realized it. Cross with herself, she made her excuses and rose from the table.

"Oh, your luck will turn, Lady Carrington, I'm sure," her neighbor said, laying a restraining hand on her arm.

"Not when the devil's on my shoulder." Judith quoted her father's favorite excuse when the cards weren't falling right.

A flash shot through Lady Barret's tawny eyes and her color faded, highlighting the patches of rouge on her cheekbones. "I haven't heard that said in a long time."

Judith shrugged. "Is it unusual? I thought it was a common expression. . . . Oh, Sebastian." She turned to greet her brother with relief. "I don't believe you're acquainted with Lady Barret."

She watched her brother as he smiled and bowed over her ladyship's hand. Could he feel that strange, disturbing aura too? But Sebastian seemed quite untroubled by Agnes Barret. Indeed, he was exerting his customary powerful charm with smiling insouciance. The lady responded with an appreciative glint in her eye and a distinctly flirtatious little chuckle.

"It's late, Sebastian," Judith said abruptly. "If you'll forgive us, ma'am. . . ."

Her brother gave her a sharp glance, then made his own farewells rather more courteously. Once out of earshot, however, he observed, "That was a bit precipitate, Ju."

"My head's beginning to ache," she offered in excuse. All her previous exhilaration had dissipated, and she wanted only to leave the hot rooms, overpoweringly stuffy with the cloying scents of the women and the heat from the massive candlebra. "And my luck was out and I wasn't watching my losses."

This disconsolate confession earned her a disapproving frown. "You should have been concentrating," he reproved. "You know the rule."

"Yes, but I wasn't thinking clearly." She wondered whether to tell him about her weird sensation with Lady Barret, then decided against it. To blame her clumsy play on a peculiar reaction to a fellow player would sound lunatic. "At least I've covered the rubies. And I've enough left for the horses."

She glanced over her shoulder. Lady Barret was standing talking to her hostess. She was a most arresting woman, tall and slender, strikingly dressed in an emerald-green gown of jaconet muslin with a deep décolletage and a broad flounce at the hem. In her youth, she would have been beautiful, Judith decided, with that massed auburn hair and the high cheekbones and chiseled mouth. The vivid color of her gown was one of Judith's own favorites. She made a mental note never to wear the color again, and then instantly chided herself for such childish fancies.

Dawn was breaking when the night porter let her in to Devlin House. She went light-footed upstairs to her own chamber. Knowing how late she'd be, she'd told Millie not to wait up for her, and the fire was almost out, the candles guttering. She threw off her clothes and stood for a minute at the window, watching the roseate bloom of the sky.

"Where the hell have you been?"

Judith spun round at the furious voice. Marcus lounged against the jamb of the connecting door, as naked as she, and his body seemed to thrum with the tension of a plucked violin string.

"To Cavendish House."

"I went to Cavendish House myself four hours ago, intending to escort you home. You were not there, madam wife." And for the last three hours, he had been lying awake listening for the sound of her return, imagining any number of scenarios, from footpads to an illicit tryst. Everything he knew of her lent itself to the worst possible construction, and within a short time, he had ceased to be able to think of any sensible explanation.

Judith tried to think quickly, aware of her mental fatigue after the hours at Pickering Street. She shrugged and asked coldly, "Were you spying on me, sir?"

He had gone to Cavendish House with the best of motives, determined to paper over their differences in the only way he knew how: a lover's insistence on seduction. But at the cold, sardonic question, all good intentions vanished. "It seems I have cause. When my wife is not where she's supposed to be and disappears God only knows where for the greater part of the night, it's hardly surprising I should feel a need to check up on you."

Abruptly Judith changed tactics. The last thing she wanted was for Marcus to decide to dog her footsteps in public. It would play merry hell with her gaming plans. She offered him a conciliatory smile, and her voice was quietly reasonable. "I was with Sebastian, Marcus. We haven't had the opportunity for a comfortable talk for some time."

Marcus knew how attached they were, how strong the bond was between them. He looked at her closely, frowning. It was distracting. The closer he looked, the more he saw of Judith in her nakedness. He felt his body stir, begin to harden. Judith's eyes flickered unerringly downward and she came toward him, extending her hands. "But since neither of us is asleep in the dawn, I can think of any number of diversions."

He took her hands, holding them tightly, examining her face, telling himself she had given him a perfectly understandable explanation for her absence.

"So can I." He drew her to the bed and fell back, pulling her with him. "Were you at your brother's lodgings?"

Judith froze beneath the stroking hand. "We had a great deal to talk about." Rolling over, she kissed his nipples, her tongue lifting the hard buds, her hand drifting down his body.

Marcus caught her hand in mid caress. "I don't think you've answered my question, Judith."

Hell and the devil. He was going to force her to lie. "Of course."

Was she lying? What reason had he for believing her? The perverse prod of disillusion drove him onward down this destructive path. "Why do I have the feeling you're being less than straightforward?" One hand still held hers, his other caressed her back in long, slow strokes.

"I can't imagine why." Her voice was muffled, buried in his skin. She still had the use of her lips and tongue, but that use didn't seem to be creating the hoped for distraction.

"If you're lying to me, my dear wife, you're going to discover that my patience and tolerance have certain limits. You are my wife, and as such the guardian of my honor. Honor and untruths make uneasy bedfellows."

"Damn you, Marcus!" Judith sat up, glaring at him. "Stop threatening me. Why would I lie?"

"I don't know," he said. "But by the same token, why wouldn't you?"

Judith closed her eyes on the hurt . . . a hurt she wasn't entitled to feel because she *was* lying. But whose fault was that?

Marcus hitched himself up against the pillows, regarding her through hooded eyes in the dim, gray light of dawn. He could feel her pain as he could feel his own, and he tried to find the words to put this mess into perspective, to salvage something out of the night.

"Judith, I can't have you running around in secret pursuits at all hours of the night, with or without your brother. It may be what you're used to doing, but your position is different now. The Marchioness of Carrington, my wife, has to be above reproach . . . whatever Judith Davenport may have done. You know that damn well."

"And why are you assuming that I was doing anything that was not above reproach?" she snapped. "I told you I was with my brother. Why isn't that enough?"

"You seem to forget I know what you and your brother get up to. Fleecing gulls with fan play . . ."

"Not anymore," she interrupted, flushing. "You can no longer have any justification for such an accusation."

"I trust not," he said. "Because let me tell you something, Judith." Reaching out, he caught her chin, his eyes and voice as hard as iron. "If I ever find that you and your brother have performed your little duet again, by the time I've finished with you, you will wish your parents had never met. Do I make myself clear?"

Judith jerked her head free of his grip, her voice frigid. "Such a statement would be impossible to misconstrue, sir."

"I had hoped to be perfectly lucid."

"You may rest assured you were."

But they were going to do it again, just once more.

And once it was over, she'd leave Marcus to find himself the kind of wife he wanted: a woman of honor and principle; meek and obedient; the epitome of virtue. And she'd wish him joy of her, she thought savagely.

"I don't think we can have anything further to discuss," she declared. "I bid you good night, my lord."

Marcus swung himself off the bed. "Good night, madam."

The door clicked shut. Judith huddled into bed, swallowing the lump in her throat, tears pricking behind her eyes. She was miserable and she was disappointed. Her body ached for some other finale to the evening, for what had been promised and then so devastatingly denied. She stared, scratchy-eyed, into the pale light of early morning, her limbs aching, her mind as clear as a bell, her body throbbing for fulfillment.

Suddenly the door between their bedrooms flew open again and then slammed shut. Marcus stood at the end of the bed, and she could feel the force of his emotion as vitally as she could see the power in his aroused body.

"Damnation, Judith. I don't know what to do about you!" His voice was a contained whisper, but the fierce frustration was all the more potent for its containment. "I want you more than I have ever wanted another woman, and yet you madden me to such a degree sometimes, I can't distinguish between the need to love you and the need to subdue you."

He came round to the side of the bed and stood looking down at her.

Silently Judith kicked aside the cover, offering her body, opalescent in the pearly dawn. Marcus came down on the bed beside her. He gathered her against him, and his hand was hard on her body as he possessed the long length from waist to ankle, the indentations and the curves. Judith felt her skin come alive under the rough touch, her thighs dampen. His fingers probed with deep, intimate insistence, and his voice demanded that she tell him what pleased her, that she open herself to him fully, that she reveal to him the sites and touches that gave her greatest pleasure.

He branded her with tongue and hand, searing her with the mark of a lover who knew her in her vulnerability, in the wild passionate soaring of her need. And finally he knelt between her widespread thighs, his body etched against the light from the window. He drew her legs onto his shoulders, slipping his hands beneath her buttocks to lift her to meet the slow thrust of his entry that seemed to penetrate her core, to fill her with a sweet anguish that she could barely contain yet could not bear to relinquish.

Tears stood out in her eyes as she held his gaze. But they were tears of joy as the ravishment of her senses began anew, this time in shared glory, a tornado, a wild, escalating spiral that swept them into the void where the world has no sway and nothing mattered but the ability to be together in this way, to be a part of each other, she in him, he in her.

Afterward, he lay holding her, her head on his shoulder, her body soft against him as she slipped into sleep. And he was filled with a great tenderness, and a tiny spring crocus of hope pushed through the heavy soil of disillusion. Surely their passion counted for something. It couldn't be a complete lie. If only he could bring new eyes to bear . . . cut through the preconceptions . . . see another Judith.

11

BERNARD MELVILLE, THIRD EARL OF GRACEMERE. JUDITH GAZED ACROSS THE
ballroom at the man who had ruined her father, the man who had
driven George Devereux and his children out of England, the man
who had ultimately driven George Davenport to his death. The slow
burn of rage was followed by the same prickle of excitement she felt
at the gaming tables, when she knew she had her fellow players on
the run.

"Charlie, are you acquainted with the Earl of Gracemere?"

"Of course I am. Isn't everyone?" Her partner executed a
smooth turn. "You dance wonderfully, Judith."

"A woman I fear is only as good as her partner," Judith observed,
laughing. "Fortunately for me, you seem to have a natural talent."

Charlie blushed.

"It's a pity it doesn't run in the family," Judith said thoughtfully.

"What do you mean?"

"Well, your cousin isn't much for the dance floor."

"No, he never has been," Charlie said. "In fact, he's such a dull stick, I don't think he cares a fig for anything outside his history books and military politics." His voice was bitter.

"Are you and Marcus at outs?" Judith asked. Charlie's frequent visits to Devlin House had for some reason ceased in the last couple of weeks. She looked at him, noticing his rather drawn look, the constraint in his eye.

"He's so damn strict, Judith. He has such antiquated notions . . . he doesn't seem to understand that a man has to amuse himself somehow."

"That's not quite true," Judith demurred mildly. "He amuses himself a great deal with sporting pursuits and horses, and he has plenty of friends who don't seem to think him a dull stick."

"I'm sorry," Charlie said uncomfortably. "I spoke out of turn. He's your husband . . ."

"Yes, but I'm not blind to his faults," Judith said with a wry smile. "He's not overly tolerant of what he considers failings, I grant you. Have you angered him in some way?"

Charlie shook his head and tried to laugh. "Oh, it's nothing. It'll put itself right soon enough. . . . have you had enough dancing? Shall I fetch you a glass of champagne?"

Judith let the subject drop since Charlie clearly didn't want to pursue it. "No, thank you," she said. "But I would like you to introduce me to Gracemere."

"Certainly, if you like. I'm not in his set, of course, so I don't know him well, but I could effect an introduction."

Judith cast a rapid eye over the ballroom, looking for Sebastian. She spotted him dancing with Harriet Moreton. He was often dancing with Harriet Moreton, she realized with a start, though shy, soft-eyed, pretty, seventeen-year-olds weren't his usual style. She fixed her eye on her brother until he looked up from his partner. He knew she was going to engineer an introduction to the enemy tonight, one on which he would intrude quite naturally, and he was waiting for her signal.

"I swear, the country is a damnably tedious place at this time of year," the Earl of Gracemere was saying to the knot of people around him as Judith and Charlie approached. "Mud . . . nothing but mud as far as the eye can see."

"Can't think why you didn't come up to town sooner, Gracemere," one of the group observed.

"Oh, I had my reasons," the earl remarked with a little smile. His eye fell on Charlie and his companion and his smile broadened. "Ah, Fenwick, I trust you're going to introduce me to your charming companion. Lady Carrington, isn't it? I've been hoping for an introduction all evening." He bowed, raising her hand to his lips.

"My lord." Judith looked upon the man who had obsessed her thoughts, both sleeping and waking, for the better part of two years, from the moment she and her brother had read their father's deathbed letter and had finally understood that his disgrace and exile had not been the simple result of his own unbridled passion for gaming.

Bernard Melville had pale blue eyes—fish eyes, Judith thought with a surge of revulsion. They seemed to be looking into her soul. She withdrew her hand from his, resisting the urge to wipe her palm on her skirt. She felt contaminated even through her satin gloves. He had a cruel mouth and a sharply pointed nose beneath the fish eyes. A dissolute countenance. How on earth was she to hide her loathing and revulsion sufficiently to charm him?

Of course she would. She was an expert at hiding her emotions . . . thanks to the Earl of Gracemere. She unfurled her fan and smiled at him over the top. "You've just returned from the country, sir. Whereabouts?"

"Oh, I have an estate in Yorkshire," he said. "A bleak place, but occasionally I feel a duty to inspect it."

Cranshaw. The estate he had won from her father. Sebastian's birthright. A hot, red surge of anger swept through her and she lowered her eyes abruptly. "I'm unfamiliar with Yorkshire, sir."

"I understand you've spent most of your life abroad, ma'am."

"I'm flattered you should know so much about me, sir." She laughed, the coquette's laugh that she'd perfected.

"My dear Lady Carrington, you must know that the news of your marriage enlivened an otherwise dull summer for us all."

"You pay me too high a compliment, Lord Gracemere. I had no idea my marriage could have competed with Waterloo as the summer's seminal event," she said smoothly. It was a mistake, but she hadn't been able to resist it.

An appreciative chuckle ran round the group and Gracemere's eyes flattened, a dull flush appearing on his cheeks. Then he laughed, too. "You're right, ma'am, to point out my foolishness. It was a facetious compliment. Forgive me, but your beauty has quite overtaken my wits."

"Now that, sir, is an irresistible compliment," she said, tapping his wrist lightly with her fan. "And an admirable recover."

He bowed again. "Is it too much to hope that you will honor me with this dance?"

"I had promised it to my brother, sir, but I don't imagine he'll insist on his prior claim." She turned to where Sebastian stood, having made his seemingly casual approach. "You'll release me, Sebastian?"

"A brother's claims are notoriously low, m'dear," he said cheerfully.

"Are you acquainted with my brother, Lord Gracemere?"

"I don't believe so," Gracemere said. "But the family resemblance is striking."

"Yes, so people say." Sebastian bowed. "Sebastian Davenport, at your service."

"Delighted." The earl returned the bow, his eyes calculating, as they scrutinized the young man, who maintained a rather fatuous smile. Agnes had seen him at Dolby's, so he must be a gamester. How good a one remained to be seen. "You must come to one of my card parties," he said with an air of condescension. "If you care for that sort of thing."

Sebastian assured him that he did and murmured something about being honored. Then Judith laid her hand on the earl's arm and Bernard Melville took her into the dance.

"So you didn't follow the world to Brussels for the great battle, my lord?"

"Alas, no. I have a shameful—or perhaps I mean shameless—lack of interest in military matters."

"Even when such matters involve Napoleon? That's indeed shameful." She laughed, peeping up at him through her eyelashes.

"I'm a lost cause, ma'am." He smiled at her. "Your husband, on the other hand, is known for his expertise on the subject."

An expertise that took him onto the battlefield, Judith reflected, remembering the agony of that day. It seemed so far away now, so far removed from this glittering round of pleasure. No wonder Marcus was often so scornful of Society's priorities. She inclined her head in silent acceptance of the earl's comment.

"Yes," he continued musingly, "your husband makes us all look like mere fribbles. It's well known that he looks down on our simple pleasures."

Judith sensed an underlying point to her partner's comments. It occurred to her that Bernard Melville didn't like Marcus Devlin. "Each to his own," she said neutrally.

The earl's glance sharpened. "But you I take it, ma'am, don't share Carrington's scorn for our idle amusements." He gestured expansively around the ballroom.

If you only knew, my Lord Gracemere, just how purposeful my idle amusements are, Judith thought. But she smiled and agreed, fluttering her eyelashes at him and watching with inward revulsion the shark of interest that swam under the flat surface of his pale eyes.

Marcus strolled up the staircase just as his hostess was about to abandon her post at its head, having decided the hour was now too advanced to expect further guests. Lady Gray greeted him with flattered surprise and the information that the last time she'd seen Lady Carrington, she'd been in the ballroom.

Marcus made his way to the ballroom. For a few minutes he couldn't see her in the melee. And then he did.

His hands clenched involuntarily as he watched her turn gracefully in the circle of Bernard Melville's arm, her eyes laughing up at him, her hand resting on his arm.

What the devil was she doing with Gracemere? But it was a futile question. She was bound to have met him sometime. It would have been too much to hope that Gracemere would have remained in rustication throughout the Season. Presumably he needed to find another pigeon to repair his fortunes at the card tables.

The dance ended and he watched the earl escort his companion off the floor. Judith was smiling in a fashion that set her husband's teeth on edge. He had watched her accomplished flirtations in Brussels with amusement and not a little admiration, and hadn't been troubled by the lighthearted coquettry that made her so popular in London. But with Gracemere, it was a very different matter. Struggling with the old rage that had barely diminished over the years, he saw the earl lead Judith toward the open French doors.

Marcus threaded his way across the crowded ballroom, acknowledging greetings with the briefest of smiles, and stepped out onto the terrace. There was no reason why Judith and her partner should not have come outside. It was a warm evening and there were plenty of people on the terrace. But the age-old rage in his soul blazed pure and bright, and he had to fight to keep it from his face and voice as he made his way to where they stood against the parapet, apparently looking at the moon.

"Good evening, my dear."

"Marcus! What brings you here?" Judith turned at his soft greeting and for a moment he could have sworn there was a flash of pleasure in her eyes. But if it was ever there, it was gone in a trice, to be replaced with what looked like vexation, and then that too was gone and her countenance was as calm and untroubled as a doll's. Marcus knew that look. Both brother and sister wore it at the gaming tables. Prickles of unease ran up and down his spine.

"Lord Gracemere and I were just identifying the constellations," Judith said.

"Your wife appears to be an accomplished astronomer, Carrington."

"My wife has many accomplishments."

The tension in the air was as suffocating as a blanket. Judith instinctively moved to lift it. She laughed. "An odd assortment, though, I'm afraid. My formal schooling was lamentably neglected."

"Growing up on the Continent must have been an education in itself," Gracemere observed, offering his snuff box to Carrington, who refused with a flat, polite smile.

"I speak five languages," Judith said. "And my mathematics are quite sound . . . in some areas, at least." She shot Marcus an impishly conspiratorial look as she said this. "I count quite well, don't I, my lord?"

"Faultlessly," he agreed, unable to resist the invitation to collusion. Such invitations were all too rare, and he felt some of his tension dissipate, the slow burn of memory rage die down. Judith had nothing to do with the past, and at this moment she had eyes only for him, and there was no ambivalence now to cloud their brilliance. "I wonder if I can persuade you to dance with your husband, ma'am?"

Judith put her head on one side, considering. "Well, it's certainly unusual, and I wouldn't want it said that we lived in each other's pockets."

"Heaven forbid. If you think there's the slightest danger of that, I'll make myself scarce immediately."

It occurred to Gracemere, listening to this byplay, that they'd forgotten his presence completely. "You will excuse me," he said, bowing and walking away.

Marcus held out his hand. "A measure, madam wife."

"If you insist." She put her hand in his. "But I can't imagine why you'd wish to torture yourself in such fashion. We both know you find dancing a dead bore."

"That may be so," he said as they took their places in the set. "But I've yet to be bored in your company."

"No, just maddened," she said with an arch smile.

"And vastly amused and aroused and fulfilled," he responded with a bland smile quite at odds with his words and the sensual glitter in his eyes.

They moved down the set and were separated by the dance movements. When they came together again, he commented, "You, at all events, seem to have been enjoying yourself this evening."

"Is that a crime?" Her eyebrows lifted in a fine and distinctly challenging arch.

Marcus shook his head. "Put up your sword, lynx. I'm not going to quarrel with you this evening."

"No?" The word was weighted with disappointment. "But we quarrel so well together."

The dance took her from him again before he could come up with a response. When she was returned to him, she was suddenly preoccupied, her eyes fixed on something over his shoulder. "My poor efforts at conversation don't appear to be entertaining you, ma'am," he drawled, when she had failed to respond to his second observation in two minutes.

"I beg your pardon." But she continued to gaze over his shoulder, chewing her lip, and whenever he touched her, he could feel the tautness in the lithe, compact frame.

"What is it, Judith?"

She shook her head. "Nothing . . . only, do you know Lady Barret?"

"Agnes Barret, yes, of course. She's the wife of Sir Thomas Barret. She's been on the scene for many years . . . a widow of some Italian count, I believe, originally. Then she married Barret this last summer." He shrugged. "Barret's a gout-ridden old fogey, but quite well heeled, so I daresay he offered a port in a storm. Although she's a damnably attractive woman; I'm sure she could have done better for herself."

"Yes, she is," Judith agreed absently. Then she seemed to shake herself out of her reverie. "Did you come here to make sure I was where I was supposed to be, sir?"

"Don't be provoking, Judith."

"I don't mean to be provoking," she protested, all innocence. "But it's only natural, when you do something so out of character, I should look for a reason."

"I came to find you," he said.

"To check up on me," she declared with a triumphant nod.

"Don't put words into my mouth," he said. "I came to find you."

"But surely it comes to the same thing. You wanted to make sure I wasn't doing something I shouldn't be."

"Well, you'll certainly think twice another time if the urge to misbehave does hit you," he remarked. "Since you won't know whether I'm likely to turn up or not."

Judith was for a moment silenced, then suddenly she began to laugh. "I do believe we're quarreling," she observed with satisfaction. "I knew it couldn't be long."

"Hornet!" He led her out of the dance.

"Shall we go home?"

"An admirable idea." He steered her across the room, one flat palm in the small of her back.

"Good evening, Lady Carrington, Marcus . . . Permit me to offer my felicitations. I would have done so earlier, but Barret was kept in the country with a touch of the gout and we've only just returned to town."

Lady Barret materialized in their path, extending her hand to Judith as she smiled at Marcus. "This wretched war," she murmured. "It played havoc with one's social life. Everyone disappeared to Brussels."

"Hardly everyone," Marcus demurred, letting his hand fall from Judith's back and lifting Lady Barret's to his lips.

"Well, now that the ogre is safely put away on that island, it's to be hoped life can go back to normal." Lady Barret shuddered delicately.

"The war lasted fifteen years," Judith remarked into the air. "Peace is hardly the normal condition."

Agnes's smile froze and her eyes seemed to shrink to mere pinpricks in her suddenly sharpened face. She laughed, a harsh sound like breaking glass. "How true, my dear Lady Carrington. Such a sharp wit you have."

Judith felt that strange aura again and the unmistakable conviction that Agnes Barret was a dangerous woman to cross. She forced a smile to her lips. "I meant no discourtesy, ma'am. But the world has been at war throughout most of my life, so perhaps I see it from a different perspective."

Agnes's eyes narrowed at this reference to their differing ages. "I hope I may call upon you, Lady Carrington," she said coldly as Marcus eased his wife away.

"I should be honored," Judith said distantly.

At the door, Judith halted and looked over her shoulder. Agnes Barret was in close conversation with Bernard Melville. They reminded her of a pair of hooded cobras, touching tongues. A shudder of revulsion ripped through her.

"What's troubling you, Judith?" Marcus asked softly. "You're wound as tight as a coiled spring. And you were unpardonably rude."

"I know. It's something about that woman." She shrugged. "Never mind. I'm just being fanciful." She moved to the staircase.

"Oh, Judith, are you leaving?" Charlie appeared from the shadows of a doorway on the landing, and Judith wondered why she felt he'd been lying in wait for them. He ducked his head at her and addressed his cousin, but without looking at him. "Marcus . . . could you spare me a few minutes tomorrow . . . a matter of some urgency?"

"I'm always available for you, Charlie," Marcus said evenly. "Shall we say at around noon, if that will suit you?"

"Yes . . . yes, that'll be fine." Two bright spots of color burned on his cheekbones. "I'll see you then . . . uh . . . Judith, good night." With a jerky bob, he kissed her cheek and then turned and disappeared rapidly into the salon.

"Damn young fool," Marcus observed without heat.

"Why, what's happened?"

"He's in dun territory again. Up to his ears in gaming debts and he's going to want me to advance him the money to settle them. He doesn't know I know it, of course."

"And how do you know it?"

He looked down at her in some surprise. "Charlie's my ward, Judith. Not much happens in his life that I don't know about. He's my responsibility."

"And you take your responsibilities very seriously," she mused. Marcus might be a strict guardian, but he was a very caring one.

"Yes, I do," he said. "And don't you ever forget it, madam wife."

"Autocrat," she threw at him over her shoulder, but she was feeling too much in charity with him to take up the cudgels with any seriousness.

It was near dawn when Marcus went to his own bed, reflecting that if they continued to burn the candle at both ends in this fashion, they would need a repairing lease in the country before the Season was half done.

He awoke when Cheveley drew back the curtains on a brilliant sunny morning. Marcus flung aside the covers and stood up, stretching. "My dressing gown, Cheveley."

The valet held the brocade dressing gown for him. Tying the cord at his waist, Marcus strolled into his wife's apartment. "Good morning, lynx."

Judith was sitting up in bed, her copper hair tumbling against the piled white pillows. A tray of hot chocolate and sweet biscuits was on the bedside table, and her knees were lost beneath a cloud of prettily penned papers.

"Good morning, Marcus." She smiled at him over the rim of her cup of chocolate, thinking how pleasant it was to be at peace with her husband.

"You have a host of admirers, it seems." He bent to kiss the tip of her nose and picked up a handful of the billets-doux, letting them fall back to the bed in a shower. "And a nosegay." The little twist of violets in a chased silver holder lay beside the chocolate pot on the table. He glanced at the card and his face darkened.

"Gracemere. You must have made a significant impression on him last evening."

Judith inclined her head in vague acknowledgment. "He writes very pretty cards, at all events. And the violets are so delicate."

"I don't think it right for you to receive such gifts, Judith."

Judith sat back against her pillows, remembering for the first time that strange tension between the two men. "In general, or Gracemere in particular?"

He shrugged. "Does it matter?"

"I think it does, sir. It's perfectly normal for a woman to receive such little attentions."

Marcus said nothing, turning instead to walk over to the window, looking out at the square. A group of children under the eye of a nursemaid were playing ball in the railed garden in the center.

"You don't like Gracemere, do you?" It seemed to Judith that the matter had better be brought into the open quickly.

"No, Judith, I do not. And you must understand that I will not have the man under my roof under any circumstances."

"May I ask why?" Her fingers restlessly pleated the coverlet as she tried to see a way through this unexpected tangle.

"You may ask, but I can't give you an answer. The issue is perfectly simple: you may not count Gracemere among your friends." His voice was level, almost expressionless, as he remained looking down at the children in the square. But he wasn't seeing them. He was seeing Martha as she had been that morning ten years before. His fist clenched and he could almost feel again the cool silver handle of his horse whip nestling in his palm.

Judith frowned at her husband's back. "Oh, no, my lord, it's not that simple," she said in soft anger. "You cannot issue such a command without a reason."

Marcus turned from the window. "I can, Judith, and I have," he stated flatly. "And I expect you to comply." He gestured to the pile of correspondence on the bed and softened his tone. "You have so many friends . . . one less can make little difference."

Judith thought rapidly. It was a damnably unexpected complication, but it was vital that Gracemere should not become a bone of contention between herself and Marcus. If she threw down the glove, Marcus would definitely pick it up, and there was no knowing to what length he would go to keep her away from her quarry. No . . . instead of defiance she must lull him into inattention. Gracemere would have to be cultivated out of eyesight and earshot of her husband.

"I have a suggestion to make," she said in a bland voice, as if the previous conversation had not taken place.

Marcus, on his guard at this sudden change of tone, raised his eyebrows slightly but said nothing.

"Supposing you asked me to do you a favor," Judith continued in a musing, conversational manner, playing idly with a copper ringlet on her shoulder. "Supposing you said *To please me, my dear wife, would you mind very much avoiding Gracemere like the plague?*" A delicately arched eyebrow rose in quizzical inquiry as she regarded her husband's set face, the taut line of his mouth.

Surprise jumped into his eyes, followed immediately by comprehension, and then his mouth curved in a slow smile. "Point taken, madam wife," he said softly. "But I think I can improve on your suggestion." He left her and went into his own apartment, returning after a minute with a bulky parcel.

He came up to the bed, to where she lay against the pillows, barely able to contain her curiosity. "What is it?"

"A present," he said with a smile, carefully placing the parcel on the bed. "I've been waiting for a suitable moment to give it to you. Now seems like the moment."

"It's a bribe!" Judith said on a peal of laughter, eagerly pulling at the string. "Shameless! You would buy my compliance."

Marcus chuckled, entranced by her gleeful excitement—like a child on Christmas morning, he thought. It occurred to him that an impoverished, helter-skelter childhood wouldn't have included too many presents. The thought produced an unfamiliar tug of tenderness as he took deep pleasure in her delight.

"Oh, Marcus, it's beautiful," she breathed, tearing off the wrapping to reveal a massive slab of checkered marble. The black squares were almost indigo, the white a translucent ivory. Almost reverently she opened the box containing the chess pieces, heavy, beautifully sculptured marble figures. Her eyes shining, she held the board on her knees and set up the pieces.

"It's not a bribe," Marcus said softly, watching her. "It's a gift with no strings attached."

She looked up and smiled at him. "Thank you."

"And now," he said, bending over her, catching her chin with his forefinger. "Will you do me that favor?"

"You had only to *ask*," she responded with an air of mock dignity.

She fell back on the pillows under the press of his body, the chess pieces scattering in the folds of the coverlet as he brought his mouth to hers. As she fumbled with the tie of his robe, pushing her hands beneath the material to find his skin, she quieted her conscience with the thought that Marcus would ultimately benefit from her plan to best Gracemere.

12

※

"WELL, WHAT DO YOU THINK, JUDITH? COULD YOU DO IT?"

As Cornelia leaned forward eagerly, the spindle-legged chair tilted precariously beneath her. She grabbed at the side table, sending it rocking.

Judith automatically put out a hand to steady the table. "You're asking me to teach you to be gamesters?" There was a bubble of laughter in her voice as she contemplated this delicious prospect and glanced around the room at her three friends.

"It's a wonderful idea," Isobel said, sipping ratafia. "We all have difficulties about money. Sally because of Jeremy; and Cornelia has to supplement her mother's jointure out of her own allowance; and as for me . . ." Her mouth tightened and a shadow of distaste crossed her expression. "Henley doles out money to me as if he's doing me the most immense favor, and only after I've asked prettily at least three times. I put off asking for as long as possible because it's so humiliating."

"I could teach you some things," Judith reflected. "The techniques with the cards . . . strategies of wagering . . . things like that. But you have to have nerve, and some natural talent to be really successful."

"I can't believe I have less talent than Jeremy," Sally said with a resigned chuckle. "He only ever plays hazard, and how can you possibly win with the dice?"

"You can't," Judith said. "At least, you can't rely upon it. Macao, piquet, quinze, unlimited loo, and whist—although the stakes there are often not high enough to be really satisfying—are the only games to play for winning rather than pure entertainment."

"I don't think I'm brave enough to play in the hells," Sally went on thoughtfully. "If Jack found out . . ." She shuddered. "He'd pack me off to the country with the children indefinitely." She glanced at her sister-in-law over the rim of her sherry glass. "Marcus would decide it was the only sensible decision."

"And Jack always does as his elder brother suggests," Judith agreed dryly. "Marcus has that effect on his nearest and dearest."

"What happened when he gave you the rubies? I forgot to ask. I was so relieved when I handed them over to Jack, I didn't think I ever wanted to see them again."

Judith chuckled. "Oh, I expressed suitable astonishment and delight at such a magnificent heirloom, and then told Marcus that actually they would suit your coloring better than mine, so perhaps he should give them back to you."

"Judith, you didn't!" exclaimed Sally, her eyes widening as the others began to laugh.

"I did," Judith insisted, laughing too. "It seemed such a delicious little twist. However," she added, "he wouldn't. It wasn't appropriate, or something." She shrugged.

"We don't *have* to play in gambling hells to make money, do we?" Isobel returned to the original subject.

"No," Judith agreed. "One can do quite well at the high-stakes tables at balls and soirees. I do think it's unfair that women can't go into White's or Watier's or Brooks's though," she grumbled. "Did you know the stakes at the Nonesuch almost always start at fifty guineas?" Her voice had a yearning note to it.

"So you'll teach us?" Cornelia asked.

"Oh, yes," Judith said. "With the greatest pleasure. We will have a school for gamesters." She refilled their glasses. "A toast, my friends: to women of independent means."

The door opened on their delighted laughter.

"Oh, Judith, I beg your pardon." Charlie hovered on the threshold. "I'm intruding."

Judith took in his hangdog expression, the white shade around his mouth, and immediately held out her hand in invitation. "No, of course you're not, Charlie. Come in. You know everyone, don't you?"

"How are you, Charlie?" Sally greeted him with a motherly smile, patting the sofa beside her.

He flung himself down and sighed, gazing morosely into the distance. Judith poured him a glass of sherry. "You've just come from Marcus's book room," she stated.

Charlie took the glass and drained its contents in one gulp. "I feel as if I've been flayed."

Sally winced and shot Judith another comprehending glance. Judith raised her eyebrows. "He told me yesterday he knew you were in debt."

"I had a sure thing at Newmarket—" Charlie began in aggrieved accents.

"Only of course it wasn't," Judith broke in. It was a familiar story.

Charlie shook his head. "The cursed screw came in last. I couldn't believe it, Judith."

"Horses are notoriously unreliable when one's counting upon them. I assume you were?" She leaned back in her deep armchair and sipped her sherry. She'd never been able to understand why anyone would bet tomorrow's dinner on a horse over which one had no control.

He nodded. "I put my shirt on it. I've had a run of bad luck at the tables, and I was convinced Merry Dancer would help me come about." He hunched over his knees, twisting his hands together, pulling at the fingers until the knuckles cracked.

Judith frowned. She knew Charlie would come into a princely inheritance when he came of age. "Surely Marcus didn't refuse to advance you enough to cover your debts of honor?" That was an inconceivable thought.

Charlie stared moodily at the carpet. "After he'd reduced me to the size of a worm, he said he would give me an advance on next quarter's allowance. And I'd have to manage on next to nothing next quarter, but at least I wouldn't find myself obliged to resign from my clubs." He laughed bitterly. "Some comfort that is. I can't possibly *eat* on what's left. But when I said that, he told me I could go into Berkshire and make myself useful on the estate, and that way I could manage with no expenses."

"It seems to me wives and wards have much in common," Judith observed, resting her chin on her elbow-propped palm on the arm of her chair.

"How's that?"

"Both live under someone else's thumb," she explained aridly.

"But for a male ward, at least there's an end to the sentence," Cornelia pointed out.

"I never know whether you're funning or not when you talk in such fashion," Charlie said, sighing.

Judith smiled. "Then you must guess."

Charlie jumped to his feet and began to pace the salon. "A man's got to play, for God's sake."

"Yes, but does he have to play as badly as you?" Judith asked with brutal frankness. "Perhaps you should join our school."

Chagrin warred with curiosity. The latter won. "What school?"

Judith explained, watching Charlie's face with ill-concealed merriment.

"Good God," he said. "You can't be serious. What a scandalous idea."

"Oh, but we are," Isobel declared, rising to her feet. "Very serious. We have every intention of earning ourselves a degree of financial independence." She drew on her lacy mittens. "I must go, Judith. It's been a most enlivening morning. Can I take you up as far as Mount Street, Cornelia?" She drifted to the door in a waft of filmy muslin.

"Thank you." Cornelia rose, tripped over her shawl, and sat down again with a thump. "Oh, dear."

Gregson announced the arrival of Sebastian just as Judith and Isobel bent to untangle Cornelia.

"Oh, Sebastian, I wasn't expecting you to call." Judith straightened as her brother entered.

"Well, I think you might have," he said, "since you're forever giving me commissions to execute for you."

"Now, what in the world do you mean?" Judith frowned.

Sebastian grinned. "I hope I haven't just bought Grantham's breakdowns for nothing. I could have sworn you asked—"

"Oh, Sebastian, you have them!" She kissed him soundly. "I didn't think you'd be able to do it so quickly."

"I have 'em right and tight." He was clearly very pleased with himself. "Only just did it, though. Steffington and Broughton were both after them."

"You're very clever, love," she said. "Where are they?"

"I put them up with my own for the moment, since I wasn't quite sure how or when you intended to spring 'em upon Carrington."

Judith pursed her lips. "Yes," she said. "I'll have to work that one out."

"What is this, Judith?" Sally refastened the ribbons of her chip-straw hat.

"Oh, I'm going to drive a perch phaeton and a pair of match geldings," Judith announced. "Sebastian has procured them for me."

"That's very dashing," Cornelia said, steady on her feet again. "And I insist on being the first person to drive with you."

"The pleasure will be all mine." Judith kept to herself the alarming images of Cornelia combined with a high-axled perch phaeton. It didn't bear thinking about. She accompanied her friends down to the hall.

Sebastian poured himself a glass of sherry while a still slightly scandalized Charlie regaled him with the story of the gaming school. It occurred to him that his sister's philanthropic, educational zeal would have done them great disservice in the days when the more fools there were at the card tables, the better it suited them. But the edge of desperate need was blunted for both of them now. And once Bernard Melville, third Earl of Gracemere, had been constrained to return what he'd stolen, the need would be gone forever. His long fingers tightened around the delicate stem of his glass, then deliberately he loosened his grip, let the mental door drop over the turbulent emotions that would muddle cool thinking.

Judith, her head full of match geldings, bumped into her husband as she hurried back up the stairs.

"You seem a trifle distracted," he observed, taking hold of the banister. "What's on your mind?"

To her annoyance, Judith felt her cheeks warm with a guilty flush. "Oh, nothing," she said airily. "I'm in a hurry because I'm going to ride with Sebastian. It's such a beautiful day."

It had been rather gray and overcast when Marcus had last looked out the window. He raised his eyebrows. "The weather is, of course, very changeable at this time of year."

Judith chewed her lip, and her husband's eyes narrowed. "What mischief do you brew, lynx?"

"Mischief? Whatever can you mean?"

"I can read it in your eyes. You're up to something."

"Of course I'm not." She changed the subject abruptly and to good purpose. "Why must you be so horrid to Charlie? He does no more than most young men in his position."

Her husband's face closed. "As you, of course, know so well, ma'am. Such naiveté has its advantages."

Judith drew breath sharply at this well-placed dart as Marcus continued in clipped tones, "How I handle Charlie is my business and has nothing to do with you. He's been my ward since he was little more than a baby, and in general we deal extremely well together."

"Yes, I know you do." Judith persisted, despite the snub. "And he's very fond of you and respects you. But he's young. . . ."

"If he were not, Judith, I would have no need to hold the reins, and we wouldn't be having this discussion." He drew his fob watch from the pocket of his waistcoat. "As I said, it is not your affair. I have an appointment. I must ask you to excuse me."

Discussion was hardly the word for it, Judith thought, standing aside as he moved past her on the stairs. She'd been most effectively put in her place when all she'd been trying to do was offer him a slant on Charlie's view of the situation. But then, Marcus Devlin had had no youth, so probably couldn't be expected to understand the ups and downs of that state. His father had died when he was a boy and his mother had been a semi-invalid ever since. Marcus had somehow jumped full-grown into adulthood, with the immense responsibility of an ancient title and an enormous estate. As far as she could tell, he'd assumed the whole without blinking an eye.

But then, she and Sebastian hadn't had much in the way of childhood either. Judith resolutely pushed aside her somber reflections as she returned to the drawing room.

13

THE ATMOSPHERE IN SEBASTIAN'S SITTING ROOM IN HIS LODGINGS ON
Albemarle Street was relaxed and good-humored. The six men sitting
around the card table were lounging back in their chairs, goblets of
claret at their elbows, all exuding the well-fed complacence of satisfied dinner guests.

Sebastian was an attentive host, and none of his guests was aware
that his single-minded concentration was on only one of their number—Bernard Melville, Earl of Gracemere.

Gracemere had accepted the invitation to dinner and macao with
alacrity, and now that the initial approach had been made, Sebastian
was confident that his strategy would keep such a hardened gamester
on the hook.

It was not difficult to play to lose against him. The earl was a
highly accomplished card player, and it was a simple matter for Sebastian to engineer a convincing loss. Gracemere held the bank. Occasionally, his eyes would flicker across the macao table to his host,
who sprawled, relaxed and nonchalant, in an armed dining chair,

apparently unconcerned that his losses were heavier than any at the table.

"Your luck is out tonight, Davenport," observed one of his guests.

Sebastian shrugged and raised his wineglass, drinking deeply. "It comes and goes, dear fellow. What do you think of the claret?"

"Excellent. Who's your wine merchant?"

"Harpers, Gracechurch Street." He pushed a rouleaux onto the table. "I'm calling." He laid his hand on the table and shook his head in resignation when the earl revealed twenty points to his own nineteen. Gracemere's tongue flickered over his lips as he noted the new loss on the paper at his side.

Rage and loathing twisted, venomous serpents in Sebastian's gut. How often had Gracemere looked like that while he was playing George Devereux for his heritage and fortune? At what point had he decided to resort to marked cards? Gracemere was a good player, but not as good as Sebastian's father had been. When had he decided he couldn't win in a fair game?

Many times Judith and Sebastian had gone over that last game, trying to picture it. The moment when their father lost the final hand, convinced Gracemere had been using marked cards. The moment when he was about to expose his opponent's cheating and thus retrieve his losses. And the dreadful moment when Gracemere had gathered up the cards and somehow "discovered" a marked card in Devereux's hand. What had happened then? Their father's last letter had not said. It had simply given them the complete explanation for the lives his children had led—an explanation that went beyond their previous knowledge of insuperable gambling debts that had forced their father's exile. This letter had been an exculpation of George Devereux, but it had not gone beyond the barest facts of Gracemere's accusation, the apparent overwhelming proof made so devastatingly public, his own innocence, and his knowledge that it was the earl who had cheated.

The ensuing scandal had sent George Devereux into exiled disgrace, disowned by his family, forced in his dishonor to relinquish the family name for himself and his children. It had driven his young wife, the mother of his children, to seek her own lonely death in an isolated convent in France. And, finally, its bitter legacy of disillusion and depression had driven George years later to follow in his wife's footsteps and take his own life.

And his children would be avenged.

The power of that conviction jolted Sebastian back to a recollection of the part he must play. Brooding in somber anger at his own table was not consonant with that part. "I think I've taken enough losses for one night," he said, yawning, pushing back his chair. "Gracemere, I'll have my revenge next time. . . ."

The earl gathered up his cards and smiled. "It'll be my pleasure, Davenport."

"Have you played often with Gracemere?" Viscount Middleton asked, standing in the narrow passage with Sebastian after the earl's departure. He looked a little uncomfortable.

"No, I understand he's only just come to town." Sebastian drew his friend back to the parlor with the inducement of a particularly fine cognac. "How about you, Harry? How well do you know his play?"

"Devil a bit." Harry squinted into his cognac. He was a handsome young man, slightly built, with a relentlessly cheerful nature that Sebastian decided had its roots in the security of an assured fortune and the confidence of an unshakeable social position. It didn't make him any the less likable.

"Don't want to speak out of turn, dear fellow," Harry continued. "But, well, fact is, it's said he can be a bad man to play with." He peered again into his goblet and swirled the golden liquid. Then he gave Sebastian a cock-eyed look meant to be shrewd.

"Fact is, Sebastian, you're new to town and—well, just a word, you understand—don't mean to interfere."

Sebastian shook his head. "You're warning me off, Harry?"

Harry swallowed his cognac. "Gracemere's a gamester with pockets to let. You wouldn't be the first pigeon—" He stopped and coughed awkwardly. It wasn't the thing to imply that one's friends could be taken in.

"Don't worry, Harry," Sebastian said. "I wasn't born yesterday."

"No . . . no, didn't mean to imply any such thing. Just thought, if you weren't aware . . . maybe you should, well, you know . . ."

"Yes, I know, and I appreciate the word." Sebastian flung a friendly arm around Harry's shoulder.

"So, you'll have a care?" Harry persisted, doggedly pursuing the path of friendship's duty. "A word to the wise."

"The wise has taken the word," Sebastian assured him with a smile. "I'm not such a gull as Gracemere might think me. Remember that, Harry."

Harry frowned, trying to absorb this, but it was too much for his befuddled brain and he soon took himself home.

Sebastian himself went to bed and allowed his mind to roam over pleasanter matters. A pair of shy blue eyes, a snub nose, a soft mouth, hovered in the air above his pillow as it did most nights these days— ever since he'd made the acquaintance of Harriet Moreton. He smiled to himself in the darkness. If he'd been asked before, he'd have said an ingenue in her first season wouldn't be able to hold his attention for five minutes. But Harriet was different. He didn't know why, she just was. She was soft and yielding and he wanted to keep her safe and untouched and . . .

Hell and the devil! He laughed softly at himself. What would Ju say if she could hear him? He must ask her to call on Harriet's mother. It would set a seal to his hitherto unmarked pursuit of Miss Moreton.

"Well, I've found my pigeon, ripe for the plucking," Gracemere declared, draining his port glass with a smile of satisfaction. "I won seven hundred guineas from him tonight." He pulled his cravat loose. "And he didn't seem in the least perturbed by it."

"I wonder where those two come from?" Agnes stretched out on the coverlet of the poster bed, greedily watching the earl disrobe, her

156

eyes narrowed with anticipation. "No one seems to know, but of course where Marcus Devlin chooses to marry, who should question antecedents? A Carrington would hardly make a mismatch."

"Oh, you know what these hybrid continental families are like. They're always rich and studded with old baronies and such like." He threw off his shirt.

"So long as the gull will suit your purpose, that's all that matters." Agnes picked up a pair of scissors from the bedside table and absently pared a loose fingernail.

"*Our* purpose," the earl corrected gently. "But for my own purpose, I've a mind to cultivate Lady Carrington." He pushed off his knee britches and kicked them into a corner. "It will certainly annoy Marcus."

"Haven't you caused him sufficient annoyance?"

Bernard's laugh was as mirthless as his smile. "I still have a score to settle, my dear. One of these days I'll see his pride in the dust." His mouth took a vicious twist.

"Tell me what happened that morning when he ran you to earth in the inn with Martha?" She wondered if perhaps this time he would tell her, but as always the earl's face closed, all expression wiped clean away.

"That lies between Carrington and myself." He put one knee on the bed.

Agnes ran a hand over his thigh. She accepted that despite all that lay between them, all that they shared, and all the years in which they'd shared it, that morning at the inn was one incident Bernard would never discuss. He had disappeared from circulation for a month after it had happened, and when he'd returned to Society with his bride, he'd seemed to be his usual self, but she had detected a new twist to his darkness, one that he still carried deep in his soul.

"So you intend to amuse yourself with coquettish Judith?" Her fingers tiptoed into his groin. "You seemed to enjoy dancing with her the other evening."

The earl's mouth curved in the travesty of a smile as he brought his other knee onto the bed. "I am going to see Marcus Devlin's damnable pride humbled, trampled in the dust, my dear. And Judith is going to help me do it. If, of course, you've no objections?" he added with an ironic rise of an eyebrow.

Agnes laughed, touching his mouth with a fingertip. "Oh, are you going to seduce her, my love? I have no objections. On the contrary, I shall enjoy every minute of it." She laughed again, a low, husky throb of amusement and desire. "Come to me, love, I've been waiting this age for you."

For a moment he ignored the plea, looking down into her face, a glitter of cruelty in his eyes that matched the gleam in hers. He knew how aroused she became at the prospect of making serious mischief. It promised a long and exciting night. He came down on the bed, his mouth moving over hers.

"But you must be careful that dallying with Carrington's wife doesn't jeopardize your chances with the little Moreton chit," Lady Barret murmured against his lips, her hand stroking his back. "A fortune of thirty thousand pounds mustn't be sneezed away, my own."

"No," he agreed. "Particularly when we both have such expensive tastes." He ran his tongue over her lips. "Such very well-matched, expensive tastes, my sweet."

Judith picked up the delicate white marble pawn, caressing it for a second before moving it to queen four. She shot Marcus a mischievous grin, seeing his puzzlement. It was not a customary opening. She hugged her drawn-up knees, feeling the heat of the fire on her right cheek.

"What the devil does that mean?" Marcus demanded.

"If you make the same countermove, it becomes the queen's gambit," she said. "It's not very common, but it can make for an interesting game."

"And what if I don't?"

"Well, you have to, really. It's Black's only logical move. It's what happens next that starts the fun."

Marcus stretched his legs in front of him and leaned back against a footstool. They were both sitting on the floor, and Marcus wore only a shirt and britches; his coat, cravat, stockings, and shoes were scattered around the room.

"You're going to have my shirt and britches within the half hour," he prophesied with resignation.

Judith chuckled. "An enticing prospect."

"Since you've lost nothing but a hair ribbon and your shoes in the last two hours, I can't help feeling the stakes are somewhat uneven."

"Well, why don't I give you a knight handicap?" She took her queen's knight off the board.

"My pride!" He groaned. "You are a devil at this game, Judith."

"But the stakes are fun," she said with another grin.

"They would be if I were not the only one being stripped of my clothes." He moved his own pawn to queen four. "There, now what?"

"Let's play piquet instead. Maybe two hours of chess is enough." Again she picked up one of the pieces, holding it up to the light. The pale marble glowed, translucent and alive with hinted streaks of color in its depths. "They are exquisite. I don't know how to thank you."

"You could always start losing pieces and thus a few articles of clothing," he suggested.

"It's hard for me to lose at chess. Let's play piquet."

"Now, just a minute. Are you telling me you will deliberately lose hands to salvage my masculine pride?"

"If necessary." She gave him an impish smile.

"What is a man to do with such a wife!" Marcus leaned forward, grabbed her upper arms, and hauled her over the board and across his thighs.

"Play piquet with her." She traced his lips with her thumb. "Otherwise, I shall never get my clothes off."

He said nothing for a minute, gazing down at her upturned face, the smiling mouth, the banked fires in the gold-brown eyes.

"I'm not as good at piquet as I am at chess," she offered. "And you are skilled with the cards."

"Nevertheless, madam wife, I doubt I have your experience."

"Perhaps not," she said. "But necessity is the mother of experience." A shadow crossed her eyes.

"Tell me about your father." The request came without conscious decision just as the evening had developed.

Judith rarely spent an evening at home, but after dinner he'd found her in the library, examining the shelves for a book to read in bed. She'd said she was tired and hadn't felt like going to the Denholms' rout party, and matters had proceeded from there. Now there was something about the firelit intimacy of the evening, something about the sensual pleasure they were taking in and of each other that made it both natural and inevitable for him to probe into areas they ordinarily kept closed.

Judith remained leaning against his chest, idly twisting a ringlet on her shoulder between finger and thumb. "He was simply a gamester who lost everything, even his lands, the family estate . . . everything."

"Tell me about him . . . about you and Sebastian."

She hitched herself up on his thighs until she was sitting straight, staring across the chess board into the fire. "He took us with him when he left the country. Our mother hadn't been able to withstand the disgrace. She went to a convent in the Alps and died there. Father hinted that she took her own life. We were no more than babies when we left England. Sebastian was nearly three and I was just two. We traveled with a series of itinerant nursemaids until we were old enough to manage alone: Vienna, Rome, Prague, Paris, Brussels, and every city in between. Father gamed, we learned how to deal with landlords and bailiffs and merchants. Then we learned to play the tables ourselves. Father was often ill."

Judith paused, looking into the flames. Absently she reached for the black marble king. The blackness was of an obliterating depth. She caressed it.

"In what way was he ill?" Marcus asked softly, feeling the currents of memory in her body as she sat on his thighs.

"Black moods, dreadful gulfs of inexorable despair," she said.

"When that happened, he would be unable to leave his bed. Sebastian and I had to fend for ourselves . . . and for him."

Marcus stroked her back, looking for adequate words, but suddenly she laughed. "It sounds horrendous, and often it was, but it was also exhilarating. We never went to school. We read what we pleased. No one ever told us what to do, what to eat, when to go to bed. We did exactly as we pleased within the constraints of necessity."

"An education of some richness," Marcus agreed, pulling her down against his chest again. "Unorthodox, but rich. An education Jean-Jacques Rousseau would have applauded."

"Yes, I daresay he would. We read *Émile* in Paris a few years ago." She stared into the fire for a minute. It was hardly an education Marcus would embrace for any child of his. But then, he was determined there would be no children of his . . . at least not conceived in *this* liaison.

"So," she said. "Piquet?"

"No," he said. "I am no longer prepared to play for your nakedness. I have a much more efficient way in which to achieve it."

"Ah," said Judith, lying back. "Well, perhaps speed is becoming of the essence, my lord."

"Yes, I believe it is."

14

LADY LETITIA MORETON FANCIED HERSELF A SEMI-INVALID AND RECLINED ON A chaise longue amid piled cushions, smelling salts and burned feathers at hand. She was a handsome woman, although her features were somewhat blurred by self-indulgence, and her voice was a plaintive thread, occasionally edged with shrillness.

"So, Lady Carrington, your brother has recently come from the Continent?"

"Yes, ma'am, from Brussels," Judith replied, performing her sisterly duty in Lady Moreton's drawing room. "After my marriage, he decided to set up in London."

Lady Moreton toyed with the silk fringe of her shawl, her eyes resting on Sebastian and Harriet. They were sitting on a sofa, Harriet's soft brown hair contrasting with Sebastian's copper head as they looked through a book of illustrations. "I'm unfamiliar with your family, Lady Carrington," she remarked.

In other words, what is your brother worth? Judith had no difficulty interpreting Lady Moreton's remark. Any woman with daughters of marriageable age would welcome young gentlemen of title and fortune to her drawing room as fervently as she would dismiss those lacking such assets. In this instance, since Harriet was an only child and a considerable heiress, her mother would also be on the watch for fortune hunters.

"My brother and I lived abroad with our father until his death," she said smoothly. "We spent much of our time in France."

"Ah, I see. A family chateau . . ." Lady Moreton's voice lifted delicately, investing the statement with questioning inflexion.

Judith smiled and inclined her head as if in agreement, repressing images of the endless series of grubby lodging houses that had comprised the family chateau.

There was more than a hint of calculation in Lady Moreton's responding smile, and the gaze she bent upon her daughter and Sebastian was tinged with complacence. Any family with which the Marquis of Carrington was willing to be allied had to be good enough for the Moretons.

"I hope you and your brother will honor us at dinner one evening," she said. "And Lord Carrington, of course, if something as ordinary as a family dinner could appeal to him."

"We should be delighted," Judith replied formally.

Their conversation was interrupted by the arrival of another caller. Agnes Barret swept into the drawing room, words of greeting on her lips, her hands extended to the room at large. She bent and kissed Lady Moreton with the familiarity of an intimate, embraced a blushing Harriet, shook Judith's hand with a degree of formality, and then turned a friendly smile on Sebastian, who kissed her hand, offering a twinkling compliment on her dress. Her green satin redingote with a tiny tulle ruff was set off by a dark-green silk hat with a bronze feather. The effect was certainly stunning. Judith was honest enough to recognize that if she hadn't felt perfectly satisfied with her own driving dress of severely cut turquoise broadcloth, trimmed with silver braiding, she might have experienced more than a hint of envy.

"Gracemere is following me up, Letitia. I knew you'd be pleased to receive him." Agnes took a low chair beside her friend's chaise longue. "He's so fond of Harriet and I couldn't convince him that she hadn't caught a chill the other afternoon when we walked in the park. The wind was particularly brisk, and he would have it that she was too lightly dressed for such weather. Of course, I explained that no self-respecting young lady would be seen in anything thicker than a wrap . . . the foolish vanity of the young!" Her laugh tinkled gently, and she patted Harriet's hand. "But such a pretty child."

"I'm sure Lord Gracemere is all condescension, Agnes," Letitia said, touching a burned feather to her nose.

"Lord Gracemere, my lady."

The earl stepped into the room before the butler had finished announcing him. "Lady Moreton . . . and Miss Moreton. I do hope you didn't contract a chill." He bowed. "I was sure you would scold me fiercely, my dear ma'am, for exposing your daughter to such a bitter wind."

"Harriet has taken no hurt, Lord Gracemere," her ladyship said. "But it's good of you to inquire."

"Oh, Gracemere has such a soft spot for Harriet," Agnes reiterated. She smiled at him and Judith recognized with a jolt the proprietorial quality to that smile. The earl's eyebrows lifted a fraction of an inch, conveying a whole world of private communication. Instantly Judith knew that Agnes Barret and Bernard Melville were lovers. But if that was so, why was Agnes promoting Gracemere's acquaintance with Harriet?

"Davenport, I see you've acquired Grantham's match-geldings." Gracemere's observation turned the conversation and Judith's contemplations. "Stolen a march on the rest of us, you lucky dog."

"Oh, they're my sister's," Sebastian said. "Although I had the charge of procuring 'em for her."

"Good God, Lady Carrington! You drive a high-perch phaeton?" The earl sounded genuinely surprised.

"As of this morning," Judith said. "The coachmaker delivered the phaeton just yesterday afternoon, so this morning is my first try-out."

"And how do you find it?"

"Splendid. The bays are beautiful goers."

"You'll be the envy of the Four Horse Club, ma'am," Gracemere said. "I know at least three men who've had their eyes on that pair since Grantham sprang 'em on the town."

"It's very dashing of you, Lady Carrington," Agnes said. "Although I confess I'm surprised Carrington countenances such an unusual conveyance. I've always thought him rather conventional."

Judith contented herself with a slight smile. Her conventional husband had not yet seen his wife on the driver's seat of her unconventional carriage. She wandered over to the window overlooking the street, where one of the Moreton's grooms was walking the horses to keep them from getting chilled. A small boy was crouching over the kennel, looking for scraps of anything that might be edible or useful. His elbows poked through the ragged sleeves of his filthy jacket as he sifted through the detritus of a rich man's street.

"I hope you'll take me up for a turn in the park," Gracemere said at her shoulder. "You must be an accomplished whip, ma'am."

"I was well taught, sir," she replied, forcing a warm smile as she looked up at him over her shoulder. "I should be delighted to demonstrate my skill."

"The pleasure will be all mine," he assured her, bowing with a smile. "I wonder, though, how Carrington would feel about your having such a passenger. He and I are—" he paused, as if searching for the right term. "Estranged, I think one could say." He regarded Judith with an air of resolute candor. "I don't know if your husband has mentioned anything." He waited for her response, his eyes grave, his expression concerned.

Judith was startled at the directness of this approach, but swiftly took the opportunity it offered.

"He's forbidden me to receive you," she said with a credible appearance of constraint, giving him a rather tremulous smile. "But since he won't tell me why, I'm not inclined to obey him." This last was said with a rush of bravado, and he smiled.

"It's a case of old wounds," he said. "Old resentments die hard, Lady Carrington . . . although, I must say, I would have thought in present circumstances that the past could be buried."

"You speak in riddles, sir." She fiddled nervously with the clasp of her reticule, hiding her acute attention to his words.

Gracemere shrugged. "A matter of love and jealousy," he said. "A matter for romantic literature and gothic melodrama." He smiled, a sad, wistful smile that Judith, if she hadn't known his true colors, would have believed in absolutely. "My wife . . . my late wife . . . was engaged to Carrington before she gave me her heart. Your husband could never forgive me for taking her from him."

"Martha," Judith whispered. What ever she'd been expecting, it hadn't been this.

"Just so. He's spoken of her?" The earl tried to hide his surprise.

Judith nodded. "Once. But your name wasn't mentioned."

"Perhaps not unexpected. I fear your husband's pride was badly lacerated, ma'am. Such a man as Carrington can accept almost anything but a wound to his pride."

Judith suspected that was the truth, although her spirit revolted against agreeing with Bernard Melville as he patronized her husband.

"You've been most enlightening, my lord," she said softly. "But I see no reason why we shouldn't still be friends." She forced herself to touch his hand in a conspiratorial gesture, and he put his hand over hers.

"I was hoping you'd say that."

Her skin crawled, but she gave him a radiant smile before turning back to the room. "I must make my farewells, Lady Moreton. I shouldn't keep my horses waiting above a half hour. Sebastian, do you accompany me?"

Sebastian was deep in conversation with Harriet and Lady Barret and looked up with both reluctance and surprise at this abrupt summons. Then he caught his sister's eye and rose immediately. "Of course. If you're going to take those beasts into the park for the first time, fresh as they are, you'd better have me beside you."

"I doubt they'll bolt with me," she said, her voice light. "I believe I have as much skill as you, my dear brother."

"Oh, surely not." This disclaimer surprisingly came from Harriet, who blushed fiercely as she realized what she'd said.

Judith couldn't help laughing. "Don't confuse strength with skill, Harriet. My brother has more strength in his hands than I do, certainly, but control doesn't rest on strength."

"Indeed not, Lady Carrington," Agnes said. Then, with a sharp look, she added, "Just as skill with the cards won't compensate for the devil of bad luck on one's shoulder. Didn't you make some such observation the other evening?"

At Pickering Street, Judith remembered. She gave a careless shrug. "It was a common expression when we were growing up. Remember, Sebastian?"

"Of course." He turned to bid farewell to Harriet and missed the interested glimmer in Lady Barret's tawny eyes.

Gracemere took Judith's hand. "Until we meet again."

"I look forward to it, sir." Judith's smile was one of defiant invitation—a child preparing herself for a major act of rebellion—and Gracemere's lip curled. What a gullible little fool she was. There would soon be a seething brew abubbling in Berkeley Square.

Judith gained the cool, crisp morning air of the street with a sigh of relief.

"What's up, Ju?" Sebastian asked directly.

"I'll tell you in a minute." She felt through her reticule for a coin, drew out a sixpence, and went over to the child in the gutter. He looked up, his eyes scared, as she approached. His nose was running, and judging by his encrusted little face had been doing so for days. He cowered, raising a hand as if to ward off a blow.

"It's all right," she said gently. "I'm not going to hurt you. Here." She handed him the coin. He stared at it as it lay winking in her palm. Then he grabbed at it with a tiny clawlike hand and was off and running as if pursued by every beadle who'd ever cried "Stop thief!"

"Poor little bugger," Sebastian said as she came back to the carriage. "I wonder how far he'll get before somebody bigger and stronger takes it from him." He handed her up to the driving seat, perched precariously high above the horses.

Judith shrugged sadly. "He'll probably steal a loaf of bread one day, and they'll hang him at Newgate. We can defeat Napoleon with great sound and fury at vast expense of money and lives. But we can't somehow ensure that a tiny child gets enough to eat. Or even change a penal system that hangs the same child for stealing the bread that would keep him from starving. At least Bonaparte brought some species of enlightenment to the penal codes in his empires."

Sebastian was accustomed to his sister's occasional tirades against the world's injustices and offered no challenge. "Now what was going on with you and Gracemere?"

"It's the devil of a tangle." She took the reins and told the groom to let go their heads. With a flick of the whip, the bays started off down the street at a brisk trot.

She waited until she had turned through the Stanhope Gate into Hyde Park before telling her brother what she'd learned from Gracemere. Sebastian heard her out in silence, then shook his head in disbelief as he realized the ramifications. "Carrington told you about this broken engagement, then?"

"Yes, before we were married. But he didn't say who the fortune hunter was, and I didn't ask. Sweet heaven, why would it concern me?"

"Of all the damnable coincidences," Sebastian muttered. "It seems as if Gracemere is entwined in every strand of our lives."

"I would like to drive a knife between his ribs," Judith said in a savage undertone, forgetfully dropping her hands so that her horses, momentarily unchecked, plunged forward.

Sebastian watched critically while she brought them under control again. "Do try to restrain yourself," he said. "I'm sure we can bring this off without resorting to murder. Gracemere deserves a lot worse."

Judith smiled grimly. "Anyway, I've decided on my strategy. I'm going to draw him into a plot to defy Marcus. He thinks I'm a silly widgeon who doesn't like being dictated to by her husband, and I'm sure he relishes the idea of conducting a flirtation with the wife of the man he's bested over a woman once before."

"You're playing with fire, my girl," Sebastian observed.

"I'll be careful," she stated with quiet confidence, acknowledging the salute of a group of army officers standing beside the driveway. Her daring equipage and its driver were drawing a fair degree of notice, she thought with satisfaction.

Sebastian also noticed the attention. "I'll lay odds that within a week your phaeton will be all the rage," he said, amused. "Every woman who fancies herself a competent whip will have to have one."

"Marcus, of course, won't give a damn about that," she meditated.

"Well, I believe your moment for convincing him otherwise has arrived." Sebastian gestured toward the pathway, where Marcus stood talking with two friends.

"Ah," Judith said.

15

PETER WELLBY SAW THEM FIRST. "DAMME, CARRINGTON, ISN'T THAT LADY Carrington?"

"She certainly can handle the ribbons," Francis Tallent observed admiringly. "I don't believe I've seen a lady driving such a carriage. Driving 'em tandem, too."

Marcus watched as the vehicle approached at a fast trot, Judith very much at home on her precarious perch, her whip at an impeccable angle. Her brother seemed perfectly at his ease beside her, but what the hell did he think he was doing, permitting his sister to behave in such fashion in public? It was the height of vulgarity for a woman to drive a sporting vehicle. But then perhaps the Davenports didn't realize that, given their unschooled and unlicensed upbringing. Marcus struggled to give them the benefit of the doubt.

"She's driving Grantham's bays," Wellby said. "I had no idea he was selling up."

"Davenport obviously has an ear to the ground," Marcus replied casually.

He moved to the edge of the pathway as Judith drew rein. "You move quickly, Sebastian. Half London was waiting to hear Grantham was selling up."

Sebastian laughed. "Handsome, aren't they?"

"Very." He moved to the side of the phaeton and spoke quietly. "I don't know what you think you're doing, Judith. Give your brother back his reins and get down from there."

Brother and sister were smiling at him with a wicked glimmer in their matching eyes.

"They're not Sebastian's reins, Marcus; they're mine. He procured the carriage and horses for me," Judith said. "I'm taking him for a turn around the park."

For a moment Marcus was speechless. "Yield your place, Davenport," he demanded grimly, laying a hand on the step.

"By all means," Sebastian replied with an obliging smile. He jumped to the ground, laying a hand on his brother-in-law's arm in passing. Marcus turned to meet his eye. That mischievous glint was still there.

"Best not to go head to head with her," Sebastian murmured.

"When I want your advice, I'll ask for it," his brother-in-law declared in a savage undertone.

Sebastian, not in the least offended, merely inclined his head in acknowledgment.

Marcus swung himself up beside his wife. "Give me the reins."

"But I'm perfectly able to handle them myself, as you must have seen," Judith responded with an innocent smile.

"Give them to me."

Judith shrugged and passed them over, together with the whip. "If you wish to try their paces, be my guest."

Marcus ground his teeth, but was forced to mask his fury as best he could under the eyes of his friends, who still stood on the path beside the carriageway. He cracked the thong of the whip, and the leader sprang forward.

"It's unwise to drive a high-couraged pair when one's in a miff,"

Judith remarked in tones of earnest solicitude as Marcus took the phaeton through the park gates. "Don't you think you shaved the gate a trifle close?"

"Hold your tongue!"

Judith shrugged and sat back, surveying her husband's handling of the reins with a critical eye. Despite his fury, he was perfectly in control of the bays and she decided her jibe had been unnecessary.

The phaeton turned into Berkeley Square and drew up outside the house. "You'll have to alight unassisted," Marcus snapped.

Judith put her head on one side, narrowing her eyes. "If you mean to drive my horses in my absence, it would be only courteous to ask my permission."

Marcus inhaled sharply, his jaw clenched. He kept his eyes straight ahead and spoke almost without expression. "You will go into the house, go to my book room, and wait for me. I will join you there shortly."

Judith alighted from the awkward vehicle with creditable grace and mounted the steps to the house.

Marcus waited until she'd been admitted, then drove around to the mews at the back of the house to leave the carriage and horses. He understood that Judith was once again demonstrating to him that she lived by her own rules. But she was his wife, and if she didn't understand that her disreputable past and unknown lineage made it all the more imperative for her to behave impeccably, then he was going to have to demonstrate that fact once and for all.

In the hall, Judith paused. She had no intention of obediently going to Marcus's book room like a naughty schoolgirl.

"Gregson, I have a headache. I'm going to rest in my bedchamber. Would you send Millie to me . . . and I'd like a glass of Madeira."

"Yes, my lady." The butler bowed. "I'll have it sent up immediately."

"Thank you." Judith ran upstairs to her own apartment, where the morning sun poured brilliantly through the long windows, dimming the fire's glow. She went to the window and stared down at the square, tapping her teeth with a fingernail. She was rather looking forward to the next few minutes. It was high time Marcus learned a few things about the wife he had taken on.

Millie helped her out of her clothes and into a particularly fetching peignoir of jonquil silk, lavishly trimmed with lace. She poured Judith a glass of Madeira and hovered solicitously with a vinegar-soaked cloth and smelling salts for the supposed headache.

"No, I need nothing further, Millie. I'll rest quietly by the fire; it'll pass soon."

After Millie curtsied and left, Judith sat in a low chair in front of the chess board by the fire. Sipping her wine, she began to reconstruct a game she had played with Sebastian several days earlier. The concentration required in remembering the moves cleared her head of emotional turmoil, and kept her from watching the clock as she waited for her husband.

She knew the exact moment when he entered the house. Despite her conviction that he had neither right nor cause for complaint, her heart speeded and she tried to cool her palms, clutching the smooth marble of a pair of pawns. She heard his step in the passage outside and swiftly bent her head to the board, feigning complete absorption as the door opened behind her.

Marcus was inconveniently struck by how deliciously desirable she looked. The copper ringlets tumbled around her bent head, exposing the slender column of her neck. His eye traveled over her body, clad in the filmy peignoir that gave her an almost insubstantial air. One narrow, bare, white foot peeped from beneath the hem, and he knew with a jolt to his belly that she was naked beneath the delicate garment.

He stood for a second in the open door, waiting for her to acknowledge him. When she didn't, he closed the door with a snap.

Judith looked up. "Ah, there you are, my lord. How did you find my horses?" She returned her attention to the chess board.

Marcus, having been informed by Gregson that her ladyship had retired to her bedroom with a headache, had decided to ignore her disobedience over the book room rather than be sidetracked from the main issue. He had also intended to keep his temper, but at this blatant provocation all good resolutions flew out of the window. He strode to the fireplace. "I will not have my wife behaving like a vulgar hoyden!"

She looked up again, brushing a wisp of hair from her brow, where a slight, puzzled frown marred the smooth expanse. "There's nothing vulgar about driving oneself in the park, Marcus."

"Damn you, Judith! Don't play the innocent with me. You know quite well that driving a high-perch phaeton is as shameless and fast as Letty Lade. You're the Marchioness of Carrington, and it's time you learned to behave properly."

Judith shook her head, and her mouth took a distinctly stubborn turn. "You're so stuffy, Marcus. I know it's an unusual carriage for a woman, but unusual doesn't necessarily mean bad . . . vulgar . . . shameless . . . fast."

"Where you're concerned, it does," he snapped.

"Oh? Why so?"

"Because, my obtuse wife, someone of your dubious origins cannot get away with things that someone of impeccable family and background might. And as my wife you have a duty to uphold the honor of my family."

Judith paled. How had she thought this would be a simple confrontation, about a simple matter? "My family and my 'dubious' background have nothing to do with this. No one here knows anything about me, good or bad, and I'm perfectly capable of setting my own style without damaging your family's honor. I tell you straight, Carrington, that I will drive what I choose to drive." Breathless, she subsided to rearm.

"Madam, you've forgotten one essential fact." His voice was dangerously quiet. "You are my wife, and you owe me your obedience. You took a most solemn vow to that intent, as I recall."

And it wasn't worth a groat in a court of law. "I have a greater right to my own freedom. I can't be expected to obey unreasonable commands that trespass upon my right to make my own choices."

"You have no such right. Obviously you don't understand the nature of marriage," he said, white-faced, his voice cold and level. "You should have thought of its uncomfortable aspects before you decided to become my wife."

"But I didn't *decide* to become your wife," Judith objected.

"Didn't you?" Marcus's eyes drilled into her.

Judith's lips were dry and she wished with all her heart that she'd never started this. "This isn't about our marriage," she said desperately. "Or not really. It's about something much more simple. I want you to trust me. My judgment has served me well all these years, and what I choose to drive is no concern of yours. I employed my brother as my agent—"

"I must remember to express my gratitude to him." The caustic interruption was delivered in the same cold, level tones. "As for you, ma'am. If your brother doesn't want those horses, then I'll send them to the block at Tattersalls first thing tomorrow." He turned away, as if the subject were closed.

"No! I won't tolerate such a thing."

"My dear wife, you have no choice."

"Oh, but I most certainly do. I shall simply keep the horses in my brother's stable and drive them whenever I please."

The gloves were well and truly off. Marcus, a white shade around his thinned mouth, advanced on her. "By God, ma'am, I am going to have to teach you that I mean what I say."

"You lay hands on me Carrington, and so help me I'll shoot you!"

Judith sprang to her feet. Her knees caught the edge of the low table, sending it flying. Chess pieces tumbled and the massive marble board fell heavily across Marcus's feet. He yelled in pain, hopping from foot to foot.

"Oh, now look what you made me do," Judith said, anger forgotten in her consternation. "I didn't mean to hurt you!"

"No, you only meant to shoot me," Marcus muttered, standing on one leg as he bent to rub his left foot. "Make up your mind, woman."

"You know I wouldn't do such a thing," she said, wringing her hands. "Oh, dear, are you very hurt?"

"Abominably." He lowered his foot gingerly to the carpet and ministered to the right one.

"I am very sorry," Judith said wretchedly. "But you made me so very cross. I didn't do it deliberately."

"God only knows what pain you'd cause if you were trying." He lowered the right foot and straightened. His eyes narrowed abruptly. In her agitation, the silk wrapper had loosened at the neck, exposing the soft, creamy swell of her breast, lifting rapidly with the raging emotions of the last half hour. The golden eyes contained anxiety and the residue of her anger; her lips were parted in dismay.

"I think," Marcus stated deliberately, "that you will conduct the remainder of this heated discussion on your back. I'll feel safer that way." Reaching across the fallen table, he caught her under the arms and lifted her clear across the debris.

"What the devil are you doing?" Judith kicked her legs as he held her with relative ease.

"What do you think I'm doing?" He lowered her to the floor, his hands sliding to her waist, his eyes still narrowed, a predatory light in their ebony depths.

"No!" Judith turned her head aside just as he was about to lower his mouth to hers. "I will not permit you to make love to me when we're quarreling."

His lips, missing her mouth, found instead the soft spot behind her ear. His tongue darted suddenly, wickedly, and she squirmed as the hot lance probed her ear.

"I haven't asked your permission," he responded against her ear.

"Damn you, Marcus, no! You don't want to do this!" She pushed against him with her hands, turning and twisting in his hold.

"I'll be the judge of that." He bore her inexorably backward until she felt the edge of the bed behind her knees. Her arms flailing wildly, she fell back on the bed, twisting her body against him, pouring forth a string of expletives in every language she knew.

Marcus hooked a finger beneath the thin silk tie at her waist and pulled it loose. He caught her thrashing arms and pulled them above her head, gazing down into her flushed face, reading in her eyes the unbidden excitement that warred with her determination not to give in to him.

He looped the tie around her wrists. Judith craned her neck sideways, gasping with a mixture of anger and excitement as he fastened the tie to the carved cherrywood pillar behind her head.

"Now," he said cheerfully, "you may fight me with your tongue, my lynx, but nothing else. However, I'm willing to wager twenty guineas that I can defeat you handsomely with the same weapon."

Judith abruptly ceased her struggles. "Twenty guineas?"

For answer, he plucked the sides of her peignoir apart. Bending his head, he drew a tongue stroke down between her breasts and over her belly. "Unless you wish to make it fifty?" He parted her thighs, holding them wide with flat palms. His breath whispered cool yet warm over the secret sensitivity of her core.

Judith lost all interest in conflict. "I'm not fool enough to defy these odds," she managed to articulate, before coherent speech was denied her under the grazing mouth, the hot, sweet strokes of his tongue.

He should have listened to his brother-in-law, Marcus thought dreamily, as he fed upon the pleasure growing within her. Direct confrontation was a crude and exhausting tactic, doomed to failure. Defeating her with delight was an infinitely more subtle strategy for achieving mastery.

Her whimpers of pleasure were building to a crescendo, her thighs tautening as the spiral coiled ever tighter in her belly, until with a shuddering cry her body arced, taut as a bow string, and then she fell back on the bed, her breath swift and shallow.

Marcus moved up her body, dropping a light kiss on her mouth, brushing her closed eyelids with his lips, and she opened her eyes, giving him a dazed smile.

"You work miracles, sir."

"One of my minor talents," he said with a smug grin, holding himself over her on an elbow, while fumbling one-handed with the waistband of his britches, pushing them off his hips. Reaching above her, he pulled loose the silk tie that bound her wrists. "I think you're sufficiently tamed now to have your hands back. You might need them for the next stage."

"I might," Judith agreed. She brought her hands down, slipping them around him, grasping his buttocks, as he eased himself into her. "Ah, that feels wonderful."

Marcus sighed in agreement, moving with gentle rhythm within the smooth, warm quiver of her body. "Sometimes," he murmured, "I think you were made to hold me as I was made to fill you."

"You only think it sometimes?" She laughed up at him, an exultant spark in her eyes as she tightened around him, glorying in the feel of him, in the light in his eye, in the absolute knowledge of the pleasure they found in each other. She lifted her hips to meet him.

"Ah, Judith, don't move again unless you're ready to be with me."

"I'm ready," she said breathlessly.

She touched his lips fleetingly, then with wicked intent moved her hand to his belly. The muscles jumped against her flattened palm and he surged against her. Their cries mingled, redolent of a primitive exultation, and his body fell heavily upon hers, sweat-slick skin melding with sweat-slick skin.

They lay for long minutes in deep, satiated silence, before Judith stirred beneath Marcus. Her legs were still sprawled around him, her arms spread out as they had fallen in the aftermath of that climactic explosion.

"Was I crushing you?" Marcus murmured, rolling away from her. He propped himself on one elbow, looking down at her, smiling at the wanton sprawl of her body.

"Only pleasurably." Her eyes opened lazily.

"Now," he said, trailing a finger down between her breasts, "to return to the vexed question of perch phaetons . . ."

Judith pushed his hand away, sat cross-legged on the bed, and regarded him. "Now, listen to me," she said calmly. "You are an old stick-in-the-mud, Marcus Devlin. . . . No, don't interrupt. When, since we've been married, have I ever caused you the slightest embarrassment?"

"Never, to my knowledge," he conceded. "And you'd better not."

Judith patted his knee. "I'm not about to. I'm going to set a new trend. I'm not about to race at Epsom, or charge down the London-to-Brighton post road at full gallop. I'm simply going to do something different—a little daring, perhaps. But you just see. . . . In a week, I'll wager any odds that there'll be quite a few others driving perch phaetons. And," she added, "you'll see that none of them exhibits anything like my style and expertise."

"Conceited baggage," he said.

"Just wait and see," she responded stoutly.

Marcus didn't immediately answer, his thoughts having taken a new direction. "How did you learn to drive so well, Judith?"

"Oh," she said vaguely, "a friend taught me two years ago."

"A friend?"

"Yes, in Vienna. He drove a team of magnificent grays and was most obliging as to teach me."

"In exchange for what?"

"Why, for my company," she said, as if it were self-explanatory.

"One of your flirts, in other words."

"I suppose you could say that. He was a very respectable flirt, though. An Austrian count of some wealth."

"Of which you and your brother relieved him, I assume."

"A few thousand," she said with cheerful insouciance. "He could well afford it, and he enjoyed my company as compensation."

"And you wonder why I sometimes question your judgment."

Judith bit her lip hard. "This is different. Why do you always throw my past in my face?" She turned her head away, blinking back tears.

Why did he? He looked at her averted profile, saw the shimmer of a teardrop on her cheek. Perhaps he wasn't being fair to her. No matter how their marriage had come about, he couldn't help but take pride in his beautiful, elegant, intelligent wife. Maybe it was time to bury the past.

He leaned forward and smudged the tear on her cheek with his finger. "If you can satisfy me that you can handle in *every* contingency a spirited pair between the shafts of such a vehicle, then you may keep your perch phaeton."

She swallowed her tears and swung out of bed. "We'll put the matter to the test immediately." Bending over, she playfully tugged at the coverlet. "Come along, lazy, get up. We'll drive to Richmond in your curricle with your grays and I'll show you how I can handle a four-in-hand. I promise you I'll prove to you that I can drive to an inch."

"Yes, I rather imagine you will." He stood up, then said consideringly, "By the way, I believe you owe me twenty guineas."

"Why, yes, sir, I believe I do," Judith replied in dulcet tones.

16

"I DON'T KNOW WHAT TO DO NOW." CHARLIE LOOKED UP FROM THE CARDS IN his hand, his expression baffled.

Sebastian, standing behind Charlie at the table, glanced down at the young man's hand of cards and grinned as he felt his sister's surging impatience. Judith was a good teacher, but she was short on forbearance. She looked up and caught Sebastian's eye. Taking a deep breath, she struggled for patience. "Do you think you want another card, Charlie?"

"I don't know exactly." He frowned. Judith was trying to explain how one could reduce the element of chance at macao. "I have eighteen points."

"Then you don't want anything higher than a three," she explained carefully. "That means there are twelve possible cards."

"Ten," Charlie said. "I already hold an ace and a two."

"You're getting there," Sebastian approved. He thrust his hands into the pockets of his buckskin britches, watching the lesson with amusement.

"All right," Judith said, gesturing to the dummy hands on the table. "We've had five rounds, two hands have folded, three are still left. What does that tell you about the three left?"

Charlie frowned. "That they have mostly low cards?"

"Exactly," she said. "Therefore, your chances of drawing one of the ten low cards that you don't have are . . . ?"

"Slim," he said with a grin of comprehension. "So I stay as I am."

"It's simple, isn't it?"

"I suppose so. What card would have been dealt me if I'd asked for one?"

Judith drew the top card from the depleted pack in front of her and slid it across to him. Charlie turned it over. It was a three.

"I never said it was an exact science." Judith smiled at his disconsolate expression.

"I always thought the fun with gaming *was* the risk."

"So it is, but doesn't it give you any satisfaction to overcome pure chance?"

Charlie looked puzzled. "Yes, it does, but it's not as thrilling as when luck smiles and I get a winning streak."

Sebastian gave a shout of laughter as his sister threw up her hands in frustration.

"Well, at least Marcus hasn't packed you off to Berkshire," she said, gathering up the cards.

"No," he agreed. "In fact, he's being deuced decent about things at the moment. I wanted to go to Repton with Giles Fotheringham for the hunting, and it was Marcus who said I needed a second hunter. He accompanied me to Tattersalls and helped me pick out a magnificent animal." He grinned slightly. "Of course, he said if he hadn't advised me, I'd have been seduced by a showy hack with no bottom, but that's just Marcus."

Judith laughed at Charlie's accurate imitation of his cousin's invariable bluntness and began to deal the cards again.

"I must love you and leave you," Sebastian said, bending to kiss his sister. "Are you going to the rout at Hartley House this evening?"

"Yes, the rest of the gaming school are going to try their wings for the first time. Cornelia and Isobel are going to play macao, at separate tables of course, and Sally's all set to try her hand at quinze."

"How're they doing?"

Judith chuckled. "Pretty well, on the whole. Cornelia has the most difficulty. It's strange, because she's so clever in so many other areas. She plays the pianoforte beautifully and composes her own music, you know. And reads Latin and Greek."

"Very bookish," Sebastian agreed. "And completely cow-handed."

"Oh, that's unkind." But Judith couldn't help smiling. "Anyway, I'm looking forward to seeing how they do. They're all absolutely determined to succeed."

"Heaven preserve the husbands of London," Sebastian teased. "How will they ensure their wives' loyalty if they can't ensure their dependence?"

Judith grimaced. "That may be a quizzing observation, Sebastian, but it has an unpleasant ring of truth. If you could hear Isobel's description of the humiliating performance . . ." Remembering Charlie's presence, she stopped abruptly. Such details were not for his tender ears.

Sebastian nodded in instant comprehension. "I take it back . . . I must be off. I promised to escort Harriet and her mother to the Botanic Gardens." He pulled a comical face.

"Whatever for? I'm sure Harriet would prefer to visit the lions at the Exchange."

"And so would I, but her revered mama does not consider it edifying, so the Botanic Gardens it is."

"Well, make sure you have a plentiful supply of sal volatile, in case Lady Moreton becomes overcome with excitement among the orchids."

"You are a disrespectful wretch," Sebastian declared.

"Yes, I'd noticed that myself" came Carrington's voice from the doorway. "How do you do, Sebastian?" He tossed his riding whip onto the sofa and drew off his gloves.

"Well enough, thank you." Sebastian grinned at his brother-in-law and picked up his hat from the side table. "Perhaps you could cure m'sister's lamentable tongue."

"Oh, I've tried, Sebastian, I've tried. It's a lost cause."

"I suppose it is. Pity, though."

"Would you two stop talking about me as if I weren't here?" Judith demanded in half-laughing indignation.

"I'm away." Sebastian blew his sister a kiss and went to the door.

"Oh, there's something I need to discuss with you, Sebastian," Marcus said. "But I can see you're in a hurry."

"Orchids await him," Judith murmured as the door closed behind her brother.

"What?"

"Orchids. He's gone to dance attendance on Lady Moreton."

"Good God, why?"

"Because he intends her for his mother-in-law."

"Hell and the devil," Marcus said. "The daughter's a considerable heiress, of course."

"What has that to do with it?" Judith demanded, bristling.

"Why, only that all sane young men with barely a feather to fly with are on the lookout for heiresses," Marcus responded casually. "What are you playing, Charlie?" He strolled over to the card table.

Charlie didn't immediately reply. He could see Judith's face and he was wondering why Marcus hadn't noticed the reaction his words were causing.

Judith said stiffly, "You know nothing about Sebastian's circumstances."

"No, but I assume he supports himself at the tables. I doubt the Moretons will look kindly upon his suit." Marcus turned to pick up the sherry decanter from the pier table.

"Well, I trust you'll be in for a surprise."

"I'd be happy to believe it, but you must face facts, Judith." He poured sherry, blithely indifferent to the effect he was having on his wife. "People like the Moretons would look kindly on an impoverished suitor only if he brought a significant title."

"I see," Judith said icily, and firmly closed her lips. Rapidly, she finished dealing the cards.

"So what are you playing?" Marcus inquired again, casually sipping sherry.

"Macao," Charlie said, eager to change the subject. Judith was looking very dangerous, and he could detect the slightest tremor in the long white fingers. "You see, I'm not very good at gaming—" he began.

"No, you're abominable," Marcus agreed, interrupting. "A baby could beat you . . . which is why you're in the trouble you're in," he added. "I'd have thought you'd do better to find some other way of amusing yourself."

"But once I learn how to win, I won't have any debts," Charlie explained eagerly. "So Judith's teaching me."

"She's *what*?" Marcus exclaimed, his cheerful insouciance gone. Sebastian had been in the room too, and the memory of another macao table in a ballroom in Brussels filled his mind and chased away all rational thought. How could he ever have thought he could bury the past? "And just *how* is she teaching you to win?"

On top of the insult to Sebastian—insults Marcus didn't even seem aware of—this was too much. Judith knew quite well what he was implying, and the last shreds of control over her volcanic temper were severed.

"Well, there's a little trick I know," she declared, the lynx eyes ablaze. "It involves nicking the right-hand corner of the knaves . . . it's almost impossible to detect if one does it aright; and then there's—"

The goad found its mark. Marcus exploded, his expression livid. "That'll do!"

With an incoherent mumble Charlie leaped to his feet and hastily left the room, closing the door behind him.

"I will not have you interfering in my family concerns," Marcus stated. "I've already told you that Charlie is *my* business, and I will not have him influenced by your dubious ethics, your views, your practices—"

"How dare you!" Judith sprang up from the table in violent interruption. "How could you imagine I would teach Charlie to be a cardsharp?"

"From what I know of you, very easily," Marcus snapped. "You forget I know full well how you go about winning."

Judith was now as pale as she'd been flushed with anger a minute before. "You are unjust," she stated flatly. "First you accuse my brother of fortune hunting, and then you accuse me of the ultimate unscrupulousness. I wish to God we'd never met." The words were spoken before she had a chance to monitor them, and there they lay, like stones on the air between them.

For a moment Marcus was silent. The hiss and crackle of the fire in the hearth was the only sound in the room. Then he said, "Do you?" His eyes were fixed on her face with an almost aching intensity.

"Don't you?" Her voice was now flat, the fire had died in her eyes, and for some reason she was crying inside. But her face showed no emotion.

"Sometimes . . . when . . . sometimes," he said slowly. *When he found himself loving her and then he'd remember her trickery, the use to which she could put her beauty and her passion—that was when he wished they'd never met.* And that knowledge was never far from the surface, however hard he tried to bury it.

He went out of the room, closing the door quietly.

Judith stood in the middle of the room, the tears now coursing soundlessly down her cheeks. If they'd never met, she would have been spared this hurt. But if they'd never met, she would have missed . . .

She drew out her handkerchief and blew her nose. Soon enough she would be free to leave him. Soon enough he'd be free of his conniving trickster wife. Only why did such thoughts make her so miserable?

17

BERNARD MELVILLE WAS PUZZLED. HE WAS LOSING TO SEBASTIAN DAVENPORT and he couldn't work out how it was happening. His opponent was playing with his usual insouciance, lounging back in his chair, legs sprawled beneath the table, a goblet of cognac at his elbow. He laughed and joked with those who stopped beside the table to watch the play, often seemed careless of his discard, and yet the points were adding up with a remorseless momentum.

Bernard had lost the first hand, won the second by a hair, and was clearly about to lose the third. The cards seemed to be running evenly, although Davenport had laughingly congratulated himself when he'd looked at his hand, counted thirty points, and declared a repique. But the earl knew his own cards were certainly good enough to give him the edge even against a major hand when playing with someone less skilled than himself. And Sebastian Davenport was a careless, inexpert player . . . wasn't he?

Sebastian watched his opponent. Gracemere was not aware of the observation, conducted as it was from beneath lazily drooping lids, but Sebastian was making a fairly accurate guess as to the earl's musings. He wondered whether to throw a guard that they would both know he should have kept. He would lose the hand, but he was ahead on points and could easily win the game with the next hand, after which he would rise the winner by a narrow margin. His fingers hovered over the cards, and a deep frown furrowed his brow. He reached for his cognac and drank.

Gracemere watched this performance of indecision with an inner smile. Despite his present success, the man was so transparent. When, with an almost defiant gesture of resolution, Sebastian threw down his only heart, the inner smile nearly broke to the surface. That was more like it. Careless, inexpert . . . positively bird-witted. Gracemere played to win the hand.

"Ah, I knew I should have retained the heart," Sebastian lamented. "I just couldn't remember what had gone before."

"I know how it is," Gracemere said with smooth reassurance, dealing the cards.

He lost the next hand so quickly, he could only put it down to the fall of the cards. "Your game, I believe, Davenport."

Sebastian smiled fuzzily as he began to count the points. "Not by much, but it makes a change, Gracemere."

"You must allow me my revenge." The earl gathered up the cards.

Sebastian yawned. "You'll have to excuse me tonight. Three games is as much as I can manage at one sitting . . . too much concentration." He laughed in cheerful self-deprecation. "Think I'll have a turn at hazard. See how the dice fall for me. I've a feeling my luck's in tonight."

"As you wish," Gracemere said, finding it hard to hide his contempt. "But I insist on a return game soon."

"By all means . . . by all means . . . wouldn't miss it for the world." Sebastian stood up, caught sight of a friend across the room, and strolled off. Gracemere watched him weave his way through the tables, an occasional unevenness in his step indication of the cognac he had been downing so liberally. He played with a wealthy man's improvidence.

Gracemere smiled. Fleecing such a careless fool would be easier than taking cake from a baby. And as for the sister . . . she'd fallen into his hand like a ripe plum with the tale of her husband's pride and jealousy. Really, such innocents shouldn't be let loose upon the world. However, his plans for her were going to prove highly entertaining for both himself and Agnes, who had declared herself a most eager partner. And he would humble Marcus Devlin at last.

For a moment, his surroundings faded into a mist and he no longer saw or heard the men at the tables, the soft slap of cards, the efficiently bustling waiters replacing bottles of burgundy, refilling the decanters of port and cognac. The flame on the branched candlestick that had lit the piquet table blurred in front of his eyes. Now he saw again the chamber above the stables on that long-ago dawn, and he saw again the pitiless ebony eyes. So vivid was the image that he could almost smell the terror he'd felt when he finally understood what Marcus Devlin was going to do to him.

Gracemere shook his head clear of the vision and slowly unclenched his fists, absently massaging his bloodless fingers. Judith would help him erase the memories and the burning wound of that unendurable humiliation.

Once out of the card room, Sebastian's step steadied, his eyes focused, his shoulders straightened. They were little adjustments, so discreetly made as to be almost unnoticeable by any not on the watch for them. Only Judith would have seen them.

"Still playing with Gracemere, I see," Viscount Middleton observed as Sebastian joined him in the hazard room.

"Yes, and my luck was in tonight," Sebastian said, watching the fall of the dice, listening to the groom porter intoning the odds, calculating how much he was prepared to lose to chance in the interests of appearances. He was supposed to be an addicted gamester, who was nevertheless unworried about his losses, and it would become quickly remarked if he chose only to play games of skill.

"Well, it's your business, I suppose," Harry observed in a tone that was not altogether approving. He tossed a rouleaux onto the baize table beneath the brilliant light of a massive candelabra. "But don't forget what I said."

"I haven't," Sebastian reassured him, making his own bet. "And if I tell you not to worry about me, Harry, I can assure you I mean it." He realized he would have liked to have said more, to repay his friend's kindness with a degree of confidence. Friendship was a dangerous thing. Until now, he'd only had one friend—his sister—and they'd both been content to have it so. But as their world had expanded, it had become harder to keep to themselves. And he'd be lying to himself if he said he didn't enjoy these new relationships.

Soon after, he left Watier's, making his way to the soiree at Hartley House where he hoped he would find Harriet, although it was past midnight.

Judith was at the macao table when he entered the card room, having discovered that his beloved had been taken home by her mama an hour earlier. He strolled casually around the table to watch her play. Judith gave him a brief smile and returned all her attention to the cards. She knew her brother was watching with the eye of a critic. He would tell her afterward if he thought she'd made any errors, and he would be able to detail every one of them from an infallible memory for every hand played. It was a service they performed for each other, although Judith was the first to acknowledge that Sebastian was the better card player.

After a few minutes' observation, he gave her a short, unsmiling nod that told her she was playing well and wandered away, pausing beside the tables where Judith's pupils were playing. Sally looked up as he stood at her shoulder and gave him the smile of one amazed at her success. He saw that she had a substantial pile of rouleaux at her place. He watched her for a minute and, when she played a weak card, said quietly, "Stop soon. You're losing your concentration."

Sally flushed and looked put out. But then she bit her lower lip and nodded. A minute later she yielded her place to one of the spectators.

"Thank you, Sebastian."

He shook his head. "No need. It's as important a lesson as any other—stop the minute your play starts going bad."

There was little advice he could give Cornelia, whose play was wildly erratic. Sometimes it verged on the brilliant, but then she would forget everything and play like a rank amateur. Her winnings fluctuated as erratically as her play, and at no point could he advise her to stop because there was no certainty that she wouldn't win the next hand.

"How am I doing?" she asked in a loud whisper, dropping her fan.

He picked up the fan, saying quietly, "It's hard to say. How much do you want to win?"

"Two hundred guineas," she whispered at her original decibel level. The other players looked up from their cards, glaring at her, and she blushed, her arm jerked, knocking over a wineglass. A servant rushed forward to deal with the mess and in the confusion Sebastian said, "Let me take over your hand."

Cornelia stood up, apologizing vigorously for her clumsiness. "I do beg your pardon, but I seem to have wine on my gown. Oh, do take my place, Mr. Davenport. Thank you so much."

Sebastian winked at her and sat down. "If the table doesn't object."

There were no objections, and he increased Cornelia's winnings to the necessary sum within half an hour. Cornelia and Sally stood behind him, watching his play intently. He rose from the table and offered them both his arm with a little grin. "Did you learn anything, ladies?"

"Yes, you and Judith are the same when you play—you don't seem to notice anything that's going on around you," Sally said. "Your expressions are completely impassive, almost as if you've ceased to inhabit your faces." She laughed. "That sounds silly, doesn't it? But you know what I mean, Cornelia."

"Yes," Cornelia agreed. "And I suspect it's because Judith and Sebastian are not ordinary card players." She looked up at her escort. "You're true gamesters, aren't you?"

"And what's a true gamester, Mrs. Forsythe?" he asked, laughing, hoping to deflect her. Cornelia Forsythe had too sharp a brain for comfort, even if she was cow-handed and inclined to erratic thought processes.

Cornelia looked at him for a minute, then she nodded her head. "You know what I mean. But it's none of my business. I'll not mention it again."

"What are you talking about?" Sally demanded.

Cornelia laughed, breaking the tension. "Nothing at all. I'm teasing Sebastian. Let's go and see how Isobel is doing."

Isobel was flushed with success. "Just look at what I've made," she said, opening her reticule to reveal the pile of shining rouleaux. I'd have had to order Henley's favorite meals for a week, and sit on his knee and beg for hours to wrest this sum from him." Then she recollected Sebastian and blushed crimson. What one confided to one's women friends couldn't be shared with a man.

But Sebastian merely frowned and said, "How very unpleasant for you."

The three women exchanged a look of amazement. What kind of a man was Judith's brother?

"Let's see how Judith's doing," Sally said, to break the moment of startled silence.

"No," Sebastian said immediately. "She won't want to be disturbed. When she's won what she intended to win, she'll stop playing."

Cornelia smiled to herself and Sebastian caught the smile. Again, he reflected that friends could be hazardous when one had secrets to keep. He suggested they repair to the supper room while they waited for Judith.

She joined them there shortly. Her eyes were tired, Sebastian thought, and her face was drawn . . . much more than an evening's intense gaming would produce. In fact, it occurred to him that she'd been crying. He gave her a glass of champagne and sat quietly as she responded to her friends' eager accounts of their various successes.

"How much did you win?" Sally asked.

"A thousand," Judith said, as if it were nothing. "I don't owe 'the fund' anything for the horses, do I, Sebastian?"

"No, Pickering Street settled that, if you recall."

"Oh, yes, I remember."

"Fund?" Sally asked.

"Private language," Judith said, smiling with an effort.

"I'm going to escort you home," Sebastian said. "You look exhausted."

"I suppose I am a little." She stood up. "I'm glad the evening was a success."

"What about Charlie?" Sally asked. "Wasn't he going to play macao this evening?"

"Yes," Judith replied with a touch of constraint. "I hope he also profited from our sessions." She touched her brother's hand. "I don't need an escort, Sebastian. My chaise is waiting outside."

Sebastian knew she was telling him she wanted privacy, and he acceded without demur. He'd find out what was troubling her when she was ready to tell him. He escorted her to the waiting chaise with the Carrington arms emblazoned on the panels and kissed her good night.

Judith sat huddled in a corner of the carriage as the iron-wheeled vehicle bumped and rattled over the cobbles. She felt chilled, although there was a rug over her knees and a hot brick at her feet. Chilled and bone-weary, although she knew the weariness was of the spirit, not of the body. Intermittent moonlight flickered through the window, shedding a cold pale light on the dim interior . . . as cold and pale as her spirit, it seemed, in the fanciful reverie of her unhappiness.

Millie was waiting up for her, but the comforting warmth and soft lights of the firelit bedchamber did little to cheer Judith. "Help me with my dress, Millie, then you may go to bed. I can manage the rest myself."

The abigail unhooked the gown of emerald silk and the apple-green half slip embroidered with seed pearls. She hung them in the armoire and left, bidding her mistress good night.

Judith sat in her petticoat in front of the mirror, raising her hands to unfasten the emerald necklace and remove the matching drops in her ears. The connecting door opened with a shocking abruptness. Marcus stood in the doorway in his dressing gown, his eyes glowing like black coals.

"No!" he said.

Judith dropped an earring. It fell on the dresser with a clatter. "No what?"

"No, I do not wish we'd never met," he stated, striding into the room to where she sat on the dresser stool. Slowly she turned to face him.

His hands clasped her throat, his thumbs pushing up her chin. He could feel the slender fragility of that alabaster column warm and pulsing against his fingers. "No," he repeated softly. "Although you're an inflammable, brawling wildcat with a tongue so sharp I'm amazed you haven't cut yourself, I could never wish such a thing."

Judith found she couldn't say anything. His eyes burned into hers and the violent, jolting current of their sexuality ripped through her.

"And you?" he asked. "Do you wish such a thing, Judith? Tell me the truth."

She shook her head. Her throat was parched and she could feel its pulse thrumming against the warm clasp of his hands. "No," she whispered finally. "No, I don't wish such a thing."

He bent his head and his mouth took hers as his hands still circled her throat. The power of the kiss blazed through her like a forest fire, laying waste the barriers of her soul, the thin defenses she might have put up to save herself from extinction in the power of his passion. She was lost in the kiss, his tongue possessing her mouth, becoming a part of her own body, and her skin where it touched his seemed no longer to belong to her.

Without moving his mouth from hers, he drew her to her feet with his hands around her throat. She obeyed blindly, inhaling the rich scents of his skin, tasting him in her mouth. He moved her backward until she felt the wall behind her, hard against her shoulderblades.

And then he lifted his mouth from hers, and she seemed to be drowning in the great black pools of his eyes, existing only in the tiny image of herself in the dark irises.

"Raise your petticoat."

It was the softest command, yet each word rang with the force and promise of fierce arousal. Slowly she drew the soft cambric up to her waist.

"Part your legs." His hands fell from her throat, opening his robe, revealing the erect shaft, poised for possession.

Obeying the jolting charge of lust, swept along on the turbulent current of passion, she moved her legs apart. Still holding her petticoat at her waist, she braced herself against the wall as, without preliminary, Marcus drove deep within her. His eyes held hers as he moved himself inside her, his hands resting lightly on his hips. Only their loins were touching, only their eyes spoke.

The black eyes seemed to swallow her as his body took control of hers. Judith felt herself losing herself, her identity, all will, joined to a power outside herself. A power that pleasured as it mastered. Her head fell back against the wall, her throat arching, white and vulnerable above the scalloped neck of her petticoat. Marcus took his hands from his hips for just long enough to pull the top of the flimsy garment down so that her breasts were bared. He nodded, a small nod of satisfaction, as he gazed down at the exposed creamy swell. He felt her submission, the yielding of her body to the power and will of his. A wave of triumph crashed over him, taking his breath away, and he surged within her as if he would make her a part of himself, indivisible, transcending her separateness, the secret parts of herself that she kept from him. For this moment, he had tamed his lynx . . . for this moment he had her bound in the chains of a delight that was in his hands to give or to withhold.

Slowly he withdrew to the edge of her body, holding himself there. Her eyes pleaded for his return but she remained mute, locked in the deep sensual silence of this world they were creating. He disengaged, and her little gasp of loss broke the silence, but he placed his hands on her hips and turned her to face the wall, fitting himself against the small of her back as she shifted to accommodate him, positioning herself so that he could slip easily within her again.

Her breasts were pressed to the wall, her cheek resting against the cool, cream paint. Denied eye contact, she was now totally possessed, submerged into his being. And Marcus gloried in an ownership that grew and fed upon the sensual purity of this union.

It was as if he had limitless resources that night. His powers of invention were unbounded, his drive and energy infinite. He commanded without words; only his hands indicated what he wanted of her, and she followed direction as blindly and willingly as if she were bewitched. There were times when she knew herself to be entranced in some fairy ring. Again and again he brought her to the outermost limit of pleasure, to the fine boundary where pleasure bordered upon pain, so intense was the delight. Again and again she surged beneath his body, his mouth, his hands, as he showed her an internal landscape she hadn't known existed; and in showing it to her, he entered the secret chambers of her soul.

There would be other nights . . . other times when Judith would take the initiative, would make her own demands and in their satisfaction satisfy in turn, but for this night, Marcus was both inventor and master of their pleasure. Through the hushed reaches of the night until dawn grayed the sky they moved silently around the room, from floor to bed, chair to couch. Sometimes she lay beneath him, sometimes over him. Her skin identified the slight roughness of the carpet, the nubby brocade of the chaise longue, the damask smoothness of the bed sheets.

Finally he laid her down on the polished, cold wood of a long rosewood table. The flat surface was hard against her shoulder blades, unyielding beneath her buttocks as he raised her legs, lifting them high onto his shoulders as he plunged for the last time deep into her body, in a fusion so complete that she could no longer tell where her own bodily limits ended and his began. The long silence of the night was at last broken when their elemental cries of a savage and primitive fulfillment mingled in the room.

Judith flung her arms high above her head, her hips arced, holding him inside her through the wild, pumping, climactic glory, then her body seemed to collapse, to go limp and weak as a newborn foal's, and she lay unseeing, unaware, a sacrifice to passion upon the cold flat altar of the table.

It was a long time before Marcus had sufficient strength to scoop her from the table and carry her to the bed. He didn't know whether she was asleep or unconscious, so deep and heavy was her breathing, so limp and relaxed her body. He fell down beside her, sinking into the mattress, as sleep rolled over him.

Judith swam upward from the dark depths of exhaustion about an hour later. She lay in the graying light, neither asleep nor awake, as memory returned to make sense of the night's excess of sensual joy. Vaguely she remembered that at the last, Marcus had not withdrawn from her body. Had he intended it that way, or was it simply that the night's loving had not admitted of such pragmatic, pedestrian concerns?

Sleep reclaimed her.

18

"How kind of you to call, Lady Carrington." Letitia Moreton smiled at her guest from the depths of her cushioned chaise longue. "Your brother isn't with you today?" Her complacent gaze rested on her daughter, sitting beside the window with her embroidery. Harriet was looking entrancingly pretty in a round gown of sprig muslin. Thoughts of weddings played most pleasurably in Letitia's head these days. Lady Carrington's brother had been making his preference for Harriet obvious, and with such a connection, Harriet would be assured of entree into the first circles.

"No, I haven't seen him today," Judith said, drawing off her gloves. "I was wondering if Harriet would care to drive with me this afternoon?"

Harriet gave her a quick, shy smile.

"Of course she would be delighted." Letitia spoke for her daughter. "Run and change your dress."

Harriet hesitated for a minute. "I understood Lady Barret was to call this afternoon, Mama. She promised to bring the topaz ribbons that we bought yesterday . . . the ones I left by accident in her barouche."

"Lady Barret will understand if you're not here. Now don't keep Lady Carrington waiting."

Harriet obeyed without further demur and Judith said reflectively, "Lady Barret's most attentive to Harriet. You must find it a great comfort to have such a friend, ma'am."

Letitia sighed. "It's such a trial to be so invalidish, Lady Carrington. And Agnes has been most kind in chaperoning Harriet."

"Perhaps you'll allow me to act as chaperone occasionally," Judith offered. "Maybe Harriet would like to accompany me to Almack's for the subscription ball next Thursday."

"Oh, you're too kind." Letitia dabbed her lips with a lace-edged handkerchief soaked in lavender water.

"Not at all. We'd be delighted if she'd join us for dinner beforehand. I'll send Sebastian with my carriage for her."

"Oh, you mustn't put yourself to such trouble."

"But I'm certain my brother will be only too happy to escort her," Judith said, offering a conspiratorial smile. It was returned with more than a hint of self-satisfaction.

"Ah, Harriet, that was quick." With relief, Judith greeted Harriet's return to the salon. "What a very dashing hat."

Harriet blushed. "Your brother was kind enough to compliment it."

Judith chuckled. "I can imagine. It's very much a Sebastian kind of a hat." She rose from her chair. "If you're ready . . ."

Outside, Harriet regarded the high-axled vehicle with some trepidation. "It's quite safe, I assure you." Judith mounted easily and held her hand down. "I can safely promise that I won't overturn you."

"No, I'm not in the least afraid of that," Harriet declared, bravely taking the helping hand and climbing up to sit beside Judith. "But it's most dreadfully high up." She regarded the restless bays with the same trepidation. They were tossing their heads, bridles jingling in the crisp autumn air.

Judith felt their mouths with a sensitive movement of the reins. "They're very fresh," she said with a cheerful insouciance that Harriet couldn't begin to understand. "I didn't drive them yesterday so they're anxious to shake the fidgets from their legs." She told the boy holding them to let go their heads and the pair lunged forward the minute they were released. Harriet shuddered and suppressed a cry of alarm. Judith drew in the reins, controlling the plunge and bringing the animals to a sedate walk.

"That's better," she said as they swung around the corner into a busy thoroughfare. "I'll give them their heads when we reach the park."

Harriet made no response to this declaration of intent, but clutched her hands tightly in her lap as a curricle dashed past, narrowly shaving the wheel of the phaeton. A scraggy mongrel ran between the wheels, a dripping piece of meat in its mouth. It was pursued by a red-faced man in a blood-smeared apron, waving a cleaver. One of Judith's bays reared in the shaft as the dog dodged its hooves and the smell of blood from the meat hit the horse's nostrils. Harriet emitted a tiny scream, but Judith calmly steadied her horse, peering down into the street to see what had happened to the dog. "Oh, good," she said. "He managed to escape. I wouldn't fancy his chances with the butcher's cleaver, would you?" She laughed, glancing sideways at Harriet.

"Oh, dear, did that scare you?" she said, seeing the girl's white face. "I promise I can handle these horses in any situation. Marcus made me do all sorts of things, including driving a bolting team through a narrow gateway, before he was satisfied I was competent to drive this pair."

Harriet gave her a wan smile, and Judith took another tack. "Do you like to ride?"

"Oh, yes, and particularly the hunt." There was real enthusiasm in the girl's voice, and Judith heaved an internal sigh of relief. Sebastian was a bruising rider to hounds, and it was hard to imagine him with a soulmate who regarded the sport with the same apprehension she regarded perch phaetons.

They turned into the park, crowded with fashionable London. Judith watched with some amusement a young lady in a dashing driving dress struggling to control a pair of blacks between the shafts of a phaeton, while a visibly anxious groom sat beside her. Not every young woman who had rushed to emulate the daring Lady Carrington had her ladyship's skills. Those who did had formed an exclusive circle with Judith at its center. Judith raised her whip several times in greeting as one or other of these friends passed, and drew up several times to acknowledge other acquaintances, introducing Harriet where necessary. Harriet seemed to enjoy the attention and soon began to relax, chatting openly about her life, her family, her likes and dislikes. She had a ready sense of humor, Judith discovered, and it gave ample opportunity to hear her entrancing, musical laugh.

"I believe Lady Barret's waving to us," Harriet observed as they started their second circuit.

Agnes and Gracemere were standing on the path, smiling and waving. Judith drew rein beside them, saying pleasantly, "Good afternoon, Lady Barret . . . Lord Gracemere. As you see, Harriet and I are enjoying the air."

Gracemere raised heavy-lidded eyes to Judith's smiling countenance. That now-familiar shark of interest darted in his gaze as he offered her a conspiratorial smile. When she fluttered her eyelashes at him, his smile broadened.

"I was coming to call in Brook Street, Harriet," Agnes said. "To bring back your ribbons."

"Thank you, ma'am," Harriet murmured. "It was so careless of me to forget them."

"Oh, young people have other things on their minds, I'll wager," Gracemere declared with an avuncular chuckle that sounded to Judith more like the cackle of a hyena.

"Do you know, Lady Carrington, I really think I must ask you to take me up beside you." Lady Barret stepped up to the phaeton. "It's such a dashing conveyance. His lordship will be happy to bear Harriet company, I know, for one turn."

Judith felt Harriet tense beside her. Glancing down, she saw the girl's gloved hands tightly clasped in her lap. "There's nothing I'd like better, ma'am, but I most solemnly promised Lady Moreton that I'd return Harriet within the hour. On another occasion, I trust you'll do me the honor."

Harriet's hands relaxed. Lady Barret's smile stiffened, her eyes chilling with unmistakable annoyance. Judith's own expression remained blandly affable.

"I shall hold you to your promise, Lady Carrington. Until later, Harriet." Agnes bowed and stepped back, laying her hand on Gracemere's arm. He, too, bowed, and Judith dropped her hands, setting the bays in motion.

"You don't care for Gracemere," she said without preamble.

Harriet shivered almost unconsciously. "I find him loathsome. I don't understand why a woman of Lady Barret's sensibility should make a friend of him."

And not just a friend. But that Judith kept to herself. "His manner's a trifle encroaching," she said.

"He's forever trying to walk and talk with me. I can't be uncivil, of course—especially as he and Lady Barret are such particular friends—so I don't know how to avoid him."

"Mmm." Judith said nothing further on the subject, but Gracemere's intentions were clearly worth exploring. If he and Sebastian were rivals for the heiress, it would add another knot to the tangle. Presumably, a rich wife needn't interfere with Gracemere's liaison with Agnes. If they deceived Sir Thomas, there was no reason why they'd scruple to deceive a young wife.

She encouraged the bays to a smart trot, weaving her way through the curricles, tilburys, and the more sedate laundelets and barouches thronging the carriageway. When she caught sight of Marcus approaching, driving his team of grays between the shafts of his curricle, she slowed her horses to a walk. An idea occurred to her that would nicely kill two birds with one stone.

"Harriet, I've just remembered an errand I must run immediately. I'm going to ask my husband to take you home."

"Oh, no . . . no, please, it's not necessary . . . I'll accompany you," Harriet stammered, utterly daunted by the prospect of enduring the Marquis of Carrington's exclusive company. What could she talk about with such an intimidatingly lofty member of the ton?

"You'll find it a dead bore," Judith stated. "And I know your mama will be pleased to see you escorted home in such irreproachable fashion."

Harriet looked up at her, startled, but then a glint of comprehension appeared in her eyes. "Yes, I'm certain she will," she said.

Judith smiled at her, well pleased. Harriet was quick on the uptake.

Marcus reined in his horses and the two carriages drew abreast of each other. "I give you good afternoon, madam wife." He greeted her with a narrow-eyed smile that spoke of many things before bowing to her companion. "Miss Moreton." Harriet blushed and returned the bow.

"Marcus, you're the very person I need," Judith said. "I've just remembered an errand I must run immediately. It'll be a great bore for Harriet, so you may escort her home for me."

Laughter sprang in the ebony eyes. Marcus, also, was quick on the uptake. "It'll be my pleasure." He tossed his reins to his tiger and sprang down from the curricle. "Miss Moreton, allow me to assist you."

Harriet's blush deepened when his lordship caught her around the waist and matter-of-factly lifted her to the ground before handing her into his own more easily managed vehicle.

Marcus stepped closer to the phaeton, resting one hand on the front axle. "Devious minx," he said. "Don't think I don't know what you're up to. You're more artful than a wagonload of monkeys."

Judith smiled demurely. "Since Sebastian has so little to offer as a suitor in his own right, he'd better make the most of his other family connections." Immediately she regretted the light, bantering words. They were too close to home, too close to the bitterness that had been so sweetly resolved.

But to her relief, Marcus chose to respond as if he had no memory of that confrontation. "You're a shameless baggage, but I've no objections to assisting Sebastian. However, I do have one crow to pluck with you."

"Oh?"

"Where is your groom?"

Judith pulled a face. "Grooms are the devil in an open carriage. They make it impossible to have a comfortable conversation."

"Nevertheless, they are indispensable."

Judith sighed. "The despot speaks again."

"And he will be obeyed."

It was a minor concession and a limited inconvenience. Matters were going so smoothly between them at the moment that she was not prepared to throw a wrench in the works over something so trivial. "Very well, if you insist, I'll not drive out again unaccompanied."

Marcus nodded. "You'd better take Henry with you for the moment."

"Oh, no!" Judith exclaimed. "That'll spoil everything. If you don't have your tiger, you won't be willing to leave your horses in order to call upon Lady Moreton when you return Harriet. The whole impact of the Marquis of Carrington's escort will be diminished."

Marcus couldn't help laughing. "I don't know why I should allow myself to be embroiled in your plots, but if you don't take Henry, then you must return home immediately."

Judith inclined her head in acknowledgment, waved gaily to Harriet, and started her horses. "Immediately" was a word open to interpretation, she decided, and she had given no verbal promise. Marcus would be safely occupied outside the park for at least forty-five minutes, and the opportunity to encourage the shark in Bernard Melville's eyes couldn't be missed.

She ran her quarry to earth near the Apsley House gate. He was engaged in conversation with a group of friends, but there was no sign of Lady Barret, which relieved Judith of the need to find a way of offering to take up Gracemere while excluding the lady.

"My lord, we meet again." She hailed him cheerfully. "Harriet has been returned home; may I offer to take you up for a turn?"

"I'm honored, Lady Carrington. I shall be the most envied man in the park."

"Fustian," she declared, laughing.

"Not in the least," he protested, swinging himself up beside her. "You're such a noted whip, ma'am. Did Carrington teach you?"

"No," Judith said, starting the horses as she prepared to water the seeds already sown. "In truth, my husband doesn't entirely approve of this turn-out." She gave her companion an up-from-under look as if to say: You know what I mean.

"But he doesn't exactly forbid it?" Gracemere asked.

"No, I don't take kindly to forbidding." She gave him an arch smile.

"I'm surprised Carrington is willing to yield. He's generally thought to have an unyielding temperament."

"He does," Judith said with a note of defiance. "But I don't see why I shouldn't amuse myself as I please."

"I see." Fancy Marcus of all men marrying a spoiled brat. It was a delicious thought and all the better for his purposes.

"However," Judith went on, her voice now low and confiding, "my husband remains adamant about refusing to receive you under his roof." She touched his knee fleetingly. "I think it a great piece of nonsense, myself, but he won't be moved." She gave him another arch smile. "So we'll have to pursue our friendship a little more . . . well, obliquely, if you see what I mean. As we're doing now."

"Yes, I see exactly what you mean." He could barely contain his amusement at having such a ripe plum fall into his lap. "But you're not afraid you might come across your husband in the park?"

Judith shook her head. "Not this afternoon. He's about some errand that will occupy him for at least an hour."

"I see you enjoy flirting with danger, Judith . . . I may call you Judith?"

"Yes, of course. It's not so much that I enjoy courting danger, sir;

but I claim the right to make my friends where I choose. If Carrington can't accept that, then I'll circumvent his disapproval." She glanced sideways at him with a coquettish little pout. "Do I shock you, Bernard, with such unwifely sentiments?"

His eyes held hers for a long minute and the shark skimmed the surface of his gaze. "On the contrary, I've always appreciated an unvirtuous wife. My tastes have never run to the milksop, and if you wish to cultivate me in order to assert your independence, then, ma'am, I'm honored to be so cultivated."

Judith allowed a moment to pass while she continued to keep her eyes on his, then a small, inviting smile touched her mouth. "Then we're agreed, sir." She held out one hand to him, across her body. He took it, squeezing it firmly.

"We are agreed."

"But it's to be our secret."

"Of course," he said smoothly. "My lips are sealed. We shall be merely civil in public and save our friendship for moments such as this."

"Just so, my lord." Judith contrived to produce a flirtatious little giggle that brought a complacent but condescending smirk to his lordship's lips.

"Miss Moreton's a very sweet-natured girl," Judith observed after a minute.

"Very," the earl concurred. "It's unfortunate her mother's ill health makes it difficult for her to be launched as she deserves."

"But Lady Barret seems willing to take a mother's place."

"Ah, yes, Agnes is all kindness," he said. "Harriet has reason to be grateful."

"I understand she's something of an heiress."

"Is she? I didn't know."

Thank you, my lord Gracemere. The disingenuous denial had told her everything she needed to know.

Shortly after, she set the earl down again at the Apsley House gate and turned her horses toward the Stanhope gate and home. It was later than she'd realized and she was now unlikely to be at home before Marcus. Sebastian, however, appeared fortuitously, just as she turned out of the gate. She drew rein.

"Sebastian, you must accompany me to Berkeley Square."

"Of course, if you like." Her brother acceded to this imperative declaration with customary good humor. "Any special reason?"

"I need to arrive home suitably escorted," she told him. "And besides, there's something we need to discuss."

"Carrington objects to your driving without a groom." There was no questioning inflexion to the remark.

Judith laughed. "How did you guess?"

"Because it's only natural he would. You're too careless of convention, Ju."

"Goodness me! Since when have you become so straitlaced?"

"I haven't," Sebastian denied, startled. "At least, I don't believe I have."

"It's Harriet's influence, I'll lay odds."

"Well, what if it is?"

"Don't be so defensive. I think she's very sweet, and if you love her then so shall I. . . . But that brings me to what we have to discuss."

"Well?"

"I believe Gracemere is courting Harriet—or courting her fortune, at any rate."

Sebastian was very still beside her. When he spoke, his voice was almost neutral. "What makes you think so?"

Judith told him and he heard her out in silence. "After all, he's married one heiress . . . snatched her from under the nose of a most desirable suitor. It doesn't seem unlikely he'd try it again," she concluded. "And I can't think of any other reason why Agnes Barret should be so sedulously cultivating an innocent girl in her first Season. The situation's perfect: Harriet's mother can't—or won't—oversee her progress. Agnes steps in, wins their confidence, and what's more natural than that she should introduce Harriet to her own friends . . . or lover, as the case may be? The Moreton fortune will benefit both of them, presumably."

"Damn the man to hell!" Sebastian hissed with abrupt vehemence. "Everywhere we turn, he's there, twisting his black evil into every thread of our lives."

"You can defeat him on this," Judith said calmly. "When you bring him down with the cards, you'll destroy every other plan he has."

Sebastian said nothing, but his jaw was tight as he stared rigidly ahead.

"Harriet loathes Gracemere."

"She told you?" Surprised, he turned to look at her.

"Yes. Although I'm sure she doesn't realize why he's so encroaching. But if she's not offering him any encouragement, he's going to have his work cut out to make any headway."

"If only this was over and done with!" Sebastian exclaimed in a vehement undertone.

Judith said nothing, knowing her brother would recover his equilibrium in his own way, and by the time they reached Berkeley Square, he was chatting quite easily again as if that impassioned wish had never been uttered.

Lacking a groom, she drove the horses to the mews herself. Marcus was standing in the cobbled yard, talking with the head stableman as his wife drove in. He strolled over to her. "One of these days, we must have a discussion on the concept of 'immediately,' Judith. It seems to be one of the increasingly long list of words we understand differently," he said in pleasant tones.

Judith scrutinized his countenance for indications of real annoyance. If there was any it was only slight. "But as you see," she pointed out, "I have an irreproachable escort."

Marcus nodded. "Do you ever object to being browbeaten and manipulated by your sister, Sebastian?"

"Not in general," Sebastian said. "I'm resigned. How about you?"

"Not yet resigned. I must persuade you to teach me how such a peaceful state can be attained."

"Oh, it's perfectly simple. The only drawback is that it takes a long time. Like rock erosion."

"I object to this habit you two have developed of talking about me as if I weren't here," Judith announced with offended dignity.

"I'm afraid you invite it, lynx. It's the only weapon we mere males have against your wiles. Let's have you down from there." Marcus reached up to grasp her waist, swinging her to the cobbles. "Do you come in, Sebastian? Or were you kidnapped en route to some other engagement?"

"The latter," he said. "I was engaged to meet some friends in the park. I daresay they've given me up now, so I may as well return home."

"If you think to make me feel guilty, brother, I can tell you you haven't succeeded." Marcus still held her by the waist and she took a step away from him. His hands tightened and she retraced the step, smiling slightly even as she wondered what the grooms and stable-hands must be thinking.

"I never attempt lost causes," Sebastian said with a grin. "And I don't think you need me around at the moment, so I'll bid you farewell."

"We have some unfinished business," Marcus said, his bantering tone disappeared. Sebastian raised his eyebrows and his brother-in-law went on, "I've been trying to catch you these last five days. Will I find you at White's or Watier's later tonight?"

"White's," Sebastian said without hesitation. Gracemere had said he would be at the faro tables at White's that evening.

Marcus felt the stirring of the air between brother and sister as if it were palpable. He'd noticed before these strange, suspended instants of tension, when they both seemed to hear something different from the actual words spoken. "Then I'll find you there," he said.

"I'm intrigued," Judith said. "What unfinished business could you have with Sebastian?"

"None of your business, ma'am."

"Oh, is it not?" A flare ignited the golden eyes.

Sebastian, chuckling, left them to it and strolled out of the yard. Matters seemed to be going less bumpily between his sister and her husband these days.

"Inside," Marcus directed. "We're going to have that discussion on semantics."

"Oh, good," Judith said happily. "That's bound to be interesting."

"Yes, I believe it will be. Walk a little faster."

Meekly Judith obeyed the pressure in the small of her back. "How did you find Lady Moreton?"

"Invalidish, in a word. Toad-eating, in another. A dead bore, in three more. *Must we encourage this connection?*"

"Yes."

"I detect a note of finality."

"Admit that Harriet is charmingly pretty, has the sweetest manners, and will make Sebastian a splendid wife."

"I accept the first two, although she's shy as a church mouse, but for the third—it seems to me a veritable mismatch."

"Sebastian knows what he wants," Judith said with quiet confidence. "And what he wants, he gets."

"Not unlike his sister," Marcus observed, but Judith could hear no sting to the statement.

19

"I DON'T KNOW WHY THE SILLY CHIT SHOULD BE SO STAND-OFFISH."
Gracemere paced the firelit salon, his mouth twisted with annoyance.

"She's shy, Bernard." Agnes poured tea. "And she's very young."

"So was Martha, but I didn't have such difficulty with her. I had
her eating out of my hand in two weeks."

Agnes refrained from pointing out that the earl had been younger
then. "Martha was ripe for the picking," she said. "Carrington's proprietorial indifference left her with so little self-esteem that she could
be easily flattered into love."

"You do me such honor, ma'am," Gracemere said with chilly
irony.

"Oh, don't fly into a pucker, Bernard. You know perfectly well
it's the truth. Harriet hasn't yet felt her wings. It's her first Season."
She rose from the sofa, carrying his tea across to him. "However,
have you noticed how Judith seems to have taken the child up? And
Sebastian seems always to be at her side."

Gracemere gave a crack of derisive laughter. "That greenhorn!
He's a ninny with more money than sense."

"So long as he's worth plucking." Agnes turned back to the tea tray.

"I only wish it could be more of a challenge," the earl said, sipping his tea.

Agnes looked up at him. "Count your blessings, my love. Why would you want to work harder than you must?"

He laughed, touching a finger to his lips in salutation. "I take your point. But to return to the Moreton chit. You must contrive to ensure she's more in my company."

"I'm not sure how much good it would do. If the child is doe-eyed for Sebastian, and Judith has decided to take up his cause, then we face some difficulties."

Gracemere's pale eyes hardened. "If the girl can't be persuaded, there are other methods."

Agnes pursed her lips. "Abduction, you mean?"

"If necessary. A night in that Hampstead inn is all that's required. It doesn't much matter if the girl spends it willingly or not. She'll be ruined either way."

"Society is so unjust," Agnes murmured with a smile. "A girl's innocence is wrested from her with an act of ravishment, and she's considered no longer fit for decent company." She glided toward Gracemere, a fluid, undulating walk, reminiscent of a serpent's slither.

"But an honorable marriage will conceal her shame," he replied, both lust and cruelty in his smile. Agnes went into his arms, her breathing swift, her lips parted, her eyes glittering with an almost feral excitement. He fastened on her mouth with a savage hunger, reflecting yet again that the planning of evil and the prospect of suffering were for Agnes the most potent aphrodisiacs. It was yet another link in the chain that bound them.

"An honorable marriage that will cost her family every penny of thirty thousand pounds," Agnes whispered against his mouth. "Poor child, I could almost pity her. Will you be kind to her?"

"I have kindness only for you, my own. The kindness that I know pleasures you." Gracemere smiled and bit down on her lower lip, his fingers closing fiercely over her right breast, pinching the rising nipple.

Agnes shuddered as the hurt blossomed and she moaned, pressing her loins against his, and the inevitable, blissful excitement surged in her blood.

The earl smiled to himself as he felt her response. Life was full of attractive propositions at the moment, with Carrington's wife begging like a fawning puppy for his help in taunting her husband and young Davenport offering himself as meekly as any sheep to the shearer.

"Judith, are you feeling quite well?" Sally looked anxiously at her sister-in-law, who seemed listless, lacking her usual burnished luster.

Judith had a headache and a dragging pain in the base of her belly. It had come on since she'd arrived at the Herons' soiree, and she didn't need a visit to the retiring room to confirm what she already knew. That wild and glorious night of lovemaking had had no fruitful consequences, and she didn't know whether she was glad or sorry.

"It's just the time of the month," she said. "And this party is so insipid." The soiree had so far featured a harpist of mediocre talent, a meager supper, and indifferent champagne. "Let's go into the card room," she suggested, putting aside her nearly untouched supper plate.

"There's a loo table in the small salon," Isobel said. "We could join that."

Judith's expression was not encouraging. "No, come and play basset instead. The stakes aren't too high, and I've explained how to make the best calculation on the card order, so at least you have some tool against pure chance."

"I don't feel clear-headed enough tonight," Sally said. "I don't think I can play properly if I haven't prepared myself beforehand."

"And all the preparation in the world doesn't necessarily help me," Cornelia declared. "I'm in favor of loo."

"But it's limited loo," Judith said disgustedly. "There's no challenge in that."

"The words of a true gamester, Lady Carrington." Agnes Barret's soft tones came from behind Judith, and it was only with the exercise of supreme self-control that she kept dislike and unease from her expression as she turned.

"Good evening, Lady Barret. Have you just arrived? I'm afraid you've missed the harpist." She offered a bland smile.

"I understand she performed magnificently."

"I fear I'm a poor judge," Judith said.

"But not of the cards. Anyone who plays at Amelia Dolby's must have both inclination and skill . . . or perhaps simply need?" she added, her eyes narrowing as she awaited Judith's reaction.

Judith bowed. "As you would know, ma'am."

Lady Barret smiled faintly. "Husbands can be so difficult about money, can't they?" Her tawny eyes held Judith's for a long minute, then with a word of excuse, she moved away.

"Good heavens," Isobel said, taking a cream puff from a silver salver presented by a waiter. "Are you at war with Agnes Barret, Judith?"

"At war? What a strange idea. How should I be?"

"I don't know," Isobel said. "But the air was crackling. Wasn't it?" She appealed to her companions as she popped the creamy confection into her mouth with an unconsciously beatific smile.

Cornelia was frowning. "There's something about her, or is it about you, Judith? I can't put my finger on it, but when she was standing so close to you . . . Oh, I don't know what I'm talking about." She shook her head in exasperation. "I'm going to play loo. It may be poor-spirited of me, but I enjoy it, and I'm perfectly content to make pin money tonight."

"I am too," Isobel declared, beckoning to the footman with the pastries. "I find high-stakes playing exciting, but it makes me most dreadfully nervous . . . one of those, I think." She selected a strawberry tart. "These are quite delicious. Why don't you try one, Judith?"

"The chicken in aspic rather put me off," Judith said. "Besides, I haven't your sweet tooth."

"It's a great trial," Isobel said a touch dolefully. "I shall become very fat, I'm convinced."

Sally laughed. "You'll be magnificent, Isobel, a plump and indolent matron of unfailing generosity, dispensing hospitality from your sofa, and taking in every waif and stray who comes your way."

Judith smiled. It was a fairly safe prediction. Isobel had a heart to match her sweet tooth.

"Very well, we'll play loo," she agreed. "I've a bellyache and a headache, so I might as well play schoolroom games." In fact, she would really prefer to be home in her bed with a book, drinking hot milk laced with brandy. And Marcus would come in later, and when he realized she didn't feel like making love, he'd make up the fire and bring his cognac and sit on her bed and talk to her. Would he be relieved that she hadn't conceived?

Judith dug up a smile and followed her friends into the salon where the loo table was set up.

The clock in the smoky room struck midnight when Marcus downed his mug of gin and water in the Daffy Club and stood up.

"Whither away?" Peter Wellby asked, watching the smoke from his clay pipe curl upward to the blackened timbers of the low ceiling.

"I have to track down my brother-in-law," Marcus told him. "He said I'd find him at White's this evening."

"Decent fellow, Davenport," Peter observed, rising with him. He extinguished his pipe and handed it to a waiting serving lad, who took it away to be hung up over the stained planking of the taproom counter until its owner came again. "Mind if I accompany you?" Peter picked up his cane. He glanced dispassionately into his empty tankard. "Had enough blue ruin for one evening."

"A glass of reasonable port won't come amiss," Marcus agreed.

Sebastian was at the faro table when his brother-in-law arrived.

He was winning steadily but with such careless good humor that the growing pile of rouleaux and vowels in front of him seemed unremarkable.

Gracemere held the bank. He glanced up as Marcus strolled over to the table. For a moment, their eyes met and again Gracemere experienced the shiver of terror of that long-ago morning, when Carrington had found him with Martha.

Hatred flickered in the earl's pale eyes and was answered with a cold, mocking disdain before the marquis turned his black gaze on Sebastian.

"A word with you, Sebastian, when the table breaks up."

"Yes, of course." Sebastian carelessly arranged several rouleaux around his chosen cards. "I think I'll close after this hand, anyway . . . while I'm ahead."

Gracemere slid the top card off the pack in front of him, revealing the knave of hearts. He laid it to the right of the pack. "That's me done for the night," Viscount Middleton said with a sigh, pushing across his rouleaux that lay beside his own knave of hearts. "The play's getting too rich for my blood."

Gracemere turned up the second card: the king of spades. This one he laid to the left of the pack.

Sebastian had bet on its counterpart and chuckled amid a chorus of good-natured groans at his continuing luck. "Never mind, tomorrow it'll have deserted me completely. The lady's a fickle mistress."

Gracemere took up the rake and pushed three fifty-guinea rouleaux across to him. "You can't walk away just yet, Davenport. Not with the luck running so completely in your favor."

There was something in the earl's voice that made Sebastian instantly alert: an eagerness that Gracemere could barely conceal. Sebastian glanced across the table and saw a shimmer of anticipation in the pale eyes. *Gracemere expected to win the next cut.*

He shrugged acceptingly and sat back, watching as the earl dealt afresh. A new pack of cards was then put in front of him. "Stakes, gentlemen." He smiled around the table.

Sebastian placed two rouleaux against the seven of clubs. The others around the table made their own bets.

Gracemere turned up the first card in the pack and laid the seven of clubs to the right of the pack.

Sebastian pushed his stake across the table without a word. The earl smiled, his eyes meeting the other's cool gaze.

"Ill luck can't last. Try another," Gracemere suggested, his tongue running over his lips.

Sebastian shook his head. "Not tonight, my lord, my luck's turned. Carrington . . . at your service."

He followed Marcus to a chair by the fire. Gracemere had placed the seven of clubs. Sebastian had expected it, though he didn't know how it had been done. He knew most of the tricks of card sharping, but he'd missed that one, though he'd guessed that Gracemere was going to try something. The earl had been playing straight up to now, and a hundred guineas was no great sum, so why had he decided to win it in such risky fashion? Was it something he did occasionally to keep his hand in, as Judith and Sebastian did once in a while? Or could he really not endure to lose even once to a man he was determined to fleece?

Sebastian knew that his strategy had succeeded and Gracemere had picked him as his next victim. He had now to draw him in deep by offering alternate wins and losses, while Judith established her own place in the earl's sphere, so that he wouldn't think twice about her presence at his side in the card room. However, if he was going to have to pit his skill against devious play so soon, they would have to think again. Only trickery could defeat trickery, and they couldn't afford to play their double act prematurely. He might have to resign himself to more losses than they'd decided he could comfortably bear.

Having reached that decision, Sebastian dismissed Gracemere from his mind for the moment and smiled at his brother-in-law, reaching for the decanter of port on the table.

"So, what is this unfinished business, Marcus? I confess you have me intrigued."

"An outstanding debt," Marcus said, taking the glass he handed to him. "Thank you. How much did you pay for Judith's horses?"

"A fraction above four hundred," Sebastian said easily. "They were a bargain."

"I won't dispute that." Marcus sat down in the winged chair, crossing his long legs in olive pantaloons. "And the coach-builder?"

"Two-fifty, I believe." He sipped his port. "It's a capital turn-out. I'd not resent the outlay."

"Oh, no, I don't in the least." Marcus made haste to reassure him. "I'll give you a draft on my bank for six hundred and fifty guineas, if that'll suit you."

Sebastian choked on his port. "Whatever for?"

"You did act as your sister's agent in this matter?"

"Yes, of course I did, but . . . Oh." Comprehension dawned. "You think I was her banker . . . No, I assure you, Carrington, Judith paid every penny herself. I did nothing more than effect the purchase."

"Judith." Marcus sat up abruptly. "Don't try to bamboozle me, Sebastian. I know full well your sister couldn't possibly have afforded such a sum. I know how much her quarterly allowance is, and I examine all her bills."

He put his glass on the table. "I've agreed to allow Judith to keep her carriage and horses, so you must understand that I can't permit you to assume an expense that is rightfully mine."

Sebastian frowned into his glass. A thorny thicket seemed to have sprung up around him. It had slipped his mind that Marcus didn't know of Judith's financial independence. But even if it hadn't, he could hardly take Marcus's money on false pretenses. After a minute he said, "Evidently your arithmetic is at fault, Carrington. I assure you that my sister paid for that turn-out herself." He added with a bland smile, "She works miracles with the smallest amounts of money, Judith does."

"What possible source of—" The question died on his lips. How could he have been so naive? So blind? He'd placed a limit on her spending and she'd simply reverted to her old ways.

"I take it Judith continues to engage in high-stakes gaming as a source of income?" His voice was level, no hint of his seething fury.

Sebastian examined his brother-in-law's drawn countenance. The white shade around his mouth, the flint in the black depths of his eyes told their own tale.

"You couldn't expect Judith to accept a humiliating dependency," he said, giving up on trying to mislead Marcus. Clearly, it was useless. "When you limited her expenditure, she had no choice but to look after her own needs."

Marcus ignored this. His voice was still even. "Do you have any idea how much my wife manages to make in a week at the gaming tables?"

Sebastian sucked in his lower lip. "It would depend on where she played and whether she needed money. But on a good evening, playing high, she could probably come away with a thousand without it seeming too noticeable. Much more, of course, if she were playing at Pickering Street."

Marcus felt as if his head were about to explode. "So she frequents hells, does she? It must feel quite like old times."

Sebastian winced. "Ju's not like other women, Carrington. She has her pride . . . maybe more than most." He shook his head, feeling for words. "But if you try to impose your will on her, she'll fight back. She's never been financially dependent on anyone. If you'd simply trusted her to keep her expenditure within bounds, none of this would have happened."

"I'm indebted to you for pointing that out to me." Marcus stood up. "However, it just so happens that my fortune is not at the disposal of every adventuress who manages to lay some claim to it. Now, if you'll excuse me, I'm going to attend to your sister. So far, I've failed to impress her with the depth of my feelings on this score. I am now going to put that right."

Heavy-hearted, Sebastian watched Marcus stride from the room. The fragile edifice of his sister's marriage was about to be cracked wide open; that much he knew absolutely. Whether it could be repaired remained to be seen. But he had to be there for Judith. She would need him very soon.

He drank another glass of port and then went home to await developments.

20

Marcus strode up St. James's toward Curzon Street. It was a dark night but he'd have been unaware of his surroundings even in brightest moonlight. His mind was a seething witches' brew of anger, disappointment, and something that he vaguely recognized as sorrow. Sorrow for the savage, abrupt destruction of his budding belief that his marriage, founded on quicksand, could be reconstructed, grounded now in cement. He had begun to lay down the burden of mistrust, gradually to allow the warmth of his feelings for Judith to overcome the doubts, to be seduced by her in every respect as thoroughly as he'd been seduced simply by her body in Brussels. And now it was all gone, ashes on his tongue. She wanted what he could give her materially, and when he didn't satisfy those wants, she gave not a thought to his position, to her position, but simply took what she wanted, perpetrating her deceitful masquerade as shamelessly as ever. She had no interest in or intention of being his wife in the fullest sense, adapting her life-style to the obligations and duties of that position even as she enjoyed its advantages. She was using him, as she had used him from the start.

At the corner of Duke Street and Piccadilly, the sounds of uproar broke through his self-absorption. A group of young bloods of about Charlie's age were drunkenly weaving their way along the pavement, arm in arm, flourishing bottles of burgundy. One of them fired a flintlock pistol in the air, and their raucous hilarity brought an officer of the watch out of an alley, his lantern raised high, throwing a yellow circle of illumination over the disheveled band. It was an error. With a fox hunter's "view halloo," the group surged forward, surrounding the man, clearly intent on one of the favorite pastimes of inebriated, aristocratic youth: boxing the watch.

Marcus's anger, already in full flame, needed only this to create a conflagration. He strode into the middle of the group, wielding his cane to good purpose, until he reached the fallen watchman. One of the young men, his face red, his eyes bloodshot, swung an empty burgundy bottle at the cane-wielding spoiler of their fun. Slender fingers gripped his wrist and the pressure made the young man wince. The marquis stared at him in silence. His grip tightened and, with a sharply indrawn breath, the young man let the bottle crash to the pavement. He fell back under the piercing menace of those ebony eyes and his companions, infected by the unspoken threat embodied in this new arrival, melted away.

The officer of the watch scrambled up, retrieving his fallen lantern, straightening his coat, adjusting his wig that had slipped over one eye. He muttered about taking the young hooligans before the Justice, but the group had gone, and soon could be heard hooting and bellowing from the safety of a reasonable distance.

"Ruffians," Marcus stated disgustedly, kicking broken glass away from his gleaming Hessians. "Too much money and time and not enough to occupy them. Sometimes I think it would have been better if we hadn't beaten Bonaparte. A few years in the army would do them the world of good." The watchman agreed, but rather nervously. His rescuer seemed to be in as dangerous a mood as his assailants, judging by those intimidating eyes and the savage way his cane had thwacked across their shoulders. He ducked his head, mumbled his thanks, and took himself off on his rounds again, swinging his lantern.

The encounter had done nothing to quell the bright flame of rage as Marcus strode up the steps of the Herons' mansion on Curzon Street. Light poured from the windows, voices and the strains of dance music greeted him as he stepped into the hall. Instructing the butler curtly to summon Lady Carrington's chaise, Marcus strode up the stairs.

His hostess came fluttering over to him, all smiles, and Marcus forced himself to respond with due courtesy, but it was clear to Amanda Heron that the Most Honorable Marquis of Carrington's thoughts were elsewhere . . . and they weren't very pleasant thoughts, judging by the look in his eye. She was quite relieved when he excused himself and made straight for the card room, casting a quick glance into the drawing room, where the rug had been rolled up and a few couples still danced to the strains of a pianoforte.

Judith was not dancing. Neither was she in the main card room. Presumably the stakes at this insipid affair were not worthy of her skill, he thought savagely, turning aside to another, smaller salon.

He heard Judith's laughing voice as he stepped through the arched doorway. "For shame, Sally, you're looed. How could you have lost that trick?"

"Oh, it grows late," Sally protested. "And I haven't your powers of concentration, Judith."

The powers necessary to maintain a deceitful masquerade. Marcus stood for a minute in the shadow of a heavy curtain. Ten people sat in a cheerful circle around the loo table. They were playing limited loo, the penalty fixed at a shilling, but Judith had beside her a substantial pile of shillings, and as he watched, a man opposite pushed the pool across the table.

"Lady Carrington, you win again."

"How very surprising," Marcus murmured, crossing to the table.

Judith experienced a start of pleasure at the sound of his voice, and missed the tone at first. She turned, smiling, as he came up

223

behind her shoulder. The smile faded as she saw his expression, a slowly creeping apprehension prickling between her shoulder blades. "Carrington, I wasn't expecting you."

"Isn't this rather tame sport for you, my dear?" he asked, gesturing to the cards and the mound of small coins. His voice was heavy with sarcasm, and the rage that he could barely contain flared in his eyes.

Two spots of color pricked her cheekbones and her scalp contracted as apprehension became absolute. She became aware of the uneasy shiftings around the table, the puzzled glances at Lord Carrington. "I've always liked party games," she offered, desperately trying to defuse whatever this was. "We've been enjoying ourselves famously." She appealed to the table at large.

"Oh, famously," Isobel agreed readily, gathering up her cards, her eyes warm and encouraging as she smiled at Judith. "Won't you join us, Lord Carrington?"

He shook his head with brusque discourtesy. "I wait only for my wife to make her excuses."

Only immediate compliance would end this mortification. Judith's head pounded as she pushed back her chair, picking up her reticule.

"You've forgotten your winnings," her husband said pointedly.

"They can go back in the pool." Judith thrust the shiny mound of coins into the middle of the table. Bidding her companions good night, she tried to smile as if nothing out of the ordinary were happening, but she could feel the stiffness of her lips and read in every eye both discomfort and consternation.

"Such winnings are too insignificant to be worth keeping, I assume," Marcus muttered against her ear as he drew her arm through his. Judith stiffened and would have withdrawn her arm, except that he tightened his grip, squeezing the limb against his body, so that to pull free would look like a struggle.

She couldn't think of anything that could safely be said in public, so she painted the stiff smile on her lips as they progressed through the rooms, bowed, made her farewells like a marionette obeying the puppeteer, and allowed herself to be removed in short order from the Herons' mansion and handed into the chaise, waiting ready at the door.

"What is all this about, Marcus?" To her annoyance, her voice shook, and she tried to deny that it was as much fear that produced the quaver as her own anger at the embarrassment he'd caused her.

"We will not discuss it here," he declared with icy finality.

"But I demand—"

"You will demand nothing."

There was such ferocity, such purpose, investing the statement that Judith was silenced. She shrank into a corner of the carriage, trying desperately to marshall her forces, to look for some clue to whatever had happened . . . to whatever was about to happen. Something dreadful had occurred. But what?

The chaise drew up in Berkeley Square. The coachman let down the footstep. Marcus sprang down and assisted Judith to alight. In silence, they entered the house, and the night porter locked and bolted the door behind them, bidding them good night.

"We will deal with this in my book room." Marcus's hand closed over Judith's shoulder as she moved toward the staircase.

There would be no waiting servants there, she realized. No one to dismiss before he could unburden himself of whatever weight of rage lay on his shoulders. She moved away from his hand, in the first gesture of independence she had managed since this debacle had begun, and walked ahead of him down the passage to the square room at the back of the house.

"Now, perhaps you'll tell me what this is all about?" Her hands shook now as she drew off her long silk gloves, finger by finger, but her voice was once more steady.

The deep nighttime silence of the sleeping house enclosed them, and for a minute Marcus didn't reply. He tossed his cane and gloves onto the table and poured himself a glass of cognac, trying to master his fury. When he spoke, his voice was relatively calm and distant.

"I've been extraordinarily naive, I freely admit. For some inexplicable and doubtless foolish reason I had assumed that once you'd achieved your goal by this marriage, you'd see no need to pursue your career at the gaming tables."

So that was it. Her lips were bloodless as she said, "When you made it clear you resented paying my expenses, I saw no alternative to paying for them myself. I prefer to do that anyway. I don't care to be dependent on a whimsical generosity, my lord."

"At no point did I say I resented paying your expenses. I did however say that as your husband, I would control your expenditure. My fortune is not at your unlimited disposal, although I now understand that you'd expected it to be." Ice tipped every loaded, humiliating word.

Judith felt herself diminishing into a small, hot ball of shame under the power of his contempt, and she fought to hold on to herself, to the essence of her pride and her knowledge of how wrong he was. "I don't and never did expect unlimited access to your money," she denied in a low voice. "But as your wife, I assumed I would be granted the dignity of an appearance of freedom, instead of being reduced to the status of a poor relation, or a child in the schoolroom, begging for pin money."

"And so in retaliation you choose to take money from my friends, to supplement an allowance you consider meager?"

"I do not *take* money from your friends . . . I win it!" she cried. "And I win it because I have the greater skill."

"You win it because you're a gamester—an adventuress, and you'll never be anything else," he declared bitterly. "I thought . . . God help me . . . I thought we were finding some truth on which to stand. But there is only one truth, isn't there, Judith? You're a manipulator and you will manipulate whoever comes your way, if they can be used to your advantage."

"No," she whispered, the cramping ache in her belly intensifying as her muscles clenched against the hateful words. She pressed her hands to her cheeks. "No, it's not like that."

"Oh, really?" His eyebrows lifted, black question marks in his dark face. "When did you decide that I would be the most useful recipient of your inestimable virtue, Judith? When you first saw me? Or did you decide later . . . even as late as when we were on the way to Quatre Bras, perhaps?"

"What are you saying?" Her eyes, huge with distress, stared at the mask of his face. "I don't understand what you're saying."

"Oh, then let me explain, my perverse and obtuse wife." He swung away from her, his fists clenched at his sides as he fought for control. He wanted to hurt her as she had hurt him, and he knew the potential power of the violence in his soul if he ever let slip the leash of control.

"When a virtuous woman loses her maidenhead dishonorably to an honorable man, she has a claim on that man. How difficult it must have been for you, reining in that passionate nature of yours, my dear, until your most precious bargaining chip found the highest bidder. Only the bidder didn't know what he was bidding for, did he? The bidder was offered the masquerade of an experienced adventuress, and only when it was too late did he discover the virgin."

Judith felt sick. Her body was one tightly clenched muscle and the nausea rose in her throat. This had never occurred to her. All this time, he believed she had deliberately led him on, offering the wiles of a wanton, in order to trap him with her virtue.

"No," she said, her voice barely audible. "It's not true. I never thought of my virginity when I was with you. I thought only of you . . . you must remember how that was . . . how it is now," she said in passionate appeal to the passion they shared. "How could you believe I could *pretend* to feel for you in that way? I don't know *how* one would pretend it." Tears clogged her throat and she forced them down.

Marcus barely heard her. He moved a hand in harsh dismissal. "You are a consummate actress," he said. "And I've watched you perform once too often. And what an amazing piece of good fortune, it must have been, when Francis and the others turned up so opportunely. It set the seal on the trap perfectly, didn't it?"

"No," she whispered again. "No, it wasn't like that." But her heart was leaden, and she was filled with tears of pain and bewilderment, and suddenly the fight went out of her. She bowed her head in defeat.

"You will now listen to me very carefully," Marcus was continuing. He articulated each word with a slow emphasis that served as much to keep a rein on his rage as it did to increase the force of his speech. "Since, for better or worse, you *are* my wife, you will begin to behave like my wife. You're not to be trusted, so I shall take responsibility for correcting your faults myself. From this moment on, outside this house, you will play only whist and limited loo. From now on, I shall watch you: every move you make." He began to count off on his fingers. "You will accept no engagement without my express permission; and you will enter a card room only in my company; and if I ever find you seated at any table other than a loo table or a whist table, then I shall oblige you to leave immediately, regardless of the embarrassment this will cause you. Do you understand?"

"Oh, yes," Judith said softly. He was going to make a prison of their marriage with himself as her jailer.

"Furthermore," he continued coldly, "you will ask for my approval before you buy anything. I shall want to know what you wish to purchase, why it's necessary, and its cost. I'll then rule on whether you may do so or not. You'll not take advantage of me ever again, Judith." There was a bleakness in his voice now, and he turned away from her, going to the long French door and pulling aside the curtain, gazing out into the starless night.

He heard the door close quietly and knew that Judith had left the room. He could hear his voice, the harsh, punitive statements, the bleakness of betrayal beneath the cold fury. They faced a lifetime together . . . a lifetime of misery for both of them. And now he wished more than he had ever wished for anything that he'd never set eyes on her. Because knowing her from now on could only bring intensified pain. He had begun to love her, but he'd been loving a chimera.

He refilled his brandy goblet and tossed the mellow golden liquid down his throat in one swallow, then he went up to his own apartment. A sleepy Cheveley jumped up from a chair beside the fire. "I trust you had a pleasant evening, my lord."

"I don't remember passing a worse," Marcus replied, wearily. The valet closed his mouth and devoted his single-minded attention to the task of putting his lordship to bed.

Next door, Judith sat on the bed, waiting. She had sent Millie to bed as soon as she'd come up and had then locked the door behind the maid, before turning the key on the connecting door. Now she listened to the soft shufflings and footfalls from next door, waiting until she heard Cheveley bid his lordship good night and the door close on his departure.

She sat hunched over the woman's pain in her belly and the shank of despair driven deep into her soul. There was no future here. The life Marcus had just decreed couldn't be lived by either of them.

The line of yellow beneath the connecting door vanished as Marcus extinguished his bedside candle. Judith stood up, straightening her aching body with a low moan. She removed her evening dress and put on a riding habit, treading softly about the room, opening drawers and armoires with exaggerated care. Into a small valise, she packed her hairbrushes, nightclothes, tooth powder, and a change of clothes. It would do to be going on with, and anything else she needed, she would buy later.

She knew only that she could no longer stay under the same roof as Marcus. Leaving him so precipitately would ruin everything with Gracemere, but she could see no option. Sebastian would understand and they'd come up with an alternative plan.

But never had she felt so desolate, or so at a loss. She couldn't stay with him, but why then was leaving him as agonizing as peeling away a layer of skin?

Delicately she turned the key and let herself out of the room. In the corridor, where a dim light came from a single candle in a wall sconce, she paused, listening. The only sounds were the creaks and rustles of the sleeping house. She crept down the stairs, still hunched over the dragging pain in her belly, and turned down the passage leading to the book room. This was not an exit to be made through the front door.

She opened the French doors and stepped into the garden, closing them quietly at her back. The gate in the wall led into the mews. Horses whickered, hooves shuffled on straw as she moved in the shadows across the swept cobbles of the yard. The stablehands wouldn't start work for another hour and Judith had the sense of being the only human awake in the whole of London town. It occurred to her that it was perhaps foolhardy to walk the streets alone in the dark hour before dawn, and her hand closed over her pistol.

It was less than a ten-minute walk, however, to Albemarle Street, and she saw no one. Sebastian's rooms were on the ground floor, and she stood on tiptoe to tap at the window. If she had to use the knocker the landlord would answer the summons and it would be hard to explain herself at such an hour. She raised her hand to tap again, when the front door opened.

"Come in, Ju," Sebastian whispered.

"How did you know it was me?" She slipped past him into the dark passageway.

"Somehow I was expecting you," he replied, picking up her valise and gesturing to the sitting room.

"I didn't wake you, then."

"No, I was waiting for you." He set down her valise and examined her carefully. "You look the very devil. Brandy?"

"Please." She threw off her cloak and drew off her gloves. "Thank you." Cradling the glass in her hands, she went to the hearth, where the ashy glow of the embers of the dying fire put out a modicum of heat.

Her brother took kindling from the basket beside the grate and tossed it onto the embers. A reassuring hiss and spurt of flame resulted. He straightened, regarding his sister with sharp-eyed concern. She sipped her brandy, stroking her stomach in an unconscious gesture he recognized as the fiery spirit warmed her cramping muscles. "You're not feeling too well," he stated.

She gave him a wan smile of agreement. "To add insult to injury."

"So, what did he do?"

"How did you know . . . ? Oh, did you tell him?"

"He wanted to repay me for your turn-out. I told him you'd paid for it yourself. He made the correct deduction. Carrington's no fool, Ju."

"I never took him for one," she said. Bleakly she recounted the scene in the book room, leaving nothing out. Sebastian listened in grim silence. It occurred to him that his brother-in-law had shown about as much sensibility as a herd of rogue elephants.

"So where do you want to go?" he asked, when she'd fallen silent.

"Some small hotel, perhaps."

"In London?"

"Yes, but in an unfashionable part; somewhere where I won't run the risk of meeting anyone I know on the street."

"Kensington . . . Bloomsbury?"

"Either . . . look, I know this ruins everything, but—"

"Not necessarily," her brother said. "We'll work out something. But at the moment, you've got to sort yourself out. We'll find somewhere for you to stay first thing in the morning." He put down his glass. "You can have the bedroom, I'll sleep on the sofa."

"No, I don't mind sleeping in here."

"Oh, Ju, don't be a bore." He picked up her valise. "Apart from the fact that you've got the bellyache, there's no need to be so tiresomely independent with me. You'll sleep in the bed and I'll be perfectly happy on the sofa. We've both slept in many more uncomfortable places in our time."

Judith gave him a ruefully apologetic smile. "Sorry. I seem to have lost the power of cool thought tonight."

He smiled and kissed her cheek. "Hardly surprising."

Judith followed him into the bedroom. "I suppose it's possible Marcus might knock on your door at some point."

"Highly likely, I would have thought," her brother agreed with a dry smile. "He can hardly pretend you never existed."

"No, but I expect he wishes he could."

Sebastian shook his head. "I admit it looks bad at the moment, but things change with time and distance."

"I can't go back," she said, pulling back the coverlet.

"No," he said neutrally. "I suppose not." He took her hands. "You're worn to a frazzle, love. We'll work something out."

"Of course we will. We always do," she assented, with a conviction she didn't truly feel. She reached up to kiss him. "Thank you."

"Sleep well."

Judith crept into bed and, despite unhappiness and uncertainty, fell instantly into the deep sleep of total, emotional exhaustion.

21

MARCUS SLEPT FITFULLY AND WOKE LEADEN WITH DEPRESSION. HE LAY IN THE big bed contemplating the bleak prospect of his marriage. After such a confrontation, after the things that had been said, he could see no possibility of anything other than a frigid, armed truce between them from now on. He knew that he would always be suspecting her of some ulterior motive, of employing some strategy to take advantage of him. He'd never again be able to trust in her responses or in her emotions . . . not even in bed. And he would watch her like a hawk. He would control every aspect of her life as it impinged upon him. And Judith's bitter resistance would fuel the vicious circle of mistrust.

He dragged himself out of bed in the cheerless dawn and padded softly to the connecting door. The handle turned but the door was locked. It didn't surprise him, but it angered him. He intended from now on that her life should be open to his inspection at all times, and he would not tolerate locked doors.

He went out into the passage to the outside door. This one opened, but the room when he stepped into it was empty. He stood in disbelief for a minute, trying to order his tumbling thoughts and a sudden morass of responses that couldn't yet be named. The bed had not been slept in, drawers stood open, their contents disturbed as if someone had gone through them in haste. The armoire was open. Judith's hairbrushes were no longer on the dressing table.

She had gone. At first, the stark recognition made no sense. His mind couldn't grasp the fact that Judith had left him. He caught and hung onto the simplest aspect: the public consequences of such an action. The response to this was equally simple: a surge of renewed anger. How dare she do such a thing? Put him in such a position? How could he possibly explain his wife's dead-of-night flight to the servants? How could he possibly explain her absence to the rest of the world? It was a piece of cowardly avoidance, something he would never have expected of Judith.

Furiously he unlocked the connecting door and stormed into his own apartment, pulling the bellrope for Cheveley.

"Her ladyship has gone into the country," he said curtly when his valet appeared. "She had news of a sick aunt and was obliged to leave immediately. Inform Millie of that fact, will you?"

"Yes, m'lord." Cheveley was far too good at keeping his feelings to himself to show the slightest surprise at this extraordinary information. He assisted his lordship into his clothes and stood patiently with a large supply of cravats in case the first attempts were unsuccessful. But the marquis seemed easily satisfied this morning and spent less than five minutes on the intricacies of cravat-tying.

He slipped a Sevres snuff box into his pocket and stalked downstairs to the breakfast parlor, throwing over his shoulder, "Gregson, have my curricle brought around."

Gregson bowed at the terse instruction.

The marquis marched into the breakfast parlor, closing the door with a controlled slam. He poured himself coffee, helped himself to a dish of eggs, fragrant with fresh herbs, and sat at the table. Slowly the conflicting emotions wrestling each other for precedence began to sort themselves out. He sipped coffee, staring sightlessly across the table, his eggs cooling in front of him. He had to find her and bring her back, of course. Whatever lay between them, whatever future they might have, she was still his wife, whether she liked it or not. Devious, scheming adventuress or not, she was his wife, whether he liked it or not. And by God, when he found her . . .

He pushed back his chair abruptly and went to the window. It was a bright morning, a hoar frost glittering on the grass. He was furious with her for putting him in this situation, but there was more to it than that. Yes, she had to come back. The scandal otherwise would be unthinkable. But he had felt more than anger when he'd stood in the doorway of her empty room . . . a room out of which all the spirit seemed to have been leeched. Even the house felt different, as if it had lost some vital presence that gave it life. Slowly he forced himself to name what he had felt as he'd stood in the doorway. He had felt the terror of loss. He felt it now, pushing up through the anger. There was no other way of describing it.

He began to pace the parlor, trying to work out what this meant. Did it mean that her deceptions didn't matter? Did it mean he was willing to endure being used, if it was the price of her presence in his life? Or did it simply mean he was willing to rescind the punishment if Judith would offer her own compromises? Could they start afresh? What was he terrified of losing—the potential for love or the certainty of lust?

He heard her laugh—that wicked, sensual chuckle in his head—and the sound winded him. He felt her body under his hands, as if in some sensuously vivid dream. He could smell the delicate, lavender-scented freshness of her skin. The burnished copper head, the great golden-brown eyes, shimmered in his internal vision. But it wasn't just that, was it? It was Judith herself. Judith with her tempestuous spirit, her needle wit, her acerbic tongue, her delicious sense of humor. Judith of the lynx pride and ferocious independence. It was the woman who carried a pistol, who didn't buckle under adversity, who didn't think twice about slaving amid the gory detritus of a battlefield, who took responsibility for herself.

It was the woman he had thought he needed to lash into submission. The foolishness of such a misguided intention now brought a sardonic curve to his mouth. Whatever she was, whatever she had been, she belonged to him. And for some perverse reason, despite the scheming and the deceit, she seemed to be what he wanted. And if that was the case, then he'd have to try to modify the bad with rather more subtlety than he'd shown so far, and what he couldn't change he'd have to accept.

But first he had to retrieve her. The initial step was obvious. If it failed, the next was less obvious.

Gregson announced that his lordship's curricle was at the door. "Thank you. Lady Carrington has gone into the country to visit a sick aunt."

"Yes, my lord, so I understand from Cheveley. Do we know when her ladyship will return?"

"When the sick aunt is recovered, I assume," Marcus snapped, thrusting his arms into the many-caped driving coat held by Gregson.

He drove to Albemarle Street. It was eleven o'clock, hopefully too early for Sebastian to have left his lodgings. He was right, to a certain extent, in that his quarry was seated at breakfast, having returned to his lodgings after an early-morning journey to Kensington.

"Good morning, Marcus." Sebastian rose from the table as his servant announced his brother-in-law. "Breakfast?" He gestured to the laden table.

"No, I've already breakfasted. Where is she, Sebastian?"

"I thought that was probably the purpose of your call." Sebastian resumed his seat. "You don't mind if I continue . . . ?"

Marcus slapped at his Hessians with his driving whip. "I haven't got all day, Sebastian. *Where is she?*"

"Well, there's the difficulty," his host murmured, taking up a tankard of ale. "I can't say, you see."

"She came to you, of course?"

"Of course." He took a draft of ale.

Marcus glanced around the room. If Judith was anywhere in the vicinity, he would know it, would feel it in his bones and through his skin. She had that effect on him, and it was getting stronger the longer he lived with her. He knew she was no longer in her brother's lodgings.

"If you don't mind my saying so, you seem to have been rather unsubtle," Sebastian observed, spearing a deviled kidney.

"I'm willing to concede that," Marcus said. "But the provocation was overpowering."

Sebastian frowned. He'd been thinking things through for many hours now, ever since his sister had fallen asleep. He hadn't said anything to her, but he had come to the conclusion that a degree of interference might be in her best interests. Of course, putting Judith's marriage together again would be in his best interests also. He couldn't destroy Gracemere without her help, and until Gracemere was dealt with, he couldn't make a formal offer for Harriet. He'd had to wrestle with the issues for a long time before he satisfied himself that what he was going to do would be certainly as much for Judith as it would be for himself.

"If you hadn't jumped to conclusions in the first place, there'd have been no need for Ju to offer you provocation," he said deliberately.

"Perhaps you'd like to explain." Marcus sat down, flicking at his boot with his whip, his eyes resting on his brother-in-law with an arrested expression.

"Ju had no idea who was in the taproom at that inn, after you and she had . . ." Sebastian waved a hand in lieu of completing the sentence.

Marcus was suddenly very still. "But she said she did."

"Did she? You sure about that?" Sebastian buttered a piece of toast without looking at his visitor.

Marcus thought. He'd asked her in that little loft on the morning of Waterloo, and she'd said . . . but no, she hadn't said anything at all. He'd asked her and she hadn't denied it.

"If it wasn't true, why wouldn't she deny it?"

"Well, you'd have to understand Ju and her eccentric principles rather better than you do to see that," her brother declared. "She'd be so insulted that you could have suspected her of such an under-hand trick that she wouldn't see any point defending herself."

"Are you telling me that all these months, she could have put my mind at rest with a single word and she deliberately chose not to?"

Sebastian nodded. It was a little more complicated than that, but he couldn't explain to Marcus that Judith had seen little difference between the accusation of manipulation and the truth of opportunism. The difference, however, struck her brother as crucial in the present turmoil. "You shouldn't have suspected such a thing of her," he said simply.

Marcus closed his eyes on a surge of exasperation that for the moment prevented his unhampered joy as he laid down the burden of mistrust. "It was not an unnatural suspicion, knowing how you and your sister were living," he pointed out after a minute.

"Oh, I beg to differ," Sebastian said. "You made a false deduction from the premise. You hardly knew her." He glanced across at Marcus. "The other matter, too," he said. "Rather delicate, but you had no grounds for—"

"All right," Marcus interrupted, a spot of color burning on his cheek. "There's no need to expand. I know what you're referring to. If your sister hadn't been ruled by that damnable lynx pride of hers, all of this could have been avoided." He slashed at his boot. "I'm not prepared to assume total responsibility for this, Sebastian."

"No," Sebastian agreed, taking up his tankard again. He drank deeply. "So what are you going to do when you find her?"

"Wring her neck and throw her body in the Serpentine," Marcus said promptly.

Sebastian chuckled and shook his head. "That might defeat the object of reconciliation."

Marcus stood up abruptly. "Damn it, Sebastian, where is she?"

Sebastian shook his head. "I'm afraid I can't help you, Marcus."

"You know where she is, though?"

Sebastian nodded. "But I'm sworn to secrecy."

Marcus regarded him through narrowed eyes, tapping the silver knob of his whip against the palm of one hand. "I daresay you'll be seeing her at some point today."

"Yes." There was cool comprehension in Sebastian's eyes.

Marcus inclined his head in acknowledgment and walked to the door. "Thank you, Sebastian."

The door closed on his visitor. Sebastian pushed his chair back from the table and stretched out his long legs. Judith would probably be annoyed at his interference, but he felt as if he'd just done some good work. He was fairly certain his sister's feelings for Marcus Devlin went deeper than she had so far been prepared to acknowledge. And Marcus, for all his autocratic temperament, felt a great deal more for Judith than he might have demonstrated.

Maybe it took a man in love to recognize the signs in others, Sebastian reflected complacently. He'd give Marcus time to set his spy in place before he went himself to see Judith.

Marcus drove his curricle round to the mews. "Where's Tom, Timkins?"

The head groom took the reins as they were tossed to him. "In the tack room, m'lord. Shall I fetch him?"

"Please."

A minute later a lad of about fourteen came hurrying across the cobbles, wiping his palms against his leather apron. "You wanted me, m'lord."

"Yes, I have a task for you." Marcus gave the boy his instructions. Tom received them in silence, nodding his head now and again to indicate comprehension. "Is that quite clear, Tom? I'm sure he'll be expecting someone on his tail and he won't try to throw you off, but I don't want you to make it obvious."

"Don't you worry, m'lord. Thinner than 'is shadow I'll be." The lad grinned cheerfully. "I could pick 'is pocket and the cove'd not know it."

"I'm sure you could," Marcus agreed. "But I beg you won't give in to the temptation."

Tom was an accomplished pickpocket, who two years earlier had had the great good fortune to pick the marquis's pocket in the crowd at a prize fight. Carrington hadn't realized his watch had gone, until an observant spectator had set up the cry of "pickpocket." The terror in the child's eyes as he'd been collared had had a powerful effect on Marcus, who'd suddenly seen the small body hanging from a scaffold in Newgate Yard. He'd taken him in charge over the protestations of the irate citizens, handed him over to his head groom with the instructions that he be taught the consequences of theft in no uncertain fashion, and then set to work. Tom had been his most devoted employee ever since, evincing a degree of intelligence that certainly qualified him for a task such as this.

The search put in motion, there was nothing to do but wait. He retreated to his book room, wondering how to apportion the blame for the misunderstanding that had caused so much grief. They both bore some responsibility, but when he turned the cold, clear eyes of honesty on the question, he was obliged to accept that he had thrown the first stone.

The barouche drew up outside a tall, well-maintained house in Cambridge Gardens, North Kensington, and three women descended, looking about them with the curiosity of those on unfamiliar territory. Kensington was a perfectly respectable place, of course, but unfashionable and definitely not frequented by the ton.

"What a strange place for Judith to choose," observed Isobel.

"What a strange thing for her to choose to do," Cornelia responded with more point, as she lifted the hem of her dress and shook ineffectually at some clinging substance. "How did that get there?" She directed a hostile stare at the material, as if it alone were responsible for its less than immaculate appearance.

Neither of her friends bothered to answer the clearly rhetorical question. "Walk the horses, we shall be about an hour," Sally instructed her coachman, before raising the knocker on the blue-painted door.

"It doesn't seem like a hotel." Isobel's experience of hotels was limited to establishments such as Brown's or Grillon's.

However, the door was promptly opened by a maidservant, who

asserted that it was indeed Cunningham's Hotel, and Mrs. Cunningham would be with them directly.

Mrs. Cunningham was a respectable female in shiny bombazine, all affability as she welcomed three such clear members of the Quality to her establishment.

"We are visiting Lady—" Cornelia stopped as Sally trod on her toe.

"Mrs. Devlin," Sally put in swiftly. "We understand that Mrs. Devlin is staying here." Judith's note, delivered to Sally by Sebastian, had warned them she was staying at Cunningham's Hotel under Marcus's family name.

"Oh, yes." Mrs Cunningham's smile broadened. "She has the best suite at the back—nice and quiet it is, as she wanted, looking over the garden. Dora will take you up and I'll have some tea sent up."

They followed the maidservant upstairs and along a corridor to double doors at the rear of the house.

Judith was sitting in a chair by the window, in front of a chess board, when her friends entered. She sprang up with a glad cry. "Oh, how good of you all to come. I was feeling thoroughly sorry for myself and horribly lonely."

"But of course we would come," Sally said, looking around the sitting room. It was pleasant enough, but nothing to the yellow drawing room in Berkeley Square. "Whatever are you about, Judith? Your note didn't explain, and Sebastian wouldn't say anything."

"Thinking," Judith replied. "That's what I'm about, but so far I haven't come up with any sensible thoughts . . . or even comforting ones," she added.

"Well, what's happened?" Cornelia sat on the sofa. "Why are you in this place?"

"It's a perfectly pleasant place," Judith said. "I have a large bedroom as well as the sitting room, and the woman who owns it is very attentive—"

"Yes, but why are you here?" Isobel interrupted this irrelevant defense of the accommodations.

Judith sighed. "Marcus and I had a dreadful fight. I had to get away somewhere quiet to think."

"You left your husband?" Even Cornelia was shaken. "You just walked out and came here?"

"In a nutshell. Marcus has forbidden my gaming and intends to control every penny I spend." Judith fiddled with the chess pieces as she told as much of the story as she could without revealing Brussels. "So, since I can't possibly accept such edicts," she finished, "and Marcus is determined that I will obey him, what else could I do?"

Isobel shook her head, saying doubtfully, "It seems a bit extreme. Husbands do demand obedience as a matter of course. One has to find a way around it."

The maidservant brought tea. "Mrs. Cunningham wants to know if you'd like some bread and butter, ma'am? Or cake?"

"Cake," Isobel said automatically, and Judith chuckled, feeling a little more cheerful. She'd been fighting waves of desolation all day . . . desolation and guilt, whenever she thought of how that moment of willful passion on the road to Quatre Bras had ruined all their carefully laid plans. And Sebastian had so far uttered not a word of reproach.

"But what are you going to do, Judith?" Sally asked, having sat in silence for some time, absorbing the situation.

"I don't know," Judith said truthfully.

"But you can't just disappear. How would Marcus explain that?" Sally persisted. "The family . . ." She stopped with a helpless shrug. The might and prestige of the Devlin family were perhaps more apparent to her than to Judith. She'd been married into it for five years. The thought of damaging that prestige, of inviting the wrath of that might, sent a fearful shudder down her spine.

"Maybe I'll just be conveniently dead," Judith said. For some reason, the thought of her mother came to her. Her mother had died quietly in a French convent, leaving barely a ripple on the surface of the world . . . if you didn't count two children.

"Judith!" Cornelia protested. "Don't talk like that."

"Oh, I don't mean *really* dead," she explained. "I'll disappear and Marcus can put it about that I've died of typhus, or a riding accident, or some such."

"You're mad," Sally pronounced. "If you believe for one minute that the Devlin family will let you get away with that, you don't know anything about them."

Judith chewed her lip for a minute. She had a horrible feeling that Sally was probably right. "I'm not thinking clearly at the moment," she said finally. "I'll worry about the details later. Tell me some gossip. I feel so isolated at the moment."

"Oh, there's a famous story going around about Hester Stanning," Isobel said. "I had it from Godfrey Chauncet." She lowered her voice confidentially.

Judith listened to the on-dit with half an ear, her mind working on some way in which she could still play her part with Gracemere. Maybe, for the denouement, Sebastian could arrange a private card party and she could make an unexpected appearance . . .

"Don't you think that's funny, Judith?"

"Oh . . . yes . . . yes, very funny." She returned to the room with a jolt.

"You weren't listening," Isobel accused, eyeing the chocolate cake that Dora had brought in. "I wonder if I dare have another piece. It's really very good."

Judith cut another slice for her. "I was listening," she said.

"When you fight with Carrington, do you lose your temper?" Cornelia asked with the air of one who'd been pondering the question for some time.

The question brought such a wave of longing washing through her that Judith was for a moment silent, lost in the memories of the times when they'd fought tooth and nail and then made up with ferocious need. "Yes," she admitted. "I have a dreadful temper, and so does Marcus."

"Good heavens," Cornelia said. "I can't imagine Forsythe losing his temper. I wonder if I should try to provoke it. It might add a bit of excitement to life."

Judith couldn't help laughing. "You're too level-headed and

even-tempered, Cornelia. You'd start arguing with yourself instead of your husband, because you'd immediately see the other point of view."

After her visitors had left, she sat in the gloom of late afternoon. Cornelia and Sally and Isobel really didn't understand. They'd stand by her, of course. They'd keep her company and keep her secret, but they couldn't begin to understand what would drive a woman to take such a desperate stance. Never having tasted freedom—the sometimes uncomfortable freedom of life outside Society—they couldn't imagine doing anything so drastic. Judith didn't blame them for it. On the contrary, she envied the simplicity and security of their lives.

It was getting dark, but she didn't ring for Dora to light the candles. The growing shadows suited her mood and she could feel herself sliding deeper and deeper into a pit of wretchedness. She hurt every time she remembered what Marcus had said to her, what he believed her to be, every time she recalled that, believing such things of her, he had still made love to her in the way he had, with such trust, such honesty, such absolute oneness with her in body and spirit. She had entrusted herself to him in those moments, as he had entrusted himself to her. And yet all the time . . .

A knock at the door shattered the grim cycle of her thoughts. Sebastian entered, and she blinked in the near darkness.

"Why are you sitting in the dark?" He struck flint against tinder and lit the branched candlestick on the table. He subjected his sister to a comprehending scrutiny, one that confirmed his suspicions and satisfied him that he'd done the right thing that morning.

"I thought you might like some company for dinner," he said, as if he didn't notice her pallor or the sheen of tears in her eyes. "Mrs. Cunningham informs me that she has a carp in parsley sauce and a boiled fowl with mushrooms. Sounds quite appetizing, I thought."

Judith managed to blink back her tears. "Thank you, Sebastian," she said with composure. "I was dreading a solitary dinner."

"I rather thought that might be the case." He bent to kiss her. "Blue-deviled?"

"An understatement," she said. "What are we going to do about Gracemere?"

"It's not important at the moment." He pulled the chess board over to the fire. "We'll work something out once you've recovered your equilibrium."

"But—"

"Which hand?" Sebastian interrupted, offering his clenched fists.

"I only want—"

"Which hand?" he repeated.

Judith pointed to his left. He opened it to reveal the black pawn.

"Oh, good, I have the advantage," he said cheerfully, sitting behind the white pieces. "Sit down, Ju, and stop looking like a week of wet Mondays."

She sat down and watched him move his pawn to king four. She moved her own in response. "Have you seen Marcus?" She tried to keep the quaver from her voice.

"He paid me a visit this morning." He moved up his queen's pawn.

She made the ritual responding move. "What did he say?"

Sebastian examined the neat center arrangement of four pawns. "He wanted to know where you were." He brought out his knight.

Judith moved her own knight and they exchanged pawns. "What did you say?"

"That I was sworn to secrecy." Sebastian sat back. The ritual opening moves made, the real play would begin.

"Was he angry?"

"Not pleased," her brother said, bringing his queen's bishop into play. "But then you wouldn't expect him to put his neck under your foot, would you?"

"I'd expect him to be more understanding," she snapped, hunching over the board. "He makes no effort to understand me."

"Oh, I wouldn't say that," Sebastian said judiciously, waiting for his sister to make her move. "I think on the whole he has a fairly good handle on you, Ju."

"How can you say that?" Judith's hand hovered over her knight.

"He knows damn well that if he allows you to ride roughshod over him, you'll have no relationship at all," Sebastian said. "Be honest, Ju. Do you want some nodcock for a husband, a man who couldn't stand up to you?"

"No," she said. "Of course not. But why do we have to stand up to each other, Sebastian? That's what I don't understand."

Her brother shrugged. "It's the kind of people you are. I don't think you're going to change that, quite frankly."

"Harriet won't stand up to you," she observed.

"She won't have to," he responded promptly. "I won't give her cause. I intend to become a country bumpkin—a squire, devoted to farming and hunting and my children."

"Yes, because when you and Harriet make your vows, you'll do it without deception," Judith said, bitterness lacing her words. "You'll be the person she believes you to be. She'll know nothing of father, of Gracemere . . . and she'll never have to know. All of that will be in the past forever. It won't come back to destroy your marriage before it's ever really begun." Her voice choked and she turned aside from the board. "I'm sorry."

Sebastian handed her his handkerchief. He had no doubts now that his interference had been justified. "Make your move, Ju," he said, indicating the board. "It's true that my marriage would be founded on something different from yours, but maybe you could move beyond that with Marcus. Once it's all over—"

"How could I possibly?" she exclaimed. "And how can you talk like this anyway? After what he believes, what he's said, what he intends to do . . . ?"

"I know," Sebastian said soothingly. "It's insupportable, I agree. I was thinking you might consider going to that little village in Bavaria, where the Helwigs are. They invited you to stay with them whenever you wished. It might tide you over an awkward few months."

"Yes," Judith agreed, wondering why Sebastian's company was so irritating. She couldn't remember ever before finding it so.

It was close to midnight when he left. Young Tom, shivering in a doorway opposite, heaved a sigh of relief.

Surveillance was a tedious business, he reckoned, setting off after the gentleman-cove in the beaver hat and long cloak. It involved hanging around for hours outside houses and clubs, going without his dinner in case the cove came out unexpectedly. However, he could take his lordship unerringly to every one of the places visited by his quarry.

Sebastian hailed a passing hackney and the jarvey pulled over immediately. If Sebastian was aware of the nonpaying passenger clinging to the back of the carriage as it swung through the quiet streets of nighttime London, he gave no sign.

Tom sprang off as the carriage turned into Albemarle Street. It seemed his quarry was going home for the night, which left his follower free to make his report to his lordship, and hopefully find some supper in the kitchen, before seeking his own bed above the stables.

Marcus had had no stomach for company that evening and had remained by his own fireside, trying to divert his thoughts with Caesar's *Gallic Wars.* The diversion was only minimally successful since he found contemplation of the war in his own back garden to be much more compelling.

The library door opened. "Young Tom is here to see you, my lord."

"Send him in, Gregson."

Tom came in on the words. "Take your cap off, lad," Gregson directed in an outraged whisper. Stableboys were not usual library visitors.

Tom snatched off his cap and stood awkwardly, twisting it between his hands. "The cove's gone 'ome to 'is bed, m'lord," he offered in explanation for his end of duty. "I thought as 'ow you'd like me report straightway."

"I would, indeed. Have you had your dinner?"

"No, m'lord. I didn't know as 'ow I could leave the doorway . . . although the cove stayed put all evening," he added, somewhat aggrieved.

"Gregson, make sure there's a good supper waiting for him in the kitchen," Marcus instructed.

The butler bowed himself out in silence, and if he felt discommoded by being instructed to see to the welfare of a stablehand he managed to keep it hidden.

"So, Tom, what have you to report?"

Tom faithfully detailed Sebastian's movements throughout the day. Uninterestingly routine for the most part: Jackson's saloon, Watier's, Viscount Middleton's lodgings, a drive in the park. However, the gem came at the shank of the rigidly chronicled day.

"Kensington, you say?" Marcus looked into the deep ruby depths of his glass of port. It sounded promising . . . unless Sebastian kept a mistress there. But Sebastian was in love with Harriet Moreton, and Marcus didn't think his brother-in-law would deem a mistress compatible with courtship, despite his unorthodox life-style.

"I could take you there, m'lord."

"Tomorrow will be soon enough, Tom. Get to your dinner now. You've done well."

Beaming, Tom left the library, basking in his god's approval that made an empty belly and the long hours of shivering in doorways well worth while.

Marcus threw another log on the fire and refilled his glass. Tomorrow he would retrieve his wife, and he'd make damn sure he hung onto her from now on.

22

MARCUS WAS UP EARLY THE NEXT MORNING, AND WITHIN MINUTES THE household was scurrying under a barrage of orders. Gregson was informed that his lordship was going into the country for a couple of weeks. Cheveley and Millie were instructed to pack for their employers and then to travel immediately to Berkshire. The traveling chaise with two outriders was ordered to be at the door by ten o'clock.

Marcus then strode down to the breakfast parlor, a distinct spring in his step. He was addressing a platter of sirloin when Charlie precipitately entered the parlor.

Marcus looked up in surprise, a smile of greeting on his lips. It died as he recognized Charlie's air of somewhat defensive bellicosity. It was a look he'd worn as a child when he considered his guardian guilty of some injustice and had screwed up his courage for a confrontation.

"What's to do, Charlie?" Marcus asked, without preamble.

"Where's Judith?" his young cousin demanded. "Gregson says she's gone to look after a sick aunt, but she doesn't have an aunt . . . sick or otherwise—at least not in England."

"Oh, how do you know that?" Marcus inquired calmly, refilling his coffee cup.

"Because she told me," Charlie stated. He glared at Marcus. "So where is she?"

"Sit down," Marcus said, gesturing to a chair. "And stop glowering at me, Charlie."

"I don't want to sit down," Charlie said. "I want to know where Judith is. I saw her yesterday and she didn't say she was going anywhere."

"Does she give you a report on all her movements?" Marcus asked gently.

Charlie's neck reddened and his scowl deepened. "Of course not, but she wouldn't go off without telling me. I know it."

Marcus sighed. "So what are you suggesting? You're surely not accusing me of disposing of her in some way, are you?" His eyebrows lifted quizzically.

Charlie's flush deepened at the sardonic question. "No, of course not . . . only . . . only . . ."

"Yes?" Marcus prompted.

"Only maybe you upset her in some way," his cousin blurted out. "I know how deuced cutting you can be when you're displeased."

Marcus frowned. "Am I really that unpleasant in our dealings, Charlie? I intend only to stand your friend."

"Yes, I know." Charlie fiddled with a fork on the table, in evident embarrassment. "It's just that you're devilish strict in some things, and you've a rough tongue that can make a fellow feel like a worm."

Marcus winced at this plain speaking, but was obliged to acknowledge there was some justice in the complaint. He examined his cousin thoughtfully. This couldn't be easy for Charlie, who was never comfortable asserting himself. Judith certainly had the power to inspire loyalty and friendship. He wondered why he hadn't been struck before by the strength of the attachments she'd formed in the few short months since she'd been in London.

"I only want to ensure that you have a fortune to come into when you reach your majority," he said mildly.

"But where's Judith?" Charlie sat down abruptly and stabbed at a rasher of bacon with the fork. "She's not hurt, is she?"

Marcus shook his head. "Not as far as I know, Charlie. And certainly not at my hands, if that's what you're thinking."

Charlie chewed bacon and swallowed. "But where is she?"

Marcus sighed. "In Kensington. But we're going to Carrington Manor today for a couple of weeks."

"Kensington?" Charlie's amazement was as great as if his cousin had said Judith was on the moon. "Whatever for?"

"Now that I'm afraid is a secret I'm not prepared to divulge," Marcus said firmly. "I appreciate your concern, Charlie, but I have to tell you that it's a matter that lies between Judith and myself. I don't mean to snub you, or to be in the least harsh, but I'm afraid it's none of your business."

Charlie stabbed a grilled mushroom from the serving platter. "But she's all right?"

"Yes, Charlie. She's perfectly all right." Marcus smiled, watching with great amusement his cousin's careless, unconscious consumption of a considerable breakfast.

"Oh, well, that's all right then." Charlie heaved a sigh of relief. "I didn't mean to pry, but, well, you know how it is with Judith . . . a fellow can't help worrying about her."

Marcus nodded. "Yes, Charlie, I know just how it is. Now, if you'll excuse me, I have things to do, so I'll leave you to your breakfast."

"Oh, I don't want breakfast," Charlie said. "I breakfasted in my lodgings before I came."

"Really? I wonder how I could have thought otherwise." Laughing, Marcus flung an affectionate arm around his cousin and squeezed his shoulders.

A short while later, he emerged from the house and climbed into the waiting chaise with the Carrington crest emblazoned on the panels.

Tom scrambled onto the box beside the coachman and proceeded to direct him through the streets to Cambridge Gardens.

Marcus stepped out and stood for a minute looking around the quiet crescent, then up at Judith's hideaway: a discreet, modest accommodation patronized by solid burghers and their ladies, he decided, stepping up to the door.

Mrs. Cunningham gazed from her front room window at the magnificent emblazoned equipage, with its two outriders, drawing up at her doorstep. Its tall, elegant occupant in buckskins and top boots, a cloak thrown carelessly around his shoulders, jumped down and stood looking at the house for a minute before approaching the front door.

"Dora . . . Dora . . . the door, immediately!" she called, smoothing down her skirt as she billowed into the hall to greet her visitor.

Dora flung open the door before Marcus could touch the door knocker. "Good morning, sir."

"Good morning," he said with a pleasant smile, seeing the ample figure of Mrs. Cunningham behind the maid. "I understand you have a lady residing—"

"Oh, yes, sir, Mrs. Devlin, sir," Mrs. Cunningham supplied helpfully. This gentleman could only be inquiring after *one* of her guests.

"Ah . . . Mrs. Devlin," Marcus murmured with another smile. He'd been fairly certain Judith wouldn't have registered under Lady Carrington and had been wondering if this would present him with any problem. But the eagerly helpful landlady had resolved his difficulty.

"And is she in?" he inquired, when the landlady seemed uncertain how to proceed.

"Oh, yes, sir. She has a lady with her, I believe."

Marcus frowned at this, wondering who could be visiting Judith here. "Perhaps you'll show me up."

"Yes . . . yes . . . of course, sir. Dora, escort the gentleman."

"Thank you." Marcus moved to the staircase, then paused, one hand on the newel post. "Lady Carrington will be leaving immediately. If you would have her account made up, I'll settle it directly."

Lady Carrington! Confusion and excitement played over Mrs.

Cunningham's countenance. "But, sir, nothing was said by Mrs. Dev —I mean, Lady . . ."

Marcus held up a hand, halting the tangle of protestation. "Nevertheless, ma'am, Lady Carrington will be leaving directly. I am Lord Carrington, you should understand."

Mrs. Cunningham gulped, curtsied. "Yes, my lord . . . I didn't know . . ."

"How should you?" he said gently, turning to follow Dora's bouncing rear up the stairs. At Judith's door, she raised her hand to knock with a flourish.

"No, I'll announce myself," he said swiftly. He waited until the disappointed maid had retreated down the stairs, then he opened the double doors.

Judith and Sally were sitting head to head on the window seat, deep in intense conversation, and both looked up as the door opened.

Judith stared at her husband, her color fluctuating wildly. "Marcus?" she whispered, as if unsure whether he was real or a vision.

"Just so," he agreed. "It seems I must be the only person in London not invited to visit you in your self-imposed seclusion." He heard the caustic note in his voice as he frowned at his sister-in-law. He'd prepared for this moment with great care, but Sally's presence threw all plans into disarray.

Sally had jumped up and instinctively moved closer to Judith, who managed to ask in cracked voice "What are you doing here, Marcus?"

"I've come to retrieve my wife," he replied, shrugging out of his cloak. "Sally, I must ask you to excuse us." He held the door in wordless command.

Sally hesitated, then stepped even closer to Judith. "I'm sorry, Marcus, but I'm here at Judith's invitation." She met his astounded stare without flinching, her shoulders stiffening as she prepared to defend her friend against all comers, including irate husbands.

First Charlie and now Sally, Marcus thought with resignation.

What on earth had got into his usually docile family these days? Silly question . . . Judith's influence, of course. He repeated calmly, "Nevertheless, I must ask you to excuse us."

"No," Sally said, closing her lips firmly.

Marcus began to laugh. "My dear Sally, what do you think I'm going to do?"

"I don't know," Sally replied. "But I'm not going to stand aside while you bully Judith."

Marcus's jaw dropped at this, and Judith recovered the power of speech. "It's all right, Sally. Why don't you wait downstairs for a few minutes?"

Sally looked between them as if assessing the risks, then she said doubtfully, "If you're sure . . ."

"Sally, I don't want to have to put you out," Marcus exclaimed in exasperation.

"That's exactly what I mean," Sally fired back. "Judith, do you really want me to leave?"

Judith had sunk back onto the window seat, covering her eyes, aware that she was on the verge of hysterical laughter. "Yes, really," she said in a stifled voice. "Marcus won't hurt me. Anyway, I've got my pistol."

"Well, if you're sure. I'll be downstairs, so just call if you need me." Sally marched to the door, shooting Marcus a darkling look as she passed him.

"Good God!" he said, closing the door behind her. "I always thought she was such a mouse."

"That's because you intimidate her," Judith said. "She's not like that at all. She's bright and funny, and a lot cleverer than either you or Jack could ever guess."

"Well, if she was intimidated just then, you could have fooled me," Marcus observed with a rueful chuckle. "I wish I knew why people imagine I'm going to do you some mischief. They've clearly never looked down the muzzle of your pistol." He took off his gloves, tossing them with his cloak onto the sofa.

Judith watched him in silence. He seemed in great good humor but that was surely impossible. For herself, her emotions were in such turmoil she didn't know what she felt.

After regarding her for a minute, Marcus said, "You really are the most exasperating creature, lynx. What on earth do you mean by running off like that? How the hell was I supposed to explain it?"

"I'm not particularly interested in how you explain it," she declared. "I'm not coming back."

"Oh, but you are," he said.

"I am not coming back to live in that prison you would construct for me!" she said, her throat closing as the hurt resurfaced. "You care only for appearances. Well, I don't give a tinker's damn for appearances, Carrington. You'll think of something to salvage your precious pride and keep up appearances, I'm certain of it." She swung away from him toward the window. "Just leave me out of it."

"Come here," he commanded.

Judith didn't move from the window, where she stood staring out at the scudding clouds, the stark lines of the bare elm trees, a black crow sitting on the wall at the bottom of the garden.

"Come here, Judith," he repeated in the same level voice.

She turned slowly. He was perched on the scrolled arm of the sofa and his eyes were quiet as they looked at her, his mouth soft. He beckoned, and she found herself moving across to him as if in response to gravity's pull.

He stood up as she reached him and reached out one hand, catching her chin. "Why didn't you tell me the truth?"

"What truth?" Her eyes seemed locked with his and the warm grasp of his hand on her chin seemed imprinted on her skin.

"That you didn't know who was in the taproom."

Shock flashed in her eyes. "How do you know?"

"Sebastian told me."

She jerked her chin out of his hand. "He had no right . . ."

"Nevertheless, he told me," Marcus said, reaching for her again. "Keep still and listen to me. It was unforgivable of me to assume the worst of you. I only wish you'd lost that formidable temper at the outset and put me in my place at once."

He smiled, but there was a hunger and a yearning in his gaze. "It was unforgivable, lynx, but can you forgive me?"

Sebastian had betrayed her. He knew the real reason why she hadn't been able to deny Marcus's accusations, and he'd chosen to ignore them in order to patch things up. Because of Gracemere? Because of Harriet?

"Say something," Marcus begged, running a finger over her mouth. "Please, Judith, say something. I can't let you leave me, my love, but I don't know how else to apologize. It was torment believing you had taken advantage of me, that you were only using our passion to your own advantage. It drove me insane to think I was no more to you than a means to an end. Can you understand that at all?"

"Oh, yes," she said softly. "Yes, I can understand it." And yet even now as his words filled her with sweet joy, she knew that she continued to deceive him. He was still a means to an end, and yet he'd become so much more than that.

"Judith?" Marcus said, softly insistent. "I need more than understanding."

She grasped his wrist tightly. "It's over. We'll put it behind us."

Marcus brought his mouth to hers in a hard affirming kiss. Judith clung to him, desperate to grasp whatever happiness they could have in their remaining time together. Desperate to believe that there was a chance he'd never find out about Gracemere.

"How did you find me?" she asked, when finally he raised his mouth from hers.

"Through Sebastian." He smiled down at her, touching the line of her jaw with a lingering finger.

"He didn't tell you!"

"Not in so many words. I had him followed."

"Good heavens," Judith said. "How very theatrical of you."

Marcus shook his head in disclaimer. "When it comes to theatricals, my love, you're unsurpassed. That dead-of-night flight through a window was an outrageous piece of melodrama." He bundled her into his arms, kissing her again.

"Just one more thing . . ." Judith murmured against his mouth. "All that other business . . ."

"Ah." He released her reluctantly. "I've instructed my bankers that you're free to draw on the account. We're joint partners in this marriage and therefore in the fortune that maintains us both. I'll not question your expenditure again, any more than you question mine."

Hiding her bittersweet emotions at his trust in her, she gave him a brilliant smile. "Now that, sir, is an inventive and generous solution to an apparently intractable problem."

"But no more high-stakes gaming." He pinched her nose. "And if I see you within a hundred yards of a gaming hell, my love, I can't answer for the consequences. Understood?"

"Understood. I'll confine myself to social play from now on."

"Good. And now we're going into Berkshire for a couple of weeks, so ring for the maidservant to pack your traps."

"Into Berkshire? Now?"

"This very minute."

"Why?"

"Because I say so," he declared cheerfully. "Now, I'd better go and reassure Sally that you're still in one piece." He shook his head in amazement. "I wonder if Jack knows what a spirited creature she is when roused."

"Probably not," Judith said, chuckling. "And it's clearly your fraternal duty to enlighten him."

In his sister's absence Sebastian devoted himself to courting Harriet. Lady Moreton watched with growing complacence, expecting each day to bring a formal offer for her daughter's hand. Sebastian fretted silently over his powerlessness to act, but until he was in possession of his birthright, he had nothing to offer a wife. Only Harriet was sunnily untroubled by the waiting, secure and trusting in the knowledge of Sebastian's love.

None of them was aware of the threat hanging over their happiness. The threat took concrete shape in a bedchamber in a tall house overlooking the River Thames. The mullioned casement rattled under the blustery winter wind from the river, and the fire in the grate spurted as needles of wind pierced tiny cracks between the panes.

Agnes drew a cashmere wrap tightly around her body as she slipped from the bed, her body languid with fulfillment despite the nip in the air. She went to the fire, bending to warm her hands.

"I swear the wretched chit sees and hears nothing that's not done or said by Sebastian," she said as if an interlude of passion hadn't broken their previous conversation. "How many times did you compliment her on her hat this afternoon before she seemed to hear you, let alone respond?"

"At least six," Gracemere responded, flipping open a delicate porcelain snuffbox. "Give me your wrist."

Smiling, Agnes straightened and held out her hand, wrist uppermost. The earl dropped a pinch of snuff exactly where her pulse throbbed and raised her wrist to his nose, breathing in the snuff. His lips lightly brushed her skin and then he dropped her hand and returned to the subject.

"Clearly Harriet's not to be wooed and won, therefore she must be taken."

"When?" Agnes moistened her lips. "You can't wait until Sebastian has declared himself."

"True enough. I will wait until I've bled Sebastian as white as it's possible—which should ruin his chances with Moreton anyway. And then we shall act." His lips tightened so that his mouth was a fleshy gash in his thin face.

"I don't doubt you, Bernard." Agnes touched his mouth with a fingertip. "Not for one minute."

He grasped her wrist again, sucking the finger into his mouth. His teeth bit down and his eyes stared down into hers, watching the pain develop, the excitement flare under the defiant challenge to endure. Agnes laughed, making no attempt to free her finger. She laughed, her head falling back, exposing the white column of her throat.

Gracemere released her wrist and circled her throat with his hands. "We *are* worthy of each other, my dear Agnes."

"Oh, yes," she whispered.

It was a long time before she spoke again. "With Judith and Carrington out of town, you must be missing a degree of entertainment."

Gracemere chuckled. "I have my plans well laid for her return. I may need you as message bearer, my dear."

"Messenger to whom?"

"Why, to Carrington, of course." A meager smile snaked over his lips. "There'd be no point compromising his wife if he's not to be aware of it."

"Oh, no," Agnes agreed. "None whatsoever. I'll convey the message of tarnished virtue with the utmost subtlety and the greatest pleasure."

"I thought the role might appeal to you, my love."

Judith clung to a shadowy corner of the conservatory. Her heart was beating swiftly with excitement and anticipation, her palms damp, moisture beading her brow from the exertion of the chase and the lush, hothouse atmosphere. The air was rich with the mingled, exotic scents of orchids, roses, and jasmine. The domed glass roof above her revealed the night sky, black infinity pricked with stars and the crescent sliver of the new moon offering the only light.

She had closed the drawing-room door that led into the conservatory, and the heavy velvet curtains had swung back, preventing the penetration of light from the house. Her ears strained to hear the sound of the door opening, the tap of a footstep on the smooth paving stones between the rows of shrubs and flowers. Would he guess where she was hiding? It was a relatively classic place for hide-and-seek. But then, it wasn't as if she didn't want to be found.

She stifled her laughter. Marcus had proved remarkably receptive to her penchant for nursery games. When she wasn't teasing him with outrageously provocative comments, which always produced the desired results, she was challenging him to horseraces through the meadow, making wagers on which raindrop would reach the bottom of the window first, throwing sticks from the bridge into the river and rushing to the other side to see which one was the first to emerge. They did nothing without laying odds, and the stakes were never for money. Indeed, they tried to outdo each other with the most imaginative and enticing wagers.

They'd spent the afternoon skating on the frozen horse pond, competing over who could make the most elaborate figures on the ice. Since Judith was no match for Marcus, who'd been skating on the pond every winter since early childhood, she'd spent a fair part of the afternoon on her backside. Marcus had made the most of the resulting bruises.

Hiding in her corner of the conservatory, ears stretched into the gloom for the slightest sound, Judith re-created the feel of his hands on her body, smoothing oil into the bruises he insisted he was discovering . . .

The door creaked, and there was a crack of light. It was extinguished so quickly, she could almost have imagined it. But she heard the faintest *click* as the door was closed again. There was silence, but she knew Marcus was in the conservatory. She could sense his presence just as she knew he could sense hers. Stepping backward on tiptoe, barely daring to breathe, she moved behind a potted orange tree, shrinking down into the deeper shadow, hugging herself as if she could thus make herself smaller. Her heart thudded in her ears as she waited to be discovered, as apprehensive as if she were truly being stalked by a predator.

Marcus stood by a bay tree, accustoming his eyes to the dimness, trying to sense where she was hiding. The conservatory was a wide, square building attached to the house, and he knew his quarry could evade him if he took off in the wrong direction. She could creep behind him to the door and be free and clear, with the rest of the vast house to offer for a further hiding place. But he was growing impatient with the game; he had another scenario in mind and was anxious to begin. The enticing curve of Judith's backside seemed imprinted on his palms, and his loins grew heavy at the thought of another anointing session, a more prolonged one—one that could continue until dawn if he chose.

He picked up a small scratching sound, tiny enough to have been a mouse. He stayed still, listening. It had come from the far corner and he stared into the gloom, straining his eyes to catch some movement in the shadows that wouldn't be a trick of the moonlight. The silence stretched, then a shower of gravel rolled across the paving from the same direction as the scratching. Marcus chuckled softly. Obviously Judith was also anxious to bring the game to a close.

Silently he removed his shoes, then trod on tiptoe toward the corner, hugging the shadows, hoping to surprise her, despite her clues. He thought he could detect a darker mass in the shadow of an orange tree, and with mischievous intent moved sideways, so that he could approach the tree from behind.

Judith crouched in her hiding place, listening for the sound of footfalls. Surely he'd picked up on her pointers. But she could hear nothing.

"Found you!"

Judith shrieked in genuine shock at the exultant statement from behind her. Marcus laughed. Bending, he caught her under the arms and hauled her to her feet.

"You lose, I believe."

Judith sank against him; her knees were quivering absurdly. "You frightened me!"

"I thought that was the point of the game. Hunter and prey . . . quarry and predator." He stroked her hair where it rested against his chest.

"I know it is, but I didn't expect you to terrify me." She straightened, pushing against his chest, her smile a pearly glimmer in the dimness. "Sebastian never terrified me when we used to play as children. I always heard him coming."

"Perhaps maturity brings greater subtlety," he murmured, glancing down at his stockinged feet.

Judith followed his gaze and burst into a peal of laughter. "You took your shoes off!"

"Observant of you . . . but, since I found you, I believe you owe me a forfeit, ma'am."

Judith narrowed her eyes. "But would you have found me if I hadn't given you those clues?"

"That, I'm afraid, we'll never know."

She chewed her bottom lip in thought. "But I still wonder if the possibility doesn't alter the original terms of the agreement."

Marcus shook his head. "No, ma'am, it does not. I discovered you . . . most completely, I would have said."

"I suppose that's true."

"So, I claim my reward."

Judith smiled. "Very well, then. And you can pay your forfeit afterward."

"Since when have winners also paid a forfeit?" Marcus demanded.

"Since I decided to make the rules," she retorted. "This was not a winner-takes-all proposition."

A long time later, Judith lay sprawled in wanton abandonment under glowing candlelight, the thick pile of the library carpet against her back and shoulders. Marcus held her buttocks on the palms of his hands, lifting her for his own dewy caresses. One couldn't draw qualitative comparisons between the joys of the pleasure giver and the receiver, she decided, her hips arcing under the fierce and fiery strokes of his tongue, the delicate grazing of his mouth.

Around them, the house was silent, only the hiss and spurt of the fire disturbing the quiet. Its heat was on her bared thigh, matching the rising heat in her loins. The coil burst asunder, taking her by surprise, as sometimes it did. She laughed softly, feeling his breath warm on her heated core as he laughed with her, in his own pleasure at her surprised release.

When he rolled, bringing her with him, she lay along his length, feeling her own softnesses pressing into the muscled concavities of his body. He parted her thighs, slowly twisted his hips, and thrust upward within the still-pulsating entrance to her body. Judith tightened around him, pushing backward until she knelt astride him. She moved herself over and around him in languid circles, teasing them both. With the same languor, she turned her head toward the uncurtained French doors. The moonlit lawn stretched beyond the windows, the frosty grass sparkling. It occurred to her that she was truly, completely happy, for the first time in her life.

There had never been room for unalloyed happiness before. But at this moment, fused in passion, even revenge somehow had lost its spur . . . was somehow irrelevant. Soon enough, they'd return to London and she would have to go to work on Gracemere again, but she wasn't going to think of that now.

She brought her mouth to his.

23

"I HOPE YOU ENJOYED YOUR RETREAT, JUDITH." BERNARD MELVILLE GUIDED his dance partner into a smooth turn.

Judith sighed. "No, it was extremely tedious. The country's so boring, and Carrington was closeted with his man of business the entire time."

"And he insisted you accompany him?" Gracemere shook his head and tutted. "How unkind of him. But then, as we know, Carrington has little interest in the preferences of others." His hand tightened on hers.

Judith controlled her shudder of revulsion and smiled up at him with a flutter of her eyelashes. "How true," she agreed. Her eyes darted swiftly around the crowded ballroom in a guilty check to assure herself that Marcus hadn't decided to abandon his own party and pay a surprise visit to the Sedgewicks' ball. Not that there was anything overtly wrong in dancing with the earl in public. Marcus himself was civil to Gracemere in company.

"My Lady Carrington was sorely missed," he assured her, a smile flickering on the fleshy lips.

"Nonsense, my lord. You know full well that redheads are not fashionable at the moment." Her laughing eyes flirtatiously invited his denial of this caveat.

He provided it without blinking an eye. "Red is not the description I would have chosen," he murmured, flicking at a copper ringlet with one finger. "And part of your charm, my dear Judith, is that you are not at all in the common way."

Judith gave him a coy look and changed the subject. "You're an accomplished card player, I understand."

"Oh, shameless evasion!" he exclaimed. "Is that your only response to my compliment?"

"Indeed, sir, a lady doesn't respond to compliments made her by stray dance partners." Her eyelashes fluttered as she gave him a mischievous smile.

"Stray dance partner! I must protest, ma'am, at such an unkind description."

"I must try to think of you in such terms, however, since I'm forbidden to consider you a friend," she responded archly.

Gracemere's pale eyes glittered. "But, as we're agreed, husbands need occasionally to be put in their places."

Judith's eyes gleamed with a conspiratorial thrill that brought a complacent smile to the earl's mouth—one that made her want to kick him hard in the shins. Fortunately, the waltz ended and he escorted her off the floor.

"My brother assures me that you're a most accomplished card player," she reiterated as they went into a small salon adjoining the ballroom.

"Your brother is a fair player himself." Gracemere offered the lie with a bland smile.

"But not as good as I am," Judith declared, closing her fan with a snap. "I challenge you to a game of piquet, my lord." She gestured to a small, unoccupied card table in the corner of the room.

"An enticing prospect," he said, with the same bland smile. "What stakes do you propose?"

Judith tapped her closed fan against her hand. "Ten guineas a point?"

Gracemere smiled at the proposal: the moderate stakes of a relatively confident gamester, who liked to think she played high. He'd seen her at the card tables and knew that Agnes had met her at Amelia Dolby's, so she couldn't be a complete novice. Presumably she played like her brother, with more enthusiasm than skill. "Stakes for a tea party, ma'am," he scoffed. "I propose something a little more enticing."

"What do you suggest, my lord?" Judith had expected him to accept her wager indulgently, and unease stirred beneath her expression of eager curiosity.

He stroked his chin, regarding her. "The honor of your company at a private dinner against . . . against . . . now, what could I offer you?" he mused.

Your head on a platter, Judith thought viciously. She had every intention of losing to him but no intention whatsoever of joining him in a tête-à-tête dinner. However, that bridge would have to be crossed when she reached it. "The chance to drive your blacks in Richmond Park," she suggested in dulcet accents. "I've envied you those horses since I first saw them."

"Then let us play, ma'am." He moved to the card table.

Judith had only one purpose behind the game: She wanted to know how he played, what habits he had, what techniques he favored. Then she and Sebastian would compare notes. As Gracemere had destroyed George Devereux playing piquet, so would Gracemere meet his own Waterloo at the hands of George's children.

She took her seat at the table with a fidgety eagerness, watching as he broke the pack. She didn't think he would bother to cheat with her; she'd been careful never to play at his table before, so he wouldn't know how well she played. He would probably assume she was a moderate player at best.

She gave him a middling performance, losing the first hand by a respectably small margin, winning the second by the appearance of a lucky retention, losing the third convincingly, but avoiding the Rubicon.

"You're certainly an accomplished player, Bernard," she said, smiling as he counted the points. "Perhaps one day you'd teach me some of your strategies." *What a delicious thought that was. . . . She knew now she was a fair match for Bernard Melville, in honest play or crooked.* She continued to smile, savoring the thought.

Bernard chuckled. "With pleasure, my dear. But first, I claim my winnings."

"But of course. However . . ." She glanced around the room. "We've already dined tonight, and this is hardly a private spot."

He chuckled again. "No, you must allow me to make the necessary arrangements, Judith. I'll inform you of the date, place, and time."

"I think, sir, that you must allow me to pick the date," she said carefully. "I'm not a free woman."

"No." Reaching for her hand, he carried it to his lips. "You are not. But are you a virtuous woman?" He smiled over her hand. "An improper question, forgive me, ma'am. . . . However, I firmly believe that you will find a tale to satisfy Carrington, when the need arises."

She would shoot him—no, that was too quick . . . a long and lingering death . . . "I daresay I could." She stood up. "But now I must return to the ballroom before anyone notices such a protracted absence."

Gracemere bowed and remained standing by the table, watching as she wafted back to the ballroom. Whatever tale she invented to put Carrington off the scent, the marquis would be apprised of his wife's intimate, clandestine rendezvous with his old enemy. The prospect of such a wonderfully apposite revenge was a heady one. But now, having played the sister, he would play her brother for rather more material stakes.

He made his way to the card room, where the serious play was taking place. Sebastian sat at the macao table and waved cheerfully at him. "Come and take a hand, Gracemere."

"Thank you." He sat down opposite Sebastian. "I just had a hand or two of piquet with your sister."

"Oh, did you win? Ju's not much of a player," Sebastian said, grinning, laying out his rouleaux.

"Calumny!" Judith's voice came from the doorway.

"But did you win?" her brother challenged, frowning over his cards before making his bet.

"No," she admitted, moving to stand behind the earl. "His lordship was more than my match, I fear."

Gracemere looked up. "The cards fell in my favor," he demurred. "I trust you're going to bring me luck now, Lady Carrington."

"Oh, I trust so," she murmured, smiling around the table. She had absorbed Gracemere's hand in a glance that barely skimmed his cards and now continued to look smilingly around the table, her fan moving lazily in front of her face.

Lord Sedgewick held the bank. His appreciative gaze rested on Lady Carrington. She was a devilishly attractive woman. Catching his eye, she smiled at him, and Sedgewick felt a distinct prickle of arousal. Marcus was a lucky dog, but then again such a woman would take a deal of handling. His lordship wondered slightly uneasily whether he himself would be up to such a task. He thought of his own wife, a matron of even temper with little interest in matters of the bedchamber beyond those necessary to ensure the succession. Lady Carrington, on the other hand, gave the distinct impression of one who might play rather nicely. . . .

Sedgewick forced his attention back to the cards. It was unseemly to think in such fashion of another man's wife. But she *was* devilishly attractive . . . and that wicked smile, when just the corners of her mouth lifted . . .

Sebastian glanced up now and again from his cards, joining in the lively conversation around the table. Judith was not the only woman standing at the table, observing the play; she was, however, the only one employing her fan. But then it was such an ordinary activity, only Sebastian truly took note.

Gracemere lost three hundred guineas to the bank in half an hour. It didn't strike him as remarkable that whenever he thought he had a winning count, Davenport played one better, declaring his hand before the earl was ready to declare his. Sebastian wasn't always the winner at the table, but Gracemere was always the loser. He put it down to ill luck.

Judith drifted out of the card room. She and Sebastian had only been practicing. They hadn't practiced in public since Brussels and both needed to see how they would handle Gracemere. The final act was fast approaching.

"Judith?"

Harriet's soft voice broke pleasantly into her musings.

"Harriet, I didn't see you here before." She drew the girl's arm through hers. "Let's go and sit by the window, it's so hot in here. You arrived late. Sebastian's been looking for you."

"Lady Barret was detained. She couldn't come for me until after eleven," Harriet confided. "And Mama is indisposed." A delicate flush mantled her cheek. "I haven't seen your brother. I thought perhaps he'd already left."

Judith chuckled. "He wouldn't leave if he was expecting to see you. He's in the card room."

Harriet received this information in silence. Her eyes were downcast while her fingers played with the silk fringe on her reticule. Gently, Judith asked if something was troubling her.

Without looking up, Harriet said, "I-I sometimes think that . . . I sometimes think that your brother plays too much," she finished in a rush.

Judith nibbled her lip. Harriet was a great deal more observant than she'd given her credit for. "He enjoys gaming," she said neutrally. "But I can safely promise you, Harriet, that he will never jeopardize your happiness, and therefore his own, with reckless play."

Harriet sighed with relief and looked up at Judith, her expression radiant, the clear eyes sparkling. "You believe that, Judith? I was so afraid he was a true gamester."

"Oh, yes," Judith said, placing her hand over Harriet's. "Not only do I believe it, Harriet, I *know* it. That doesn't mean he's not a gamester," she added judiciously. "But if he's away from the tables, he'll not miss them."

"Secrets . . . do you exchange secrets?" Agnes Barret's falsely cheery voice sounded from behind them.

"Good evening, Lady Barret," Judith said, unable to disguise the chill in her voice. "No, I don't believe Harriet and I share any secrets."

"No, indeed not," Harriet agreed, blushing and transparently flustered.

Lady Barret's gaze rested on her for a minute, a slightly contemptuous smile on her lips, before she turned back to Judith, who met the now cool and calculating scrutiny with one of her own. The animosity between them seemed to crackle and even Harriet was aware of it, her eyes darting between the two women.

"I understand you've recently returned from Berkshire, Lady Carrington." Agnes bowed.

"My husband had some estate business to attend to," Judith said, returning the bow.

Minimal courtesies satisfied, Agnes turned back to Harriet. "Harriet, my dear, should you object to remaining a little longer? I've promised to take up Lord Gracemere as far as his house when we leave, but he's engaged in the card room." A trilling laugh accompanied the explanation. "I don't think your mama will worry, since she knows you're with me."

Harriet mumbled something, but her eyes flickered toward Judith in a distinct plea.

"I'm about to order my own carriage," Judith suggested immediately. "If Harriet's fatigued, I'd be glad to take her home on my way. I'm sure Lady Moreton will find nothing to object to in such an arrangement."

"Oh, no," Harriet agreed hastily. "And, in truth, Lady Barret, I do find myself a little fatigued." She touched her temples and offered a wan smile. "I fear I'm getting the headache . . . it's so hot in here."

Judith read naked malevolence in the split-second glare Agnes directed at her. It chilled her, yet she met it with a slightly triumphant lift of her eyebrows. They *were* on a battleground . . . but what battleground and over what issue?

Routed, Agnes bowed, offered Harriet her sympathy, promised to call upon her and Letitia in the morning, and left them.

"Thank you," Harriet whispered.

Judith chuckled. "Don't thank me. Your performance was impeccable. I could almost believe in your headache myself. Let's go and drag Sebastian from the card room, and he will escort us home."

The suggestion found immediate favor with Harriet, and the two went in search of Sebastian. However, when they entered the card room, a strange expression crossed Sebastian's face. He cast in his hand immediately and came over to them.

"You shouldn't be in here," he said to Harriet almost brusquely, leading her back to the ballroom.

"We came to fetch you," Judith said, puzzled. "We thought you might escort us both home."

"With the greatest pleasure." He seemed to recollect himself, but his expression was still a little black. "I'll order your carriage immediately."

"What's the matter?" Judith whispered, as Harriet went off to fetch her cloak.

"I don't want Harriet in the card room," he stated with low-voiced vehemence. "It's no place for her."

"Oh." Judith followed Harriet to the retiring room, considering this. Sebastian wanted no taint of the gaming tables to touch his future wife. Interesting. For Sebastian, such places were associated with all that he intended to put behind him once Gracemere had paid his dues. They carried the taint of unscrupulous play, of desperation, of poverty and anger and injustice. But didn't they also carry the memories of the bond between himself and his sister? Of the years when all they'd had was each other? The thought that she and Sebastian could be growing apart saddened her.

Marcus had just arrived home when the chaise deposited his wife at her own door. "I was about to come in search of you at the Sedgewicks'," he said as she came into the hall. "Did you have a pleasant evening?" He held open the door to the library.

Flirting with Gracemere and cheating at cards. An evening of deceit. She'd thought she'd be able to carry it off by reminding herself of the vital need for secrecy, of how much rode on maintaining that secrecy, but instead, at the sound of his voice, waves of panic broke over her. She could feel the color flooding her cheeks, sweat trickling beneath her arms, moistening her palms. How could Marcus possibly not sense her guilt? Her instinct was to plead fatigue and run upstairs without further conversation. Instead she forced herself to behave normally.

"Pleasant enough, thank you." She went past him into the library.

Now why the devil wouldn't she look at him properly? He could feel her jangling like an ill-hung bell.

"A glass of port before bed?" Marcus suggested, lifting a decanter from the salver on the pier table.

"I'd prefer Madeira, I think." She shrugged out of her evening cloak, dropping it on the couch, and went over to the window overlooking the square. She drew back the curtains, saying brightly, "It's a frosty night."

"Yes," he agreed, setting her glass of wine on a table, regarding her with puzzled amusement as she continued to stare out of the window. "What's so absorbing in the square at this time of night?"

She shrugged, laughed faintly, and turned back to the room. "Nothing, of course. For some reason I feel restless."

Marcus decided the insouciance lacked conviction. "I wonder why you should feel restless." He sipped port, looking at her over the rim of his glass. "What have you been up to, lynx?"

"Up to? Whyever should I be up to anything?"

"You tell me." He continued to scrutinize her until her color deepened.

"It was a tedious crush," she said, taking an overlarge sip of her wine. "I daresay that's why I feel so restless."

"That would of course explain it," he observed gravely.

Judith shot him a suspicious glance. Her husband looked amused but far from satisfied. She yawned. "I'm tired. I think I'll go up to bed."

"But I thought you felt restless," he pointed out unhelpfully.

Judith nibbled a fingernail. "I do and I don't. It's a very peculiar feeling."

"Perhaps we should take a turn around the square," he suggested. "A little exercise in the night air might help you decide exactly which of the two you feel."

"Oh, stop teasing me, Marcus!" she exclaimed in frustration, wondering desperately how she could deflect the course of this inquiry. He *could* sense her guilt, although never in a blue moon would he be able to guess at how dire it was. However, that was no particular help.

"My apologies, ma'am." He came over to her and took the glass from her hand. "Let's go upstairs and I'll endeavor to wrest the truth from you by some other means of persuasion."

"There is no truth. I don't know what you're talking about."

"Don't you?" His eyebrows lifted. "Well, let me explain. I know that either you *have* been wading hip deep in trouble this evening, or that you're planning to do so."

"How can you know that . . . I mean, you can't know it because there's nothing to know." Crossly she bit her lip at this inept denial.

Marcus shook his head. "If you'd not been up to mischief, lynx, you'd tell me what was bothering you. Since you're trying very hard to persuade me to drop the subject, I can only assume it's something I won't like."

This was dreadful. "You're talking to me as if I were a child, instead of a grown woman who's just come back from a tedious ball," she said, trying for an assumption of affronted dignity.

Marcus shook his head. "It won't do, Judith. Cut line, and tell me what mischief you've been brewing."

Desperately Judith cast around for something harmless to confess that would satisfy him. "I'm just being silly," she mumbled finally. "I don't want to talk about it." *Silly about what? Talk about what?* She had no idea, and crossed her fingers behind her back, hoping he would leave it at that. A vain hope.

"You're rather closing out my options," he observed, regarding her consideringly.

There was something about the look that put Judith instantly on her guard. The amusement was still there and there was a deeply sensual glimmer in the background, but these were not as reassuring as they might have been. There was a coiled purpose in the powerful frame, determination in the set of his mouth and the firmness of his jaw.

"You're making a mountain out of a molehill." She tried for a light touch again. "I'm out of sorts because I had a tedious evening and have the beginnings of a headache." It was feeble, and she wasn't much surprised that it didn't work.

"Fustian!" was Marcus's uncompromising response. "You're up to something, and it's been my invariable experience that when you decide to keep something from me, it develops into the most monumental bone of contention. I am not prepared to join battle with you yet again . . . either now, or at some point in the future when whatever it is is finally brought unassailably to my attention. So you will oblige me with chapter and verse, if you please."

If she hadn't had such a weight on her conscience, Judith could have responded to this provocation in the manner it deserved. But tonight she was too cowed by the truth to fight back. "Please," she said, pressing her temples. "I am truly too tired to be bullied."

"Bullied!" Marcus was momentarily thrown off balance. "I want to know what's troubling you, and I'm bullying you?"

"You don't want to know what's the matter," she cried, stung by this clear misrepresentation of the conversation so far. "You believe

I've been up to something and I'm keeping it from you. That's not the same thing, I'll have you know."

"In my book, where you're concerned, Judith, it is." He shook his head with every appearance of reluctant resignation. "Oh, well, have it your own way. Don't say you weren't warned."

"Marcus!" Judith shrieked, as she found herself lifted onto a low table. His shoulder went into her stomach and the next instant, she was draped over his shoulder, staring at the carpet, her ringlets, falling loose from the ivory and pearl fillet, tumbling over her face.

"Yes, my dear?" he asked, all solicitude as he strode with her to the door.

"Put me down!" She pummeled his back with her fists and sneezed as her hair tickled her nose. The absurdity of her position struck her with full force as they reached the hall. Her gown of emerald taffeta was hardly suited to such rough handling, and the pearl drops in her ears dangled ludicrously against Marcus's back. She kicked her feet violently in their white satin slippers.

"When we get upstairs," he said calmly, placing a steadying hand on her upturned rear, but other than that ignoring her gyrations.

"But the servants." Judith gasped. "You can't possibly carry me through the house in this mortifying fashion."

"Can I not?" Laughter quivered in his voice. "You've had every opportunity to be cooperative, lynx."

Judith subsided with a groan, closed her eyes tightly and prayed that everyone had gone to bed . . . everyone, that is, except for Millie and Cheveley. She reared up against his shoulder at the thought. "Oh, God. Marcus, you have to let me walk into my room."

"Do I?"

"Please!"

He stopped, halfway up the stairs. "If you tell me straightway what I want to know, I'll allow you to enter your room on your own two feet."

"Oh, God," Judith muttered again. But inspiration came to her in the same instant. It must have something to do with all that blood rushing to her head. It wouldn't be a lie, either, just half the truth.

When she didn't immediately reply to his ultimatum, Marcus resumed climbing the stairs, carrying his burden seemingly with the greatest of ease.

"Please!" she yelped as they reached the head of the stairs. "Put me down and I'll tell you as soon as we're in my room. I will, I promise."

Marcus made no reply, merely continued down the corridor to Judith's chamber. At the door, however, mercifully, he stopped. "Word of a lynx?"

"Word of a Davenport," she said with a gasp. "I couldn't bear to be carried in there like a sack of potatoes."

Laughing, he lowered her to the floor, holding her waist as her feet touched ground. "I did tell you I had various methods of persuasion to hand."

Judith brushed her hair out of her eyes and tried to smooth her much-abused gown. She glared up at him, her face pink with indignation and the results of her upside-down journey. "How could you?"

"Very easily." He opened the door for her, gesturing she should precede him, offering a gently mocking bow.

"Lawks-a-mercy, my lady!" Millie squawked, jumping up from her chair. "Look at your dress." She stared with some disbelief at Judith's rumpled gown and wildly tumbled ringlets.

"I feel as if I've been dragged through a hedge backward," Judith declared, shooting her husband a fulminating glare.

Marcus grinned. "You may have fifteen minutes to prepare yourself for bed, ma'am. Then you will fulfill your side of the bargain."

"Some bargain," Judith muttered as the connecting door closed on his departure. "Help me undress, Millie. Fifteen minutes is no great time."

"No, my lady. But whatever's happened?"

"It's his lordship's idea of a joke," Judith told her, peering at her image in the cheval glass. "What a mess!"

Millie helped Judith into her nightgown and brushed her hair, returning order to the copper cloud. "If that'll be all, I'll take this for sponging and pressing, m'lady." She picked up the much-abused gown on her way to the door.

"Yes, thank you, Millie. Good night."

Judith blew out all but one candle and hopped swiftly into bed, propping the pillows behind her head, pulling the sheet up to her chin, offering her husband a demure bedtime image when he came in to hear her explanation. Her guilty panic had vanished under the spur of action, and now she knew how to handle the situation, she was as calm as if she were playing for high stakes on Pickering Street.

"Well, madam wife?" Marcus closed the door behind him and trod to the darkened bed. "You may look as if butter wouldn't melt in your mouth, but I know better. Out with it!" He snapped his fingers.

Judith frowned and sat up straight against the pillows. "I told you it was silly and I was making a mountain out of a molehill, but since you insist, then I'll tell you. It's Agnes Barret." She sat back again, with the air of one who has discharged a difficult but possibly point-less duty.

"Agnes Barret?" Marcus sat on the end of the bed. "Explain."

"I don't know how to," she said, and the ring of truth was in the admission. "She upsets me dreadfully. I feel as if we're fighting some war to the death, but I don't know what the issue is or what the weapon is. Whenever I'm obliged to talk to her, I feel as if an entire regiment is tramping over my grave."

"Good God!" Marcus lifted the candle, holding it high so that her face was thrown into relief. He could read the truth in her eyes. "So what happened tonight?"

She shrugged. "We just had words . . . or, at least, not even that, but I prevented her from driving Harriet home and she was furious. We exchanged looks, I think you could say. For some reason, she's cultivating Harriet." She plucked at the coverlet. "I believe Agnes and Gracemere are lovers."

Marcus frowned. "It's not inconceivable, I suppose. I gather they've known each other from childhood. Why should it concern you?"

"It makes things awkward," she said, catching a loose thread on the sheet and twisting it restlessly around her finger. "That's why I didn't want to talk about this. I think Gracemere is trying to court Harriet—only she won't have anything to do with him—and Agnes is constantly trying to throw them together."

"I see." It was a flat statement. Harriet wouldn't be the first heiress to receive Gracemere's attentions, Marcus mused. But if she was holding him at arm's length, she was no Martha. Presumably Sebastian was a more potent counterweight to Gracemere's courting than he had been.

"You're scowling," Judith said. "And I haven't said anything yet to annoy you."

He banished the scowl with the memories and smiled. "Oh, dear, lynx, are you about to?"

"I don't know whether it will or not," she said judiciously, still twisting the thread.

"Out with it!"

"Well, whenever I'm with Harriet and she's with Agnes, Gracemere is usually not too far away." She looked up at him, her dark eyebrows in a quizzical arch. "I didn't want to bring up a potentially contentious subject."

"My dear, Gracemere is not a contentious subject so long as you don't encourage him. You can't help but be in his company on occasion, and I won't shrivel and die at the mention of his name," he commented with a wry smile.

"I didn't want to run any risks," she said with perfect truth.

Marcus leaned over to catch a ringlet, twisting it around his finger. "So that's what's been bothering you this evening?"

"Yes," she agreed. "But now that you've made me confess it, I feel as if I'm being fanciful about Agnes, so now I feel particularly silly."

Marcus laughed and threw off his brocade dressing gown. "Well, I'd better restore your self-esteem. Move over."

Judith obligingly did so, reflecting that she had pulled the chestnuts out of that particular fire without singeing herself too severely. She wondered how long her luck would hold.

24

"I CAN'T UNDERSTAND HOW YOU CAN BE SO NONCHALANT ABOUT Gracemere's attentions to Harriet." Judith clasped her gloved hands tightly within her swansdown muff. It was a bitterly cold afternoon, not a comfortable one for walking at the fashionable hour in the park. However, Society's dictates always won out over comfort, and there were almost as many promenaders today as on the most clement afternoon.

Sebastian swished at the bare hedgerow with his cane. "Harriet detests him, you said as much yourself," he replied. "And she loves me," he added with a touch of complacence. "Why should I concern myself with Gracemere? If it were anyone else, I might even pity him on such a fruitless quest."

"Agnes Barret is his accomplice."

"Oh, Ju, don't be so melodramatic. Accomplice, indeed. What kind of conspiracy are you imagining?"

Judith shook her head. She didn't know, she just knew she sensed that Agnes and Bernard were pure evil. "They're lovers," she said.

Sebastian shrugged. "Maybe so. So what?"

Judith gave up and abruptly changed the subject. "You will come to Carrington Manor for Christmas?"

"Where else would I go?" He laughed down at her.

"You might prefer to spend it with Lord and Lady Moreton," Judith declared loftily. "I'm sure they'll make an exception for Christmas and put something other than gruel and weak tea on their table."

"Stuff!" her brother responded amiably, well aware that Judith intended to invite Harriet to Carrington Manor, while delicately excluding the parents.

Judith waved at a passing laundelet in response to the vigorous greetings of its passengers. "There's Isobel and Cornelia." The laundelet drew up beside the path.

"Judith, that is the most divine hat," Isobel said. "Good afternoon, Sebastian . . . I saw a hat just like that in Bridge's, Judith, but it didn't look like anything at all. I didn't even try it on. I thought it might make me look bald or something."

Sebastian noticed the hat in question for the first time: a tight helmet that completely enclosed his sister's head, hiding her hair, leaving the lines and planes of her face to look upon the world unadorned. It wouldn't suit everyone, he decided.

"Bone structure," Cornelia commented. "You've got to have bones in your face." Her nose was reddened with the cold and she dabbed at it with her handkerchief. "I do wish I hadn't let you persuade me into this, Isobel. It's freezing and I'd much rather be beside my fire with a book."

"Oh, it's good for you to get some fresh air," Isobel said. "You can't spend all day buried in some Latin text, can she, Judith? Sebastian, what's your opinion?"

Sebastian regarded the red-nosed and distinctly disconsolate Cornelia. "I think there's much to be said for firesides and books . . . although I can't say I'm a great one for the classics."

Cornelia sniffed and blew her nose. "As it happens, I wasn't reading Latin, I was reading *Guy Mannering*. Have you come across it, Judith?"

Judith nodded. "I have a copy, but I haven't yet read it. It's said to be by Walter Scott, isn't it?"

"Yes, it has the same touch as *Waverley* . . . although he won't admit to having written that either."

A gust of wind set the plume in Isobel's hat quivering, and the coachman coughed pointedly as the horses stamped on the roadway.

"Your horses are getting cold, Isobel," Sebastian said, stepping back onto the path. "It's no weather for standing around."

"It's no weather for walking either," Judith declared, huddling into her pelisse.

After waving the laundelet on its way, she turned back to her brother. "Sebastian, I think it's time to step up the play for Gracemere. We should aim to have the business over by Christmas."

Sebastian nodded. "We've got him exactly where we want him. I'll begin taking increasingly heavy losses to whet his appetite for the last night."

"I trust we still have the funds we need?"

He nodded. "Enough."

"Has he cheated again?"

"Twice. I lost carelessly, of course. He has no idea I know why I lost."

"The Duchess of Devonshire's ball is in three weeks," Judith said thoughtfully. "A week before Christmas. It would be the perfect occasion for exposure—everyone will be there."

Sebastian thought for a minute, then nodded briskly. "I'll play mostly piquet with him from now on. Winning a little, losing a lot. The night before the ball, I'll lose so heavily he's bound to think I'm on the verge of ruin. On the night, he'll move in for the coup de grace."

"And on that night . . ." Judith shivered, but not with cold. On that night, together, they would destroy Bernard Melville, Earl of Gracemere.

With a resumption of briskness, she continued. "I'll become involved in the 'duel' you and he are engaged in—a playful thing, you understand. He'll think I'm wonderfully naive, to be seeing it as a game, not realizing that my brother is a fat pigeon that he's going to pluck clean."

"You'll have to make sure Marcus is somewhere else that night," Sebastian said matter-of-factly.

"Yes," Judith agreed. Then she said in a rush, "I don't know how much longer I can keep up this deceit, Sebastian. I feel such a traitor, so disloyal."

"Three more weeks," Sebastian said quietly. "That's all. I can't wait much longer either, Ju."

"No, I know that." She caught his hand, crushing his fingers in a convulsive grip. A minute later she spoke cheerfully, diminishing the intensity of the last few minutes. "Have you thought how you're going to manage Letitia?"

Sebastian groaned. "I'm hoping Yorkshire will prove too far for frequent visitations."

"Is Harriet able to stand up to her mother?"

Sebastian considered. "Yes, with support," he said finally. "She hasn't done so yet, of course, but I think, when we're married, she'll prefer to upset her mama than me."

Judith went into a peal of laughter. "Such a sweet, accommodating creature she is, Sebastian. It's fortunate she's fallen in love with someone who'll never injure her." That graveyard shiver ran across her scalp again and her laughter died as the twinned images of Agnes and Gracemere thrust themselves forward.

"I must go home," she said as they reached the Apsley gate. "Lord Castlereagh, Lord Liverpool, and the Duke of Wellington are dining with us."

"Such exalted circles you move in," Sebastian declared with a chuckle. "The prime minister and the foreign secretary no less."

"I suspect Marcus is turning his interests to politics, now that there aren't any wars being fought," Judith said. "And Wellington is certainly turning his attention that way. Marcus says it's because the duke has a very simple political philosophy: He's the servant of the Crown and obliged to do his duty by it in whatever way is necessary —on the battlefield or in Parliament. He's the most popular man in the country and he has such influence in the Lords, he can probably coordinate the Tories in a way that Liverpool can't." She frowned. "I wonder if Marcus is looking at a post in any ministry Wellington might set up. Funny, I only just thought of that."

"My sister a cabinet minister's wife," Sebastian said with mock awe. "You'd best hurry home and charm your husband's guests."

"Curiously, I don't find Wellington in the least intimidating," Judith said. "Maybe because I once spent the night sleeping on a table in his headquarters. And he's a shocking flirt," she added.

"Then I'm sure you and he get on like a house on fire," her brother teased.

Judith arrived home to find a note waiting for her. It was from the Earl of Gracemere, calling in her debt of honor with the request of the pleasure of her company the following night at a public ridotto at Ranelagh. Frowning, Judith took the note up to her bedchamber and rang for Millie. She thrust the invitation to the back of a drawer in her secretaire while she waited for her abigail.

Bernard had chosen a curious location for the payment of her debt. A public ridotto was a vulgar masquerade, one not in general frequented by members of the ton. But perhaps that was the point. Maybe he was considerately ensuring the secrecy of the rendezvous. And then again . . . What she knew of Gracemere didn't lend itself to consideration. He was much more likely to be making mischief.

She wasn't going to go, of course. But how to refuse the invitation without Gracemere's questioning her good faith in their friendship? If she put his back up this late in the game, she'd have little enough time to repair the damage before the Duchess of Devonshire's ball, and on that night she would have to stick closer to Gracemere than his shadow.

"My lady . . . which gown, my lady?"

"I beg your pardon, Millie?" Abstracted, she looked up. Millie was standing patiently beside the armoire.

"Which gown will you wear this evening, my lady?"

"Oh." Judith frowned, turning her attention to this all important question. "The straw-colored sarsenet, I think."

"With the sapphires," Marcus said from the connecting door. He lounged against the door jamb, fastening the buttons on his shirt cuffs, his black eyes twinkling. "They'll draw attention to the décolletage of that gown, which, as I recall is somewhat dramatic. The duke will appreciate it."

Judith chuckled. "And one must please one's guests, after all."

"It's the duty of a host," he agreed with gravity.

"And of a wife to further her husband's ambitions," she said in dulcet tones.

Marcus's smile was wry. "So you guessed?"

"What post appeals? Foreign secretary . . . home secretary, perhaps?"

He shrugged. "I don't know yet. It depends on what Peel and Canning want. Anyway, nothing's going to happen for a while. I'm just interested in preparing the ground."

"Well, I'll charm your guests," she said. "But Castlereagh's a dour individual. I'm sure he disapproves of flirtation."

Marcus laughed. "Never mind. It's with Wellington that my political future lies, my love."

Judith put her problem with Gracemere out of her head for the evening, devoting her single-minded attention to her husband's interests. It was a fascinating evening and she fell asleep in the early hours of the morning, thinking that she might well enjoy a role as political hostess.

It was bright sunshine when Marcus was awakened the next morning by the pretty chiming of the clock on the mantelshelf. It was nine o'clock, but Judith was still unstirring beside him. He hitched himself on one elbow to look down at her.

She lay on her back, her arms flung above her head, her lips slightly parted with the deep, even, trusting breath of a secure child. In sleep, without the usual vibrancy of expression, she appeared younger than her years and definitely more vulnerable. Her skin smelled warm and soft, redolent of a curious, babylike innocence— an innocence quite at odds with the charming, sophisticated hostess of the previous evening.

Perhaps he should have expected an upbringing spent racketing around the Continent to produce such a poised, well-informed, worldly cosmopolite. But he didn't think she'd been mixing in the first circles on her travels. And yet she never put a foot wrong; she behaved with all the assurance of an aristocrat, all the confidence of one who'd never gone without anything in her life. And Sebastian was the same. George Davenport must have been quite a character to have produced two such children in such unfavorable circumstances. Not for the first time, Marcus wondered about the Davenport antecedents. Judith always said she knew nothing about her family origins. Their father had insisted they were irrelevant and as a family they had to create themselves. Marcus supposed he could see the reasoning.

He lay down beside Judith again, his thigh resting against the warm, satiny length of her leg. It was impossible to resist the slow, gentle heat rising in his loins at the feel and the scent of her. With a tiny sigh of contented resignation, delicately, as if reluctant to wake her, he turned her onto her side, facing away from him. She murmured, but it was a wordless sound that came from sleep. He fitted his body against hers, and in sleep she nuzzled her bottom into his belly. He slipped his hand between her thighs, feeling for the sleep-closed entrance to her body with a tender, gossamery caress. He smiled as he felt her body responding without any prompting from her mind. She murmured again and drew her knees up, pushing backward in wordless invitation.

He slipped inside her, his hands caressing her breasts, his face buried in the fragrant burnished tumble of her hair, and she tightened around him, the soft, sweet velvet sheath enclosing him, so that he became a part of her. He felt her body come alive as she returned to full awareness, and it was as if his own body were a part of her waking process. He could feel the blood beginning to flow swiftly in her veins, vigor to fill the muscles and sinews of her body, the sharp clarity of a newly awakened brain. Fancifully he imagined he was giving birth to her, creating her for the new day.

"Good morning, lynx," he whispered into her hair as the ripples of pleasure filled her body.

She chuckled sleepily. "That was a very thoughtful way to wake someone up." Rolling onto her back again, she blinked up at him as he hung over her, his black eyes soft with his own pleasure. She touched his mouth with a fingertip. "Did you sleep well?"

"Beautifully." He swung himself out of bed, stretched and yawned. "What plans do you have for the day?"

Judith sat up against the pillows, enjoying the view. Marcus, naked, was a sight for sore eyes. However, the question brought the day's main issue to the forefront of her mind again. "Oh, I think I might ride with Sebastian this morning," she said vaguely. She would take the problem to her brother and between them they would come up with a solution.

Marcus blew her a kiss and left her, and Judith threw off the covers, pulling the bellrope for Millie.

In fact, the solution was remarkably simple. "Go to Ranelagh," Sebastian said. "And I'll ensure that I'm there with a large group of my own friends. We'll all be a trifle foxed, of course, very jolly and quite impossible to shake off. Gracemere will have your company, but you'll also be in the unexceptional company of your brother. You'll tell Marcus as soon as you get home, but you won't need to mention Gracemere, and I'll lay odds he'll think nothing of it. If he objects to your going to such a vulgar masquerade, you can put up with a scolding."

Judith pulled a rueful face. "Marcus's scoldings aren't much fun."

"In this case, it's a small price to pay."

Judith wasn't so sure, but she said no more.

25

SEBASTIAN'S PLAN WORKED LIKE A CHARM. MARCUS WAS ENGAGED TO dine with friends and was not in the house to see his wife leave, a cream domino and loo mask over one arm. Awaiting her in a hired chaise at the corner of the square was Gracemere.

Judith greeted him with a brilliant smile. "Such an adventure, my lord," she gushed with all the enthusiasm of a child being given a treat. "I've never been to a public ridotto before."

The earl bowed over her hand. "Then I'm honored to be the first to introduce you to its pleasures." He handed her into the chaise and climbed in after her. "I trust you'll be pleased with Ranelagh. It's said by some to be prettier than Vauxhall."

It was a relatively mild evening and Judith would have been enchanted by her first sight of the gardens, brilliantly lit by myriad golden lanterns, if she hadn't had other things on her mind. She had to ensure that she and her companion met up with Sebastian's party before they all became lost in the anonymous throng parading along the gravel walks in dominoes and masks.

"I'd like to dance," she said. "May we go to the pavilion?"

"By all means." The earl bowed and took the loo mask from her. "Allow me."

She endured the feel of his fingers deftly tying the strings of the mask, struggling to hold herself away from him without giving him any indication of the depths of her revulsion. She left the cream domino hanging open from her shoulders, revealing her ball gown of sapphire taffeta. It was a startling color that set her hair on fire, and Sebastian would have little difficulty recognizing his sister in the crowd, despite the mask.

They had circled the ballroom only once, before Sebastian saw them. He was in a group of friends, lounging against the wall, ogling the dancers with the appearance of those who've escaped from the restraints of convention and are determined to enjoy themselves in whatever outrageous fashion presented itself. They held tankards of porter and blue ruin, and were imbibing freely as they exchanged indelicate observations on the company.

"Good God, it's m'sister," Sebastian declared, his voice slightly slurred, as Judith and Gracemere came within earshot.

Judith felt her partner's sudden rigidity. "Sebastian," she called, breaking free from the earl. "What are you doing here? Isn't it a famous adventure? I've never seen such people. Do you know, there were people chasing each other around the lily pond just now. They'd taken their masks off . . . Oh, my lord, I beg your pardon." She turned with a radiant smile to the earl, whose expression was well hidden by his mask. "What a coincidence. My brother's here, too."

"So I see." Gracemere bowed. "Your sister had a great desire to sample the delights of a public ridotto, Davenport. I offered my services as escort."

"Why, Ju, you know I would have escorted you m'self," Sebastian said reproachfully. "But let me make you known to my friends."

A woman in a green domino moved out of the window embrasure

as Judith took her brother's arm. There was no mischief to be wrought here, no tale of tarnished virtue to bear to the Most Honorable Marquis of Carrington. Agnes Barret went home.

From then on, the earl's carefully constructed scheme of seduction disintegrated. Sebastian, in the merry fuzziness engendered by gin and porter, remained convinced that Gracemere could only be as delighted as they all were at this serendipitous meeting, and nothing would satisfy him but that they should join together and have supper in one of the rotundas, where they could observe the cits and the ladies of the demimonde to their hearts' content. Several jesting references were made to the Marquis of Carrington's possible reactions to his wife's indulging herself in such vulgar fashion, and Judith seemed to become as tipsy as her brother and his companions as the evening wore on.

Gracemere could do nothing but sit amid the rowdy group, waiting impatiently for the evening to end. He felt like an elderly uncle who'd strayed into a party of exuberant youth. Judith's behavior was certainly inappropriate for the Marchioness of Carrington, but her identity was well concealed behind her mask, should any other members of the ton have also decided to pass such an unconventional evening. But in any event, she could be accused only of an excess of high spirits. There was nothing of which to make a public scandal, and no capital that the earl could make out of his escort. Instead of a private, intimate supper in a dimly lit box, they were supping very publicly under the full glare of a dozen candelabra in the company of Judith's brother. If it ever became known, Society's censure would be slight, tempered with indulgence. Instead of moving flirtation down the paths of overt seduction, he was obliged to watch his prey's disintegration into a giggling ingenue, leaning against her brother for the physical support she needed so vitally. He assumed Agnes had returned home.

At the end of the evening, he was forced to endure Sebastian's rollicking company in the chaise. He couldn't refuse his request for a ride home without it seeming most peculiar, so he sat in the corner of the chaise balefully listening to the brother and sister's drunken giggles and infelicitous observations.

When the chaise drew up in Berkeley Square, Sebastian lurched down the step. "I'll walk m'sister to her door," he said, hiccupping through the window at Gracemere. "My thanks for the ride. Famous evening . . . famous sport." He grinned crookedly, and put a finger to his lip. "Mustn't let it get about, though, must we?"

The earl sighed and agreed faintly, before taking Judith's hand and raising it to his lips. "You'll understand, I'm sure, my dear Judith, when I say that I don't consider your debt paid. The terms of the agreement have not been met by tonight's little entertainment."

Judith blinked at him, squinting as she tried to focus. She seemed to be struggling with an errant memory. "Debt, sir? How did it come about that we . . . Oh, yes." She smiled triumphantly. "I remember now. We must play piquet again, you know. Next time *I'll* win the wager and I'll drive your blacks in Richmond Park."

"Maybe so," he said with a dry smile. "But first we must settle the original debt. You'll not renege, I know."

"Oh, no . . . no . . . course not." Judith hiccupped, smiled fuzzily, and tripped down the step to the pavement, where she turned and waved merrily at him through the window. He knocked on the panel and the coachman set the horses in motion. Gracemere looked back through the window as they turned the corner of the square. Brother and sister were still giggling as they stumbled up the steps to the house.

Of all the wretched pieces of ill luck . . . and the gullible simpleton couldn't even hold her drink. He would contrive better next time.

"I think we pulled that one off rather neatly," Sebastian observed, reaching for the door knocker.

Judith shook her head. "So neatly that I fear he's going to call the payment null and void and demand a rerun."

"We'll find a way around it," her brother assured her.

Judith chuckled. "Yes, of course we will. But I'm sure he thinks you're even more of a nincompoop than ever."

They were still laughing when the night porter opened the door. "Good evening, my lady."

"Good evening, Norris. Is his lordship returned?"

"Yes, my lady. He's in the library, I believe."

A wicked idea occurred to Judith, borne on the ebullience of a successful masquerade. It was one of her more asinine ideas, she would subsequently admit. Wishing her brother a swift good night, she went into the house, making her way directly to the library as she retied her loo mask.

Marcus, ensconced beside the fire, awaiting his wife's return, looked up from his Tacitus as the door opened.

"I give you good night, my lord," Judith said, leaning against the door, smiling rather vaguely at him. "Did you pass a pleasant evening?" The question was punctuated with a discreet hiccup.

"Yes, thank you." Marcus closed the book over his finger, regarding his wife with some puzzlement. She seemed to be sagging against the door in a boneless kind of way, and her smile was rather unfocused. "How was your evening?"

"Oh, famous!" She said with another hiccup. "I beg your pardon . . ." She covered her mouth with one hand. "It just seems to happen . . . so silly . . ." A giggle escaped her.

Her loo mask was askew, Marcus noticed. "Judith, are you foxed?" It seemed an extraordinary explanation, but he was familiar enough with the condition to recognize it.

She shook her head vigorously. And then hiccupped again. "Course not . . . just a trifle bosky." She swayed and giggled again. "Oh, don't look so prim, Marcus. It's not kind when I feel so warm and woolly."

"Come here!" he commanded, putting his book aside.

Judith pushed herself off the door and weaved her way toward him, knocking against a spindle-legged drum table. "Oh, dear." She grabbed it and steadied it with great deliberation, swallowing another hiccup. "Careless of me. Didn't see it there."

"So how was your evening, truly?" She plopped onto his lap with a sigh of relief. "My legs are tired. I'll lay odds you were not as entertained as I was . . . oh, I beg your pardon." A spasm of hiccups overtook her for a minute, then she rested her head against his arm, smiling that skewed smile, her eyes heavy-lidded in the slits of the loo mask.

"Where the devil have you been?" he demanded, reaching behind her head to untie the mask, torn between amusement and disapproval.

"To Ranelagh," she said with a cozy smile. "A public ridotto. Very vulgar, but famous fun. Went with Sebastian and his friends." Her eyes closed but the smile remained.

Participating in a vulgar masquerade was one thing, coming back thoroughly under the hatches was another altogether. "What the hell have you been drinking?"

"Gin," she said.

"Gin!"

"Oh, and porter," she offered, as if in mitigation. "Blue ruin and porter." She snuggled into his shoulder, her body boneless in his lap. "You should have come."

"I don't recall receiving an invitation," he said drily. "But if I had done, you wouldn't have come home in this state, I can assure you."

Her eyelids fluttered coquettishly. "You're not going to be a prude and scold, are you?"

Marcus sighed. "There would be little point in your present condition. Anyway, the condition carries its own punishment. I wouldn't want your head in the morning."

"Stuff," she said on a renewed attack of hiccups.

"Just wait. Come on, I'll put you to bed." He stood up, lifting her in his arms. She flung one arm around his neck, burying her face in his neck.

"For God's sake, keep still. I don't want to drop you."

"Oh, no," she muttered. "Wouldn't want that. Think I told Millie not to wait up for me."

"With some foresight. I can't imagine what she'd think if she saw you like this."

"Oh, you are being a prude." She tweaked his nose.

"Stop it, Judith." Disapproval was gaining the upper hand over amusement.

In her bedchamber he dropped her onto the bed. She bounced and yawned, flinging her arms and legs wide. "I'll go to sleep now."

"You can't go to sleep in your clothes." He lifted her feet, pulling off her satin pumps and tossing them to the floor. Pushing up her skirt, he unfastened her garters and drew off her silk stockings. "Stand up." He hauled her to her feet and unhooked her gown, while she swayed, humming to herself, that beatific smile still on her lips.

The gown fell to the floor in a rich rustle of taffeta and Marcus was reminded of the first time he'd undressed her in the inn on the road to Quatre Bras. It was a memory that in any other circumstances would have aroused him. Not tonight. He pulled her petticoat over her head.

Judith chose that moment to fall back on the bed with a sigh. Marcus bent over her, his lips tightening as he unfastened the tapes of her pantalettes. "Lift up." Obligingly she raised her hips so he could pull the garment down.

Her eyes opened suddenly in sleepy, seductive invitation and she ran her hands over her body, naked except for the pearl collar she wore at her throat and the pearl drops in her ears. She offered him the same skewed but rather delightful smile.

"God in heaven," Marcus muttered. "Where's your nightgown?" He found it in the armoire and pulled her into a sitting position, dropping the fine lawn over her head. "Where are your arms?"

"Here," she mumbled from within the voluminous folds of material, flapping her arms helpfully.

"Dear God!" he muttered again, thrusting the unwieldy limbs into the long sleeves. "From now on, madam wife, outside these walls you drink nothing but orgeat and lemonade, is that clear?" He removed her jewelry before pulling back the covers and maneuvering her under the sheet. Then he stood looking down at her, shaking his head.

Suddenly her eyes shot open and she was laughing up at him, all traces of befuddlement gone from her expression, the curiously smudged lines of her face snapping back into their customary firm delineation. "I fooled you, and I really didn't think I'd be able to."

His jaw dropped. "Judith, you . . . you *devil*!" He stared at her, not trusting the evidence of his eyes. But it was absolutely clear that she was as sober as she'd ever been.

Judith hitched herself up on the pillows, chuckling. "You ought to know me well enough by now to know that I'd never really get foxed. It's just an act that Sebastian and I perfected. If you think I'm convincing on my own, you should see us together."

"I imagine it serves to disarm quite a few gulls," he said in a flat voice.

"Well, yes," Judith agreed. "On occasion it did. But it's perfectly harmless."

"Harmless? You are a baggage, and I cannot imagine how you've escaped being whipped at the cart's tail through every capital on the Continent." He turned from her, seething with fury. "How dare you play your tricks on me?"

Judith suddenly realized the magnitude of her error. In the exultant aftermath of foiling Gracemere, she'd allowed herself to get carried away. Of all the tactless, stupid ideas—to play Marcus for a fool with the tricks of her disreputable past!

"Oh, Marcus, it was just a little fun," she said, leaping out of bed. "I'm sorry if you don't like being teased." She put a hand on his arm but he snatched it away. "Oh, please," she said, putting her arms around his waist, laying her head between his shoulder blades. "*Please* don't be cross. I really didn't think you'd mind being teased, but I accept it was wrong and thoughtless of me."

"It isn't a matter of being teased," he said. "You played me for a fool, and I will *not* be treated like one of the simpletons you and your brother have been exploiting all your adult lives."

"I'm sorry," she said again. "It was a grave error of judgment, I understand that now, but I really didn't mean any harm by it. Please forgive me."

There was no mistaking the contrition in her voice. Marcus allowed his anger to subside, recognizing that it had two causes: his own feeling of foolishness at having fallen for such a trick, and his dislike of any reminders of her past life. He probably should have guessed the truth. Judith was too much in control of herself and her life to yield to intoxication . . . only the appearance of it as and when it suited her.

"Don't you *ever* treat me like that again."

"I won't, I promise." She squeezed his waist. "But you haven't said you forgive me."

"I forgive you."

"Penance?"

He pulled her arms free of his waist and hauled her around in front of him, placing his hands on her shoulders. "I'll think of something appropriate once you've told me just what you were doing at Ranelagh."

"But I have told you. I went to the ridotto with Sebastian and some of his friends."

"Why didn't you mention it before?"

"Because I knew you'd be stuffy about it." She gave him a roguish smile. "And you would have been, so don't deny it."

"I wasn't going to. A public ridotto is no place for the Marchioness of Carrington."

"I know, but no one recognized us . . . there was no one there to recognize us."

"Your brother's idea of evening entertainment leaves much to be desired. However, I assume he didn't escort his prospective fiancée?" he asked aridly.

"No, of course not," Judith said. "He doesn't even like it when Harriet goes into a card room. But it's different with me."

Marcus wondered how Harriet would feel once she came face to face with the exclusivity of her husband's relationship with his sister. "It would seem that Sebastian and I have similar attitudes to what's appropriate for a wife," he observed. "I could wish that occasionally he'd remember that as well as being his sister, you're also my wife."

"He doesn't forget that. But neither does he make decisions for me," Judith pointed out. "As it happens, going to Ranelagh was my idea." Not entirely true, but near enough.

"I would have escorted you if you'd asked." His hands slipped from her shoulders to clasp her arms. "Do you prefer Sebastian's company to mine, lynx?"

"No, how could you think such a thing?" She was genuinely distressed at such an interpretation, but the sticky threads of deceit were entangling her again. She couldn't tell the truth about the evening, but without the truth, it appeared that she had chosen her brother's company over her husband's—indeed, had deliberately excluded her husband.

"It's very easy to think such a thing," he said quietly.

"I didn't think it would have amused you," she improvised, with a touch of desperation. "London is still quite new to us and we're accustomed to thinking of different things to do in new places. We just fell into an old habit."

He let it go, although the ring of truth was somehow lacking despite the plausibility of the explanation. "Very well, let's leave it at that." His hands slipped from her arms.

It sounded rather grudging to Judith. She turned back to the bed, ebullience vanished in a fog of dejection.

"Just a minute."

Something in his voice banished melancholy. She paused, one knee on the bed, the other foot on the floor.

"There remains the small matter of penance."

Judith looked over her shoulder at him, her eyes now sparkling with anticipation. "Yes, my lord?" Eagerness laced the dulcet tones.

He trod over to the bed. "I think I'll let you choose your own . . . later. For the moment, kneel on the bed." Reaching across her, he pulled the pillows out, tucking them against her belly as he unfastened his britches.

Judith laughed softly, drawing her nightgown up to her waist, falling forward over the piled pillows. "A fitting end to a ribald evening, sir."

"Abominable woman," he said, one hand in the small of her back as he guided himself within her. "If I had a grain of common sense, I'd banish you to Berkshire, where you couldn't get up to any more mischief."

Judith had no immediate rejoinder and shortly was beyond any coherent verbal response, although her body spoke to him with perfect fluency.

26

"So what now?" Agnes said, looking up from the hothouse roses she was arranging in a wide crystal bowl. "Are you still set on revenge?"

"Certainly," Gracemere said. "It was annoying, meeting Davenport like that, although I wish you could have seen the pair of them. They couldn't see straight." He smiled contemptuously at the memory. "They're such simpletons, I almost wonder if they're worth the trouble I'm taking."

Agnes tossed a fading bloom into the basket at her feet. "One must never underestimate, Bernard."

"No," he agreed, taking snuff. "And I have every intention of holding Judith to her wager. She will pay her debt at a private dinner at a place of my choosing. And this time there'll be no possibility of unwanted company. You will see her with me and you'll accidentally let the gossip fall within Carrington's earshot. Since his wife's an eager participant in this amusing liaison, he won't be able to challenge me over it, without exposing both of them to public ridicule, so he'll have to swallow it . . . and his pride."

"It'll ruin his marriage," Agnes commented with a cynical laugh.

Gracemere shrugged. "But of course. The main object of the exercise, really. I don't believe Judith cares a whit for him, anyway. She's all too eager to flout his authority." He smiled. "Where shall I arrange this intimate little dinner, my love? Somewhere rather more compromising than Ranelagh this time."

"A private parlor in a small hotel on Jermyn Street," Agnes suggested casually. "I'm sure you know such a one."

Gracemere gaped at her, then roared with laughter. "You never cease to amaze me, my dear. A brilliant idea. I'll entertain Carrington's wife in a whorehouse."

"It *is* an amusing idea," Agnes agreed. Her lip curled. "There's something about that little bitch . . . I don't know what it is, but whenever I'm in the same room with her, I feel she's trouble." She shook her head. "She never misses an opportunity to do or say something to annoy me. And I don't understand why I should allow myself to react to her insolence. But I can't help myself." She sucked a bead of blood off her finger where a rose thorn had pricked. "I shall really enjoy watching you humble her."

"Then you shall do so, my love," Gracemere said. "I shall entertain Carrington's wife in a house run by a lady of the night, and I'll lay odds his naive bride won't understand where she is."

"Therein lies the cream of the jest," Agnes assented. "She'll flutter and feel it's all most improper, but she'll have no idea *how* grossly improper . . . how could she?"

"How indeed?" Gracemere went to the secretaire. "Come and help me compose my second invitation. It needs to be a little more inviting—or do I mean compelling—than the last, but still couched in terms of calling in a debt of honor. Whatever second thoughts she may have had, she'll not renege when it's put in those terms. She likes to think of herself as a true gamester, willing to play high and lose with panache." He laughed, shaking his head. "I wonder where the Davenports sprang from."

"Oh, as you said before, one of those hybrid foreign families." Agnes drew up a chair to the secretaire. "Now, let's compose this compelling missive."

Half an hour later the earl sanded the single sheet, folded it, and sealed it with his signet ring. "You struck just the right note, my love: a challenge to the chit's willingness to play high and take risks. She'll not be able to resist the temptation to prove herself daring and reckless, pursuing an amusing adventure to pique her husband."

Agnes smiled. "And once you've finished playing games with the Devlins, what do you intend with Harriet?"

"Simple abduction. She's always in your company. You'll bring her to me in a hired chaise. Perfectly straightforward, my love."

"You'll marry her out of hand." Agnes nodded. "One night is all it will take to persuade her to go before a preacher in the morning. And once she's married, then her parents will be able to do nothing. They'll want to put the best light upon it, for fear their precious reputation be ruined. We'll have our thirty thousand, my dear, and the story will be of a runaway love match—the exigencies of a powerful passion, et cetera, et cetera." Her cynical laugh hung in the air, and Gracemere recognized as always that when it came to cold-blooded assessments of human nature, his mistress matched him step for step.

The invitation arrived in conventional fashion with Judith's chocolate the following morning. The dinner was set for that very night, the arrangements crisply laid out. She would find an unmarked chaise awaiting her as before. The destination was a secret, but it was one the earl thought she would enjoy, appealing as it would to her sense of adventure and the gamester within her.

Judith crumpled the sheet with a soft exclamation. There was no way out of this one. She couldn't refuse without annoying Gracemere and, as before, she couldn't afford to annoy him, not this close to the endgame.

She dressed and went in search of Marcus. He was in his book room, closeted with John, but looked up, his eyes crinkling with pleasure at her entrance. "Good morning, my love. What can I do for you?"

Sweet heaven, how she hated lying to him. She smiled at John to take her mind off what she was saying. "I just wanted to tell you that I'm going to a very private dinner this evening."

"Oh," Marcus said, putting down his quill. "Am I not invited?"

"No, I'm afraid not." She turned her eyes to him, hoping she was now in control of her features. "It's all women, you see."

Marcus laughed. "Cornelia and the others?"

"Just so. I'm sure I won't be late, though."

John coughed apologetically. "Excuse me, your ladyship, but you and Lord Carrington are engaged to the Willoughbys this evening—the musicale," he said. "The harpist, if you recall?"

"Oh, I'd completely forgotten," Judith said. "And I do so want to spend the evening with my friends. Marcus . . . would you mind?"

He couldn't resist the appeal in those golden brown eyes. "I must go alone, it would seem."

"You are a prince among husbands," she said, reaching across the desk to kiss him. John averted his eyes.

"I shall expect compensation," Marcus said.

"That goes without saying." She went to the door. "And as I said, I won't be late."

In fact, if she managed matters aright, she wouldn't be out of the house for much more than an hour. Bernard Melville, Earl of Gracemere, was not going to enjoy the clandestine company of his enemy's wife . . . whatever he might think.

Thus resolved, Judith felt a little better about her lie. Circumstances were working in her favor, since none of her friends had been invited to the musicale. The Willoughbys were an elderly couple who didn't go about much in Society, but were friends of Marcus's mother and he had felt obliged to accept the invitation to a small and select gathering of elderly music lovers. By the time he came home, his wife would be virtuously abed, having spent the greater part of the evening irreproachably by her own fireside.

She dressed with care that evening, choosing a gown with an unusually high neckline and arranging her hair in a demure braided coronet. Her conduct tonight would be the antithesis of flirtatious. Before leaving, she sent Millie on an errand to the kitchen that greatly puzzled the abigail. However, questions were not invited so she fetched what was required and saved her curiosity for later in the servants' hall, when her ladyship's strange request could be discussed at length.

Judith dropped the small package into her reticule, adjusted the shawl about her shoulders, and went downstairs. The Willoughbys kept early hours and Marcus had already left.

The unmarked chaise awaited her on the same corner as before, and as before the earl was inside to greet her.

"Good evening, Bernard," Judith said cheerfully. "I must say, sir, that you don't give much notice of your invitations."

"Adventures are supposed to take one by surprise," he said. "And you do like adventures, don't you, my dear Judith?"

Judith allowed a little giggle to escape her. "Life would be very dull without them, sir."

"Just so. And the so-staid husband . . . how was he disposed of for the evening?"

Judith gritted her teeth. "Marcus had his own engagement," she said. "Where do we go, Bernard?"

"Ah, that's a surprise," he told her. "I trust you'll be pleased."

"I'm sure I shall." She clapped her hands softly, her eyes glowing in the dim light of the chaise. "I like surprises as much as I like adventures."

"Splendid," he said, reaching across to take her hand. "I hope this one will be all that you expect."

"And I hope the evening will be all that you expect, Bernard," she said, smiling a little shyly.

He carried her hand to his lips.

The chaise drew up in front of a tall town house, its door lit by a lantern, light glowing from behind curtained windows. Judith stepped out and looked curiously up and down the street. "Where are we?"

"Jermyn Street," Gracemere said casually. "A small and very discreet hotel I frequent on occasion. Come, my dear." He escorted her to the door that was opened by an elderly butler in a powdered wig.

"My lord . . . madam." He bowed. "Madame is in the salon."

Judith allowed herself to be ushered into the salon. She looked around at the gilt moldings, the heavy satin draperies, the deep armchairs, and the women in their elegant gowns with just a little something out of place. The air was heavy with the fragrance of musk, a decadent, overblown scent, and Judith knew immediately what Gracemere had brought her to. She'd been in such places before: the luxurious bordello catering to the wealthy and whatever tastes they might have. There was nothing these women wouldn't do if the price was right.

She glanced sideways at her escort and saw the smile flickering on the cruel mouth as he greeted their ostensible hostess. He wouldn't think she knew what the place was, she realized. After all, what respectable lady of the ton would? He wasn't to know that her father had had many good friends who ran places like this one—friends who would provide free lodging on occasion to the impoverished gamester and his children . . . lodging and comfort to the lonely widower. Her father had never been short of female company, Judith remembered. Something about him appealed to women. She suspected he'd never paid for the comfort offered him in places such as this. Once his children had reached a certain age, however, George Davenport had stopped accepting this kind of hospitality, but Judith's memory was crystal clear.

Madame greeted her courteously, but her eyes were shrewdly assessing and she too seemed to share in the jest with Gracemere. They obviously knew each other well.

"Your private dining room is ready, my lord," she said. "Bernice will show you up." She beckoned to a young woman in crimson satin, who came over immediately. Her gown was rich, the fall of lace at the neck delicate, but the lace was slightly awry, and the neckline so low that it barely covered her nipples.

"This way, sir . . . madam." She barely acknowledged Judith but smiled at Gracemere, who chucked her beneath the chin with a lazy forefinger.

They went upstairs to a small parlor, as ostentatiously decorated as the one downstairs. A fire burned in the grate, and a round table was set for two. A richly cushioned divan was the only other furniture, apart from a worked screen in the corner. It would conceal the commode, Judith knew. Rooms such as this were equipped to cater in total privacy for all needs.

"Goodness me, Bernard," she said with an amazed little titter. "What a strange place. It's almost more like a bedchamber than a dining parlor."

"It's a very private hotel," he said, pouring wine into two glasses. "A toast, my dear Judith."

She took the glass. "And what shall we toast, sir?"

"Adventure and the confounding of dictatorial husbands." He raised his glass, laughing at her as he drank.

Judith took a sip, smiling, then, carrying her glass, she strolled over to the window and drew aside the curtain to look down on the street. Under cover of the curtain, she took the packet from her reticule and shook the contents in her wineglass.

"Are there many such hotels on this street, Bernard?" she asked in tones of innocent curiosity, turning back to him, giving him a wide-eyed smile as she drained the contents of her glass. "May I have some more wine?"

"Of course, my dear." He brought the decanter over to her. If she became foxed again, it would only add spice to the affair this time. She probably wouldn't remember what had happened, and he'd deposit her at her doorstep for her husband in a distinctly shop-soiled condition.

Judith raised the refilled glass, then gasped, slamming it back on the table. Her hand went to her throat and, under Gracemere's astonished, horrified gaze, she turned a delicate shade of green. With a sudden gasp, she flew behind the screen to the commode from whence came the most unromantic and unladylike sounds.

Marcus made his wife's excuses to the Willoughbys, offering a polite white lie. He did what was required of him, making the rounds of his fellow guests, most of whom he'd known since boyhood, ate an indifferent dinner, enjoyed good burgundy, and followed his fellow guests to the drawing room for the recital.

"My Lord Carrington, this is an unexpected encounter." Agnes Barret materialized on the arm of her elderly husband just as the harpist took her place. "We are come so late," she whispered, sitting beside the marquis. "We had another dinner engagement, but we couldn't offend the Willoughbys. Such old friends of my husband's." She fanned herself vigorously and looked around the room, nodding and smiling as she met recognition.

Marcus murmured something suitable, thinking that she was a most attractive woman, with those fine eyes and high cheekbones and that curiously familiar wicked curve to her mouth.

"Lady Carrington isn't with you?" Agnes turned her smile upon him.

"No, she had a previous engagement," he said.

"Ah." Agnes frowned as if in thought. "Not in Jermyn Street, of course."

Premonition shot up Marcus's spine like flame on a tarred stick. "I hardly think so, ma'am."

Agnes shook her head. "No, of course not. Silly of me, I had the unmistakable impression I'd seen her alighting from a chaise . . . it must have been a trick of the light. The lantern over the door was throwing strange shadows."

Marcus sat still, a smile fixed on his face, his eyes on the harpist as she began to pluck her instrument. He felt enwrapped in tendrils of malice, the evil mischief emanating from the woman beside him seeming to weave around him. Judith had been right. Agnes Barret was not harmless. Agnes Barret was dangerous. And if Agnes Barret was Gracemere's lover, then Judith was in danger. How or why, he couldn't guess. But he was as certain of it as he was of his own name. Martha's battered little face rose vividly in his memory, the despairing whimpers filling his ears anew.

He rose without excuse from his chair and left the room, while the harpist's gentle music continued behind him.

Agnes, startled, watched him stalk from the room. She'd done no more than sow the first little seed. She hadn't mentioned Bernard. That would come tomorrow or the next day, a whispered word to set the gossip on its way. What could possibly have driven the marquis to leave so precipitately?

Marcus left the house without making farewells and walked fast to Jermyn Street.

Gracemere listened for a minute in horrified impotence to the sounds of violent retching behind the screen. Then he strode to the door, flung it open, and bellowed for help. Madame came up the stairs, two of her girls on her heels.

"Whatever is it, my lord?"

He gestured to the room behind him. "Her ladyship appears to be unwell. Do something."

Madame listened for a minute, gave the earl a most telling look, and hurried into the room, disappearing behind the screen.

Gracemere paced the corridor, unwilling to return to the scene of such a horribly intimate disintegration. He thumped a fist into the palm of his other hand, cursing all women. It couldn't have been the wine, she'd only had one glass and she'd been perfectly sober when they'd arrived.

Judith staggered out from behind the screen, supported by Madame and one of the women. She was waxen, a faint sheen of perspiration on her brow, her hair lackluster, her eyes watering.

"My lord, I don't know what . . ." She pressed her hand to her mouth. "Something I ate . . . so mortifying . . . I don't know how to apologize—"

"You must go home," he interrupted brusquely. "The chaise will take you."

She nodded feebly. "Yes, thank you. I have to lie down." Staggering, she fell onto the divan, lying back with her eyes closed.

Madame took her fan and began to ply it vigorously. "My lord, I can't have sick women in my house," she said, an edge to the refined accents. "It doesn't look good, and what my other guests would think, listening . . ."

"Yes, yes," Bernard interrupted. "Have her taken downstairs and put in the chaise. Tell the driver to take her back to Berkeley Square."

Somehow, a limp and groaning Judith was bundled down the stairs and into the waiting chaise. Bernard stood at the window, watching as the vehicle moved off down the street. Some devil was at work here, throwing all his carefully engineered schemes awry. He went to the table and flung himself into a chair, moodily refilling his glass. He might as well eat the dinner he'd ordered with such care.

Marcus turned onto Jermyn Street from St. James's. He was amazed at his own calm as he looked down the street. Three houses had lanterns outside their doors. Behind one of those doors he was certain he would find his wife in the company of Bernard Melville, Earl of Gracemere. He had no idea why she was there, why she would have allowed herself to be trapped by Gracemere, but the reasons didn't interest him at the moment. There would be time for that later. He had but one thought, to reach her before she was hurt.

The first door had no knowledge of the Earl of Gracemere. The butler in the powdered wig behind the second door bowed him within immediately. Madame emerged from the salon, all smiles, ready to greet a new customer.

"Where is Gracemere?"

The clipped question, the burning black eyes, the almost mask-like impassivity of expression impressed Madame as nothing else could have done. "I believe his lordship is abovestairs, sir. Is he expecting you?"

"If he's not, he should be," Marcus said. "Direct me to him, if you please."

Madame made a shrewd guess as to the business the new arrival might have with the earl. She gestured to Bernice. It was none of her business if Gracemere chose to invoke outraged husbands, and she wasn't prepared to have a scene in her hall. "Show this gentleman to Lord Gracemere's parlor."

Marcus strode up the stairs after the girl. At the door, he waved her away. He stood for a second listening. There was complete silence. After lifting the latch gently, he pushed the door open. The room had a single occupant.

Gracemere was sprawled in a chair at the table, a glass of claret in his hand, his eyes on the offensively cheerful glow in the grate. His head swiveled at the sound of the door opening.

"Ah, Gracemere," Marcus observed, deceptively pleasant. "There you are."

"I'm flattered you should seek me out, Carrington." Bernard sipped his wine. "To what do I owe this unlooked-for attention?"

"Oh, a simple matter." Marcus tossed his cane onto the divan and took the chair opposite the earl. He examined the place settings for a minute before returning his attention to the earl. "A simple matter," he repeated. "Where is my wife, Bernard?"

Gracemere gestured expansively around the room. "Why ask me, Marcus? I dine alone."

"It would appear so," Marcus agreed. "But you are clearly expecting a guest." He picked up the fork at his place, examining the tines with careful interest, before reaching for the second wineglass on the table. It was half full. "Has your guest made a temporary departure?"

The earl gave a crack of sardonic laughter. "I trust not temporary."

"Oh? You interest me greatly, Gracemere. Please explain." He turned the stem of the wineglass between finger and thumb, regarding the earl intently across the table.

"Your wife is not here," the earl said. "She has been here, but she is by now, I trust, safely tucked up in her own bed."

"I see." Marcus rose. "And the circumstances of her departure . . . ?"

Gracemere shuddered. "Quite innocent, I assure you. Your wife's virtue remains untainted, Marcus. Now, perhaps you'd leave me to my dinner."

"By all means. But allow me to give you a piece of advice. If you should have any further plans involving the health and welfare of my wife, I suggest you drop them forthwith." He picked up his cane and tapped it thoughtfully into his palm. "I would hate to use a horse-whip on you again, but if it did become necessary, I can safely promise you that this time it will be no secret. It will be the most talked of on-dit of this or any other Season."

He bowed, mockery in every line of his body, but there was no concealing the menace in his eyes as they rested for a second on Gracemere's flushed face. "Don't underestimate me again, Bernard. And just remember that another time I'll not let pride conceal the truth. I'll face whatever I have to to expose you. That is all I have to say."

He walked out of the room, closing the door quietly behind him.

27

Marcus walked back to Berkeley Square. Whatever reasons Judith had had for involving herself with Gracemere initially, she'd been perfectly capable of extricating herself from trouble. Judging by the half-full wineglass, she'd left in haste, and she must have made some considerable scene if her putative host hoped she wasn't going to return.

But why the hell had she been with Gracemere in the first place? Had she been defying her husband for principle's sake? But that didn't make sense—they'd resolved the issue amicably as far as he remembered. She'd agreed to do as he wished if he moderated his dictatorial manner. So why would she persist in cultivating such an acquaintanceship. No, it was much more than that. Acquaintances didn't dine tête-à-tête. So why?

The old serpents of mistrust began to wreathe and writhe in his gut, and he felt cold and sick. Did he know her at all? Had he ever known her? Had she colluded with Gracemere to wound him? But if that was so, why had she left her dinner companion against his will? Perhaps she hadn't expected seduction. His ingenuous wife had believed an invitation to a clandestine dinner to be completely innocent? Impossible. There was nothing ingenuous about Judith; she was far too worldly to fall for such a fabrication. But perhaps Gracemere had led her to believe the invitation was different—not a private party but one in company she knew. And when she'd discovered the truth . . . This explanation was more plausible, and he began to feel a little comforted. And then he remembered how she'd lied to him that morning—a party with her women friends. The serpents hissed and acid betrayal soured his mouth.

Judith was standing at her window, looking down on the square, when he came in sight of the house. She had been waiting for him, knowing what she had to do. She had known that Gracemere was capable of ruining a man with cheating and lies. She knew he was capable of running off with another man's fiancée. But this evening she had glimpsed the depths of maleficence that outdid anything that she already knew. A clandestine rendezvous was one thing, but to pick such a place for the kind of woman he believed Judith to be was evil beyond anything. Somehow Marcus was to have been injured by Gracemere's plotting and Marcus's wife had been just a tool. Judith was now convinced of it. Was Marcus to be somehow confronted with the information of his wife's rendezvous? Confronted and humiliated? Was it to be made public perhaps?

She stood at the window with her arms crossed over her breasts, still feeling weak and shaky after her violent vomiting but knowing that unless she could circumvent Gracemere's ulterior motive, she might just as well have yielded to seduction. If a public scandal was to be made, the simple fact of her willing presence in such a place with the earl would be sufficient cause.

She was going to have to tell Marcus the whole. If he heard it from her lips, he would be forewarned and forearmed. The thought of what she risked by such a course filled her with dread.

Marcus disappeared from view as he climbed the steps beneath her window.

She went out to the hall at the top of the stairs as Marcus was admitted to the house, then she sped lightly down the stairs toward him.

"Marcus, I need to talk with you."

He looked up, and despite the gall and wormwood of his suspicions, his eyes anxiously raked her face. She was pale and tense, but other than that, as far as he could tell seemed quite well.

"Did you enjoy your evening?" he asked, unsmiling as he handed his cloak and gloves to Gregson. Until he decided how to deal with the situation, he would pretend he knew nothing about it.

Judith shook her head dismissively. "Could we go into your book room? I have to talk to you."

Surely she wasn't going to tell him? A thrill of hope coursed through him. "It's a book-room matter?"

"I believe so." She was clasping her hands tightly, her expression one of painful intensity.

Marcus knew he wanted her confidence now more than he had ever wanted anything. Only her honesty would have the power to erase the suspicions, defang the serpents of mistrust. But just in case he was wrong, he continued the charade. "Oh, dear." He managed a faint smile of rueful comprehension at this choice of venue. His book room seemed to have become the arena for discussion of all potentially explosive issues. "Could it wait until morning?"

"I don't think so."

"Very well. Let's get it over with, whatever it is."

Judith led the way. The candles were extinguished but the fire was still alight. She relit the candles while Marcus tossed a log onto the embers.

"Am I going to need fortification?" He gestured to the decanters on the sideboard.

"I imagine so. I'll have a glass of port also."

Marcus filled two glasses, watching as Judith bent to warm her hands at the fire, its light setting matching fires aglow in the burnished ringlets tumbling about her face.

"I have a confession to make," she said eventually, turning to face him, her pallor even more marked. "I'm afraid you're going to be very, very angry."

She was going to tell him. He kept the joy from his expression and said evenly, "I'm duly warned. Let me hear it."

"Very well." She put down her glass and squared her shoulders. "It's about Gracemere." She paused, but Marcus said nothing, although his eyes had narrowed. He sipped his port and waited.

Quietly she told him how she had played piquet with Gracemere, what the stakes were, and where he had taken her that evening. "I'm afraid he intends to create some scandal that would humiliate you," she finished. "I had to tell you . . . warn you. I couldn't bear you to hear it from anyone else."

She fell silent, twisting her hands against her skirt, her expression taut with anxiety as she waited for his response.

"You recognized the place for what it was?" His voice was level, and his eyes had not left her face.

She nodded. "As children we spent some time in similar establishments . . . but that's another story."

"You must tell me sometime," he commented calmly. "You didn't stay very long tonight, I gather."

"No, I put mustard in my wine and made myself very sick," she said. "It's a trick I've used before to get out of a ticklish situation." A gleam appeared in her eye, a hint of the customarily mischievous Judith. "I'm afraid the earl was rather put off by the results."

The Earl of Gracemere's disgruntlement was now explained. Against all the odds, laughter bubbled in Marcus's chest. "You vomited?"

She nodded. "Prodigiously . . . mustard has that effect. It's also very wearing," she added. "I still feel weak and shivery."

Marcus asked his most important question. "Am I to be told why you've been cultivating Gracemere despite our agreement that you would hold him at arm's length?"

Judith bit her lip. This was where it became tricky. "There is something I wasn't intending to tell you—"

"Dear God, Judith, you have more layers than an onion!" Marcus interrupted. "Every time I think I've peeled away the last skin and reached some core of truth and understanding, you reveal a dozen new layers."

"I'm sure you've never peeled an onion in your life," Judith said, momentarily diverted.

"That is beside the point."

Judith sighed. "I know that it was Gracemere who took Martha from you—" Marcus's sharply indrawn breath stopped her for a minute, but when he said nothing, she continued resolutely.

"Gracemere told me, as an explanation for why you held him in such enmity. I wanted—" She paused, casting a quick look up at him. His expression was impassive, neither encouraging nor threatening.

"I wanted to know something about Martha," she rushed on. "You wouldn't talk of her . . . except that once in the inn at Quatre Bras, and then you said you never wanted to talk about her again. You said she was my antithesis in every way, and I wanted to know what she was like—what that meant. It was almost an obsession," she finished, opening her hands in a gesture appealing for understanding.

Marcus stared, for the moment unable to respond. Feminine curiosity! Was that all it was? Judith simply wanted to know what her predecessor had been like? The simplicity of the answer confused him. It seemed too simple for someone as complex as Judith. And yet it was perfectly understandable. He had been adamant in his refusal to discuss that aspect of his past.

"I've never liked Gracemere, Marcus," Judith said when he remained silent. She was thinking fast now, and the distorted truth tripped convincingly off her tongue.

"I've never trusted him either, which is why I took the mustard. But I didn't think it would do any harm to cultivate him long enough to satisfy my curiosity. He was playing with me. I knew that. And I thought, so long as I knew it, I'd be able to play along without anything serious happening. I'd find out what I wanted and that would be that. I didn't intend to hurt you . . . I . . . oh, how can I convince you of that?"

He scrutinized her expression for a minute, then nodded slowly. "I believe you. Did he satisfy your curiosity?"

Judith shook her head. "There wasn't time. Once I realized what he was up to this evening, I had to move quickly."

Marcus turned to the fire and threw on another log. When he spoke, his voice was businesslike.

"It's true that Martha fell in love with Gracemere. It's true I think that had I been more attentive, she wouldn't have done so. I grew up with her. Her family's estates marched with my own, and it had always been assumed, from the cradle almost, that we would unite the two estates. I saw no reason to question the plan, but neither did I see any reason to pay Martha any particular attentions on that account."

A log slipped in a shower of sparks, and he kicked it back with a booted foot. "I amused myself in the manner of most young sprigs with too much money and not enough to occupy them. Martha was a meek dab of a girl, a little brown mouse."

He glanced across at Judith, who was all burnished radiance and luster despite the events of the evening. "You and she are chalk and cheese," he said. "Both physically and in temperament. Martha was meek and easily influenced. The perfect prey for someone like Gracemere, whose pockets were always to let and who spent his time dodging bailiffs and the Fleet prison. But he's of impeccable breeding, has considerable address and a honeyed tongue when it suits him. They eloped, putting me in the guise of a loathsome suitor forced upon an unwilling woman."

He turned his back to the room, leaning his arm along the mantelpiece, staring down into the rekindled fire as the memory of that time flooded his mind as vividly as if it were yesterday.

Martha's father had been a sick man, and she'd had no brothers. It had fallen to the hand of the jilted fiancé to go after the fugitives and bring Martha back before they joined hands over the anvil. He'd found them very quickly. Gracemere had had no intention of immediately taking Martha to Gretna Green.

She'd been a battered, gibbering wreck when he'd come up with them. Her lover, desperate to ensure there would be no possibility of annulment, had raped her within a few hours of their flight. Ruined, and possibly pregnant, Martha had had no option but to accept as husband the only man likely to offer for her.

"I backed out of the engagement with as much grace as I could muster," he said in the same level tones, giving no indication of the violent swirling of the age-old rage—a rage that had led him to thrash Bernard Melville to within an inch of his life.

"And nine months later Martha died giving birth to a stillborn child. Gracemere inherited her entire fortune except for the estate which her father left to a nephew. He was determined that Gracemere shouldn't take that . . . for which I can only be grateful, having been spared such a neighbor."

He looked up, his eyes unreadable. "Does that satisfy your curiosity, lynx?"

Judith nodded. But in truth the curiosity that had been a convenient fabrication was now reality. Marcus was leaving something out; she could hear the gaps in the story as if he'd underlined them. And she could feel the deep currents of emotion swirling behind his apparently bland expression. However, she had no choice under the circumstances but to accept what he'd said without question. The ease with which she'd managed to deceive him was somehow harder to endure than the deception itself. He now trusted her enough to believe her lies.

"I don't know why I needed to know so badly," she said. "It happened a long time ago, after all."

"Yes, when you were a little girl of twelve," Marcus responded with a dry half smile.

"Are you very angry?" Judith regarded him somberly. "You have the right, I freely admit it."

Marcus frowned, pulling at his chin. Her confession seemed to have made all the difference to his feelings. "No, I'm not angry. You put yourself in a highly dangerous and compromising situation, but you managed to extricate yourself neatly enough. However, I'm disappointed you didn't feel able to ask *me* your questions. I would have thought matters were running smoothly enough between us for that."

Oh, what a tangled web we weave, Judith thought, hearing the hurt in his voice. She couldn't possibly enter into any discussion about why she hadn't felt able to share her invented curiosity with him. She offered him a slightly helpless shrug of acceptance that he acknowledged with a resigned shake of his head.

"What are we going to do if Gracemere does decide to create a scandal?" She changed the subject.

Marcus's expression hardened. "He won't." It was a sharp, succinct statement.

"But how can you be so sure?"

"My dear Judith, don't you trust me to make sure of it?" he demanded in a voice like iron. "Believe me, I am a match for Gracemere."

Judith, looking at the set of his jaw, the uncompromising slash of his mouth, the eyes like black flint, didn't doubt for a minute that her husband was more than a match for Gracemere, or anyone else who might decide to meddle in his affairs.

And where did that leave his wife? His lying, conniving trickster of a wife. A shudder ripped up her spine, and she crossed her arms, hugging her breasts, staring up at him in silence.

His expression abruptly softened as he saw her shiver. "You need to be in bed," he said. "An evening spent hanging over the commode is enough to exhaust anyone." A smile tugged willy-nilly at the corners of his mouth as he imagined the scene. He could almost feel sorry for Gracemere. He picked up her discarded wineglass and handed it to her, saying lightly, "Be a good girl and finish your port, it'll warm you."

Judith's responding smile was somewhat tentative, but she obediently finished the wine and found it comforting in her sore and empty belly.

"Upstairs now." Marcus took the glass from her. "I'll come up later, when you're tucked in."

"I seem to need to be cuddled," Judith said in a voice that sounded small.

Marcus put his arms around her, holding her tightly against him, feeling her fragility. "I'll hold you all night," he promised into her fragrant hair. "I'll come as soon as Millie's helped you to bed."

He held her throughout the night, and she slept secure in his arms, but her dreams were filled with images of things cracked and broken under a tumultous reign of chaos.

28

A FEW DAYS LATER, AS HE SAT OVER THE BREAKFAST TABLE, MARCUS RECEIVED an invitation from his old friend Colonel Morcby of the Seventh Hussars, requesting the pleasure of his company at a regimental dinner in the company of Arthur Wellesley, Duke of Wellington; Field Marshal Gebhard Leberecht von Blücher; and General Karl von Clausewitz, at eight o'clock in the evening of Wednesday, December 12 at regimental headquarters on Horseguard's Parade. December 12 was the night of the Duchess of Devonshire's ball.

Marcus drank his coffee, wondering how Judith would react if he cried off from the ball. It was the high point of the pre-Christmas festivities, and all fashionable London would be there. Would she feel neglected if she had to go alone? But her friends would be there, and her brother, he reasoned. It wasn't as if he'd see much of her all evening, even if he did escort her. Besides, Judith was not a woman to demand her husband's company when he'd received an invitation so vastly more appealing. He didn't doubt she'd understand the appeal of the invitation from Colonel Morcby.

He left the breakfast parlor and went upstairs to his wife's chamber. The atmosphere in the room was steamy and scented. The fire had been built as high as safety permitted and heat blasted the room, augmenting the steam wreathing from a copper hip bath drawn up before the hearth. Marcus blinked to clear his vision and then smiled.

Millie was pouring more water from a copper jug into the tub while Judith stood beside the bath, one toe delicately testing the temperature. Her hair was piled on top of her head and she hadn't a stitch of clothing on.

"Good morning, sir." She greeted him with a smile. "I think that'll do for the moment, Millie. But perhaps you should fetch up some more jugs from the kitchen for later. . . . I'm taking a bath, Marcus," she informed him somewhat unnecessarily.

"So I see." He stepped aside as Millie hurried past him through the doorway, carrying empty jugs.

"I intend to spend the entire morning luxuriating in hot water," she informed him, stepping into the tub. "It's a pity you can't join me."

"Who says I can't?"

"Well, no one." She let her head fall back against the rim, drawing her legs up so that her dimpled knees broke the surface of the water. "I simply assumed, since you're dressed for town, that you were not in the mood for beguilement."

"Sadly, I'm in the mood but unable to indulge," he said. "I'm on my way to Angelo's."

"Ah," said Judith, sitting up suddenly, slopping water over the edge of the bath onto the sheet spread beneath it. "I should like to learn to fence."

"You amaze me," Marcus said, shrugging out of his coat and rolling up his shirt sleeves. "I didn't think there was anything you didn't know how to do. Weren't you able to find an admirer to teach you?"

"Sadly, no," she said, sitting back again, regarding his preparations through narrowed eyes. "Perhaps you would like to take on the task."

"It'll be a pleasure." Marcus picked up the lavender-scented cake of soap from the dish beside the bath and moved behind her. "Lean forward and I'll do your back."

"You'll ruin your pantaloons, kneeling on the floor," she pointed out, remaining with her back against the tub.

"They are knitted, my dear, and mold themselves to my wishes," he observed. "Unlike my wife, it would seem." He slipped an arm around her, bending her forward so that he could soap the smooth plane of her back with firm circular movements, occasionally scribbling down her spine with a tantalizing fingernail.

Judith arched her back like a cat beneath the hard hands, bending her neck for the rough exploration of a fingertip creeping into her scalp.

"Oh, I was forgetting," Marcus murmured, sliding his hand down her back beneath the surface of the water on a more intimate laundering. "I've received an invitation to dine in Horseguard's Parade on Wednesday. Would you mind if I don't accompany you to the ball?" Gentle pressure bent her further over his encircling arm, and the sudden tension in her body, the ripple of her skin, he ascribed to its obvious cause.

"Who invited you?" She tried to sound casually interested, even though she knew the answer. Charlie had engineered the invitation from his own regimental colonel. Initially, he'd been puzzled by Judith's request that he do so, until she'd explained that she wanted it to be a surprise for Marcus, who would find the ball a dead bore and would much prefer to dine with his military friends.

Marcus was unable to hide his pleasure in the prospect of such an evening in such company as he told Judith what she already knew. It was slight balm to her guilty conscience.

Millie's reappearance with fresh jugs of hot water put an end to tantalizing play, and Marcus dropped the soap into the water, dried his hands, and stood up, rolling down his sleeves. "I'll leave you to your bath, lynx."

"Don't forget to tell John to accept the colonel's invitation before you go."

"I won't." Fleetingly he touched the topknot of copper ringlets as he went to the door. "An understanding wife is a pearl beyond price."

Oh, what a tangled web we weave. The desolate refrain seemed to have become a part of her bloodstream these days, thudding in time with the life blood in her veins.

Bernard Melville cast a covert glance at his opponent across the card table. Davenport was drinking heavily. His hair was tousled, flopping untidily over his broad forehead, and every now and again he would run his hands through it with a distracted air. He had been losing steadily for three hours and Bernard felt the gut-twisting excitement of the gamester who has his opponent on the run. He had ceased to keep count of his winnings, and knew from his own experience that Sebastian, in the grip of the same fever, would have no idea how much he'd lost. He had run out of rouleaux long since and now scribbled IOUs without apparent awareness; the pile of vowels mounted at Bernard's elbow.

Twice Bernard had used marked cards, when Sebastian had won the preceding hands and the earl, so addicted now to winning against him, hadn't been able to endure even the slightest possibility of further losses. He could smell blood, the taste of it was on his tongue. In another hour, he reckoned, Sebastian Davenport would be a ruined man.

"Sebastian, you've been at cards all evening." Harry Middleton strolled across to the table, trying to conceal his concern as he took in the vowels and rouleaux at Gracemere's elbow. "Leave it now, man, and come and be sociable."

Bernard was unable to conceal his fury at this interference and his breath hissed through his teeth. "Leave the man alone, Middleton, can't you see we're in the middle of play?"

Sebastian looked up and smiled in rather dazed fashion at his friend. "Devil take it, Harry, but I lost track of the time." His eyes focused again on his cards. "Last hand, Gracemere. I'm all rolled up for tonight." He laughed with an assumption of carelessness and discarded the knave of hearts.

Bernard had no choice but to accept the end of play when, at the end of the hand, Sebastian threw down his cards and yawned. "What's the damage, Gracemere?"

Bernard added up the points. "Ninety-eight."

"Rubiconed, by God!" Sebastian yawned again. "Tot up my vowels and I'll send you a draft on my bank in the morning."

The staggering sum handed to him had its effect. The earl examined him covertly, noting the sudden slight tremor of his hands, the tightening of his mouth. Then Sebastian looked up, raised his eyebrows in an assumption of carelessness, and whistled. "You'll give me a chance to come about, I trust, my lord?"

"But of course—tomorrow, at Devonshire House?" Bernard almost licked his fleshy lips in anticipation.

Sebastian nodded, tried to laugh, but it had a hollow ring. "Why not? It'll be a dull enough affair otherwise, I'll lay odds." Flinging a comradely arm around Harry's shoulder, he strolled off with his friend.

"It looked like you lost a fortune," Harry remarked, giving his friend an anxious stare.

Sebastian shrugged. "I'll get it back, Harry, tomorrow."

"I told you, Gracemere's a bad man to play with."

Sebastian looked down at his friend and Harry saw a different light in his eyes. He spoke softly. "So am I, Harry, as Gracemere is going to find out. You'll see."

Harry's scalp prickled. He had never seen Sebastian look like that, never heard that note in his voice. He suddenly saw Sebastian Davenport as a dangerous man, and he didn't know how or why he should have formed such an impression.

29

"Gregson, when my brother calls you may send him straight up to the yellow drawing room. But I'm not at home to anyone else." Judith crossed the hall to the stairs the following morning, pausing to rearrange a display of bronze chrysanthemums in a copper jug on a marble table.

"Very well, my lady."

"These are past their best," she said, giving up on the flowers. "Have them replaced, please."

"Yes, my lady." Gregson bowed. There was an unusual sharpness in her ladyship's voice this morning, a slight air of irritability about her.

Judith ran up to her own sanctum, where she sat down immediately in front of the chess board. The problem set out was sufficiently complex to occupy her mind for the next hour while she waited for her brother. They would spend the greater part of the day training for the evening's play, separating at the end of the afternoon with time enough to rest and compose themselves before the game began.

It was a pattern they had established long since, on their travels, but it had been many months since they'd used it. Despite her anxiety, the immense value of the stakes, Judith was aware of the old familiar prickle of excitement, the surge of exhilaration.

Sebastian arrived before midmorning. He greeted her briefly, then shrugged out of his coat and sat down in his shirt-sleeves, breaking the pack of cards on the table. "Let's go over the code for aces. The movement you make for the spade is very similar to the one for the heart. I want to see if we can sharpen the difference." Judith nodded and picked up her fan.

They worked steadily until noon, making minor adjustments to the code of signals, then they played a game of chess until Gregson announced nuncheon. Marcus walked into the dining room to find his wife and her brother eating scalloped oysters and cold chicken in absorbed silence.

"If I didn't know you both better, I'd think I was interrupting a quarrel," he observed, helping himself to oysters.

"No," Judith said, managing a smile. "We were just absorbed in our own thoughts. How was your morning?"

Marcus began to regale them with a tale he'd heard at Brooks's, and then realized that they weren't listening to him. He paused, waited for one of them to notice that he hadn't finished the story, and when neither of them did, shrugged and turned his attention to his plate.

"Are you dining at home this evening, Ju?" Sebastian asked abruptly.

"No, at the Henleys'," she answered. "Isobel's giving a dinner party before the ball."

"Oh, good." Marcus refilled his glass, smiling across the table at her. "I didn't like to think of you dining alone, lynx."

"Oh, I can usually avoid such a fate, if I wish to," she said with a lift of her eyebrows. "I'm not dependent upon my husband's company, my lord."

Ordinarily, the remark would have been bantering, but for some reason Marcus sensed a strain in the words, and her smile seemed effortful. Perhaps she *had* quarreled with Sebastian.

"Do you have something important to do this afternoon, Judith, or would you like to ride with me in Richmond Park? It's a beautiful afternoon," he asked at the end of the meal.

She shook her head. "Another day I'd come with pleasure, but this afternoon Sebastian and I have plans that can't be put off."

"Oh." He tossed his napkin on the table, concealing his hurt and puzzlement. "Then I'll leave you to them."

"Oh, dear," Judith whispered as the door closed softly behind him. "I didn't mean to sound so dismissive, but I couldn't think what other excuse to make."

"After tonight, you won't have to make excuses." Sebastian pushed back his chair. "Let's get back to work."

By five o'clock, they knew they had covered every eventuality, every combination of hands that skill and experience could come up with. They knew how Gracemere played when he played straight, and Sebastian knew what tricks he favored when he played crooked. They now had in place their own system that would defeat the earl's marked cards.

"We've done the best we can," Sebastian pronounced finally. "There's an element of chance, of course, but there always is."

"He's a gamester who's scented blood," Judith said. "We know what that madness is like. Once in the grip of it, he'll not stop until he's at *point non plus* . . . or you are."

"It will not be I," her brother said with quiet confidence.

"No." Judith held out her hand. They clasped hands in silent communion that held both promise and resolve. Then Sebastian bent and kissed her cheek and left. She listened to his feet receding on the stairs, before going up to her room to lie down with pads soaked in witch hazel on her eyes, and a swirling cloud of playing cards in her internal vision.

Gracemere escorted Agnes Barret to Devonshire House some time after ten o'clock. They were early, but not unfashionably so, and spent an hour circulating the salons. They danced twice and then Agnes was claimed by a bewhiskered acquaintance of her ailing husband's. "I shall enjoy watching you pluck your pigeon later," she said softly as they parted. Her lips curved in a smile of malicious anticipation, and her little white teeth glimmered for a minute. Gracemere bowed over her hand.

"Such an audience can only add spice to an already delicious prospect, madam."

"I trust you'll have another audience also," she murmured.

The earl's pale eyes narrowed vindictively. "The sister as well? Yes, ma'am. I trust so. It will add savor to the spice."

"It's to be hoped she doesn't vomit over you again." Agnes's soft laugh was as malicious as her earlier smile, and she went off on the arm of her partner.

Gracemere looked around the rapidly filling salon. There was no sign as yet of Sebastian Davenport, but he saw Judith enter with Isobel Henley and her party and his lips tightened. Since the debacle at Jermyn Street, he had continued to cultivate her as assiduously as ever, although always out of sight of Marcus. His motive now was simple. A beloved sister would watch her brother's downfall. Judith would suffer in impotent horror as she witnessed her brother's destruction, and the earl would have some small satisfaction for the mortification she had caused him. Marcus's pride would be humbled at the public humiliation of his brother-in-law, and Gracemere and Agnes would have Harriet Moreton and her fortune.

The earl made his way over to Judith. "Magnificent," he murmured, raising her hand to his lips. His admiration was genuine. Emeralds blazed in her copper hair and around the white throat. Her gown of gold spider gauze over bronze satin was startlingly unusual, and a perfect foil for her hair.

"Flatterer," she declared, tapping his wrist with her fan. "But, indeed, my lord, I am not immune to flattery, so pray don't stop."

He laughed and escorted her to the dance floor. "Your husband doesn't accompany you?"

"Alas, no," she said with a mock sigh. "A regimental dinner claimed his attention."

"How fortunate." A smile touched his lips and Judith felt clammy. "I don't see your brother here either."

"Oh, I daresay he'll be along later," she said. "He was to dine with friends."

"We have an agreement to meet at the card table," the earl told her, still smiling. "We're engaged in battle."

"Oh, yes, Sebastian told me. A duel of piquet." She laughed. "Sebastian is determined to win tonight, Bernard, I should warn you. He says he lost out of hand last night and must recoup his losses if he's not to be completely rolled up." She laughed, as if at the absurdity of such an idea, and Gracemere allowed an answering chuckle to escape him.

"I'm most eager to give him his revenge. Dare I hope that his lovely sister will stand at my side?"

"Well, as to that, sir, it might seem disloyal in me to appear to favor my brother's adversary," she said archly. "But I shall maintain an impartial interest. I confess I derive much pleasure from watching two such accomplished players in combat." She leaned forward and said almost guiltily, "But I do believe, Bernard, that you have the edge."

"Now it's you who are guilty of flattery, ma'am," Gracemere said in barely concealed mockery. Fortunately, Judith appeared not to hear the mockery.

"But you did win last night," she pointed out very seriously. "However, perhaps the cards weren't running in Sebastian's favor. It does make a difference, after all."

"Oh, of course it does," he agreed. "All the difference in the world, my dear Judith. Let's hope luck smiles upon your brother tonight . . . just to even things up, you understand."

"Yes, of course." The music stopped and the earl was obliged to relinquish her to a new partner . . . but not without reminding her of her promise to be in the card room later. Judith agreed, all smiles, and then took her place in the set. *So far so good.*

When Sebastian arrived, he was all smiling good humor, greeting friends and acquaintances, obliging his hostess by dancing with several unfortunate ladies who were without partners, imbibing liberally of champagne, and generally behaving like any other young blood.

To his relief and Harriet's not-so-secret chagrin, Harriet had not received an invitation to the ball. It was her first Season and she was too young and unknown to move invariably in the first circles. Once Sebastian declared his suit and her engagement to the Marquis of Carrington's brother-in-law was known, that would change, as Letitia told her, but this was small comfort to Harriet, spending the evening in dutiful attendance upon her mama.

It was after midnight when Sebastian and Gracemere met in the card room. Judith was watching for the moment when they both disappeared from the dance floor. It had been agreed that she wouldn't make her own appearance at the table until after they'd been playing for a while, by which time Sebastian would have established a winning pattern and they assumed that Gracemere would be ready to resort to marked cards.

For nearly an hour she continued to dance, to smile, to talk. She ate supper, sipped champagne, and forced herself not to think of what was happening in the card room. If it was going according to plan, Bernard Melville would by now be wondering what was happening to him.

At one o'clock she made her way to the gaming room. Immediately it was clear that something unusual was happening. Although there were people playing at the hazard, faro, macao, and basset tables, there was a distracted air in the room. Eyes were flickering to a small table in an alcove, where two men played piquet.

Judith crossed the room. "I've come to keep my promise, my lord," she said gaily.

Gracemere looked up from his cards and she recognized the look in his eye. It was the haunted feverishness of a man in captivity to the cards. "Your brother's luck has turned, it would seem," he said, clearing his throat.

Judith saw the pile of rouleaux at her brother's elbow. The earl was not yet resorting to vowels, then. She took up her place, casually, behind the earl's chair.

Gracemere was confusedly aware that the man he was playing with was not the man he thought he knew. Davenport's face was utterly impassive, he was silent most of the time, and when he spoke it was with staccato precision. The only part of his body he seemed to move were his long white hands on the cards.

Initially, the earl put his losses down to an uneven fall of the cards. When first he thought there must be more to it than that, he dismissed the idea. He'd played often enough with Sebastian Davenport to know what quality of player he was. True, occasionally he had won, sometimes puzzlingly, but even poor gamesters had occasional successes. As Gracemere's losses mounted, the ridiculousness of it all struck him powerfully. He increased the stakes, knowing that everything would go back to normal in a minute—it always did. All he needed was to win one game when the stakes were really high, and he would recoup his losses in one fell swoop. With that knowledge in mind, he played his first marked card. His sleight-of-hand was so expert that Judith missed it the first time and he won heavily.

Sebastian was unmoved, merely pushing across a substantial pile of rouleaux. Judith gave an excited little cry, saying in an exaggerated whisper, "Oh, well done, sir."

Gracemere didn't seem to hear her. He increased the stakes yet again. By now people were drifting toward the table, attracted by the tension. It was warm and Judith opened her fan.

Gracemere began to have a dreadful sense of topsy-turvy familiarity. This scene had happened before but there was an essential difference. He was not winning. He played with a dogged concentration, writing vowels now much as his adversary had done the previous evening. He played his marked cards, and yet he still didn't win. At one point, he looked wildly across the small table at his opponent as he played a heart that would spoil a repique. But Davenport seemed prepared and played his own ten, keeping his point advantage. How could it be happening? There was no explanation, except that his adversary had changed from a conceited greenhorn to a card player of awesome skill. And not just skill—it would take a magician to withstand the earl's special cards.

He glanced up at the woman, gently fanning herself at his shoulder. She smiled reassuringly at him, as if she didn't understand what was happening to him . . . as if she simply thought her brother was having a run of good luck for once.

He was a gamester. He knew he needed only one win. If he staked everything he had left, then he could recoup everything and bring his opponent to the ground.

George Devereux had at the last wagered the family estates in Yorkshire. Bernard Melville drew another sheet of paper and wrote his stake, the estate he had won from George Devereux, pushing it across the table to his adversary. Sebastian glanced at it, then swept his own winnings, rouleaux and vowels, together with his own IOU to match his opponent's extraordinary stake, into a pile at the side of the table. He put his hand in his pocket and deliberately drew out an elaborately carved signet ring. This last game he played for his father. His eyes flicked upward to his sister, who nodded infinitesimally in acknowledgment, before he slipped the ring onto his finger, shook back the ruffles on his shirt-sleeves, and broke a new pack of cards, beginning to deal.

Agnes Barret stared at the ring on Sebastian Davenport's finger. Her world seemed to turn on its axis, a slow roll into a nightmare of disbelief. She wanted to scream some kind of a warning to Bernard, so powerful was her sense of the danger embodied in that ring, but no sound would emerge from her throat. Her eyes were riveted on it: the Devereux family ring. She tore her eyes from Sebastian's long slender fingers and gazed at his sister. For a second Judith's golden brown eyes met Agnes's gaze, and the shock of her own recognition stunned Agnes with its primitive, vital force. And she wondered with a horrified desperation why she hadn't known it before . . . why some instinctive maternal essence had failed to recognize the children she hadn't seen since their babyhood.

Marcus Devlin, Marquis of Carrington, stood in the open doorway of the card room. The buzz of the attentive crowd around the players was so low as to be almost subliminal. He could see across the throng. He could see his wife, the steady, purposeful movement of her fan. He knew what she was doing. She and her brother were defrauding the Earl of Gracemere under the eyes of fashionable London. He couldn't imagine why, he knew only that he could do nothing about it. Only by exposing them could he stop it.

Distantly, in abject cowardice, he wished his evening had not ended when it had, or that he had gone straight home from Horseguard's Parade instead of following temptation and coming to find his wife. Wretchedly he wished he could have been spared this knowledge, because it was a knowledge he didn't know what to do with. It was a knowledge that destroyed love . . . that made impossible any kind of trust and confidence on which love and marriage could be based.

The moment when the Devereux estate passed back into the hands of its rightful heir, Agnes Barret understood everything. Bernard Melville had been beaten at his own game by the children of the man he had destroyed twenty years earlier. She didn't know how they'd done it, but she knew both brother and sister were partners. The nincompoops, the greenhorns, the simpletons, had been working toward this moment from the day they'd set foot in London.

A sick, impotent rage filled her throat as she saw Bernard's blank incomprehension as he lost the final hand. Agnes's eyes rose again to the face of her daughter standing behind him. Judith's gaze met hers —met and read the wild fury, the depths of a vindictive rage. And Judith's eyes carried a cold triumph that met and matched that vindictive rage. Agnes dropped her wineglass. It fell from suddenly nerveless fingers to smash on the parquet at her feet, splattering ruby red drops.

The low buzz increased in volume. Desperately Gracemere struggled to control his disordered thoughts. There was one chance to salvage everything. Twenty years ago he had placed a marked card in the hand of his opponent. And George Devereux had been dishonored and destroyed. If he could do the same now, at this moment publicly expose his adversary, he would recoup his losses. A cheat would not be permitted to keep his dishonorable winnings.

Hope soared and his confusion died as his thoughts became icily clear. "Well played, Davenport," he said into the tense hush. Lightly he shook down his sleeve, palming a card.

Judith's fan snapped shut.

"You won't mind if I take a look at—"

Before he could finish the sentence, before his hand could reach to caress his opponent's cards on the table—to remove and substitute —Sebastian Davenport suddenly spoke, and the words sent a wave of nausea through the earl, bile filling his mouth.

"Permit me," George Devereux's son said, grasping his adversary's stretched wrist. "Permit me, my lord."

It was at this moment that Marcus moved. He pushed through the crowd, reaching his wife's side. He said nothing, but he grasped her elbow and the knuckles of his other hand punched into the small of her back, compelling her forward, away from the table.

She hadn't known he was there, and when she looked up at him, at the rigid set of his jaw, the fine line of his mouth, the black, adamantine eyes, she knew that he had seen it all. In that moment she fully understood what she was about to lose.

Marcus saw the dazed look in her eyes . . . the look of someone who has been inhabiting another world, a world of acute, single-minded concentration. He continued to compel her toward the door, oblivious of the scene still at the table.

"No . . ." Judith said, her voice thick. "Please, wait, just one minute. . . . It must be completed."

The intensity in the low voice caught him off balance, and he stopped. Sebastian's voice was cold and steady in the now totally hushed room.

"May I see the card in your hand, my lord."

Sebastian's long fingers were bloodless as they gripped Grace-mere's wrist, forcing his hand over to reveal the card lying snug in the palm.

Marcus turned his head slowly, although he maintained his hold on Judith. He watched in amazement as his brother-in-law slid the card from the earl's now-slack grasp. He heard his brother-in-law

334

say, "Such an interesting pip on the corner, Gracemere. I don't think I've seen its like before. Harry, do you care to look at this card?"

Judith sighed, her entire body seeming to lose its rigidity as Harry Middleton took the card from his friend. Marcus wondered if he would ever understand anything again. And then with cold ferocity he decided that he would understand this if he had to put his wife on the rack to do so.

"March!" he spat out, and the pressure of his knuckles in the small of her back increased.

Judith made no further protest. She had now to face the one thing she'd feared more than anything.

They left Devonshire House without so much as a polite farewell and journeyed home in a silence weighted with dread. When the chaise drew up, Marcus sprang to the pavement, lifted Judith down before she had a chance to put a foot on the step, and swung her in front of him, propelling her up the steps and into the hall with his knuckles still pressed deeply into her back so she began to imagine she would always bear their imprint.

Inside, she glanced bleakly up at him. "Book room?"

"Just so." But he still didn't allow her to make unhindered progress and drove her ahead of him down the passage.

He pushed her into the room and flung the door shut with similar roughness. Judith shivered, afraid not so much of what he would do to her but of what she had done to him. He let her go as the door slammed and went to the fireplace, leaning his shoulders against the mantelshelf, his expression black as he stared at her standing silently in front of him.

"You are now going to tell me the truth," he said flatly. "It's possible you have never told the whole truth in your life before, but now you are going to do so. Everything. You will dot every 'i' and cross every 't,' because, so help me, if you leave anything out—if you obfuscate in any way whatsoever—I will not answer for the consequences. Now, begin."

It was the only chance to salvage anything out of the ruins. But it was a desperate chance at best. Judith took a deep breath and began at the beginning—twenty years earlier.

Marcus listened, unmoving, unspeaking, until she fell silent and the room seemed to close around them, the weight of her words a leaden pall to smother trust.

"I now understand why your brother was so anxious to make peace between us," he said, speaking slowly and carefully, articulating every word as if formulating the thought as he spoke. "Estranged from your husband, you wouldn't be much use to him, would you?"

"No," Judith agreed bleakly. What defense was there?

"So you were both looking for the perfect gull . . . that is the right word, isn't it? The perfect gull who would facilitate your long-planned vengeance."

Judith shook her head. "No, that's not true. I can see why you would think that, but it's not true. I didn't plot to marry you. Sebastian told the truth."

Marcus raised a skeptical eyebrow. "Deny if you can that I have been very useful to you."

"I can't deny that," she said miserably. "Any more than I can't fail to understand your anger and hurt. I ask only that you believe there was no deliberate intention to use you."

"But you didn't feel able to confide in me," he stated. "Even after matters were going smoothly between us. What have I done in these last weeks, Judith, that would deny me your trust?"

She shook her head again. "Nothing . . . nothing . . . but if I'd told you what we intended to do you would have prevented me, wouldn't you?"

"Oh, yes," he said savagely. "I would have locked you up and thrown away the key if it was the only way to prevent my wife from disgracing my honor in such despicable fashion."

Judith flushed and for the first time a note of vibrancy returned to her voice. "Gracemere got what he deserved. He's been robbing Sebastian blind for weeks now. Just as he defrauded our father . . . defrauded him and then accused *him* of cheating. Would you be so poor-spirited as to allow a man who did that to *your* father to go scot free? Can't you understand the need for vengeance, for justice, Marcus? The driving power that closes one's mind to all else but the need to avenge . . . to take back what has been stolen?"

Marcus didn't respond to this impassioned plea. Instead, he inquired in a tone of distant curiosity, "Tell me, was it pure coincidence that I received an invitation from Morcby for tonight?"

Judith's color deepened and the fight went out of her again as she saw the hopelessness of her position. "No," she confessed dismally. "Charlie—"

"Charlie? Are you telling me that you have involved my cousin in this deception . . . this betrayal?" His eyes were great black holes in his white face.

"Not exactly. . . . I mean, I did ask him to procure the invitation but I didn't tell him why." She stared at him, her hands pressed to her burning cheeks, devastated by what she had said, by what he was entitled to feel.

He drew a deep, shuddering breath. "Get out of my sight! I can't trust myself in the same room with you."

"Marcus, please—" She took a step toward him.

He flung out his hands as if to ward her off. "Go!"

"Please . . . please *try* to understand, to see it just a little through my eyes," she pleaded, unable to accept her dismissal, terrified that if she obeyed him, the vast gulf yawning between them would become infinite.

He took her by the upper arms and shook her until her head whipped back and forth and she felt sick. Then his hands fell from her as if she were a burning brand, or something disgusting that he couldn't endure to touch any longer. While she stood dazed in the middle of the room, rubbing her bruised arms, he stormed out, leaving the door swinging open.

Judith crept into a deep chair by the fire and huddled into it, curling in on herself, racked with deep shuddering spasms of devastation.

She didn't know how long she'd been crouching there like some

337

small wounded animal in emeralds and spider gauze and satin before Marcus returned.

He stood over her and spoke with a distant politeness. "I'm sorry if I hurt you. I didn't intend to. Come upstairs now, you need your bed."

"I think I'd rather stay here, thank you." She heard her voice, as stiffly polite as his.

Marcus bent and scooped her out of the chair. He set her on her feet. "Must I carry you?"

She shook her head and started out of the room. Neither of them could endure such physical contact tonight—not with all the rich, sensual memories embedded in such a touching.

She walked ahead of him up the stairs and into her own room. Marcus turned aside through his own door.

30

JUDITH LAY AWAKE THROUGH THE LAST REMAINING HOURS OF DARKNESS. She stared upward at the canopy over the bed, her eyelids peeled back as if they were held open with sticks, her eyeballs feeling shrunken and dried like shriveled peas. Despite a bone-deep bodily fatigue and total emotional exhaustion, she couldn't imagine sleeping. She lay straight-limbed in the bed, the sheet pulled up to her chin, her body perfectly aligned on the mattress, feeling the throbbing bruises on her arms where Marcus had held her and shaken her as the only truly alive parts of herself.

There ought to have been a sense of completion: The long dark road to vengeance had been traveled. Sebastian was in possession of his birthright and whatever depredations Gracemere's profligacy had worked upon the estate, Sebastian would work to put right. George Devereux was avenged; his children had a place in the world he had been driven from.

There ought to have been a sense of completion, of satisfaction. But there was only emptiness. Where there should have been gain there was only the greatest loss. What price vengeance when set against the loss of love? She had tried to have both and what she'd won was ashes on the wind.

Except for Sebastian, she reminded herself. Sebastian could now have the love of his Harriet, now that he had something to offer her. Sebastian could retire to the country and fulfill his bucolic dreams. And for herself . . . ?

The only thing she could do for Marcus was to remove herself as gracefully as possible from his life. There was no legal impediment to such a disappearance. She would tell him so as soon as she could. On which melancholy decision, she managed to fall asleep just as the sun came up.

She awoke at midmorning, rang for Millie, rose and dressed in desultory silence. "Is his lordship in, do you know, Millie?"

"I believe he went out after breakfast, my lady." Millie brushed a speck of lint from the sleeve of a blue silk spencer before holding it out for her. "You're looking a trifle fatigued, my lady," she observed with concern. "A little rouge might help."

Judith examined herself in the glass. Her eyes were dull and heavy in a pallid complexion. She shook her head. "No, I think it would just make things worse." She fastened a string of coral around her throat and went downstairs to the yellow drawing room.

"Mr. Davenport left his card an hour ago, my lady." Gregson presented the silver salver.

"Thank you, Gregson. Could you bring me some coffee, please?"

Sebastian had scrawled a note on the back of the card: *Why aren't I jubilant? I feel as if we lost not won. Come to me when you can. I need to talk to you.*

Judith tossed the card into the fire. She would probably be feeling the same as her brother even without the catastrophe with Marcus. The intensity had been too great to leave one feeling anything but drained. And she needed Sebastian now as she'd never needed him before.

"Lady Barret, my lady," Gregson intoned, entering the room with a tray of coffee.

Judith saw Agnes's face as it had been last night, a mask of rage and hatred. Her heart jumped then seemed to drop into her stomach. She opened her mouth to tell Gregson to make her excuses, but Agnes walked in on the heels of the butler. Her face was almost as pale as Judith's.

"Lady Barret." Judith bowed, hearing how thin her voice sounded. "How kind of you to call. Another cup, Gregson."

"No, I don't wish for coffee, thank you," Agnes said. She didn't return Judith's bow but paced the room, waiting for Gregson to finish pouring Judith's coffee.

When the door closed on the butler, Agnes swung round on her daughter. Her eyes blazed in her face, where two spots of rouge burned in violent contrast to her pallor. "Let us take off the gloves, Judith. I don't know *how* you did it, but I know *what* you and your brother did last night."

"Oh?" Judith, struggling for calm, raised an ironic eyebrow. "And what was that?"

"Somehow, between you, you cheated Gracemere." Agnes's voice shook and her pallor had become even more pronounced. Her hands trembled and she clasped them tightly together. "You ruined him!" Her voice was a low hiss and she advanced on Judith, who stepped back, away from the force of this vengeful rage.

"He would have ruined my brother as he ruined our father," Judith said, a quaver in her voice. There was no point in denying the truth with this woman, who seemed somehow to know everything anyway. Unconsciously her hands passed through the air as if she could thus dispel the enveloping evil miasma.

Agnes laughed, a shocking crack of amusement. "Unlike you and your brother, your father was a weak fool. He had no idea how to stand up for himself . . . or to hold onto what he owned."

Judith stared at the woman. Even through her fear and outrage, she recognized the truth of what Agnes had said. But she had always assumed exile and poverty had destroyed George's stability and will-power. Agnes was implying that it had an earlier genesis. "What do you know of my father?" she demanded. "What could you possibly know of the life he led?"

Agnes laughed again and abruptly Judith turned from her. "Get out of my house, Lady Barret."

"I'll leave when I've said what I came here to say, Judith." Her voice dropped to barely a whisper, but each word had bell-like clarity in the still room. "You will pay for what you did . . . you and your brother."

"Oh, I am paying," Judith said softly, almost to herself. "You don't know how much." Then her voice strengthened. "But my brother will now enjoy his birthright. Sebastian will take his happiness with both hands now. *His* happiness and place in the world is assured."

"He will pay," Agnes reiterated with a cold certainty that sent renewed chills up Judith's spine.

She could think of nothing to say to combat the menace in the room and, when Gregson opened the door, turned with blind relief toward the distraction.

"Lady Devlin, Lady Isobel Henley, and Mrs. Forsythe."

"Judith, it's the talk of the town," Isobel exclaimed, swirling into the room in a cloud of muslin. "Your brother exposed the Earl of Gracemere as a cheat!"

"I left before midnight," Cornelia put in. She tripped on the edge of the rug and caught herself just in time. "But Forsythe was full of it over the breakfast table. He says Gracemere will never be able to show his face in Society again . . . Oh, I beg your pardon, Lady Barret. I didn't see you standing there."

Under Judith's incredulous stare, a complete change came over Agnes. The ice left her eyes, a tinge of normal color returned to her cheeks. Her voice was as light and nonchalant as ever. "As Lady Isobel says, it's the talk of the town. I'm sure everyone will be beating a path to your door, Lady Carrington, to talk of your brother."

"I wonder how long the earl has been cheating," Sally commented, sitting down beside the fire. "It couldn't be that he only began last night, could it?"

"Unlikely," Judith said, trying to respond normally. If Agnes Barret could behave as if there were no history and the things that had been said in this room had never been spoken, then so could she. She drew on a lifetime's experience with a masquerade and showed her own mask of insouciance.

"But how did Sebastian know?"

"He's been playing with the earl for the last two months," Judith said, shrugging, averting her eyes from Agnes. "I imagine he realized something wasn't quite right before."

"Miss Moreton, my lady." The door again opened and an excited Harriet bounced in.

"Oh, Judith, I could barely contain myself . . . such extraordinary news. Is it true that Sebastian discovered the Earl of Gracemere cheating? Oh, how I wish I could have been there." Then Harriet saw Agnes and subsided, blushing furiously.

"You have, of course, never cared for Gracemere, have you, my dear?" Agnes remarked. "Nevertheless, one shouldn't gloat over another's misfortune."

"I find it hard to call it misfortune, ma'am," Isobel said, scrutinizing the plate of sweet biscuits on the coffee tray. "When a man deliberately sets out to injure another man and is unmasked, misfortune seems a misnomer." She selected a piece of shortbread.

Agnes bowed coldly and began to leaf through a periodical on a console table. Cornelia kicked Isobel's ankle with lamentable lack of delicacy and an uneasy silence fell for a minute. Then Sally spoke with customary good nature. "It's quite shocking news, of course. But one can only assume that the earl had a compelling reason to play in that manner. Debts of unmanageable magnitude . . . what other explanation could there be?"

"You're right," Cornelia said. "We shouldn't be the first to throw stones."

"No," Sally agreed, thinking of four thousand pounds' worth of pawned rubies.

In the next half hour, it seemed that half London was indeed beating a path to Judith's door, agog to learn any details that might not be generally known. Judith dispensed hospitality, asserted she had no inside snippets of gossip since she hadn't seen her brother since the previous evening, and all the while her head spun with conjecture. What possible revenge could Agnes and Gracemere have in mind? The speculation took her mind off her trouble with Marcus to some extent, but did nothing to restore her equilibrium. She waited impatiently for her guests to take their leave, so that she could go to Sebastian.

"Judith, I must go home, Annie has the croup." Sally appeared at Judith's elbow. "Nurse is quite good with her, but the poor little love frets if I'm away too long."

"I'm sorry." Judith received this information with less than her usual attention. "It's not serious, I hope."

"No . . . Judith, is something the matter?" Sally regarded her friend closely. "You seem *distrait.*"

"It's hardly surprising," Judith said, trying to pass it off, gesturing around the crowded room. "After last night."

"I suppose not. What did Marcus have to say?" It was a shrewd guess, but Sally was good at guessing games when it came to Devlins.

Judith shook her head. "Not now, Sally."

Sally accepted this with a nod and a compassionate kiss. "Oh, I was forgetting, Harriet had to leave . . . some errand she has to run for her mother. You were deep in conversation and she didn't want to interrupt, so I said I'd say good-bye for her."

"Thanks. I expect Sebastian will be able to answer all her questions later." Judith smiled, but the strain in the smile was obvious. Sally pressed her hand briefly and left.

Judith looked around the room and realized that Agnes Barret had also made a discreet departure. But then she wouldn't have expected her to make any farewells.

Judith walked to Albemarle Street as soon as the last visitor had left. Sebastian had been watching for her from his front window and came to open the door himself. "I've been hiding," he confessed. "I saw Harry Middleton this morning, but I've had Broughton deny me to everyone else."

"Wise of you," she said. "My drawing room's been full since

midmorning with people trying to pry some additional tidbit out of me." She unpinned her hat and drew off her gloves.

Sebastian poured sherry. "You look the very devil," he said frankly. "What happened to you last night? I looked up and you'd gone."

"Marcus took me away just as you were exposing Gracemere."

Sebastian whistled soundlessly. "He saw."

She nodded. "All of it."

"Bad?"

She nodded again. "Very. As bad as we knew it would be if he found out."

"I'm sorry, love." Sebastian took his sister in his arms and she wept quietly for a few moments while he stroked her hair. "When he's had time to calm down, to look at it clearly, he'll understand. He knows you love him. He'd have to be a blind man not to know it."

"I hoped he loved me," she said drearily. "But love is easily killed, it seems. He despises me." She heard again his voice telling her to go away . . . to get out of his sight. Such furious contempt.

"Stuff," her brother said. "Of course he doesn't despise you."

"Yes, he does. Anyway, let's not talk of it anymore now. Agnes Barret paid me a visit this morning."

She explained what Agnes had said and Sebastian listened attentively. "There's nothing she could do," he said at the end. "Neither of them has any redress, Ju. Gracemere will have to leave London. He's already been obliged to resign from his clubs, according to Harry. He can rusticate in the country or go abroad. But there's no place in Society for him now . . . or ever again."

"And Agnes?"

"She's untarnished. She can continue as before."

"But without her lover. And if her fortunes are tied with Gracemere's then his ruin is hers, one way or the other."

"Either she ends her relationship with Gracemere, or she abandons her place in Society and joins him in exile. Not comfortable choices. Now, what are we going to do about Marcus?"

Judith shook her head tiredly. "I don't believe there's anything to be done. I'll leave him as soon as I can decently do so without causing remark. We'll concoct some story to put me out of the way, and Marcus will be free to marry or to continue to live as he did before he met me."

Sebastian could think of nothing to say in the face of this dreary future. Any option he might offer would be just as wretched when compared with what might have been.

Judith reached for her hat and gloves. "I'd better go home. Maybe Marcus will be back by now."

She walked back to Berkeley Square and found Harriet's maid on the doorstep. "Beggin' your pardon, m'lady, but Lady Moreton sent me." The girl bobbed a curtsy. "She asks as 'ow could you send miss 'ome as soon as possible."

"Send her home?" Judith stared at the girl. "But she went home a long time ago." It was a mere ten minutes' walk from Berkeley Square to Brook Street. "Oh, but she said she had some errands to run for Lady Moreton. I expect that's where she is."

"Oh, no, m'lady," the girl corrected. "Miss already sent the footman home with her ladyship's tonic."

"You'd better come in," Judith said, and the girl followed her into the house.

"Gregson, did you see Miss Moreton leave earlier?"

"Oh, yes, my lady. She left with Lady Barret."

Judith felt the blood drain from her face. Harriet . . . with Agnes. She saw again those tawny eyes, glittering with maleficence, heard again the hissed threats.

She thought of Harriet, the perfect means of revenge upon Sebastian.

"Tell your mistress that Miss Moreton went with Lady Barret. I'm certain she'll be returning shortly," she instructed the maid. "Gregson, send someone to find his lordship." Her voice was crisp, offering no hint of the terror she felt. "In fact, send as many people as necessary. He may be at one of his clubs, or at Jackson's Saloon

. . . at one of his friends' houses. But he must be found immediately."

"Is there a message, my lady?"

"Simply that he's needed at home immediately."

Judith went up to her drawing room. Once private, she paced the room in agitation, feeling completely helpless. What would they do with Harriet? Marcus had an inner knowledge of Gracemere, he'd have some idea of what he intended. She was far too agitated to worry about how she would face him after last night's hideous scene; neither did it occur to her that her husband would withhold his help, however deeply disgusted he was with his wife and her brother. Marcus was not vindictive. With the greatest difficulty, she resisted the urge to send a message to Sebastian. What could he do, except join her in impotent fear?

Marcus was in Gentleman Jackson's Saloon, when one of the six footmen ran him to earth. Stripped to the waist, pouring sweat, he was attempting to exorcise misery and disappointment in a violent bout with a punchball.

He had passed no better a night than Judith, but the sharpest spur of his hurt was becoming blunter and some elements of rationality beginning to offer a spark of light in his darkness. He could hear her voice clearly now demanding that he understand the driving power of vengeance. He knew that power. Once he'd obeyed its spur himself . . . and with Gracemere. There was a perfect appropriateness to the vengeance Judith and Sebastian had taken. But still he couldn't reconcile himself to the knowledge that he'd been used. If only she'd taken him into her confidence . . .

But how could she have done so? He would have stopped her. However sympathetic he might have been to her brother's situation, to her father's ruin, he would never have permitted Judith to do what she'd done. And the destruction of Bernard Melville, Earl of Gracemere, was central to Judith's view of the world. Until that had been accomplished, nothing else could take precedence . . . not even her husband. Had he the right to believe she should have dropped the most powerful imperative of her life—and her brother's life—simply because *he* had come on the scene? Her bond with her brother was too complex and too strong to be severed by the simple ties of passion . . . of lust and a burgeoning love.

He didn't countenance what she'd done, but he understood it. From understanding could come acceptance . . .

"My lord, one of your men has a message for you."

Marcus grabbed a towel, rubbing the sweat from his face. "Someone for me, Jackson?"

"Yes, my lord." Gentleman Jackson indicated the lad in Carrington livery, standing at the far side of the room, gazing wide-eyed at the sparring couples.

"What the devil can he want?" Marcus beckoned and the lad trotted across, his message spilling from his lips. "Her ladyship, my lord, wishes you to return home immediately."

"Her ladyship!" His heart lurched. Only the direst necessity would send Judith in search of him in this fashion.

"Is her ladyship well?" he demanded, toweling his sweat-soaked head.

"Yes, my lord," the man said. "I believe so, my lord. Gregson said we was all to search London for you."

"All?"

"Yes, my lord. There's six of us."

"Go back to Berkeley Square and say I'm on my way," Marcus instructed tersely, his heart slowing as he went into the changing room. If Judith was well and unhurt, that was all that mattered. Surely she wouldn't have sent all over London for him just to tell him that she was leaving him . . . although, knowing his lynx, maybe he shouldn't be so sanguine. So far, he hadn't managed to keep a step ahead of her. Why should he assume he could do so now?

He dressed in haste and took a hackney home. Gregson had the door open as he ran up the steps. "Her ladyship . . . ?"

"In the yellow drawing room, my lord."

He took the stairs two at a time. "Judith, what is it?" The question was on his lips almost before he had the door open. Her white face and scared eyes stopped him on the threshold. "What is it?"

"Harriet," she said, moistening her lips. She wanted to run to him, but the memory of the previous night was too raw. "I believe Agnes and Gracemere have abducted her."

He closed his eyes for a minute. He didn't ever want to hear the name of Gracemere again. He had no interest in his old enemy and Agnes Barret. If he was to pick up the pieces of his shattered marriage, Bernard Melville, Earl of Gracemere, had to be consigned to the pits of hell. And then he saw Martha as she'd been that morning, ten years before, crouched in a corner of the room, her face bruised, her eyes sightless with tears, soft whimpers coming from her mouth as she'd rocked herself in her hurt. A man who raped once could do so again.

"Tell me what you know."

Judith explained, finding it possible to slow her thoughts and present facts rather than impressions under Marcus's calm attention. "I'm so frightened," she said at the end. "I've always felt the evil in both of them. What will they do to her, Marcus?"

Marcus thought swiftly. There was no point exacerbating her fears. Later, when it was over, he would tell her the truth about Gracemere and Martha. But for now he had to prevent the violation of another innocent. He had to get there in time. He had failed once; he wouldn't fail again.

He spoke suddenly with precision and clarity and Judith quailed at the fury and the purpose in his eyes.

"I will not permit any harm to come to Harriet. This lies between Gracemere and myself. You are to say nothing to anyone and you will stay here until I return. You and your brother will not involve yourselves in this. I'll brook no interference. Do you understand?"

"I understand," Judith said as he strode from the room.

But I don't accept it.

31

JUDITH RAN UPSTAIRS, THREW A CLOAK AROUND HER SHOULDERS, THRUST HER pistol and a heavy purse into the pocket, and left the house through the French doors of the book room.

Marcus's curricle was being led from the mews as she crossed the cobbles. Drawing her hood over her head, she followed the curricle into the square and there hailed a passing hackney. "Wait on the corner, and then follow that curricle when its driver takes the reins," she instructed the jarvey, handing him a guinea. He touched a forelock.

"You don't want the cove to know 'e's bein' followed, lady?"

"Not if you can avoid it," she agreed, climbing inside. She peeped around the strip of leather shielding the window, watching as Marcus came out of the house and climbed into the curricle. She called softly up to the driver. "There's another two guineas in it if you don't lose him *and* he doesn't realize we're behind him."

"Gotcha!" The jarvey cracked a whip and the vehicle lurched forward. Judith sat back, taking shallow breaths of the fusty air. The last occupant of the vehicle must have been eating raw onions and smoking a particularly noxious tobacco.

Marcus never looked back. He drove fast through the city, taking the northern route out to Hampstead Heath. It was a journey he'd made once before in the same urgency, consumed with the same desperate fury. How long had Gracemere had with the girl? Four hours at the most. Was Agnes Barret with him? Having procured the girl, was she going to hold her for him? The nauseating images spun before his internal vision.

The Reading stage lumbered down the road toward him, the postboy blowing his horn. The postboy grabbed the side of the box and closed his eyes tightly as the curricle didn't slacken speed. The two vehicles passed with barely a centimeter to spare.

"Lord-a-mercy!" the jarvey yelled down to his passenger. "That's drivin' for you. Didn't even shave the varnish, I'll lay odds. He's in a powerful 'urry, your cove."

Judith clung onto the strap as the hackney swayed and swerved along the rutted road, trying to keep the curricle in sight. It occurred to her somewhat belatedly that she had no idea how far Marcus was going. He could be going anywhere—Reading, or Oxford. Somewhere well out of the ordinary reach of a hired London hackney. But how did he know where Gracemere had gone?

The road wound over the heath and she leaned out of the window. "Can you still see him?"

"Aye, he's just turned off at the crossroads. Reckon he's 'eaded for the Green Man," the jarvey called back. "It's the only place 'ereabouts. Folks don't much relish livin' too close to the gibbet."

"No, I don't suppose they do." Judith retreated into the fetid interior again, averting her eyes from the rotting corpse swinging on the gibbet as the carriage turned left at the crossroads.

Marcus drew up in the courtyard of a dark, shabby inn under the creaking sign of the Green Man. He jumped down, tossing the reins to a small lad picking his nose by the wall, and strode into the pitch-roofed building, ducking his head under the low lintel. He held his driving whip loosely in one hand.

Voices came from the taproom to the left of the hall, and the smell of boiling greens wafted from the kitchen at the rear, mingling with the reek of stale beer. The innkeeper came bustling out from the back regions, wiping his hands on a grimy apron. When he saw his visitor, his eyes widened as the years rolled back.

"Ah, Winkler, still in business I see," the marquis observed in a pleasant tone not matched by his expression. "I'm amazed the Bow Street Runners haven't caught up with you yet."

The innkeeper shuffled his feet and looked Marcus over with a calculating shiftiness that carried a degree of apprehension. "What can I do for you, my lord?"

"The same as before," Marcus said. "Nothing overly demanding, Winkler. Your . . . your *guests* are to be found above the stables as usual, I assume?"

The landlord licked his lips and glanced anxiously around, as if expecting to see a Bow Street Runner spring up out of the dust in the corners of the hallway. "If you say so, m'lord."

"I do," Marcus said aridly, turning on his heel. "Oh, and should you hear any undue disturbances, you will be sure to ignore them, won't you? I know how deaf you are, Winkler."

The landlord wiped his forehead with his apron. "Whatever you say, m'lord."

"Just so." Marcus smiled with the appearance of great affability and walked back outside. He crossed the yard at the back of the inn. The stable was a substantial red-brick building at the rear of the courtyard. Beneath its sloping roof were two connecting rooms available to those who knew of them and were able to pay substantially for their use. No questions were ever asked of the various, generally felonious, occupants, and what went on in those rooms was known only to the participants. So far, Winkler and his clients seemed to have escaped the attentions of the law.

Marcus glanced up at the latticed, tightly curtained windows overlooking the stableyard just before he entered the building. He saw no flicker of movement at the curtains and he could hear no sound of voices as he trod softly up the wooden stairs at the rear of the dim interior. He paused, listening at a door at the head of the stairs. His heart had started to thud and he realized he was listening for the sounds he'd heard once before at this door. The sounds that had sent him bursting into the room with his whip raised. But there were no whimpering cries this afternoon. A chair scraped on the wooden floor and then there was silence.

He lifted the latch, then kicked the door open with his booted foot.

Gracemere leaped to his feet, a foul oath on his lips. The chair clattered to the floor behind him. *"You!"*

"Surely you were expecting me, Gracemere," Marcus said. "You must know that I always keep my promises." He glanced around the room. The curtains were pulled tight over the windows blocking out the afternoon's sunlight. The room was lit by thick tallow candles and the bright glow of the fire.

Harriet huddled on a wooden settle beside the fire. At the sound of Marcus's voice, she sat up with a cry, staring wild-eyed at him as if he were an apparition. Her eyes were swollen with weeping, her hair in disarray, her expression distraught, but he could see no marks of brutality.

He crossed the room swiftly. "Are you hurt, child?"

She gulped, tried to shake her head, then burst into a torrent of weeping that mounted alarmingly toward hysteria.

Marcus wasted no time in soothing her. He turned back to the earl, who still stood as if stunned. "Foolish of you to return here, Gracemere, but then a rat usually goes back to its own dung heap," he observed, cracking the thong of his whip on the floor. His eyes went to the door in the middle of the wall; he knew of old that it connected this room with its partner. "Where is Lady Barret? I should like her to witness the next few minutes."

Gracemere's face was bloodless. He looked desperately around the room and then grabbed for a bread knife on the table. Marcus's whip snapped, catching him across the knuckles. He gave a cry of fury, of fear, of pain, snatching back his hand.

Marcus advanced on him, taking his time, his eyes never leaving his face, the whip curled loosely at his side. Suddenly the whip cracked again and his quarry jumped backward. Again the thong whistled and snapped, and again Gracemere jumped back. In this fashion, Marcus pursued his prey until the earl stood backed against a heavy armoire.

"Now," Marcus said softly. "Now, let us begin in earnest, sir."

"Let us indeed begin in earnest, my lord." Agnes Barret stood in the door connecting the two rooms. She held a serviceable-looking flintlock pistol in her hand, pointing directly at the marquis. "Give the whip to Gracemere. I think he might enjoy putting it to good use."

The earl chuckled and held out his hand.

"Don't think I won't shoot, Carrington," Agnes said with a tight smile. "Of course, I won't kill you. The consequences of your death might be a little difficult to avoid, but I will break your knees. We shall all three be long gone from here by the time you recover your senses sufficiently to drag yourself down the stairs."

Harriet screamed. Gracemere snatched the whip from Marcus.

Within the inn, the landlord was struggling for breath as the jarvey cheerfully tightened his boldly checkered scarf around his throat, inquiring for the second time, "Where'll we find the gennelman cove, friend?"

"Perhaps he can't speak," Judith suggested as the innkeeper flailed desperately in the jarvey's choke hold. "You are squeezing him rather tightly."

The jarvey slackened the material a trifle and Mr. Winkler gestured outside with a hoarse but informative, "stables." His expression clearly indicated that he no longer had the least interest in preserving anyone's privacy, and would willingly yield up whatever secrets of his house and its guests were demanded of him, and even those that weren't.

"Stay here and keep an eye on him," Judith instructed the jarvey, taking the pistol from her pocket. "If I need you, I'll call."

"Right you are, lady," the jarvey said. "'Andy with that popper, are you?"

"Handy enough," Judith said.

Gathering up her skirts, she ran to the stable building, having no idea what she would find. In the dark, manure-scented interior, she stopped and looked around. Then she heard Harriet's scream and the sickening hiss and crack of a whip.

She hurled herself at the stairs, stumbled, picked herself up, and flung open the door at the head. Her eyes, accustomed to simultaneous observation and assimilation of half a dozen hands of cards, instantly took in the tableau. Agnes Barret with her pistol raised, aimed at Marcus; the two men swaying, grappling for possession of a whip; Harriet, paralyzed with horror, her mouth open but now no sound issuing forth.

Judith didn't pause for reflection. She fired her pistol and the flintlock spun out of Agnes's grip. Agnes stared numbly at the hand that had held the gun. Blood welled from the torn flesh and dripped to the floor.

"Dear God in heaven!" Marcus breathed, wrenching the whip from Gracemere's abruptly slackened hold.

Judith sprang across the room to retrieve Agnes's pistol. She directed the flintlock at Gracemere and looked properly at Marcus for the first time.

"That's quite an aim you have," he observed. "But I can't imagine why that should surprise me."

No response seemed required and Judith glanced toward the settle where Harriet sat, now looking utterly bemused. "Harriet . . ."

"She's frightened but has taken no serious harm," Marcus said. "What interests me rather more is what the devil you think you're doing here." He pulled out his handkerchief and went over to where Agnes stood, still staring in disbelief at the blood welling from her hand.

"It seems fortunate I am here," Judith responded rather tartly. "You didn't really expect me to leave you to conduct this business alone?"

"I had thought I'd made it crystal clear that was exactly what I expected." Taking Agnes's hand, he wrapped the handkerchief over the wound.

"But I *love* you," Judith cried with an edge of exasperation. "I couldn't possibly stand by when you might be hurt."

Marcus looked up from his bandaging, and a smile touched his eyes, then spread slowly across his face. "No, I suppose you couldn't," he said. "Where you love, you love hard and long, don't you, lynx?"

"And you?" It was a tentative question and she seemed to be perched on a precipice with joy on one side, desolation on the other.

"I've never loved before," Marcus said, still smiling. "But it does seem to be a very powerful and exclusive emotion."

Despair, anxiety, tension drained slowly away, leaving her empty of all but bone-deep relief and a well of loving warmth. It was going to be all right. She hadn't lost Marcus and his love. "And forgiveness?" she asked. "Can love include that?"

"It seems to promote it," he said, tying a knot in the handkerchief. "Is that comfortable, Lady Barret?"

"Comfortable is hardly the word I would have used," Agnes stated. She looked across at Judith with a strange smile quirking her lips. "I have to say, Charlotte, that for two such mewling babes, you and Peter have certainly turned out unexpectedly. Whatever could George have done, I wonder, to have given you both so much strength of character?"

Gracemere flung himself on the settle beside a shrinking Harriet and began to laugh. It was an unsettling sound, totally without mirth.

Judith stared at Agnes. "What do you mean?" But she knew. She knew as she had always known. Only the knowledge had been in blood and bone and sinew, in the threads of a primitive instinct, not in absolute words speaking absolute truths.

"Can't you guess, my dear child?" Agnes said, a taunting note in her voice. "But yes, I see that you can. Curiously, I find you a worthy daughter. I hadn't expected George's children to have any red blood in their veins."

"I thought you were dead," Judith said, her voice hollow.

"Alice Devereux is dead," Agnes said. "She died a convenient death in a convent somewhere. And then she rose again, as you see." She passed her uninjured hand down her body in mocking explanation.

"Marcus . . . ?" Judith spoke his name hesitantly, her eyes searched for his, her free hand went out toward him in apprehensive plea.

"I'm here," he said softly, taking her hand, squeezing it tightly as her mother continued to talk.

"Your father was so blind. He never knew . . . never guessed that Gracemere and I had been lovers since we were little more than children. Since between us we hadn't a feather to fly with, one of us had to marry for money. But it didn't work out as it was supposed to. In the end, we had to get rid of George."

She was speaking quietly, cradling her bandaged hand, almost as if unaware of her audience. "He was in the way, always making demands . . . protestations of love. He wouldn't leave me alone. He made it impossible for me to be with Gracemere as I had to be. And there was Peter and then you, ten months apart, for heaven's sake. I had to get away from him."

Judith felt nauseated but she could no more move away or even interrupt than the fly stickily entwined in the web. She gazed at her mother, who continued her explanation with almost an assumption of shared comprehension.

"I couldn't simply leave your father, you must understand, because then I would have been as penniless as if I'd never married him. What were we to do?" It was a genuine question. "I could only leave your father if we had possession of his money. So Gracemere took it from him. We did what was necessary."

"Sebastian and I would have been in your way, of course," Judith heard herself say. "You'd hardly want to be saddled with a pair of brats when you started on your new life."

Agnes shook her head impatiently. "I never wanted children but George insisted. If he chose to take you with him when he left, why would it matter to me?"

"Why indeed?" Judith agreed distantly. "I quite see that." She shook her head as if to dispel the cobwebs of confusion. In some essential way, the story seemed to have nothing to do with her at all, but she couldn't quite clarify how or why that should be so.

"It seems that the affair has come full circle, ma'am," Marcus said into the silence, still holding Judith's hand. "Your children have ruined you and your lover as completely as you and your lover ruined their father. There's a nice symmetry to it, I'm sure you'll agree." And it did now seem to him that it was the only right thing to have happened. Listening to the evil in this woman, who for passion's sake had condemned her children to a life as outcasts, he felt only satisfaction for what Judith and her brother had achieved. Vengeance was an ancient and savage imperative.

"But my mother needn't be ruined. Perhaps she would prefer to remain with her present husband in London," Judith suggested with a razor-edged smile, her voice hard. "I'm sure Sebastian—or rather, Peter—and I would really enjoy getting to know her properly."

Agnes regarded her daughter with a glimmer of respect. "That could almost be an amusing prospect. However, my dear, you'll never see me again. You must make my farewells to your brother." She turned and went into the connecting room. Gracemere rose from the settle, offered a mocking bow to Judith, and followed his mistress.

Harriet whimpered. "I don't understand . . ."

"No, of course you don't," Judith said swiftly. "What a terrible time you must have had, love. There's a hackney downstairs. The jarvey is most reliable and he'll convey you back to Brook Street immediately. In fact, I'll accompany you—"

"No, you will not," Marcus interrupted. "I'm not letting you out of my sight again. Come, Harriet." He picked up the bewildered, tear-streaked girl, who lay limply in his arms. "I'm going to put you in the hackney and direct the jarvey to take you to Sebastian. I think you'll find greater strength there than in your mother's company, and he will know just how to explain matters to your parents so that they have no idea of the truth. Davenports are very good at that." He cast

358

his wife a darkling look that nevertheless carried a hint of rueful amusement. "Stay here, Judith, until I come back."

"I'll be here," she said. She stood looking at the closed door to the other room. How much of her mother did she have in her? Was she infected with her mother's evil? But she knew she wasn't. The person she was had more to do with the circumstances of her childhood than to any blood, bone, and sinew she shared with Agnes Barret. Her mother's abandonment had been the greatest service she could have rendered her children. If she'd stayed in their lives, they would probably have learned to be as warped as she.

She went to the window, watching as Marcus carried Harriet across the yard. She felt curiously at peace, despite the dreadful revelations of the last minutes. It was as if something had been completed. The last piece of her past was fitted in place. She knew her mother, had avenged her father. Now she was free to be her own person.

"I can't imagine how Sebastian is going to adapt to life with a woman who collapses in the middle of adventures," Marcus observed, when he returned. "After a lifetime with you, my love, it seems impossible to imagine."

"I expect he'll find it a pleasant change," Judith said. "How did you know Gracemere would be here?"

"That's a story for later . . . much later."

Marcus came over to her, taking her hands in his. The black eyes gazed down at her intently. "How do you feel after all that?"

"I was shocked at first, but now it seems oddly irrelevant. She's nothing to me." She shrugged. "It's strange, but I really don't feel any connection with her at all. In fact, now I know *who* she is—*what* she is—it's a great weight off my mind. She's been disturbing me ever since I met her. It's a relief to know why."

Marcus nodded. "She is nothing to you. Now we can put all this behind us and start afresh."

Judith bit her lip. "Yes, well, there's just one thing more—"

"Oh, no." Marcus groaned, dropping her hands. "Not something else, Judith, *please.*"

"I wasn't going to tell you—"

"Judith, don't do this to me!"

"I have to," she wailed. "If you hadn't discovered about Gracemere and all this muddle, I would have kept quiet about it. Sebastian said it wasn't important because we create our own truths, but it *is* important, and since you know all the rest, you had better know this, too. In fact, it'll probably occur to you, anyway, at some point, when you have time to think."

Marcus closed his eyes briefly and said with heavy resignation, "Go on. What truth have you created now?" He moved away to the fireplace and stood waiting.

"Well, you see . . . you see, we aren't married," she blurted, wringing her hands.

"What!"

"Judith Davenport isn't a legal person; neither is Sebastian Davenport. I didn't think about it in the church, how should I have? It was only afterward, when I looked at the register. But we're Devereux . . . I don't ever remember being called Charlotte, but . . ." She saw comprehension in his eyes and fell silent, judging she'd said enough.

Marcus strode across the room. His fingers clamped one wrist, tightening around the fragile bones, as he dragged her to the door. She tripped over an uneven flagstone on the threshold but his pace didn't slacken as he hauled her after him, down the rickety stairs. She stumbled in his wake, her manacled wrist at full stretch, and they emerged in the sunlit stableyard. Judith blinked at the brightness of the light after the gloom above.

"Marcus, what are you doing? Where are we going?" she demanded breathlessly.

"I'll tell you where we're going," he replied in clipped accents. "We're going to find a bishop and a special license, and we're going to finalize this marriage beyond all possible doubt. After which I intend to exercise *all* my marital rights—including the one involving a rod no thicker than my finger. The only question is in which order I decide to exercise those rights." He caught her around the waist and tossed her unceremoniously into his curricle.

"Can't I have an opinion?" Judith asked, picking herself up and scrambling onto the seat.

"No, you may not!" He jumped up beside her. "If you have a grain of common sense, which I doubt, you'll sit very still and keep your mouth shut."

Judith sat back, smoothing down her skirt, catching her breath, as the thong of his whip flicked the leader's neck and the team plunged forward. They kept up a furious pace, pounding across the heath, and swung onto the deserted post road at the gibbet. Judith examined her companion's profile with a mischievous glint in her eye.

"Marcus, you're laughing," she stated.

"What the hell have I got to laugh about?" he demanded, keeping his eyes on the road ahead. "For the last seven months, I've been living in sin with a woman who took part in an illegal marriage ceremony, and if circumstances hadn't forced a confession from her, fully intended to leave me in ignorance for the rest of my mortal span!"

"Ignorance is supposed to be bliss," Judith offered, not a whit fooled by his ferocious tone. "Anyway, what's in a name?" A strange little sound came from him and his shoulders shook. "I *know* you're laughing," she insisted. "You once said it was very bad to repress laughter . . . I'm sure you said it would give one an apoplexy."

Marcus checked his horses and drove the curricle off the road into a stand of trees. There they stopped and he turned toward Judith. Her mischievous glint deepened as she saw the merriment in his eyes. "I knew you were laughing," she said with satisfaction.

He caught her chin. "Ever since I met you, I have taken leave of my senses. Why else would I permit a tempestuous, manipulative, unscrupulous wildcat to lead me the craziest dance a man has ever been led?"

"For a man who hates dancing, it does seem a little inconsistent," she agreed, smiling. "But, judging by my own experience, one doesn't choose where to love. Why else would I fall body and soul in lust and love with a tyrannical, stuffy despot, who insists on keeping me under his thumb, and is only happy when he's laying down the law to all and sundry?"

"But you do love him nevertheless?"

"Oh, yes," she said, reaching up to grasp his wrist. "As he loves a designing adventuress."

"Beyond reason," he said softly. "I love you beyond reason, you abominable lynx."

He brought his mouth to hers, his hand moving to palm her scalp as she reached against him, and his tongue plundered the sweetness of her mouth even as she drank greedily of the taste and scent of him, of the promise of an untrammeled future, where loyalties were simple and trust was absolute.